THUNDER GAME

THE CARPATHIAN NOVELS

DARK HOPE	DARK WOLF	DARK MELODY
DARK MEMORY	DARK LYCAN	DARK SYMPHONY
DARK WHISPER	DARK STORM	DARK GUARDIAN
DARK TAROT	DARK PREDATOR	DARK LEGEND
DARK SONG	DARK PERIL	DARK FIRE
DARK ILLUSION	DARK SLAYER	DARK CHALLENGE
DARK SENTINEL	DARK CURSE	DARK MAGIC
DARK LEGACY	DARK POSSESSION	DARK GOLD
DARK CAROUSEL	DARK CELEBRATION	DARK DESIRE
DARK PROMISES	DARK DEMON	DARK PRINCE
DARK GHOST	DARK SECRET	
DARK BLOOD	DARK DESTINY	

ANTHOLOGIES

EDGE OF DARKNESS
(with Maggie Shayne and Lori Herter)

DARKEST AT DAWN
(includes Dark Hunger *and* Dark Secret*)*

SEA STORM
(includes Magic in the Wind *and* Oceans of Fire*)*

FEVER
(includes The Awakening *and* Wild Rain*)*

FANTASY
(with Emma Holly, Sabrina Jeffries, and Elda Minger)

LOVER BEWARE
(with Fiona Brand, Katherine Sutcliffe, and Eileen Wilks)

HOT BLOODED
(with Maggie Shayne, Emma Holly, and Angela Knight)

SPECIALS

DARK CRIME
THE AWAKENING
DARK HUNGER
MAGIC IN THE WIND

RED ON THE RIVER
MURDER AT SUNRISE LAKE

THUNDER
GAME

CHRISTINE
FEEHAN

BERKLEY
NEW YORK

BERKLEY
An imprint of Penguin Random House LLC
1745 Broadway, New York, NY 10019
penguinrandomhouse.com

Book design by Kelly Lipovich

Library of Congress Cataloging-in-Publication Data
Names: Feehan, Christine, author.
Title: Thunder game / Christine Feehan.
Description: New York : Berkley, 2025. | Series: GhostWalker novel |
Identifiers: LCCN 2024049358 (print) | LCCN 2024049359 (ebook) |
ISBN 9780593819630 (hardcover) | ISBN 9780593819654 (ebook)
Subjects: LCGFT: Paranormal fiction. | Romance fiction. | Novels.
Classification: LCC PS3606.E36 T49 2025 (print) |
LCC PS3606.E36 (ebook) | DDC 813/.6—dc23/eng/20241021
LC record available at https://lccn.loc.gov/2024049358
LC ebook record available at https://lccn.loc.gov/2024049359

Printed in the United States of America
1st Printing

The authorized representative in the EU for product safety and compliance is
Penguin Random House Ireland, Morrison Chambers, 32 Nassau Street,
Dublin D02 YH68, Ireland, https://eu-contact.penguin.ie.

For Leila, my beautiful granddaughter.
This one is for you.

FOR MY READERS

Be sure to go to ChristineFeehan.com/members/ to sign up for my private book announcement list and download the free ebook of *Dark Desserts*. Join my community and get firsthand news, enter the book discussions, ask your questions and chat with me. Please feel free to email me at Christine@ChristineFeehan.com. I would love to hear from you.

ACKNOWLEDGMENTS

Thank you to Diane Trudeau. I would never have been able to get this book written under such circumstances. To Cheryl Wilson for her invaluable help. You always come through. To Sheila English for taking care of all the details in my life! What would I do without you? To Brian Feehan for keeping me on track. To Denise for handling all the details of every aspect of my life, which is so crazy. And to my amazing invaluable researcher Karen Brownfield Houton—you are a miracle to me! Thank you all so very much!

THE GHOSTWALKER
SYMBOL DETAILS

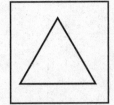

SIGNIFIES
shadow

SIGNIFIES
protection against evil forces

SIGNIFIES
the Greek letter psi, which is used by parapsychology researchers to signify ESP or other psychic abilities

SIGNIFIES
qualities of a knight—loyalty, generosity, courage and honor

SIGNIFIES
shadow knights who protect against evil forces using psychic powers, courage and honor

nox noctis est nostri

THE GHOSTWALKER CREED

We are the GhostWalkers, we live in the shadows
The sea, the earth, and the air are our domain
No fallen comrade will be left behind
We are loyalty and honor bound
We are invisible to our enemies
and we destroy them where we find them
We believe in justice and we protect our country
and those unable to protect themselves
What goes unseen, unheard and unknown are GhostWalkers
There is honor in the shadows and it is us
We move in complete silence whether in jungle or desert
We walk among our enemy unseen and unheard
Striking without sound and scatter to the winds
before they have knowledge of our existence
We gather information and wait with endless patience
for that perfect moment to deliver swift justice
We are both merciful and merciless
We are relentless and implacable in our resolve
We are the GhostWalkers and the night is ours

THUNDER
GAME

1

It took a moment of time. One heartbeat. A split second. Diego Campos had grown up in a cruel, unrelenting world and knew for a fact that everything you planned, everything you held dear, could be lost in that single space of time. Despite all the plans you made, all the precautions you took, that single moment would change your life.

Those horrible life-altering moments had happened to him many times, setting him on dark paths he could never come back from. And he was damned tired of trying.

He had come home to die. The only thing he wanted from life now was to be cremated and have his ashes buried next to his parents and five siblings in the graveyard behind the cabin his father had built so many years ago, there in the Appalachian Mountains.

He was on his way home to the old cabin now. With the exception of his brother Rubin, most of the rest of his family were already there, interred in the rocky soil that had been their home for so many years. It was important to him that his ashes were laid to rest beside them, and he knew, being a GhostWalker, that wouldn't happen if he died anywhere but at the cabin, where Rubin would find him. Even grieving, Rubin would follow his wishes to the letter.

And he would grieve.

Rubin had followed others into the military and into the volunteer program of enhancement of psychic abilities. Diego had followed Rubin. Both scored exceptionally high and were accepted into the program. In the end, not only had their psychic abilities been enhanced, but they had been altered genetically. Given animal, bird and even reptile DNA. Those traits allowed them to do extraordinary things, but they also brought out every negative trait any volunteer in the GhostWalker program had. Diego had quite a bit of darkness in him. That had never stopped Rubin from having intense loyalty toward Diego, however.

Diego had driven up to the old trail that led the way up the mountain. He was miles from home, having to travel mostly by foot to reach the family homestead. He pulled off the pitted dirt road into the shelter of trees and brush. It was one of the places Rubin would look for his vehicle. They had often returned to the mountains and would leave supplies for each other in the truck they'd hidden in the bushes. There was an old road leading up the mountain, but they rarely used it. Neither liked to leave tracks.

Despite the shit show that was his life, Diego could never say he hadn't been loved. But Rubin would be grieving for a man who had ceased to exist years earlier—hell, a man who never truly had existed. All the good in him had died during his brutal childhood years.

He was sorry Rubin would be the one to find him. If there were a way to spare his brother that, he would. But ending it at the cabin, knowing Rubin would be along in the next week or two to visit the neighbors who needed a doctor, was the only way he could think of to ensure his last wishes were carried out.

Wildflowers grew everywhere, splashes of color springing up in every direction, vying for space with ferns and various bushes. The moment he saw the verbesina, memories of his sisters making crowns from the bright yellow flowers flooded his mind. They'd been so young, laughing as they wove the strands of flowers together and placed them on one another's heads.

His heart clenched in his chest. Years earlier, he and Rubin had planted verbesina and other wildflowers his sisters had loved in the family graveyard located behind the cabin. They made a point of keeping the little family cemetery nice when they returned each year.

August was ending, and it was time for their semiannual trek home. Rubin hadn't questioned that Diego wanted to go up a little early. He knew Diego preferred being in the mountains, and it was natural for him to go a couple of weeks early. Besides, Rubin was married now and had commitments to his wife. Diego was counting on Rubin's love for Jonquille to get him through the next few weeks.

Rubin was ten months older than Diego. They'd been seven years old when their father had died, leaving their mother with nine children and only the land to sustain them. Together, Rubin and Diego had dug the grave and buried their father in that small cemetery behind the cabin.

Hoping to bring in money to feed the family, their two oldest brothers, at fourteen and fifteen, had gone off looking for work but never returned. After two months with no word, Diego realized his older brothers had to be dead, or they would have returned to aid the family, so he made up his mind to protect the others. He had gifts, dark ones perhaps, but incredible gifts he knew he could develop. He set about doing just that every chance he had, determined to protect those he loved. But it cost him dearly.

As the next-oldest male after their missing brothers, Rubin had become the de facto head of the family just days before his eighth birthday. The expectation had been for him to run the family, to provide for them, even though he was only eight. Diego was his shadow, watching over him, honing his skills with his rifle, to better protect Rubin when they went out in the rugged terrain during every type of weather to hunt, fish, and forage for food to bring home to their mother and sisters.

Rifle skills weren't the only thing Diego worked on. He had a close affinity with animals. He could understand them, and they could understand him. He worked hard to establish as many connections as he could with the wildlife and birds surrounding them. That led to better hunting skills and gave them an added layer of protection. His mother, a stern, religious woman, was certain he practiced witchcraft. Her punishments didn't stop him though, not when it was for the survival of all of them.

Diego shifted the pack carrying his favorite weapons as he came upon a stream where he'd fished for trout with Rubin and his older sister, Mary. They'd laughed so much together, and Rubin had caught the biggest trout in his life. Their family had eaten well that night, Diego and Mary contributing with their smaller but tasty fish. He could not only remember his sister's laughter, but he heard the sound of it in his mind. He could see them all so clearly, their lips pink and stained with grease from the fish they'd fried up in Mama's old cast-iron skillet. Even Mama had been smiling, a rare thing, but she had that day, her eyes warm as she watched her children eating and laughing.

Man, that trout had tasted so good. That was a good day. He stood by the stream, a half smile on his face at the memory until he remembered the tragedy that had come a few weeks later. Diego's fingers flexed around the strap of his backpack, knuckles going white as his grip tightened. That was the terrible truth that dogged him. There was never any good in his life that bad didn't soon follow.

Rubin and Diego were nine when Mary left home to get married. Mathew Sawyer had been a good man, but she was barely of age. She died in childbirth nine months later, leaving behind her newborn son. Rubin and Diego dug the grave and buried her beside their father.

Diego had been particularly close to Mary, and he was devastated by her death. He knew Rubin was as well. But they were quiet about their grief, doing their best to comfort their mother and sisters.

Diego toed a large rock beside the stream and watched as several bugs crawled out from under it. Memories continued to flood his mind, and even the beetles couldn't distract him.

The year they turned ten was a decent year. They managed to put together a generator from old parts they found in a mine. They came up with a way to bring gravity-fed running water to the house, the first their mother ever had.

Diego shifted his pack once more, used to the heavy weight of it, and began to follow the winding stream up toward Luther Gunthrie's place. Rubin and Diego had often snuck past Luther's homestead to get to the best fishing spots. Night fishing for catfish or bass often saved them from starvation.

Diego had begun to get very proficient at calling wildlife to him, but he felt guilty each time they had to kill a deer or rabbit he'd summoned. He didn't feel quite so guilty when he practiced on the fish in the streams. He'd had to hide his abilities from his mother. Although his connection with animals saved his family from starvation, she believed the devil was in him and she'd try to beat the affliction out of him.

The thought of night fishing brought up one of his worst

memories. That next summer, Lucy, their twelve-year-old sister, had gone night fishing with eight-year-old Jayne. Four men hiking the Appalachian Trail had run across the two girls. When their sisters didn't come home, Rubin and Diego went to find them. Lucy was dead, and Jayne was nearly comatose from the brutal attack.

After carrying the girls home, they went back to track their sisters' attackers. Rubin and Diego caught up with the men the following night. By morning all four men were dead. Rubin and Diego left them where they lay for the vultures and wildlife to take care of. They lived in a remote part of the mountains, and neither of them worried about the bodies being discovered.

They were thirteen when the flu took Jayne and then their sister Ruby. They buried both girls next to their father and sisters. Their mother never spoke a word after that. She sat in a chair, rocking, barely eating or sleeping. Just rocking, staring straight ahead with a vacant stare.

Their fourteenth winter was brutal. The snow fell every day, and they ran out of food. Rubin and Diego had no choice but to go hunting. When they returned to the cabin, their mother was dead. She had hanged herself, and Star, their last living sister, blamed herself for falling asleep. Star snuck out that night, leaving a note that said she'd gone to join the Catholic nuns in a convent. Alarmed, they tracked her and found her frozen body near the stream where Lucy had been murdered. It took days to bury their mother and sister in the frozen ground alongside the rest of their family.

After that, Diego decided that his sole purpose in life was to protect Rubin. He knew his brother was a good man. He didn't have that dark place inside him that Diego did. Diego also knew he had to be very careful that Rubin didn't realize his younger brother possessed the same gifts he had and was using them to protect Rubin, even after they joined the GhostWalker program.

Until Rubin and Diego discovered the truth about Luther Gunthrie and the government experiments done on him, they'd believed Whitney had been the man who conceived the GhostWalker program and psychically enhanced the soldiers who tested high in psychic ability. He'd also genetically altered them without their permission, making the GhostWalkers enhanced physically as well as psychically. They'd signed on for the psychic enhancements because they believed they would be a help to their country and fellow soldiers. The genetic enhancements, however, they hadn't known about and had never agreed to. Still, they were soldiers who had joined a top secret military program, and they did their jobs, no matter how dangerous it was or how many times they were betrayed by factions of the government.

Each branch of the service had one GhostWalker team, consisting of ten members. The first team experimented on had a few major problems. Some needed anchors to drain away the psychic energy that adhered to them like magnets. Others had brain bleeds. Every subsequent team had fewer and fewer flaws until Whitney had achieved his goal and created his prize group, the Pararescue Team. They might have what Whitney considered fewer flaws, but they also had more genetic enhancements than any of them cared for. Most of their talents were hidden from Whitney and never documented.

Diego might have been ten months younger than Rubin, but they may as well have been twins. Each gift that should have been unique to one was shared. It was just that Diego never allowed anyone to see him use some of the stronger and more valued talents his brother was known for. Once those gifts had been enhanced by Whitney, both men's abilities had continued to grow in strength, though Diego and even Rubin had kept the full extent of their power increase a closely guarded secret. As for hiding most of his psychic talents entirely, well, Diego had his reasons, and he would take those to his grave.

Diego turned away from the stream to take a shortcut through the denser forest. The trees were tall, and the canopy overhead cut out a great deal of light. This grove of trees was at the very bottom of the mountain as it began its climb upward. Although a long hike from their homestead, Diego had favored practicing calling birds and wildlife to him in the heart of that dense forest. He was protected there, and the animals were diverse. His mother's friends or the other children couldn't spy on him and tattle to her. She might think she knew what he was doing, and she often punished him for disappearing all day and sometimes overnight, but he felt the punishments were worth what he was gaining.

That proved to be true when Rubin came looking for him once in an effort to keep him from getting whipped with a switch. Their mother had been ranting and raving. Rubin wanted Diego to hunt food and bring it back so their mother would think that was what he'd been doing each time he disappeared. Diego no longer cared if he was beaten. His mother refused to love or want him no matter what he'd done to try to earn her affection, and he had given up. He went his own way unless Rubin asked him to do something. And he protected Rubin. Was his shadow, whether his brother wanted it or not.

His first huge success at commanding animals had taken place right there in that very section of the forest. Not only his first success, but the worst lesson possible in responsibility and the consequences of meddling with nature.

The memory washed over him, and for the first time he felt weak, so much so he had to stop and crouch down in the brush, breathing deeply, reliving that moment when he'd nearly lost his brother. When he'd been utterly responsible for the demise of a pack, animals that he loved.

It had been a bad winter with slim pickings for the wildlife, including coyotes. They'd grown bold in places, snatching cats and even small dogs right out from under the noses of the homesteaders. Their mournful howls could be heard throughout the mountain trails, adding to the mystique of the fog-shrouded forest.

Diego had a plan to aid them and cull some of the old, dying deer at the same time. He worked patiently to connect with the pack occupying the thick groves close to Luther's homestead. If he could eventually use the coyotes as scouts, the beatings he received for disappearing over long periods would be worth it. The pack accepted him, responding to his calls when he aided them in hunting.

The pack was hungry. Starving, just like his family. The more time he spent trying to connect with the animals, the more he felt part of their pack. The first time he was able to help them bring down an aging doe—a huge sacrifice when his family was hungry— he had felt intense guilt for not packing the meat home, but at the same time, the hunger of the pack had been overwhelming.

It had never occurred to him that the pack would hunt a human being. He'd never seen evidence of it. He'd never heard of coyotes doing such a thing, but that particular day, the pack that he'd been helping to feed surrounded Rubin when his brother came to find him. They darted in, trying to knock him to the ground. Rubin shot two of them, and Diego had no choice but to dispatch the others until all six were lying dead.

After much thought and soul-searching, Diego had to admit to himself that he had been responsible for the change in behavior of the coyote pack. Until he had helped them pull down bigger game, they had survived on small animals like rabbits and mice. They'd eaten carrion and plants. But once they learned they could pull down a larger animal and consume it, humans appeared as prey to them. Diego had to accept that responsibility. That particular lesson had been heart-wrenching, and it took him years to get over it.

Now he no longer had to ensure that Rubin remained alive and well in the world. Rubin had met and married Jonquille, a perfect match for him. He was happy and healthy and in a good place. Their GhostWalker unit would protect him. Rubin was a psychic surgeon, a very rare and sought-after talent. That alone would ensure he was guarded. It was the kind of talent every unit wished they had, but Rubin and Diego's unit kept it very quiet. No one outside their close-knit division could know. If Whitney—or the government—found out, Rubin would be taken and studied. Most likely they would take his brain apart in an attempt to make others like him.

Diego had a very persuasive voice. At times he could use compelling energy to get others to do what he wanted. He wanted Rubin safe, and time and again, he ensured that every member of their unit wanted the same thing. Diego was considered an amazing sniper, but there were others in his unit who could shoot as well as him or better. At least so it appeared to everyone observing them. He made certain he was never considered the best. He kept his talents in the shadows even while he played the front man, doing paperwork and setting up whatever Rubin needed. He always appeared quiet but approachable. He was very, very careful not to draw undue attention. Ever.

Luther Gunthrie's property was situated at the base of the mountain and ran upward into the heavy forest. Diego happened to know there was a network of caves the old man didn't reveal to anyone. He'd even hidden his moonshine still there. Rubin and Diego had discovered one of the secret entrances when they were tracking him, knowing he'd been severely injured.

Diego decided visiting with Luther Gunthrie on the way up to his cabin was a practical idea. Luther was getting up there in age and never went to a doctor. He made moonshine, and since his beloved wife had died, he kept to himself. The trail leading to the rugged holler back to his home was so overgrown one couldn't recognize that it had ever been an actual path. Gunthrie had planted wildflowers along the trails and paths until it was impossible to know a road had ever been there.

Since his beloved Lotty was gone, Luther discouraged visitors, particularly the official kind that he believed came looking for his still—or were government men determined to bring him back to their labs. Over the years he'd built up a mystique with his neighbors. Although families lived miles from one another, they knew each other—or thought they did.

Most people had no idea that Luther was an original Ghost-Walker, the ones who'd existed long before Whitney began his experiments. In the Vietnam era, there were a small number of recruits who had volunteered to be enhanced physically. The hope had been to produce supersoldiers. In retrospect, it made sense that Whitney wasn't the first to come up with the idea. Whitney was ambitious, narcissistic and a monster. He was quite brilliant, there was no doubt about that, but he built everything he did on someone else's research.

Throughout the intervening years, Luther had been "worked on" more than once. Despite his age, after serving his country in Vietnam, he was sent to Iraq and Afghanistan. Like Diego and Rubin, he had been sent out on countless missions, all of which he had completed. Each time he returned to his home in the Appalachian Mountains, he hoped he would be left alone.

Luther's one wish was to be buried beside his beloved wife, Lotty. The man had expressed to Diego and Rubin that he knew the government would come for his body. Diego and Rubin would never allow him to fall into the hands of the enemy. Diego knew it would be the same for him. It was the reason he had come home to the Appalachian Mountains. He knew Rubin would find him and ensure he was cremated and his ashes buried in the family cemetery.

The persistent cry of a red-tailed hawk alerted him to possible danger. The bird uncharacteristically darted through the trees, flying low to keep his attention, banked and then flew back toward the road, giving him the impression of three vehicles covered with branches and vines tucked into the outer border of the tree line.

Diego's heart dropped when he came onto the three trucks. There were no identifying plates, but he knew immediately they were military. He'd seen vehicles like that before, when men had come for Jonquille months earlier. He opened each hood, prepared to disable the vehicle, but just like before, when Jonquille had been in trouble, someone had been there before him. He guessed Luther. Little got past Luther when someone was on his land.

He picked up the pace. To get to Luther's home, one had to trek a long way from the main trail to find the entrance to the holler. It was another mile or so before the cabin came into view. The land belonged to Luther, and he had a lot of acreage. He knew every inch of his property. Diego was the same way about his family's land.

As a young boy, he had explored continuously, and he did so each time he returned. He was very familiar with the wildlife, flora and fauna on the vast acreage Rubin and he owned together. Each time a property bordering their land came up for sale, they bought it with the idea of better protecting the old homestead.

Luther's cabin was nearly hidden among the trees and overgrown grasses and brush. Diego knew that just another forty feet to the west of the cabin was the most magnificent clearing surrounded by forest. Luther had worked at transplanting every kind of wildflower growing in the woods to that meadow because Lotty loved them so. Luther had built a fence to protect Lotty's vegetable garden from deer. Whatever his wife wanted, Luther made it happen. In return, she spoiled her man, patching every hole in his clothing and mending his socks. He always had a warm meal waiting no matter when he returned. She lavished attention on him and turned the cabin into a warm, welcoming, peaceful home for him.

Diego was halfway to the cabin, making his way through the profusion of wildflowers covering the trail, when he heard it—the moment that would change the course of his life once again. The sound of gunfire was distinctive. And the shooters weren't firing off one or two shots, like hunters might. No, this was a volley.

These were no hunters illegally poaching on Luther Gunthrie's land. And those were no hunting rifles being fired. Diego had spent most of his adult life in the military. He knew an M4 when he heard one. He was hearing more than one.

Whoever these men were, they hadn't taken their time to get to know their adversary. Like many before them, they made the mistake of taking Luther at face value. He was at least eighty, although he appeared ageless. But despite his age, Luther Gunthrie was a man who could handle weapons and any kind of combat. Any kind. In fact, the crusty old wolf welcomed combat. Not only could he outhunt and outshoot men a quarter his age, his property was riddled with bolt-holes and depressions in the ground Luther could fit into, as well as countless weapons caches secreted away. At any time of the day, he was more prepared for war than most militaries.

Diego normally didn't travel with quite as many weapons as Luther had stashed around his property, but on this trip, he had brought a small arsenal with him. From the first moment he had planned his exit from life, he'd intended to leave everything he valued for his brother Rubin, including his guns. As a result, he was carrying his favorite sniper rifle, as well as his hunting rifle, a Glock, a Sig Sauer and plenty of ammo for each. He was also armed to the teeth with his favorite knives.

His weapons weren't the only advantage Diego had on his side. He glanced up at the trees, spotting a red-tailed hawk perched on the branch of a large oak tree not far away. Diego could sense another two hawks within a mile radius of his current position.

Ever since he could remember, Diego had always had a special affinity with birds. It was one of his many abilities that all the psychic and genetic manipulations of the GhostWalker program had enhanced. Prior to entering the program, he had already developed a rapport with the birds in this area, using them to hunt or scout for him.

With a thought, he sent the three hawks into the air to pinpoint the shooters.

He could connect with each hawk separately and view the enemy from the bird's perspective. When he did that, however, it took so much energy it often left him feeling weak. He couldn't afford that until he knew what he was facing. Instead, he instructed the hawks to scout and return to him. Almost immediately, he received the impression of men dropping from the sky to land in the trees above the clearing. More men had come from the road below the cabin. They were surrounding Luther, coming in from various directions, utilizing a ground crew and those parachuting in. This was a very serious attack.

Diego quickly made his way up the side of the mountain, using a deer trail and staying hidden within the brush. He had scouted Luther's land many times and knew the best locations to oversee the cabin, the meadow and even part of the forest. Luther's adversaries had parachuted in and, wanting to avoid the trees, were mostly at the lower edge of the mountain. Those coming in from the road were swarming behind Luther's cabin.

Luther should have made his way into the cabin, where he had access to the caves, or at least headed toward one of the cave entrances, but instead, he was caught between the cabin and the meadow, in high grass with little protection. How was that even possible? The explanation was that Luther wasn't alone. With him were two women.

One woman was a fighter, armed and clearly familiar with her weapon. She had dark auburn hair pulled back in a thick braid. She wore cargo pants and appeared armed to the teeth. Even with all the guns and ammunition hanging from her belt and slung around her neck, Diego could see she was slender with a woman's figure. He wished she wore a vest. Bullets were hitting too close. Luther shouted instructions to her, and she nodded, staying low as she crawled through the brush toward a small depression behind several large rocks.

The other woman was curled up in a ball, rocking back and forth, hands over her ears. She was directly behind Luther, and he kept his body between her and the incoming fire. It was clear both Luther and the unknown warrior woman were protecting the woman on the ground. Diego couldn't tell if she'd been wounded. She had darker hair than the fighter, but it had shades of red in it. From what he could see, she had a similar build, though she might have been a little lighter.

A five-man team kept the three pinned down, but Diego could see they hadn't come alone. Behind Luther and the two women, another five-man team was creeping through the brush behind the cabin toward them. Another five-man team was spread out in the forest, ringing the meadow. That was fifteen men they'd sent after Luther. Diego's earlier estimation of the attackers went up a notch. Clearly, they did know who they were confronting. So what was their endgame? Were they trying to acquire Luther? The women? Or kill them all?

Diego let out the loud screech of a red-tailed hawk to warn Luther he'd joined the party. He repeated the screaming message three times to ensure that Luther would realize the cry was a code.

Luther knew every bird on his property and the sound of their voices. He said something to Warrior Woman. She looked up at the mountains in his direction and then nodded.

Luther cupped his hands around his mouth and screeched a reply. *Enemies. Lethal force.*

One of the men with an M4 shot at the woman, spitting bullets around her. It was covering fire to allow the team behind them to advance. Without hesitation, Diego shot him between the eyes and then switched targets to a man with an M5, killing him the same way. Two down and less than a second had passed. He moved position, knowing they would be looking for him.

Even as he rolled into the deeper depression and crawled backward, a volley of shots rang out, bullets sweeping across the mountain near his location. They hadn't spotted him, but they were experienced and had zeroed in on his position quickly. Too darned quick. Someone was directing these men, and that someone had to be found.

He crawled through the brush, using the impressions the circling birds sent to him to guide his way. Through the birds in the air, he was aware of the positions of his enemies. It was important to find the commander, the one directing the others. He sent one of the hawks to cover more of the territory in the direction he considered most likely for the man to have set up his command center. The soldiers in the brush behind the cabin were creeping closer to Luther and the women. The unit at the edge of the forest was more cautious, but they were advancing stealthily.

Diego reached his next destination point, an outcropping of boulders jutting out of the mountain. The brush was thick, but there were few trees. He let out another series of hawk cries, warning Luther of the danger. Warrior Woman quickly scanned the forest as if she understood the message he'd sent to Gunthrie.

When she moved her head slightly, rays from the sun settled in her hair, lighting the thick braid to various shades of red from dark to fiery. It was unexpected when her hair had appeared dark in the shadows and shade of the trees. And distracting.

A frisson of alarm crept down his spine as he eyed the woman through his scope. She had a face so beautiful that it captured his attention and held it fast. He drank in the sight of her, rapt with a single-minded focus that turned the frisson of alarm into a blaring warning. Diego catalogued people when he saw them, filing their images in his mind with near-robotic precision. He could recall anyone he'd met in great detail, but he never took such notice of a woman's beauty. He certainly didn't pay particular attention to her high cheekbones and large green eyes. Or the fact that her mouth was perfectly shaped. Perfectly.

Nothing distracted him. He wasn't that kind of a man. When he hunted, he did so with a single-minded purpose. The fact that he not only noticed but was practically fixated on the details of this woman's physical appearance was truly disturbing.

Who was this mystery woman? What was she doing there? He had a feeling she was the cause of the assault on Luther.

Another volley of shots spat at his previous location, snapping Diego out of his fascinated preoccupation with the woman. The gunfire sounded like a combination of rolling thunder and angry bees, but he wasn't anywhere near where the bullets struck. It was clear the attackers weren't familiar with the terrain.

Diego wasn't a man who cursed often, but the activity surrounding Luther suddenly doubled, going from three five-man teams to six. Someone had sent an army after Luther.

Diego needed to get down there and find out what was going on. He switched rifles, inserting the trackers Mordichai Fortunes, a fellow GhostWalker, had made. It would be impossible for those hunting Luther and the women to detect the trackers in the bloodstream. That was the beauty of having a few geniuses in his Ghost-Walker unit.

Again, he let out the cries of the hawk, this time a series of hunting cries, warning Luther he was about to be overrun and that Diego was going to shoot darts into all three of them. He didn't wait. They didn't have that kind of time. Luther turned his head to speak to the women, and Diego fired the first dart. It penetrated the skin in Luther's neck, and Diego knew from experience that the dart felt like the sting of an angry bee.

Immediately he switched targets, going for the female behind Luther. She dropped her hands in response to Luther's command and turned her head, giving Diego a better target. He took the shot and switched to Warrior Woman. If the man running the soldiers was watching, he didn't want him speculating when the first young woman clapped her hand over her neck. Luther had been stoic, not even flinching. He hoped Warrior Woman would be the same.

The tracker was a needle-shaped dart filled with nano-transmitters that flooded the bloodstream and then adhered to the walls of the veins and arteries. They lasted about three months before they naturally dissolved. The needle carrying the liquid was slim and also dissolvable. It still stung like hell entering the body. Warrior Woman was clearly arguing with Luther, shaking her head adamantly. Diego didn't have to be good at reading body language. Warrior Woman did not want a transmitter in her.

She turned her head toward Luther gesturing, every line of her body protesting. Diego took the shot, uncaring that she was adamantly opposed to the transmitter. Hell was about to rain down on them.

She had discipline, he had to give her that. She didn't cover her neck or even jerk when the needle went in, but she did turn her head and flick a scowl at the side of the mountain where he was concealed. At the same time, she gave him the finger. It was an elegant movement, her gun in her fist, the finger riding the barrel. She looked beautifully defiant. Unexpectedly, he found himself smiling. A genuine smile. Strange that she could make him smile in such a dire situation.

He let out another shrieking cry, warning Luther to move toward one of his bolt-holes that would lead to the caverns. The moment Luther signaled to the women to retreat, to press back into the brush, a volley of shots rang out, the bullets spitting all around the three. Warrior Woman returned fire, and two of the enemy shooters went down. Diego took out three who were coming up behind them. Luther shot one soldier at nearly point-blank range and another as the soldier fired from the cabin roof.

Diego was certain the soldiers were attempting to herd the three to a specific spot with their gunfire. Warrior Woman must have thought so as well. She backed into another depression and scooted into deeper brush, angling away from Luther and the other woman. Diego could see her deliberately moving brush to keep attention centered on her. At the same time, she fired at the wave of soldiers spreading out to capture them.

Luther caught up to the other woman and ran, slinging her over his shoulder, staying low but firing rapidly at any soldiers he could see. Instantly a volley of shots rang out, returning the fire. Luther stumbled and nearly went down but kept moving, trying for one of his bolt-holes.

Diego shot three soldiers as they sprayed bullets at Luther and the girl on his shoulder. Warrior Woman spat bullets as well and two more soldiers went down. Movement up higher on the mountain, above the first wave of soldiers, caught his attention. The hawks in the sky screamed warnings at him.

More soldiers. Luther and the women didn't stand a chance even with him picking off soldiers. He doubted they had time to escape into a bolt-hole. He continued firing, trying to give Luther cover, but the soldiers were swarming around him. Luther staggered, went down to one knee and gently deposited the girl on the ground. He leaned close to her, whispering something. She clutched his arm for a moment and then nodded before letting him go.

Diego knew immediately that Luther was going to try to make it to one of the entrances to the caves. By abandoning the young woman, he gave them both a chance to live. Luther had to believe the soldiers wouldn't kill the girl, who had once again curled up in a ball. She waved him away, and Luther was up and running. Diego rapidly shot as many of the soldiers gunning for him as possible, but there were so many. Inevitably Luther went down, rolling and tumbling, leaving a trail of blood splotches until he disappeared in the higher grass surrounding a pile of boulders.

Diego shot one of the soldiers who shot Luther, but even as the bullet plowed through the man's chest, a secondary spray of blood spewed close to the first. Warrior Woman had turned back and was firing as well. She seemed to be an excellent shot. When she tried to get to the other two, she was instantly cut off.

From his vantage point above them, he could see the soldiers swooping in on the young woman on the ground. They surrounded her, guns out, but she didn't put up any resistance as they approached her. It didn't appear she had any weapons on her, and it was apparent to anyone looking at her that she was violently ill.

They secured her and turned away from the firefight still waging between Warrior Woman and other soldiers. They began to run back toward the meadow. Diego had to let them go and turn his attention to aiding Warrior Woman. She was game, that was certain. She didn't flinch from a fight, even though the odds were overwhelming.

Diego didn't miss, and he was dropping the soldiers closest to her as quickly as possible. She had no choice but to move from the depression she was in and head up the mountain to evade the wave of soldiers. She couldn't get to the other woman, and she probably had no idea where Luther had gone. He'd vanished, as was his way. There were times when Diego wondered if he could teleport. He knew a couple of men who could do so, but they'd been enhanced in ways he hadn't thought Luther had been.

Warrior Woman refused to give up or go down. She sighted target after target as her guns spat thunder. He tried to help her, picking off every enemy combatant he could. But no matter how many soldiers they took out, more took their place.

He swore as a bullet smashed into her, driving her backward and down. It appeared as if she might have been hit with a second bullet while she was going down. Diego retaliated, killing the two shooters, but soldiers swarmed around her, kicking her weapon from her hand and hastily dragging her into a more sheltered position, where a man, presumably a medic, crouched over her.

Diego didn't like the way his heart accelerated or the way a terrible cold fury burned through him. He'd felt that same kind of icy rage when his sister had been murdered. He'd been just a boy at the time, but he'd gone hunting nevertheless, and he hadn't stopped until all four offenders were food for scavengers.

He knew just how unrelenting and merciless he could be when the cold fury took him. It was not a sensation he enjoyed. He didn't want to be a man who gloried in revenge. Or one who would kill out of anger, no matter how righteous that anger might be.

No, he preferred to be detached and coolheaded. To know that every bullet he fired, every life he took, was a necessity, a task he performed solely to defend others, protect his own life or serve his country.

After a few minutes, the men hoisted the limp, unconscious body of Warrior Woman and started hiking up the mountain with her. Clearly, they were making their way up the mountain, through the forest, to a clearing where they could rendezvous with a helicopter. Reluctantly he let them go.

He studied the soldiers. There was now a division of thirds. One-third had taken the girl with the darker hair toward the road where their vehicles had been left. They were going to find that Luther had rendered them useless. It would slow them down but not stop them. The second faction, the soldiers who had parachuted in, were taking Warrior Woman into the forest and up the mountain. The last third were scouring Luther's homestead, looking for him.

Diego made his way down the mountain in a careful retreat. He had trackers in both women. Admittedly, he was concerned about Warrior Woman. She'd taken some nasty hits. His instinct was to go after her, but with the transmitters he could follow her easily enough. It was the only logical decision. He had to find out what he was dealing with before he made his plans.

Finding Luther was the most important first step. If Luther was in good enough shape, he'd be able to go after the other woman.

Luther would be able to tell Diego what was going on. Why so many soldiers were determined to take the women and why those soldiers were still hunting Luther. Once he secured Luther, he would then follow the soldiers who'd taken Warrior Woman. He hoped Luther was in good enough shape to go after the other woman. That was his best course of action, but he couldn't do anything for either woman until he ensured that Luther was alive and would stay that way.

Diego scanned his surroundings. He knew there was an extensive cave system running below the property. He knew several ways into the cave system, though the caves weren't on any map. Luther had discovered them accidentally and established several hidden entrances to them, including one from inside his cabin. The cabin entrance was closest. To reach it, Diego just had to get through the line of soldiers and sneak into the cabin without being seen. The soldiers had already searched it looking for Luther. He had a big property, and the chances of them returning to search it again were low. They might guard it, and he particularly needed to rid them of their commander. He would have to do that before he got to the cabin.

Diego called on the red-tailed hawk he'd sent out to find the commander in charge. He would have to be secreted somewhere up high, where he could oversee Luther's property. He was directing the remaining soldiers in a grid pattern. The hawk reacted with a dizzying vision of a man perched on the branch of a tree. Diego would need a clear line of sight to take him down.

The cabin wasn't exactly in the open; there were too many flowering bushes growing tall and wide around it. That provided him with cover as he made his way through enemy lines to a large bush growing near the cabin's front door. He used his ability to feel the ground and felt the crush of heavy boots coming down on tall grasses and brush.

The flame azalea standing sentry beside the cabin's door was in full bloom, the showy double blossoms bright and gorgeous and plentiful, the low-hanging branches providing a curtain for him to slide behind. The last time he'd hidden in this bush, he'd had to wait for enemies close to the cabin to move past, and it was no different this time.

The flowers were gorgeous. The bush had been Lotty's favorite, and Luther babied it until it thrived, the abundance of fiery red-orange flowers a testament to the great love he'd borne for his wife.

Rubin loved Jonquille the way Luther had loved Lotty.

The deep connection between them left Diego feeling isolated and alone. Rubin and Jonquille didn't mean for him to feel that way. His brother and sister-in-law included Diego in their lives, but just seeing them, he felt apart. Just as when he'd observed Lotty and Luther when he'd been a child. Outside their circle of love. Unworthy of being included in it.

He knew he hadn't been loved as a child by his mother. She'd withdrawn from her children but still tried to take care of them—with the exception of Diego. Diego had never been able to do anything right. He'd learned fast that he was going to get into trouble no matter what he did. Somehow, it didn't matter to him. He'd adopted Rubin's code and stayed with it. Loyalty. Family. Community. Survival. Rubin had been the leader in all things moral, and Diego followed him.

He could honestly say he knew how to love. He loved his brother and Jonquille. He loved Ezekiel, Mordichai and Malichai Fortunes. When teenage Rubin and Diego hopped a train and headed for anywhere but here, they landed in Detroit, where Ezekiel eventually found them on the street trying to survive. They had no problem in the woods, but learning the ways of city streets was much more difficult, and they had a tendency to defend themselves to the death. Ezekiel took them under his protective wing and guided them through those perils. And there were many perils. Just as many as living off the land in these mountains provided, only in the city, the dangers were different.

The faint vibration in the ground ceased, confirming the soldiers had moved away from Luther's cabin.

Once the soldiers were completely away from the cabin, Diego made it onto the roof. Thanks to the red-tailed hawk, he knew where the commanding officer was secreted while directing the search for Luther. It took only seconds to set up and begin his sweep of the trees.

The terrain rose into a good-sized hill with a large grove of trees covering it. Using his enhanced vision, he saw the commander's face come into sharp focus.

Diego took a breath, let it out and squeezed the trigger. The moment he did, he rolled from his vantage point, taking his gun with him. He hit the ground, caught up his pack and entered the cabin.

2

Entering the caves tracking a wounded Luther was a bit like hunting a wounded cougar or leopard. Diego knew the way through the cabin into the narrow, low man-made tunnel Luther had dug to connect to the cave system. The dark, twisting uphill tunnel was reinforced with metal, rebar and cement. Diego followed along, bending nearly double in places as he made his way uphill and then down toward the woods.

At first the tunnel was uncomfortably warm, but that gave way to cold air abruptly as he came to a wide-open cavern. Layers of rock were of unexpected colors and quite beautiful. The cave was a good distance underground, so he knew his voice wouldn't carry to any soldiers sweeping the area looking for Luther.

Diego sang a few notes of a female morning bird, the indigo bunting. Lotty loved those birds, the male with his brilliant blue feathers and the female with her paler, much more subdued coloring. Luther had learned their songs to lure them close so she could watch them. Silence greeted his call, but he was certain Luther was in the caves. He could feel the waves of pain coming off the man. He hurried, ignoring the chandelier overhead in the form of a stalactite. The color was nearly pure white but had a wide band of red at the top, tapering as it came toward the bottom. There were several stalactites on the ceiling, some bigger than others and all beautiful.

The stalagmites rising from the cavern floor were in columns of pale blue, purple and a shade of rust red. In two places the stalagmites nearly touched the stalactite above it to form a long pillar. Water dripped continuously as he made his way around the limestone. Rocks gave way to a shallow stream. The rock walls appeared orange with the peculiar red rust running along the edges of the water. The water was dark in places, forming pools, but Diego knew the floor was solid rock.

Water trickled from the walls of the cave on either side as he walked through the pools of water. The colors and various formations seemed ever changing as minerals mixing with calcite changed subtly. The walls were thick with tubes of yellow. On the floor were enormous tubes resembling shawls. Some were pencil-thin while others were huge, round and fat. Pale blue stalactites hanging from the ceiling gave way to ones of royal blue. Large and thick, there were so many they appeared nearly impenetrable.

He spotted the narrow corridor that veered off from the main direction of pools of water. The tunnel was dark and foreboding. He'd been down that tight, shadowy passage that was really a wide crack in two giant slabs of rock.

This was Luther's refuge when he was in bad shape and knew it would be difficult to protect himself. Those coming for him would have to do so in single file. He felt the older man ahead of him, pain coming off him in waves. The scent of blood permeated the air.

Diego gave the birdcall one more time as he hurried forward through the narrow, mud-slick tunnel. Then he called out.

"Coming in, Luther," he announced.

Strangely, that well of healing energy stirred, drove him toward the old man's hiding spot, the need to help him stronger than anything he'd ever experienced, even with the animals he loved so much. He'd never had such a powerful response to a human being in trouble.

It felt like déjà vu as Diego rounded one more bend to see the larger hollowed-out chamber where Luther lay, blood covering his clothing so it was impossible to tell where the wounds were until he got right beside him. An arm for certain, and the worst wound was on Luther's left leg.

"Tell me what's going on, fast," Diego instructed as he ran his hands over Luther's arm and leg.

"They came for the girls. My nephew Collin's girls. I had no idea they existed. When Collin and his wife died in an accident, rather than bring the girls to me as their parents requested, Bridget was taken to Whitney, and Leila was sent to the lab with the people I work with." Luther sounded grim.

"Whitney did that?"

Luther shook his head. "A man by the name of General Pillar oversees the lab in Maryland where volunteers are enhanced and trained. Pillar made the decision to take the girls when Leila was ten."

"Which one is Bridget and which one is Leila?" Why knowing that was important, Diego didn't want to dwell on, but he wanted to know which was Warrior Woman.

"Bridget was curled in the ball and Leila is the fierce fighter."

Diego found himself turning the name over and over in his mind. Leila. He couldn't be paired with her since she hadn't been sent to Whitney for enhancement. But he was inexplicably interested.

"The lab experimenting on you does the same thing Whitney does to women and children?" Diego sounded mild enough, but he didn't feel that way. He knew Whitney had many facilities all over the world. He had hoped the division responsible for Luther was different.

"No, to my knowledge the government lab only took soldiers who volunteered. They made an exception for the girls because they're interested in natural genetics and what they can do with them. My fault. They knew I had psychic abilities and figured my kin would also. I didn't think about family. I lost all contact with them after Vietnam."

Diego understood what he was saying. The post-Vietnam years were a time of turmoil, and the returning soldiers weren't treated in a respectful manner to say the least. Many became estranged from their families when they needed them the most.

"I had Lotty," Luther said as if reading Diego's thoughts. "She was my world and made everything I faced in my life worthwhile. I'd take nothing back, Diego. Not one thing, just to know I could have those years with her." He looked up at Diego's face. "Just heal the damn thing. I know you're a doctor, but you can also do that mumbo jumbo your brother does."

Diego drew back, deliberately lifting his eyebrow. "What makes you think that? Rubin is . . ." He broke off, trying to search for a word that would adequately describe his brother. "Elite. One of a kind. There is no one like Rubin."

Luther gave a snort of derision. "You had everyone fooled, but you gotta remember who you're talkin' to. Spent a lifetime foolin' folks myself. You can bet I spotted your game back when you were a little kid. You might be ten months younger than your brother, but you shoulda been twins. You're exactly alike. Could be the same person. Fix the leg and arm so we can go after the girls."

Diego was a little disgusted with himself. He should have known a man who ran a con his entire life would see right into him. "Rubin and I are alike in some ways; we share the same gifts, but he doesn't have the kind of darkness in him that I do."

He passed his hands over the wound in Luther's leg. At once that well inside him opened, heat and healing energy pouring out. "Our mother saw it in me. She talked to me often, explaining I was born to be the opposite of Rubin, that he was pure light and healing energy. I had the darkness in me. She described me as the executioner. She told me my sole purpose was to keep my brother safe. Our mother had gifts and she could see things others couldn't." He spoke matter-of-factly because he'd accepted his mother's assessment of him before he was eight. He'd lived with that knowledge and done his best to make the most of his life.

Luther eyed him with a kind of shock. "Boy, you had to know your mother was ill. Mentally ill. She was always too soft inside for the kind of life she had. After your father died, and she lost your two older brothers, she had a mental break. She made you and Rubin responsible for your sisters and her. You were just little kids, and she forced you to take on the role of adults."

"That doesn't negate what she knew. She was a seer." Diego placed his hands above the wound on Luther's arm. That healing energy welled up strong. He'd never used it on humans, but he'd healed countless animals. His gift hadn't gone to waste. He'd never revealed to anyone, including Rubin, that he had the same gifts his brother had.

"Children have no idea their parent is mentally ill. How they are raised and the things the parent says and does are normal to those children even when it's abuse. You were abused both emotionally and physically, but you and your brother simply accepted it as how parents raised children because you never saw any other way. You accepted that you were responsible for bringing your family food. That required hunting. I know you got beat if you ever missed and came home a bullet short. I saw the evidence on more than one occasion. I used to bring fresh meat to the cabin in an effort to spare you boys when the weather got rough. Your mother had no right to expect eight-year-old boys to go out in the middle of a snowstorm and bring back food to the family."

"Someone had to do it," Diego pointed out.

"Not in the middle of the storm. Your father would never have gone out in that weather, but your mother insisted that you and your brother go. She didn't recognize your genius—finding the parts to put together a generator, bringing water to the cabin. Diego, think back to your childhood. You had to have questioned her orders and decisions at some point. You had to realize she was putting your life in danger."

Diego shrugged. He didn't want to pull up those memories. None of them were good. "She was certain I was born to sacrifice for the family and to keep Rubin alive. It makes sense that I went out hunting when things were rough."

"Why Rubin? Why didn't he stay home? One never went without the other."

"Rubin didn't allow me to go alone. He ignored her when she was angry with him; he just picked up his rifle and went out the door. Rubin doesn't argue." Diego shoved a hand through his hair and then was annoyed that he'd given Luther any indication that the conversation was getting to him.

"What happened when Rubin left the cabin?"

"I followed him. I always have his back."

"What did your mother say or do when you returned?"

Diego didn't allow himself to think much about his childhood. He tried another casual shrug. "She blamed me for not going on my own. That was just the way it was, Luther. No big deal."

"That's the problem with a child living with mental illness in the house. It could be years before they realize their mother or father are ill. By that time, the damage is already done. You think the way your mother treated you was normal. You believed her when she told you Rubin was special and the 'good' one. From the time you were a little boy she treated you as the bad child. Not only did you accept that treatment, but you came to believe her. I'm telling you it's bullshit."

Diego gave him a false smile. "You saying that doesn't make me a believer, Luther. I've lived with my strange detachment all my life. I know for a fact Rubin is not like me when it comes to killing anything. Even when we hunted for food for the family, he agonized over taking the shot. I feel more of an affinity with animals than I do with people, but I never hesitated or thought about it. For me it was a simple matter of survival. Of necessity. With the people we hunted, it was just as simple. They committed a crime against our family or against our country or against my unit. I don't hesitate, and I don't lose sleep. Rubin does."

"Why should that make you evil? Or ill? You do your job, just like the rest of us. You should thank the Lord that you're so good at it. Who do you think gave you the abilities you have? If you didn't use them to save lives, that would be wrong."

Diego couldn't help the small smile that escaped. "You see in black and white, Luther."

"I see *you*. Your own brother doesn't see you, but I can. I would rather have you fighting at my side than anyone else I know."

Diego took a few minutes to spread healing energy through the wound in Luther's arm. He sank back, sitting abruptly. Healing drained strength. The more psychic energy spent, the harder the crash.

"Tell me about your nieces."

"Bridget is in bad shape. She doesn't have filters and needs an anchor. I didn't even know what an anchor was. I didn't have Whitney experimenting on me. I volunteered to be enhanced physically because I wanted to serve my country to the best of my ability. I also had it in my head that I would be able to save my fellow soldiers. At the time, I was young and not so smart about life."

Luther shifted his weight and reached behind him to the small red cooler tucked in the shadow of the corner of the cave. He handed Diego a water bottle and took one for himself. Diego knew from his past experience that Luther had cached supplies for any occasion in the cave.

"Leila was trained as one of us and she's hell on wheels. What they didn't count on was her loyalty to her sister. She never once let on that she was furious that General Pillar took them and then separated the two of them. Pillar is a lieutenant general. First chance Leila got, she tracked down her sister and broke her out of the hellhole she was kept prisoner in. Guess Whitney and the commander of the lab, General Phil Chariot, want their experiments back. Chariot is a major general."

"We search for Whitney all the time. He has too many friends in high places warning him if we plan to make a move against him. How is it possible she tracked down her sister?" Diego didn't comment on the subtle warning Luther gave him by mentioning the ranks of Luther's opponents. Enemies were enemies as far as Diego was concerned. He tended to see the world in black and white. What had been done to those girls was wrong. It was that simple.

Luther sighed. "It's clear you have gifts you've developed, Diego. I have a few, but they aren't as strong as yours. I practice daily to strengthen them, but you're clearly enhanced. Leila is like me. She's very gifted, but she hasn't been enhanced; at least she told me they didn't do the kinds of experiments on her that Whitney did on her sister. In all honesty, I'm not certain she's telling the truth. I made the mistake of getting angry when I found out the government had stepped in and taken the two girls away from me when I didn't even know they existed. I told her I was going to go to war with them. That was a very bad mistake on my part. She protested vigorously and said they wanted to be left alone. That the girls needed me. She told me Bridget was in a bad way. She also told me she would have to disappear for a short time and needed me to take care of her sister. She wanted me to work with Bridget to develop barriers in her mind. It's possible they did enhance her psychic gifts and she didn't want me going after them."

"Why would she leave her sister here and go off somewhere?"

"Leila keeps her own counsel. She reminds me of me. She's careful with information."

"She was asking a pretty big favor."

"That's so, but they're my only living relatives. She believed I would have the same kind of loyalty she does. And she is loyal. There's no question, if she heard I was under attack or injured, she would have come to my aid. If they tested her, my guess is they would have found her protective nature and loyalty to family to be off the charts."

Diego found satisfaction in that. He knew Luther was shrewd at reading people. A segment of society made the mistake of dismissing seniors—Diego wasn't one of them. Luther was an excellent judge of character. He was extremely observant. Diego was also an observant man, and from the time he was a child he had watched Luther. He'd had no idea the man had been enhanced as a soldier. That was how good Luther was at hiding in plain sight. Diego couldn't help but admire the man. If Luther said his great-niece was like him, Diego believed him. That made her . . . extraordinary.

"You go after Leila," Luther said. "They're headed up the mountain with her. That's your backyard. You'll get to her faster, and she needs medical attention. I'll go after Bridget."

"Chances are good they'll get both to a vehicle or plane before we can stop them." He was extremely worried about Warrior Woman. She hadn't looked good when the attackers had carried her off. A part of him hoped her captors had already transported her to a facility where there was good medical. He didn't share with Luther. "You have a phone? I can send you the app to track both women. It's encoded, so I'll have to send you the key. Just remember, if you get captured, your phone has to be destroyed."

"That won't happen," Luther assured. "I may be old, Diego, but I can still run rings around these young soldiers. They look at me and see an old man, so they discount all my experience. That is their biggest mistake." His eyes, shrewd and almost cunning, stared directly into Diego's eyes. "Never forget that, son. Experience always counts."

Diego nodded, understanding that Luther was passing on good advice to him. He knew Luther didn't bother to educate very many others, and Diego felt privileged to have the old man impart his wisdom. Luther mostly didn't bother to speak to people, keeping strictly to himself. The old man had always been considered eccentric, but he had evaded detection for years thanks to his secretive lone-wolf ways.

"They're going to know you'll be following them, Diego," Luther continued. "They have no idea who you are, but they're afraid of you. You took out their commander, and that's stirred up a hornet's nest. They lost too many men and didn't expect that either. Their orders are most likely to stick around and find us no matter what. And they'll be looking to identify you."

Diego gave him a faint smile. "I'm a ghost in the woods, especially my woods. They won't see me, Luther. Be careful and don't take chances. If they bring Bridget to Whitney, we'll have a way into Whitney's compound. If not, we'll be able to find her no matter where she is."

Luther nodded and straightened his body slowly. He had learned years earlier that haste wasn't a good thing. A smart operator planned his actions and took care of the wounds in his body before making any fast moves. Death came to anyone who moved without thinking it through. Luther had the patience of a hunter. Diego had the patience of a predator.

Diego wanted to point out that subtle difference to Luther, just to get his opinion. Luther was one of the few people he admired and would listen to. Luther didn't believe Diego was evil at heart, but Diego knew there was darkness living inside him. It had grown heavier over time. Depression was the curse of his family. He knew his mother suffered from depression and two of his sisters had. He hadn't considered that he did, but now, after making the decision to end his life, he was fairly certain he carried it as well.

Diego wished Luther good hunting and made his way out of the cave. He avoided the soldiers still searching for Luther and him. It was easy enough to do when he knew the terrain like the back of his hand.

Hunting in the woods, however, always made him feel alive. Part of nature. He was a natural predator, and the moment he slipped into the trees and began tracking his prey, his world changed. Every sense became more acute. The wind spoke to him, bringing information on his surroundings. Lizards, voles and ants scurrying through the bracken on the forest floor were like extensions of his own senses, their movements absorbing information and funneling it back to him.

The Appalachian Mountains were different from any other mountain range. They were old, with an eerie, spooky atmosphere amplified by the fog and the high canopies blocking out light to many areas. The terrain was steep, the forests overgrown, making it very difficult to navigate and easy to get lost. The extreme weather of snow and rain created a tropical rainforest in many areas.

The forest was once again home to moose, bear and elk; even wolves were returning, helping the ecosystem. Many species now thrived when not long ago they'd been hunted nearly to extinction. Sightings were rare, but Diego had roamed those mountains for years and he was familiar with the wildlife.

He ran with the ease of the deer, his enhancements making it

easy for him to lengthen his stride and cover the rough, steep terrain with inhuman speed. This was his backyard. He'd been born
and raised here. He'd hunted the mountains from the time he was
three. The forest was dark and intense, but he was used to it.

Hikers often chose to backpack the Appalachian Trail. Although it was shorter than the Pacific Crest Trail by several hundred miles, it took longer due to the difficulty. Often tourists
discounted the mountains because they were smaller than many
others. What they didn't realize was that people disappeared often.
The mountains were easy to get lost in due to the dense foliage, fog
and unexpected weather. Going off the trail even for a short distance could turn someone around and they'd be lost.

He was certain he was getting close to the intruders and Warrior
Woman, within a mile, but he was in dense forest. It was impossible
to see ahead without going up into the trees. He ran unerringly to the
nearest tree that gave him the best vantage point. He climbed the tall
trunk with the ease of long practice and perched near the top. He
had jogged more than halfway up the mountain, and by the look of
the tracks he was catching up, but he still had a ways to go. He
wanted to get a visual if he could. He put the scope from his rifle to
his eye and did a slow sweep of the mountain.

It didn't take long to spot the small group. They'd stopped in a
clearing just north of a steep gorge.

The five men had formed a loose semicircle, standing around
Leila as she lay on the ground. He turned the scope on each of
them as they spoke.

"She's dying," one with massive shoulders and arms stated.
"Why bother taking her with us the rest of the way. What's the use
of putting up with the bitch making it hard for us?"

Diego's gut tightened as the man toed Leila's leg. The temptation to take the man out was nearly overwhelming. He couldn't get
them all, not from the position he was in. Another man, a blond,

said something, and he switched the scope to magnify his mouth so he could read his lips.

"I say we put a bullet in her and let's be done with it," the blond said.

"Been a long time without a woman," the first man said. "Might as well take advantage of the situation before she croaks on us."

The blond burst out laughing. "Jeez, Harold, she's nearly dead."

"That just makes it easier." Harold smirked.

None of the other men raised an objection. If anything, they shifted closer in the circle surrounding Leila.

Instantly Diego moved. He wasn't going to physically catch up with them in time to stop them from assaulting Leila. It didn't matter that the woman was shot all to hell and in obvious pain. The five men were abandoning all attempts to save her life and were in agreement about assaulting her. It mattered little to him whether they would participate or not; they weren't stopping Harold.

He needed to get into position fast to take all of them out. He didn't bother to climb down the tree but instead ran along the most stable branch to leap into the tree next to the one he'd been in. He knew exactly where he had to be, and he got there in under a minute. Part was knowledge, part instincts, but when he was in hunting mode, he could run the branches of a tree with the ease of a cat, leap to the next one, landing in perfect balance, still running without pause. All the while he knew the exact angle he needed for any shot.

His speed at setting up his rifle was legendary. He didn't waste time looking to see what any of the men said; it was too late for them. They were still in that same loose semicircle around the fallen woman. No one had made a move to help her or push the disgusting Harold away from her. Diego could see blood on her abdomen, a lot of it. Way more than any minor wound could produce.

Again, he didn't waste time worrying. He pushed his fear for her out of his head and practiced each shot in his mind, one after another, easily switching targets until he could find them in his sleep. That took under a minute. His mind calculated and built a pattern as if programming a computer.

Harold pulled out his gun and gestured toward the woman to the others. Diego shot him and then the blond. He got off two more rounds before the bodies began to drop. All four shots sounded nearly simultaneous. The fifth man was the farthest from his warrior woman, and when the four bodies crumpled, he started to lift his gun toward Leila. The fifth shot took him before the gun was even aimed at her.

Diego slung his rifle around his neck and kept to the trees, using them as an arboreal highway. When he ran out of strong branches, he hit the ground running. He could go for miles thanks to his enhancements. Instinctively he leapt over rotted logs and termite hills. He went up the mountain with long strides, covering the mile quickly. Once he encountered a thin stream bubbling over rocks with a herd of deer drinking. Startled, the animals scattered, but he was gone before they could decide which way to run.

When he was a few feet from Leila, Diego slowed to a walk. "Coming up on you," he warned. She had her eyes closed, but she gripped a knife in her fist. "Friend of Luther's," he added.

Her lashes fluttered. She even had splatters of blood on her face. He didn't wait for an invitation. She might think she was fast enough to gut him, but she wasn't.

He dragged the dead bodies away from her and tumbled them into the ravine. It didn't take long, but it was one more thing to take his energy when he needed it for healing.

"I'm a doctor, a healer. I'll need to take a look at your wounds to see how best to help you." He kept his voice low and soothing. He had a compelling voice and could influence others. He also could do the same with energy. He had used his gifts shamelessly to build the compulsion to protect his brother. He'd never once felt remorse. He didn't now as he crouched beside her, but he did feel regret. If he ever tried to pursue a relationship with her, he'd always know she was influenced to trust him by his voice.

The tip of the blade came up. "Not going to get raped. I'd rather be dead."

"No, you're not going to get raped. I'm going to look at your wounds, and I'll have to take a look under your clothes." His brother was far better at soothing patients than he was. He'd just as soon use his gifts. In this case, he didn't have time to argue with her or reassure her. He used his voice the way others used a knife, the energy looking to slide into her brain with precise precision.

Those lashes fluttered again, but she didn't seem able to open her eyes.

"Just killed five men for you, Warrior Woman. Give me the knife and let me get to work saving your life."

"I hear you knocking, but you can't come in." There was the slightest trace of amusement in her voice.

Despite the severity of her wounds and the dire situation, he found answering humor somewhere deep he hadn't known existed in him. He was somewhat shocked that his compelling voice and the strong energy didn't work on her. At the same time, there was satisfaction. She was the first. He was inexplicably pleased she wasn't affected by his voice.

He reached in slowly. "Coming for the knife."

Her body tensed, and she winced. Gasped. He took the blade from her and set it aside. "I have to know what we're looking at here."

"I knew it was bad, but thought I would be all right." Her teeth bit down on her lower lip hard and then eased. "I can sometimes slow my heart. I practice. I tried to slow the flow of the blood internally. But a few minutes ago, the two running with me dropped me. I felt something tear. It doesn't feel good." Her voice was thin and weak.

Diego laid his hands over the bloody mess that was her abdomen. The bullets had done quite a bit of damage, but the jarring fall had wreaked a lot of havoc on a body already torn apart.

"I'm going to stop the bleeding, but the repairs are just temporary, like putting a Band-Aid on it. I can't do surgery until we're in a safe place. I can't move you far. You won't survive it." He believed in being truthful.

A faint smile curved her lips. "Tired. Cold. I don't think you have a chance saving me, and it's all right. I'm just so tired. Go after my sister."

"You're not giving up, Warrior Woman." He kept his voice low, but used a more commanding tone. Whether she responded to compulsion or not, she was trained as a soldier. She would respond to commands.

Using the kind of psychic energy it took to stop the internal bleeding was going to leave him weak. There was nothing else for it. If he didn't get it stopped now, she didn't have a hope in hell, and he wasn't about to lose her.

He felt the heat welling up in him. When it happened, he was always a little shocked that he had that in him. He was cold as ice, but apparently there was a deep well of fire he could tap into.

"You're going to feel heat. A lot of it. Stay very still."

He directed his hands over the wound and sent healing energy into her body. Light burst under his palms, which grew hot, almost scorching. The worse the wound, the more energy demanded. He willed energy into her wound and hoped he was going about it the right way. He'd honed these particular healing skills on animals over the years, not humans. Sure, he'd gone through medical school to become a surgeon, but in their GhostWalker unit there were several surgeons, so he rarely had to put his physical surgical skills to use on his team members. Now, however, he was grateful he knew every muscle, organ and bone in the body. Knowledge of the human body was essential when he was healing this way.

"You don't get to give up, Leila. I know you're tired, but you have gifts no one else in the world has, or at least very few. It doesn't matter how you acquired them; you have them. Even without your skills, you're unique."

Her lips pressed together, and she gave a small shake of her head.

"I said don't move," he reiterated. What he was doing was going to be barely enough to sustain her until he could perform surgery on her. He tried not to think about that and what it would reveal to the world about him. He didn't need to get ahead of himself. At the moment, his concentration had to be on the ugly wounds inside her body.

"My sister," she whispered. "You don't understand about her."

"It doesn't matter if your sister can stop the plague," he said. "She isn't worth more than you. I need you to fight. Make up your mind you're going to live."

"I was supposed to look after her," she admitted. "They did terrible things to her."

The hypocrisy of what he was spouting got to him. The trouble was, he believed what he was saying. This woman was unique. Gifted. The world had need of her. It didn't matter if her sister was ten times what Warrior Woman was. Leila had her place in the world.

He shook his head to get rid of the thoughts Luther had planted, but he couldn't very well spout off as gospel the things he was saying to her without turning the spotlight back on himself. He was a man who believed in scrutinizing all traits in himself and fixing whatever he didn't like if it was possible. If he couldn't do it immediately, he worked hard to change over time.

"You aren't responsible for anything that happened to her. We'll find her, and we'll get to the people who hurt her. To do that, you have to live. Stay still."

"It burns."

She didn't whine. There was no whine or even pain in her tone. She'd stated a fact. He admired her all the more for that.

"I know it does. I'm sorry for that, but we have to stop this bleeding. I'll give you a transfusion before I move you to a safer place."

She shuddered. "You can't move me. It hurts so bad."

"I've got painkillers with me. I'll be gentle. It will be a while before I can safely finish working on you. I have to set up a camp for us that anyone looking won't be able to find. Healing like this wipes me out. Surgery will be worse." He hesitated. "I don't allow anyone to know I'm capable of psychic surgery. Not ever. I'm trusting you to keep my secrets." He hoped she understood what he was giving to her. "Even my brother is unaware of this particular gift."

"Healing? Why would you hide it? It's amazing."

"Not healing, although I don't heal humans as a rule and don't want others to know I'm capable of that either. That's my brother's gift."

She was silent. Her lashes fluttered as if she were trying to open her eyes again, but she subsided. Diego lifted his hands away from her abdomen. He'd done the most basic, temporary holds to stop the bleeding. The damage to her body was so extensive he was already feeling drained just from stopping the various sites from bleeding.

His body wanted to lie back and rest, but he forced himself to grab his backpack and pull out his medical kit. "Setting up for a transfusion." He heard the tired note in his voice. She did too. Those long lashes fluttered again.

"You don't know my blood type."

"I'll be compatible."

"Can't move me. You're draining yourself for no reason."

"Got a good reason right in front of me. Make up your mind to live. You're a warrior woman. You don't lie down because some peckerwood tries to kill you. You get up and you go after them."

That faint smile he found unexpectedly endearing curved her bottom lip, briefly creating a bow. He thought he caught a glimpse of dimples on either side of her mouth, but he couldn't be certain.

"That easy?"

"Didn't say it was easy, woman, just that it had to be done. When it's a necessity, you just do it. You don't fret about it. Right now, my job is to get some blood in you and then rest so I can build us a shelter close."

"I still don't think you can move me." Another little shudder went through her body, and he realized she knew it would hurt like hell.

She'd lost enough blood that she was cold and shivering. After he managed to get a decent vein, he covered her with his emergency blanket that had been folded into a tiny square and was in a zip pouch. Making himself comfortable beside her, he linked them together through the line.

"How do you know your blood is compatible with mine?"

He detested that she was shaking. He moved closer so their bodies were touching, his thigh against hers. "My blood type is compatible with just about everything, another fact I don't want getting out."

This time there was no denying the dimples. "My mystery man has many secrets." She said it in a fake-spooky voice that made him want to laugh.

"I'm giving you a painkiller. Try to sleep for a little while. I'm going to rest as well."

"There were more soldiers than the ones you killed. Five men went up the mountain to contact someone."

He sighed. "You might have told me sooner."

"Sorry." Again, the lashes fluttered, and this time she was able to partially lift them, revealing startling vivid green eyes. "I'm not thinking clearly. You could give me a gun."

"I will," he acknowledged, "but—later, when I know your brain is clear and you haven't gotten it into your head that I'm the most annoying man you've ever met and shooting me appeals to you."

"Don't make me laugh; it hurts," she admonished. "Are you annoying?"

"Probably. I like things my way. And I make decisions based on logic, not emotion, which can be annoying to some people."

"What you're saying is you think you're right."

He pushed back the strands of hair falling across her face. "What I'm saying is I *know* I'm right." He did his best to sound pompous, but there was too much humor in his tone. "Go to sleep."

He reached for the birds. He would need lookouts if they were going to be hunted.

3

I t took far too long to build a refuge that couldn't be seen from the air or any trail. Once he had Leila inside, he would erase all tracks leading to their shelter. He had gone half a mile off trail through heavy brush and trees. There was a particularly tall tree with a huge root system reaching for a thin trickle of running water that came from above. The small stream ran all year round, sometimes doubling in size, but always there was a source of water for the animals and plants. The tree provided shelter for wildlife and was home to birds, squirrels and lizards.

The tree was full, thick branches reaching in all directions, darkening the forest floor. Tall ferns grew around the tree, blocking the view from any direction. Years earlier, Diego had discovered the spot when he followed an owl through the forest. Just to the left of the root system was a steep berm, a drop-off that was covered by years of foliage, needles, leaves, branches and twigs falling to form a massive mound that appeared solid.

He had patiently climbed down the ridge, exploring, and had found the entrance to a cave. It wasn't really a cave, more of a deep depression in the mountain hidden by the root system, ferns and the hundred-year-old accumulation of debris at the edge of that berm. It would be impossible to find unless you knew where it was.

Diego worked as fast as possible knowing Warrior Woman didn't have much time. They would need a place with room for both to lie down and easy access to water. He had rations with him—he rarely went anywhere without them—and he knew how to hunt for food in the forest, but he wouldn't be in very good shape after performing a psychic surgery.

The truth was if he didn't have to hurry, he would have tried to find a way to back out of using his greatest gift. A psychic surgeon was extremely rare, and the gift required a completely selfless sacrifice. He didn't think of himself in that light. Rubin was a man who would sacrifice everything for others. He didn't always base his decisions on logic. The compulsion to heal was extremely strong, and Rubin was very empathetic. There were times when he risked his life when he should have known better.

Diego was far more pragmatic than his brother. He had never allowed emotions to rule him. With a gift such as psychic surgery, he knew to succeed he had to be willing to sacrifice his own life for his patient. He was never one hundred percent certain he would make the exchange once he was deep into surgery and things were going wrong. He'd seen it happen to Rubin dozens of times. He'd been the watcher, ensuring his brother stayed alive during the process, but he had never let on that he had that same gift.

He prepared the small den with everything he could think of that they would need when both would be weak and vulnerable. He was meticulous, paying attention to details. Those could mean the difference between life and death. Throughout his life in the mountains, he'd befriended the great gray owl, and he called on them now, asking them to stay alert for any signs of intruders. Only then did he go back to Warrior Woman.

It was a testament to Leila's strength of will that she hadn't moved when he cautioned her not to. Even with the painkiller he'd given her, she had to be in agony. He found himself admiring her and was even more determined to save her life.

The journey to the shelter was a nightmare. He was a member of the Air Force GhostWalker's Pararescue Team. Countless times he'd carried the wounded on his back over impossible terrain. He'd done so automatically, without thought, getting his patient to a safe place where they could save his life. Carrying Leila felt different, personal, as if he shared every bone-jarring bump as he took her over the rough terrain and through the dense forest. The half-mile hike felt like ten. It was virtually impossible to avoid the brush and low-hanging branches as he made his way to the shelter. She didn't make a sound, but her breathing was erratic.

Diego was good enough in the forest that he could cover his tracks, but if he broke branches or bruised leaves, a good tracker might be able to follow him. He knew he would have to erase all evidence of their passing.

Once in the shelter, he settled Leila on the soft raised area he'd made for her. The sleeping bag was on top of a bed of leaves he'd compacted to make it softer for her.

"We don't have much time. I want you to listen to me carefully. I know you're struggling to stay conscious, but you need to hear me and follow my directions to the letter. I'm going to remove all traces of us coming here. It will take a few minutes. Beside you are water and rations. I'm placing three guns within your reach." He guided her hand to each one. "Extra ammo is next to the food. I'm giving you three knives."

Her lashes did lift then, and she looked him directly in the eye. "Are you leaving me?"

"Just for a couple of minutes to wipe out our tracks, but when I come back, I'll be doing the surgery on you. I'm going to talk very plainly. There has to be truth between us at all times. I'm not going to hide that this situation is dire." While he spoke, he set up for the operation.

"I prefer truth."

"If we survive, I expect that you will never give away the fact that I performed this surgery on you."

"We?"

He ignored the fact that he wanted to rub his finger over the little frown lines appearing between her brows. "If I live through this, I'm going to go down hard. Very hard. It will leave us without protection. I expect that during that time, the men who went up the mountain will come looking for their friends. They're going to find five dead bodies, and they won't be happy. Hopefully, I'll have concealed our tracks and they won't be able to find us."

He saw the protest welling up and turned away from her. He didn't have time to argue or explain. He hurried away and double-timed back. Systematically he erased every trace of them. There was one fern with a broken stalk and a small branch that had been snapped but hadn't fallen. He didn't try to fix those, just hightailed it back to the shelter.

Leila opened her eyes the instant he returned. He stripped off his jacket and boots and knelt beside her.

"Tell me what you meant," she greeted.

He didn't pretend he didn't understand. "There's a risk in doing this type of surgery. An exchange between us. You won't live if it isn't done, Leila."

As he passed his palms over her abdomen, he was already feeling the well of energy that signaled he could tap into that healing fire buried deep inside him.

"I'm not exchanging my life for yours," she protested.

"You don't have a choice. Close your eyes and just be still. When I go down, and I will, I'll need to heal just like you. Hopefully, we won't have any visitors. I've got sentries scattered throughout the forest. They'll alert us when the men reach the bodies and if they come close to us."

"Diego." She whispered his name. "You shouldn't do this."

He gave her a vague smile. "I should. Now let me concentrate."

That was all he could give her. Psychic surgery wasn't completely different than physical surgery. Every artery and vein had to be repaired around any wounds. The muscles and organs had to be dealt with. The damage to Leila was extensive. Once he could see inside her body, mapping everything out with heat first, he didn't understand how she could have spoken to him let alone lived through such traumatic wounds.

Once she stopped fighting it, she slid under quietly, succumbing to the pain and trauma, giving herself up to him. It told him a lot about her that she didn't continue to try to argue. She accepted the inevitable and allowed him to take over.

Psychic surgery required a transfer; it was brief, but the surgeon, as he meticulously repaired a shattered body, took on the wounds for a brief period of time. Opening the deep well of healing energy, he began, with his mind, to move the damaged pieces of Leila's bone, muscle and veins back into place, meticulously mending each one. There were so many damaged parts, and he lost himself in the work. Once he started, there was no turning back. Healing her had become a compulsion.

Her spleen was ruptured. It was a wonder she hadn't bled out. He knew she had gifts and she'd managed to slow the bleeding in order to give herself time to defeat her captors. He had no choice but to remove the organ. He knew she could live without a spleen, but she would have to always watch out for infections.

Her liver and gallbladder were intact as well as the large intestine, but there was some trauma to her stomach and small intestine. The bullet had entered at a strange angle, and he mapped the trajectory through the damage, making certain to clear every fragment left behind so there was no shrapnel or metal in her body. It was a painstaking process.

There was no one there to wipe the sweat that ran down his face into his eyes or hand him water. He didn't have a partner to support his body when his strength gave out and he had to continue without rest. He'd known the surgery would be difficult, but he hadn't realized how many hours it would take or how drained he would become so quickly. He had no other recourse than to continue no matter how tired he got. When he finished, he would be lying right next to her, unable to move, and that was if he lived.

The pain was horrendous. It crashed through him each time he moved to a new organ or vein. The bullet had exited at an odd angle through her back, breaking a rib in its path and cracking two others. It was well after dark before he finished.

He knew the crash was coming, and it was going to be bad. Already, his vision was blurred, dark around the edges. His head pounded and his body hurt beyond belief. Still, he wasn't finished until he gave her what she needed. He hooked himself up to an IV after he removed the equipment for the blood transfer, and then it was over.

Diego went down hard, just as he feared he would. He was thankful he hadn't been standing. One moment he was half sitting beside her, and the next everything went black.

Leila became aware of sound first. Insects droning. She registered that was a good thing but she was disoriented and at first couldn't figure out why. Her head pounded and her abdomen felt on fire. She was afraid to move. Breathing hurt. She reached for the weapons Diego had promised would be close, just to reassure herself that she wouldn't be taken a second time. She'd never felt so vulnerable.

It took another few minutes, or at least it felt that way, to pry her eyes open. Despite finding herself hooked up to a needle with what appeared to be an empty bag of fluids, her entire body felt dry, and her eyes and mouth were desperate for fluids.

She turned her head, and for one moment, her heart accelerated. She slowed the beat immediately and took in the man who had most likely saved her life. He hadn't left her or given up. He'd treated her with respect, telling her step-by-step what he had to do. He'd left supplies and weapons for her, giving her every chance for survival.

Light filtered through the branches and brush covering the small den where they sheltered. The early morning rays fell across Diego's face, illuminating the sharp angles and planes of his cheekbones and jaw. His face was a perfect sculpture of masculine beauty. She had never seen a man so gorgeous. Everything about his features appealed to her. *But* . . . Her heart sank. Was he breathing?

Her heart sped up in alarm, and once again, she deliberately slowed her pulse. It wouldn't do any good to have both of them dead. She couldn't do more than turn her head, fearing that moving around would destroy all the work Diego had done. She felt as if she'd had an operation, her insides sore, but she felt different from when she'd gone under.

The scent of blood was disturbing. She knew that many of the predators in the forest would be attracted to their shelter. Leila tightened her fingers around the gun. She would have to be ready to defend them. First, though, she had to determine if Diego was alive.

His body lay very close to hers. Thighs touching. She began to feel around for his arm or hand. She had to stay very still, that was what he'd said, but she was uncomfortable. Her clothes were a mess and felt sticky against her skin. That wasn't the only problem. She couldn't get up to use the bathroom, not that there was one. Diego hadn't thought of that. Or had he? She hadn't looked around for a bucket. He said he'd put everything she needed within her reach so she wouldn't have to move. She wasn't wearing her trousers, just her bloodstained, very tattered shirt. He'd had to take off her trousers and underwear to operate on her.

She lay there unmoving, feeling exhausted, scared, with tears leaking out of her eyes. It took several more minutes to get the courage to continue exploring for Diego's arm. She didn't dare try to turn on her side to face him. She wasn't even certain she could. Finally, after moving her palm along his thigh, up his hip and rib cage, she brushed his arm with her fingers. One arm was down along his side.

Leila traced a path to his wrist and settled her fingers over his pulse. She found herself holding her breath. Waiting. He had to be alive. It was as necessary as her next breath. For a moment, she couldn't see or hear anything but her own wild heartbeat thudding in reaction. Then she felt it: a faint, fluttery beat that sent her emotions soaring. The relief was overwhelming.

His wrist and that heartbeat acted like some kind of a security blanket for her. She lay there beside him, just breathing, grateful that he was alive. She was more grateful for his life than her own. It took another few minutes before she began searching with her other hand for anything he may have left to aid her in relieving herself. She didn't want to ruin the makeshift bed she was on, and she was becoming a little desperate.

Her fingers touched something soft and round, and she dragged it onto her chest. The roll of toilet paper made her smile. Of course he would be traveling with toilet paper. He seemed to have a magical pack with everything she needed. The next thing she found was a lightweight plastic rectangular container she could slide under her. It wasn't easy, and she hurt like hell, but she managed to lift her hips just enough to get the shallow basin beneath her. Relief was tremendous. Even overwhelming. She could feel tears on her face.

Leila wasn't a crier. She had always been stoic, refusing to allow anyone to see what she was feeling. Once she started, she was unable to turn off the faucet, especially when she realized it wouldn't be as easy to remove the container as it was to slide it under her. She had to worry about spilling. It took effort and pain to manage, but she was able. Exhausted, she fell asleep with tears still running down her face.

~

Leila woke hours or days later, she didn't know which and didn't care. She didn't especially want to be awake. Night in the forest was spooky. She had no idea why. She'd spent hundreds of hours training in forests. This one felt different—ancient. Eerie. Each time she heard movement outside the shelter, she half expected some mythical, monstrous creature to stick its head inside and confront her with a mouthful of teeth and glowing eyes. The gun in her hand and holding on to Diego's wrist, feeling his heartbeat, kept her wild imagination from conjuring up every creature she'd read about that was supposed to occupy the Appalachians.

"Smoke wolf," she murmured aloud. She'd read he was a red-eyed, enormous fierce predator rarely seen. He would eat any livestock, wildlife or human, he encountered.

"Aw, the smoke wolf. You need to rattle chains to deter him."

Her heart stuttered. She turned her head to look at Diego. He hadn't moved.

"You do? Chains?"

"Yep. He's called a smoke wolf because he can shift into a cloud of smoke. You can see why he's not been tracked far or caught."

The amusement in his voice charmed her. She really liked the sound of his voice. She told herself it was because he had saved her, but she knew it was far more than that.

"I would be more concerned about the raven mocker finding us," he continued. This time the note of amusement seemed to stroke over her skin like healing fingers. "He hunts the sick and dying at night."

"That's just great," she played along, wanting to keep him talking. "What does he look like?"

"Very large, raven feathers and sharp wicked beak. It would drain our life force, and that allows him to extend his life."

She gripped his wrist tighter. "Well, at least we'd go together. What else could be out there?"

"Warrior Woman, we've got bigfoot, but he might be likely to help us, so we'll discount having to protect ourselves from him. These mountains have many scary creatures. There's the massive silver giant with his fur-covered body and glowing eyes."

"Glowing eyes seem to be a common theme in these mountains."

The briefest of smiles curved his lips and made her heart stutter. He really was a stunningly gorgeous man.

"The giant is about ten feet high and weighs in around five hundred pounds, but he's agile and said to be very fast. I, personally, have never encountered him but have met a few who glimpsed him. They said just seeing him foreshadowed tragedy. He eats wildlife, livestock and humans."

"So, a lovely fellow. He wouldn't be likely to help us."

"I doubt he'd offer his services. I'm just telling you what a couple of old-timers swore to me. They'd caught glimpses of him and hid."

"How can he be defeated, just in case he shows up while you're asleep? Should I try flashing him?" She did her best to sound innocent and must have managed, because she was rewarded with that same faint smile.

"I was told to defeat him you needed divine intervention or powerful magic. I imagine you flashing him would be considered either."

She laughed. Even though laughter hurt, she was extremely happy she could. Right in the middle of one of the worst messes she was trapped in, he made her laugh. It was genuine too. She could pretend when needed, but there was no need around Diego. It didn't make sense, other than that they were thrown together in dire circumstances and he made her feel alive when she shouldn't be.

He was silent for a moment. "Couldn't save your spleen, Leila. There was no use in trying, it was shredded. If you hadn't controlled the blood and your heart, you'd be dead. You did a good job. Wanted to make it right for you, but there was no getting that back."

"You saved my life. I don't know how, but you did. Thank you for that." And he'd risked his own life for her. No one had ever done that for her.

"You'll have to be careful of infections. You can live without a spleen, but you're susceptible to everything that comes along. I did what I could to stimulate your ability to fight off diseases, but honestly, I was exhausted at that point and knew I'd crash hard. I'll go in another time and do what I can for you."

He sounded so tired. Too tired. That alarmed her. Inadvertently, she dug her fingers into his wrist as if she could hold him to her.

"Don't," she implored softly. "Diego, don't leave me."

"Not leaving you, beautiful," he murmured softly. "Just too tired to stay awake. Hydrate. That's important. Stay hydrated for me."

"What about you? Drink water."

"Can't move yet." Again, his lips curved into that faint smile. "No worries about the legends coming to life and trying to do you in. I protected our den."

She didn't know how he would protect it, but she was becoming a believer in him. "Do you want me to try to get you water?"

"No. Do you have any idea how many hours or days have gone by?"

"I don't."

He fell silent. In the darkness, his labored breathing was all she could focus on. She had to work to keep her heart under control. She wasn't afraid of a predator finding them because of the scent of blood. She didn't fear smoke wolf, silver man or bigfoot. She was terrified to lose him. Not because she would be alone. She'd spent a good deal of her life alone. It was Diego. He was a compelling, charismatic man, and she found herself actually enjoying his company, as brief a time as she'd had with him.

"I'll examine you again the next time I come to."

His voice reached her out of the darkness, a soothing blend of velvet and heat.

"I can tell I'm getting better. The pain is a thousand times less," she assured him.

"Don't want you to have *any* pain, woman."

This time she didn't get one of his killer, barely there smiles. She wished she had the energy to trace his lips. Map out his entire face. His bone structure was sharp, cutting edge.

"If I were reading a romance novel, which I will never admit I had access to, the author would describe your features as 'chiseled.'"

That got her the smile. "Is that a good thing?"

"Yep. You really are a thing of physical beauty, Diego," she said sincerely, wondering why she couldn't stop her mouth from announcing every thought in her head to him.

Again, she got that brief flash. "Woman, you're high as a kite still. We can't have been out that long."

"No, it's the truth. I wouldn't just say something not true. It isn't drugs." Although it was entirely possible she was blurting out the truth because there were still drugs in her system. "Which reminds me. Why are you carrying drugs with you? Isn't that illegal?"

"My brother Rubin—who, by the way, is a brilliant doctor—and I come up a couple times a year to check on some of the locals. There are several who mistrust outsiders, especially doctors. We like to make certain they get care and any vaccinations they may need. If they need an operation and we're capable, Rubin does the honors. In this case, I brought supplies with me. He'll be coming up to do the rounds."

"You're kind of brilliant yourself," she felt compelled to point out.

"I'm brilliant at killing, Warrior Woman, not saving lives."

She bit down on her lower lip while she contemplated what he said. "Do you save lives by killing? Or do you just kill willy-nilly?"

She got an actual laugh that turned into a cough. Her breath caught in her throat. He really seemed worse off than she was.

"Willy-nilly?" There was more of that velvety masculine amusement. "I hear all kinds of phrases up here, use a few of them myself, but 'willy-nilly' coming out of your mouth was unexpected."

"At random. I'm asking if you just go around shooting anyone at random. That's what 'willy-nilly' means." She did her best to sound snippy, but it was impossible when she wanted to laugh.

"Let me give this a little thought."

"Usually, if a person is going to lie, they think things over. And I already know the answer. I'm going to keep you talking so you don't fall asleep."

"I'm not dead."

"How would I know? You don't make a sound. You don't even snore. Can't you at least do that? You're gorgeous. You killed those five men trying to rape and kill me in like under five seconds, prepared us a shelter, gave me blood, operated and set everything up for me so I'd have anything I needed at my fingertips. That's brilliant in my opinion."

"You're good for my soul, Warrior Woman. Coming from you, who I have all the respect in the world for, it means something that you think I'm brilliant."

He fell silent again, and she listened to his breathing. Just the sound, like his heartbeat, was reassuring to her, even when it continued to sound a little ragged. She wrapped herself up in his compliment. She had heard the honesty. He respected her and had no problem saying so. Meaning it. No one had ever complimented her. Not a single person. He called her "Warrior Woman," and not in a sarcastic, demeaning way. He meant that title out of respect. Once she thought he might have used "my" in front of "Warrior Woman." She would have liked that a lot if it was true. That made no sense at all to her, but she admitted she was a little screwed up at that moment. Still, she kept her hand on his wrist, staying connected to him.

"Forgot to tell you, old man Gunthrie perpetuated his own myth."

That voice. Like black velvet caressing her skin. She needed it there in the darkness. She could even admit she was afraid. She rarely allowed herself to feel fear. It wasn't of dying or being alone—she'd been alone all her life—but she felt totally vulnerable and helpless. She knew the other men in the unit sent after her would be returning, and they would never stop hunting her when they discovered the bodies of their companions.

"The gigantic hornet. It would come to his call and land in his meadow, that little clearing where he planted all the wildflowers for Lotty," Diego continued in his mesmerizing voice.

Goose bumps formed on her skin, but it was the unfamiliar longing that made her want to turn her body toward his, wrap him in her arms and hold him close so he couldn't possibly slip away from her.

"He had all the kids terrified, but we'd sneak out and try to make our way down the mountain to get a glimpse of the hornet when we knew it was around the time it was most likely to show up."

She forced herself to go along with his story. She was interested, especially since it had to do with her uncle, but more to keep him alert and talking. "The hornet was on a schedule to greet my uncle?"

"Give or take a day or two. It was always risky to go, especially at night in the forest, even if you know it well. But we were boys and we had to be brave. Our courage may have been fueled by moonshine."

His little grin revealed a crease at his mouth that intrigued her.

"We grew up on ghost stories and the various folklore from different parts of the Appalachians. The scarier, the better, and we all believed. Luther was a legend all by himself even without the giant hornet with its glowing eyes. Put those two together and his reputation grew until he was all but mythological himself."

Not only did Diego sound amused, but he sounded respectful. She considered that he didn't realize how much he admired her uncle.

"The rumors continued to grow that gigantic flying insects would land on the property, right in Lotty's meadow, and Luther would duck his head to avoid it being bitten off, lean against the creature and pet it while he communed with it."

A giggle slipped out. She hastily pressed her fingers over her mouth, shocked at the sound. She'd never giggled in her life. She didn't even know how.

"Is that what everyone said?"

"Whispered. It was old man Gunthrie. He scared the bejesus out of everyone, adults and children alike. We were all told to stay clear of his land. He was likely to shoot and bury you so no one would ever find the body. Or some thought he might eat the bodies."

"Eww." She wrinkled her nose. "No one really believed that, did they?"

"Of course we did. At any event where the boys got together, we'd talk about Luther and the gigantic hornets. We were sneaking moonshine, and that added to our stories and courage. I was about eight or nine, so the idea of creeping up on the old man without being detected was the ultimate challenge, especially if he had his army of gigantic hornets."

"You drank moonshine at eight or nine?" She didn't know why that shocked her, but it did.

"Naturally. Did a lot of things at eight and nine." The laughter faded from his voice.

She wanted it back. Clearly, his memories of his childhood weren't all happy. "Did you ever manage to sneak up on him and catch him with the hornets?"

"I saw the hornet a time or two from a distance through trees and shrubs. It looked like a yellow-and-black body with a long tail that spun at the end. The front of him was a bubble of black and yellow. His wings were on top of his head and spun instead of flapped."

"You said the eyes glowed. Every monster up here has glowing eyes."

"The eyes were so bright red you didn't dare look into them. Luther always seemed to know when there were spies about. Every time those things set down in Lotty's clearing, the fog would be particularly heavy, making it difficult to see through the trees.

None of us had binoculars in those days, and we didn't dare get too close. After all, Luther might shoot and bury us, or worse, feed us to his hornets."

She could hear the humor in his voice, and she found herself liking him even more. A man who could laugh at himself was worth his weight in gold. "I don't know much about children, but in all the books I've read, little boys are always mischievous."

"That wasn't what my mother called it."

There was that note in his voice that sent alarms skittering through her. Once again, she did her best to drag him back to good memories.

"Did you figure out the myth of the hornets?"

"Yeah, but it took a couple of times traipsin' through the woods at night in the fog and risking that old man shooting us. Glowing eyes, wings on its head, long tail."

It was a clear challenge. She thought it over. She knew her uncle now. He wasn't Hornet Man. He was a soldier through and through.

She burst out laughing. "A helicopter. Uncle Luther was rendezvousing with a helicopter."

"Yep. Much more fun for us to think he was Hornet Man and commanded an army of gigantic hornets. Naturally, when Rubin and I figured it out, we didn't tell anyone, not even our friends."

"That would spoil the fun and mystique."

"Yeah, it would have. And all the young boys coming up behind us. We weren't able to get together often. Life was hard. It took a lot of work to survive in these mountains. We were much more remote than a lot of others. Once my father died, we went to other homes less and less, even for the celebrations. But Luther would come. He'd bring us meat and other goods. Leave it on the porch or visit with my mother briefly. Sometimes he'd have a talk with Rubin and me about fishing or hunting. Even tracking. We learned a lot from him. He'd show up even in the worst weather. Be abrupt, brisk, but always gave good advice. We learned fast to believe him."

She was losing him. Panic set in for a moment, but she took a couple of deep breaths and let him slide into sleep. She followed not long after, her hand curled over the top of his wrist like a delicate shackle.

4

The sound of rain woke him. Diego lay quietly for a moment just listening. He'd always loved the sound of rain, especially when he was out in the forest. There was music to the way the drops fell. The wind through the trees, the way each drop fell on various trees and shrubs, all of it was a soothing symphony to him. The rain cleared the air, brought life to everything: plants, wildlife, stock and humans. Tonight, the rain was light, nearly a mist, a soft, quiet song that caught at his heart the way the rain in the forest often did.

After allowing himself a brief moment to be fully relaxed, Diego breathed away the pain crashing through him and focused on the sounds of the forest. With his enhanced hearing he could identify and position wildlife in the vicinity. He would know when intruders were close. Every noise, rustle, flutter or squeak gave him information necessary to survive.

Survive. He was a grown man and a doctor. He should have recognized all the signs of a child indoctrinated with a parent's depression and near hatred. Luther was right. That old man had tried through the years to save Rubin. To save *him*. As a child he hadn't recognized that his mother was mentally ill. He hadn't realized how much her opinion of him shaped him into thinking he was worthless other than as his brother's protector. Had he accomplished what he'd set out to do, he would have missed meeting an incredible woman—a survivor against all odds. That would have been the true tragedy of his life.

Diego opened his eyes, focused on the ceiling of woven branches and vines, and then turned his head slowly to look at the woman lying so still beside him. He felt the heat of her through their touching thighs. Her palm curled around his wrist. He didn't move his arm away from her as he studied her. He had excellent night vision, thanks to all the enhancements done to him, and it was easy for him to see her high cheekbones, that delicate curve along her jaw, the length of her lashes and her full, bow-shaped lips. She'd called him a gorgeous man. She'd gotten that wrong, but he knew beauty when he saw it.

He found himself admiring her all the more. She was lying in a makeshift shelter with a total stranger, totally vulnerable after getting shot all to hell, nearly raped, and operated on in a manner she had no knowledge of, but she lay with a gun at her fingertips and one hand on him. On his pulse. Looking after him. There wasn't a doubt in his mind that she would have shot anything poking its head through the entrance to their den. This was a woman who would protect her children. He knew with absolute certainty that she would never single one out and label them a demon from hell.

He studied her face, feature by feature, while the rain played a symphony to him. There was both strength and softness in that ultrafeminine face. This woman would be a wonder—a miracle for a man to wake up to every morning and fall asleep with the image of her in his mind to carry him through the night.

With some reluctance, he forced his body to move. He was careful. Taking on life-threatening injuries was always risky. Seeing the severity of her wounds, he'd known there was a better-than-average chance he wouldn't make it, but the compulsion to heal her was far too strong to deny.

He took his time checking every muscle, stretching to loosen his stiff body before he sat up. His body didn't like the new position, his insides protesting, but he needed to get outside and then do a few chores, hopefully before she woke.

The cool, wet air was refreshing to him. He rarely was inside. His preference would always be the outdoors, where he could see and feel anything coming at him or anyone he loved. There was a freedom he felt deeply when he was in the forest—or swamp. He'd adapted to the swamp in Louisiana, and it felt like a second home to him. Never the city. He couldn't breathe there. He faked it, using his enhanced abilities to get by. Charming, smiling and appearing easygoing when none of it was real.

Diego buried Leila's bloody clothing, along with the shirt of his that had bloodstains on it from carrying her. He didn't worry about wild animals finding them through the scent; he could control the animals. But if the soldiers sent to find the others were enhanced trackers—and he was certain these men were sent from the laboratory Luther and Leila had been enhanced in—then one of them could easily have an acute sense of smell. He did. Gino Mazza, one of his teammates, could track anyone with drops of blood lingering in the air.

He replenished their water supply after he thoroughly washed and cleaned the basin he'd provided for Leila to relieve herself. After hydrating and spending more time staring down at her face and admiring her, he knelt beside her and spread his hands over her, reaching for the well of energy inside him. At once, heat rose, moving through his body to his mind and hands, allowing him to examine her.

Her long lashes fluttered and then lifted, a distraction he didn't need.

"That's very warm."

Her voice was drowsy, sexy, sending a different kind of heat down his spine. "Don't distract me, woman. Give me a few minutes to make sure everything is going to hold before you go getting all flirty with me."

"I don't get flirty. Not ever."

Even just coming out of a deep sleep, her sense of humor was at the forefront, recognizing he was teasing her. That was another point in her favor. He needed a woman with a sense of humor. The thought came before he could censor it. He shook his head and tried again to focus, shoving his strange addiction to her away so he could take care of her.

She was healing nicely. She had a long way to go, but the surgery was holding. He needed to get her legs and hips moving so there was no chance of blood clots. Now that he wasn't as weak, he could go back in and boost her antibodies against infection and make certain each organ affected by the bullet would be strong enough to hold while she moved around. In a hospital, with normal surgery, she would be discharged in three days to a week if it was just her spleen removed. Her stomach and small intestine had also been compromised.

He sat back, eyeing her sternly. "Do not give me your cute smile and expect I'm going to let you talk me into letting you up."

Her perfect bow of a mouth curved, drawing his immediate attention. That got him right in the gut. Women were attracted to him. He never went looking; they found him. He always made it clear it would be for a night. He had no interest in adding a woman to his life. Never. Until now. There was something about her he had a bad feeling he might not be able to live without. Anything different in his life put him on edge. Leila was as different as it got. And his reaction to her was a mystery to him.

"What?" Her voice was low, creating an intimacy between them. "Tell me. I'd rather you be honest with me."

Her palm found his wrist. He felt her fingers slide over his pulse. That small, telling gesture was enough to set his heart stuttering. It made no sense that he was so attracted. If he'd been eyeing her for one night, he wouldn't have given it a second thought. She was beautiful and funny and obviously intelligent. Courageous. He could go on listing her qualities, and that was the problem right there. That reaction was completely foreign to his nature.

Diego had a bad feeling that everything he'd ever wanted was right there, lying on the small bed he'd made for her. Looking up at him with those eyes of hers. She was everything he wanted without knowing he wanted it.

"You're unexpected." He decided honesty with her was the only recourse he had. He had no idea why he made that decision when he wasn't honest with his brother, the one person he loved and held in the highest regard. "I've lived in the wilds a long time, and my enhancements include many predatory animals. That's made me have more animal instincts than is probably good."

Her brows came together. Of its own volition, his finger rubbed along that little frown line, smoothing it out.

"What are you thinking? Is something wrong?" Her voice was tinged with worry.

"Not with you. You're healing nicely. I'm just in unfamiliar territory. I like to think things through before I make a move."

"Do you think I'm a threat to you? You saved my life. I'm grateful for everything you've done for me."

He had the unexpected urge to brush his lips against hers just to see what she tasted like. To inhale her breath, take her inside him where he could study her from every angle and see what it was that he found so intriguing. That alone made her dangerous to him, whether she thought so or not.

He asked himself if it was possible she'd been paired with him. He knew that was an ongoing experiment Whitney enjoyed. He would use scent to enhance an attraction between two people, especially if he thought he would be able to get a child from his soldiers he deemed worthy.

"You were never given to Whitney?"

She shook her head. "If I had been, I would have killed him. He didn't raise me and remove all my filters the way he did my sister. She's a mess, and he deliberately did that to her. If I'm ever introduced, I would consider it a worthy exchange: my life to take him with me."

His ability to breathe stopped. His lungs felt raw and burning. His heart did that weird stuttering thing in his chest that actually hurt. He found himself shaking his head. "No, you're not going to get killed just because you get a shot at him. You're a bloodthirsty, hotheaded little thing. It looks like I might have to stick around you and keep you from doing anything crazy on the spur of the moment."

She narrowed her eyes at him. "You did *not* just call me a 'little thing.' There's nothing little about me."

He felt the grin before it flashed through him. "You're right, Leila. My mistake."

"Has anyone ever just wanted to carve a small reminder not to be arrogant into you? Not kill you, just give you a few cuts making up some symbol so you learn to behave?"

"Actually, yes."

"And I don't mean enemies. Someone you live around and know very well."

"Rubin has threatened to shoot me on many occasions. He's thrown knives at me. Once he shaved the skin off my arm."

She gasped, her large green eyes looking like two jewels pressed into her face. Her fingers dug into his inner wrist. "He really did that?" She sounded indignant after just having threatened him with similar behavior, making him want to laugh.

He shrugged, drinking her in. Her reactions to things fascinated him. "Yep. Apparently, I can be quite annoying." He knew he didn't sound in the least remorseful because he wasn't.

He gently took his wrist back so he could move around behind her, setting up a backrest between her and what would be a very uncomfortable wall. "I'm going to lift you. Let me do the work. You just stay relaxed. You're going to feel it because you haven't moved for a while, but everything looks good, and I reinforced the weaker spots I found."

He slipped his hands under her arms and as gently as possible eased her into a sitting position. Her breath hissed out, but she didn't make any other sound. Sweat broke out on her forehead, but she tilted her head back and gave him a smile that could have melted the devil.

"Thank you. You're a pretty amazing man." There was open admiration in her voice.

He settled her against the backrest and rolled his jacket to shove under one arm to help keep her upright. He sat beside her on the other side, sliding his hand down her arm to catch her hand. Threading her fingers through his, he wove them together.

"Woman, you're going to make me think you still have drugs in your system if you start that nonsense again."

She laughed just as he knew she would. He put a bottle of water in her free hand. "Hydrate. It's important to keep hydrated."

She made a face. "Then I'll have to go to the bathroom. I'm not complaining about the accommodations, because you made it as nice and as easy for me as possible, but it's seriously ugh."

He raised his eyebrow. "'Ugh'?" he deliberately repeated. "You're a soldier. You must be used to going into terrain without a clean bathroom."

"Just because I'm used to it doesn't mean I have to like it." She ducked her head, refusing to look at him. "I know I'm a mess and I look more a soldier than a woman, but I can assure you, I've got a side that is all girl."

He caught her chin and brought her head up. Her green eyes collided with his. Her expression was heartbreaking, as if she expected her admission to lessen his opinion of her.

"When we get to the cabin, there's a shower and a decent bathroom. I like the fact that you have that side to you. It means I might have a shot."

A look of utter confusion crossed her face. "A shot? At what?"

"If we're both total alphas, how do we get along? And I want to get along with you. I don't say that to many people. In fact, giving it some thought, the only woman I've ever thought that of is Jonquille, my sister-in-law. It was important for her to accept me as her family. She needed a family. She's like your sister, no filters. Rubin is like me. We can anchor those without filters and give them some relief from the continual bombardment."

"Do you like her? On her own, without being your brother's wife, do you like her for who she is?"

He nodded slowly. "Yeah, she's special. I'm grateful Rubin has her. He's very much in love with her, and she deserves him." He smiled down at her without really feeling like smiling. "I'm not such a bargain."

She gave him that frown he found both adorable and offensive. He didn't like her disturbed over anything, and this time the frown was genuine. She didn't agree with him. He found himself liking the fact that she stuck up for him, even when he was the one putting himself down.

"You have to have women throwing themselves at you, Diego." She made it a statement.

He wasn't going to deny it, so he shrugged instead. "It happens. That doesn't mean I'm not lonely or don't want a woman of my own."

"Have there been a lot of women?"

He recognized treacherous waters when he saw them. "Probably too many." He turned her hand over and brought her fingers to his mouth. It was difficult to resist biting the tips gently. The desire was there. He felt a little like a wolf coaxing a mate to accept him. He realized he was courting her in his strange, wild way.

"How come you aren't with one of them? What went wrong?"

"Nothing went wrong. We weren't in a relationship. I don't date. I didn't see any of them for more than a few hours."

Her eyebrow shot up, but she didn't pull her hand away from his, and her body stayed relaxed against him. Trusting. He didn't deserve her trust, not yet, but he was determined that he would.

"A few hours?" she repeated, staring straight into his eyes.

He could fall into all that vivid green and just live there. She was mesmerizing. "Yeah. I don't like admitting I'm that big of a dick, but I made it clear going in that I wouldn't be sticking around."

"You know they didn't believe you."

"They believed me, but they didn't want to. They mostly tried to convince me that we would be good together."

"But you didn't think so."

"Honey, seriously? They sought me out, but they didn't know the first thing about who I am or what I do. They only knew I was a doctor in the service, and they liked how I looked. There are a lot of women who like to marry servicemen. Doctors are at a premium. Not one of them took the time to have a conversation with me. It wasn't like they cared enough to find out who I am."

"They weren't very intelligent," she pointed out. "Why be with someone if you aren't going to be best friends and have a relationship where you communicate? Where you *like* that person? Shouldn't a relationship be like that?" Her fingers tightened around his.

"It matters to me what you think. What kind of relationship would you like?" He felt as if he were holding his breath. Everything in him went utterly still. Waiting for the crash. Waiting to be told a man like him would never stand a chance with her.

"When I think about having a husband and family, which, in all honesty, I didn't ever believe could happen to me, I know I want us to be best friends first. I want to laugh with him all the time. If we have children, I want their father to laugh with me at their antics. My parents were like that. Always together. Always laughing. My dad would dance my mother around the kitchen. Or the living room. Music was always playing in our house, and he would just catch her around the waist and spin her around and then pull her close. The way they looked at each other was priceless."

"What were you doing when they danced together?" He wished he could have seen her as a young child in a happy home.

"Dancing with my sister. We'd all hold hands sometimes, or Dad would dance with me and Mom with Bridget." She pressed her lips together, and he tightened his fingers around hers, wanting to comfort her. "I miss them every day."

Did he miss his father? His mother? He missed his siblings but not his parents so much. He hadn't thought about that, or why. He'd just tucked them away in a compartment in his mind and firmly closed and locked the door.

"Your parents sound like good people. Luther was that way with Lotty. We'd sneak down to visit her occasionally, and when

Luther would show up, we'd just fade into the forest, but we always watched them together before we slunk off for home. Luther knew we were there, but it never stopped him from picking her flowers or sweeping her off her feet and carrying her into the house. Sometimes he did dance with her, and he sang. Don't ever let on I told you that or he'd likely take my head off. He loved Lotty more than anything."

"What was she like? She would have been my great-aunt."

"Lotty didn't have a mean bone in her body. No matter how long Luther was gone when he disappeared, she waited for him. She kept their little house perfect and comfortable for him. Everything was about him. And for him, everything was about her. When he was gone, and we always thought he was on a trip of some kind, something to do with his moonshine, Rubin and I hunted and fished for Lotty. Luther never left her without supplies, but we always checked on her. We liked being around her, and sometimes we'd sneak our sisters out. We'd bring them down here. At times we could convince my mother that Lotty needed the company, then it wasn't so bad when we went back home."

"My mother told me my grandmother admitted to saying horrible things to Luther after the war," Leila said. "She was an activist, as were her friends. They all were very mean to Luther. She said the moment she hurled the insults at him, she regretted it, but she didn't apologize right there in front of her friends as she should have. My mother told me to always think before speaking and never say things to a loved one you can't take back. My grandmother never had the chance to apologize to him and make things right between them. He disappeared."

"He was still working for the government. They would have helped him disappear."

"My father always hoped to meet him. He knew he was Luther's nephew because my grandmother would always tell him wonderful stories about him. My grandmother said that was her one regret, and it was a heartbreaking one. She really did love him. She didn't want Luther to die thinking no one loved him. She always told me she loved him very much."

"Lotty loved him," Diego said. "Men like us, like Luther and I, don't expect to be loved. We don't, so if it happens, it would feel like a miracle. Lotty was Luther's miracle."

Her thumb stroked along the outside of his fingers. It was the lightest of touches. He doubted she was aware of it. It was gentle. Comforting. Instinctive in her to want to soothe him. She was born with that trait. His warrior woman, lethal as hell, but all woman. The good kind. He couldn't help but think of the stark difference in what she wanted for her home and family and what his mother had created for them.

"Diego, what did you mean when you said the kind of men you and Luther are?"

He leaned his head beside hers against the makeshift backrest. "I promised myself I'd give you the real me, even though I know it will screw up any chance I have with you." He kept his gaze fixed on her face. She had the most appealing bone structure.

"That implies you don't give others the real you. Why bother with me?"

"I hide in plain sight. I have to. My brother is hanging out there, vulnerable, whether he likes to think so or not. That doesn't discount his abilities to fight. He's a man to have on your side, and he brings all kinds of assets to the table with him. It's just that his surgeries are incredible. His speed and skills are light-years ahead of mine. He's saved so many lives during our rescues, it's unbelievable. There are a couple of others with his ability, but he's hands down the master."

She rubbed her cheek against his shoulder. "Why aren't you including yourself with those miracle workers? You are, you know."

"You took a big chance letting me work on you. I heal animals, and have, hundreds of them, but I've only helped a couple of humans. Your operation was the first major one like that I've done. I travel with Rubin, and I always ensure he's safe when he's healing. He's extraordinary at it."

She was silent for a short period of time, thinking things over, the way she seemed to do. "I was pretty out of it, but I recall you telling me you were trusting me not to give away your secret. I took that to mean to our government or anyone who would dissect you to see how it worked. But you meant anyone. No one knows you can do what your brother does, do they? You don't want *anyone* to know."

She turned her head when she asked the question, staring him straight in the eyes. Two emeralds. That was what it was like looking into. A beautiful green jeweled sea. He could get lost looking into her eyes, and he wasn't the poetic type. He knew Rubin wrote poetry. He'd never invaded his brother's privacy, but he knew Rubin had a poet's soul. He, however, did not. There wasn't a bone in his body that could be labeled romantic, or poetic, yet looking into her eyes, all he could think about was the beauty of emeralds.

He'd promised himself he'd be real with her. She would ask him uncomfortable questions, questions he no longer had the answers to. "You and Luther. That's it."

"Luther is so tight-lipped when it comes to confidences, you know he'd never give anyone the smallest detail about you, even if they tortured him."

"That's true. How long were you with your great-uncle before you were attacked?"

"About eighteen hours."

"He didn't know much about either of you. I needed information quickly, and he wanted me to go after you, so he didn't have much of a choice. He told me you were his great-nieces. He blames himself for what happened to you."

"That seems to be a running theme in our family. I blame my-self for not taking care of my sister, and Luther blames himself for what happened to us when he didn't even know we existed. You know what that proves? We are human after all. Making us some kind of souped-up elite soldiers still doesn't make us think we're all that."

Again, there was that faint note of humor. She had no trouble laughing at herself. He thought that was a much better way to handle life than being morose, as he often found himself getting to be. He flashed a small self-deprecating grin.

"I need to hang out with you more. You make me laugh when I thought I'd forgotten how." He tugged at her hair. The braid was coming loose, and stray strands were beginning to behave on the wild side. He wanted to see that mass of silk shiny and naturally wild.

Once again, her green eyes moved over his face as if commit-ting his features to memory. She seemed to make it a habit, when she looked at him, to focus completely on him. The intensity in her direct stare gave him the feeling she could see right into him. In-side. He had a lot of secrets, most of them needing to stay con-cealed, never to see the light of day.

Diego wanted her to see him, and yet that was the very thing he feared. He found humor in the dichotomy, needing her to see him but not wanting her to. That ability to laugh at himself was always there, but she was bringing it out stronger than ever. A good thing, he decided.

"When I signaled to Luther I was there, you knew where I was," he changed the subject. He was genuinely curious. "How?" His birdcalls were so close to reality, he couldn't imagine she could hear the difference.

A small frown flitted across her face. "Before I answer that, how did you know I was aware of you?"

This time Diego couldn't resist smoothing that little frown line between her eyebrows. "You glanced up toward my location."

"I did?" She sounded horrified. "If the enemy was watching, I could have given your position away. Or just tipped them off that help had arrived. That would have put your life in jeopardy."

"It was extremely brief. First, I doubt anyone but me noticed. And second, they would have thought you were looking for their positions."

She ducked her head. "Don't make excuses for my mistake. That was a big one. Huge. You don't do things like that in combat and jeopardize your allies."

"Woman." He brought their linked hands toward his mouth and then was unable to prevent himself from brushing a kiss over the back of her hand. "Stop. You didn't give anything away. I had a weird, compulsive need to keep looking at you. I used my scope, not just enhanced vision. I could have given my position away if the sun had caught it."

"You had a weird compulsion to look at me?" Once again, she turned the power of her large eyes on him. "That's what it felt like? A compulsion?"

"Yeah. I couldn't have stopped myself if I wanted to." What difference did it make if he was honest with her? He had the feeling she would see inside him, no matter what he said or did, and he was adept at hiding in plain sight.

"Me either." Her voice was so low he barely caught her admission, even with his acute hearing. "I didn't hear any difference in the warning call from the bird. The notes were exact."

"Almost," he corrected. "Not sure anyone produces perfect birdcalls, but it's as close as I can make them, practicing all the time. I started when I was a kid." He pressed the back of her hand to his jaw. He needed a shave, and the stubble on his jaw scraped against her skin. She didn't pull away from him.

"Diego?" She tilted her head back and then rested it against his shoulder. "I honestly think I would know where you were if you were within a mile of me. I think I could pinpoint your exact location. I have gifts, strong ones, but never anything like the awareness I have of you. It's very strong." She hesitated.

"Tell me. I'm choosing to be honest with you. This is all new for me, just like I suspect it is for you. New is alarming."

"It's more than the attraction being new for me. It's the intensity of it. The quickness of it. I'm a loner. I wasn't trained to be part of a unit. I was always sent out on my own, and I had no desire to be around the other soldiers. We were all training. My training was very specific, and I was always monitored, or I would have gotten away to look for my sister a lot sooner."

"How did you find her? We track Whitney, and by the time we acquire his location, he moves, taking the women with him."

Again, that little frown appeared. "I don't know how I track people. Gut instinct? I just have some kind of built-in radar. If I follow it, I get results."

"A gift, then. You've been enhanced." He made it a statement.

"Physically. Genetically enhanced, but not psychically. The gifts I have are extremely strong, but the lab where they experiment on the volunteer soldiers doesn't do the kinds of experiments Whitney does."

"Were you ever around Whitney, even as a child?"

"No. They took Bridget to him. I heard them talking. I was combative and exhibited the ability to act independently, even as a young child. When they tested us, I tested high in the protective area. The lab wanted me and gave Bridget to Whitney. She was always much easier than I ever was. I questioned everything and had problems with authority. Bridget was sweet and loving."

There was a note in her voice that told Diego that Leila had regrets. He understood what that was like. Children did and said things they shouldn't, or didn't do what they were told. Once they lost parents or siblings, there was no way to take back whatever was said or done.

Diego pressed a kiss to the back of her hand, needing to comfort her. He found it interesting that the compulsion was a *need*, not a want. She didn't show her distress, but every instinct he had told him that little betraying note in her voice gave away her true feelings. It was odd that they had the same issues, both feeling it was their duty to protect their sibling.

He didn't want Leila to ever feel that Bridget was more important than she was—but he knew she did. He felt that way about Rubin. His brother was the better man. There was nothing Luther could say to make him feel differently because he had grown up with Rubin. He knew the man was sensitive and compassionate. It wasn't that Rubin never lost his temper—and when he did, he could annihilate everyone around him—it was just that it didn't happen often and it was always justified. Diego thought of himself as cold as ice. Leila was anything but cold.

"Asking questions is a good trait to have. The more information, the better. I was a big proponent of asking questions until it was beaten out of me." He said it matter-of-factly, using a casual tone. It was history. He didn't dwell on it. But if he spoke it out loud, that door to his childhood creaked open and he felt the lash of the belt or the switch across his back, buttocks and legs.

He felt Leila's instant, visceral response. Every muscle in her body tensed, and her breath exploded from her lungs. "Your parents beat you because you asked questions?"

His warrior woman had a hot temper. He'd have to remember that. "Yep."

"Someone should have beat them so they could see how it felt," she snapped.

He burst out laughing. It was the first time he could ever remember laughing over a dark memory. Her eyes widened.

"Diego."

The softness in her voice created an intimacy between them. Without thinking, and he was a deliberate man, he caught her chin and brushed his lips over hers. He couldn't have stopped himself if someone put a gun to his head. The compulsion—the need—was too strong. The touch of her soft mouth was electric. Hot sparks of desire flashed down his spine. Leapt through his bloodstream. He lifted his head, shocked at his reaction to that brief touch. He'd kissed before, too many times, but nothing could have prepared him for the heady reality of simply brushing his lips against hers. She tasted like wild strawberries. She tasted like his.

She lifted her long lashes, and once again, he was falling into those emerald pools. "What was that?"

"I figured if you didn't want me kissing you, if you didn't like it, you'd use that knife that's right there next to your hand."

A faint smile curved her lips. "Guess I liked it. You're still alive."

5

A low, growling bark sounding the alarm came from a great horned owl, instantly alerting Diego. He came awake, every sense flaring out to read the forest outside their sanctuary. The female owl was a particular favorite of his. She was very familiar with him and his touch, allowing him to communicate with her easily.

The raptor was a ferocious hunter. She defended her territory relentlessly, without fear. She could be a deadly killing machine when her ire was aroused. She would drop silently out of the darkness with no warning, coming in low and fast, her talons and beak lethal weapons. He was fond of her. More than once, she'd protected him. In fact, she had saved his life.

Diego had fallen asleep with his arm around Leila. The pads of her fingers rested on his inner wrist, unerringly over his pulse, as if that steady beat reassured her. He pressed his face into her neck and inhaled.

"Wake up, Warrior Woman." He kept his voice low and soft,

not wanting to startle her. He should have known better. She was instantly alert. Her breathing changed, but she lay still, clearly doing as he had done, reaching for information outside their shelter.

"The men pursuing you are about three miles out and coming this way fast. They have to know something is wrong since not one of the soldiers from their unit contacted them. Once they find the bodies, they'll be out for blood."

"I can get up," she said. "I'll back you up. The pain is less today."

"No, sweetheart, you're going to stay right here and defend our den. You have a couple more days to heal before we can move you up to the cabin. Let's take care of getting you ready."

She made a face. "Lovely. My favorite thing is waking up and having you have to take care of me like that."

"Are you getting modest on me?" He traced her cheekbone with the pad of his finger. "I'll go out for a few minutes and start to set things up. You'll have some privacy that way."

"Thanks, Diego. I appreciate everything you do for me."

He didn't acknowledge her gratitude. He wasn't used to having anyone thank him or treat him the way she did. He had a bad feeling that she was capable of ripping out what was left of his heart. It wouldn't take much to fall off the proverbial cliff with her.

He examined her before he did anything else, needing the assurance that she was healing. Each morning, he performed another healing session on her, in the hopes it would speed up the process. Without her spleen, he knew she was susceptible to infections. He wanted to stimulate her immune system and defenses as best he could. Moving her was going to be difficult on her. He wanted her in the best shape possible before they started the long trek up the mountain to his cabin.

Leila caught at his arm when he made a move to go. "Tell me what you're going to do."

"What I do best. Hunt." He was abrupt and he didn't mean to be. Those men looking for Leila had been part of the attack on her, and his intention was to leave their dead bodies for the vultures and ants. He didn't want her to see that ruthless side of him, although it would be best if she did.

"Are you upset with me, Diego? I know it must be difficult to stay here taking care of me. I'm getting stronger, and then I'll be able to take care of myself," she assured him. Her voice was strong, but once again he caught that small note that tugged at his heartstrings. Deep down, she believed he wanted to be away from her.

He swore under his breath as he leaned directly over her, forcing her to tilt her head back, her vivid green eyes meeting his. "We're a pair of idiots. You know that, don't you? Doesn't matter that we might have high IQs. The bottom line is we're letting others dictate how we feel about us. Luther would not be happy with either of us."

Her eyes widened. "My uncle?"

"The man can give a lecture, woman. You haven't experienced the full extent of Luther's annoyance. He'll tell you something most likely spot-on, and if you don't learn right there and then, he thinks you aren't quite bright, and he has no problem letting you know."

He found her confusion adorable. *Adorable.* Good grief, it was too late for him to act normal or to run. He was already gone. It made no sense unless he considered they were in life-and-death circumstances and they'd formed a bond to survive. He told himself that was the reason he was head over heels for her, but he wasn't a man to lie to himself.

"You think Luther would lecture me?"

"I know he would. He would tell you to quit thinking you aren't worthy of love and admiration or respect. You are. I am. We're just doing this crazy dance around each other, and we've got to stop.

Every time you think badly of yourself, change your thinking. Tell yourself you're a good person."

At once her face flushed and she lowered her chin, but not fast enough. Her eyes had welled up with tears, and she gave a little shake of her head. "I'm not, Diego. You don't know the terrible things I've done. I don't want you to think that I'm something I'm not." She sounded near panic-stricken. Her fingers tightened on his wrist. "You can't go out there and put your life on the line for me. You've already done it and you shouldn't have. I shouldn't have allowed it. I stayed alive because . . ." She broke off, turning her face away from him.

He curled his palm around the nape of her neck and traced the line of her jaw with the pad of his thumb. Her body trembled, betraying her very real agitation. "Share with me, Warrior Woman. I realize you have no reason to trust me, but I swear to you, I'll help you figure it out."

He knew she was used to being alone. She'd only had herself to rely on. She may have had a good early childhood with her parents, but he knew from experience that age ten was still very young. She'd had to make decisions regarding her life. Her sister had been ripped away from her—the sister she'd promised her parents she would look after.

Growing up in a laboratory, even if it wasn't a facility like Whitney's, was brutal on a child. He couldn't imagine what Leila's training had been like, especially when he'd witnessed the way the soldiers had callously treated what amounted to a dying woman. That revelation struck him. He'd thought the soldiers coming from the lab would be decent men, because Luther, his one example, had been. But the five soldiers he'd killed to keep them off Leila had failed to show compassion, empathy or even decency. Had she been exposed to those kinds of men after she'd turned ten?

"Leila, talk to me. You have to trust someone. Let that someone be me. I don't consider myself the best of men, but I'm loyal, and I don't break promises."

Leila shook her head and looked at him. He read despair in her eyes. All that look did was make him want to gather her up and shelter her in his arms.

"You are the best of men, and that's the problem, Diego. I know you think because you killed a few men that makes you irredeemable in some way, but it doesn't. You were at war. Fighting for your country. It doesn't matter if war was declared; you know we sometimes don't have choices."

His thumb continued to stroke along her delicate jaw, tracing that line, committing her features to his physical memory. That declaration shook him, whether he wanted to admit it or not. She wasn't a liar. She spoke to him what she believed was truth. And she saw into him, past the bullshit persona he put out there for others to see. He knew she could see into that place in him that was all killer. Almost pure predator. The hunt was sacred to him. As necessary as breathing. Why didn't she see that as a negative trait?

"Sweetheart, you're looking beyond my worst characteristics because you think you need me to survive. Or you feel you owe me a debt." He tried to be practical, not let her opinion of him wrap her around his heart. Who knew she would manage to gut him in such a short time? He had a high respect for Leila and the gifts she obviously had. "You're at a place where you could do this on your own. It would be difficult, but you don't need me."

Her lashes were so damned long. That little flutter, the sweep up and down, veiling her expression and then revealing the vivid green of her eyes sent flickering flames dancing through his veins.

"I might not need you, Diego, but I want to be with you. I see darkness in you. You view that as a bad trait. I believe it's what allows you to be so effective at what you do." Her gaze shifted from his and then returned, the green going so vivid it appeared as though two jewels had been pressed into her face. "I have a child. A daughter. I killed her father."

Diego heard the defiance in her voice. The expectation that he would condemn her. A child? He should have seen that when he was examining her. All he saw was the mess the bullet had made of her body.

"There's no doubt in my mind that if you killed him, he deserved killing." He kept his voice mild. Soothing. "And don't cry." He swept his finger under her left eye to remove the glittering liquid. "You'll break my heart, and you've already put the damn thing in jeopardy."

She blinked rapidly, her soft lips parting slightly. His body reacted in an inappropriate way for a doctor. Her doctor. He needed to keep reminding himself of that.

"He wasn't the only one I killed that day. He had two friends with him. They were fellow soldiers, men I trained with. I kept to myself for the most part because many of the soldiers were amped up and seemed off to me."

His gut tightened. He couldn't abide men who beat or raped women. It was a huge trigger for him after the experiences of his childhood. He had a bad, bad feeling his little warrior woman had been exposed to men like the ones who had tried to rape her when she was at her most vulnerable.

"With that experience, it's a wonder you went to your uncle with Bridget." It was an effort to keep his voice mild and soothing, but he managed.

"Believe me, I was ready to kill him if needed. Bridget was in a bad way, and I needed to go back for my daughter. Before I could, I had to ensure Bridget would be safe. Luther was my only choice. I counted on the fact that my feelings of loyalty and need to protect family were just as strong in him."

A daughter. That was the reason Leila had told Luther she had to leave but would come back. She had killed the child's father along with two of his friends.

"They tried to rape you." Diego made the statement for her.

"Leon succeeded. That was how I conceived."

So the bastard who raped her had been named Leon. That name would forever haunt him because he was determined to take that memory onto his shoulders and find a way to lessen the impact on her.

"And you kept the baby." Again, he was very careful of his tone. He didn't want her to think he wouldn't accept another man's child, no matter the circumstances of conception. Her daughter was Leila's. He would welcome—and love and protect—any child of Leila's.

The tears in Leila's eyes did more than gut him. His heart felt as though it clenched in his chest so hard he feared a heart attack. That didn't bode well for their future. He was going to be a push-over for the woman. Maybe that was what she needed. He hoped so, because he was already feeling possessive toward her. Protective. It felt as though she was always meant to be his. Maybe he'd been created and shaped into the monster he knew himself to be just to be able to protect her. To be whatever she and her daughter would need.

"I'd been alone so long. It wasn't her fault that those men were jacked up from the enhancements. I needed her."

She spoke low, a confession when he wasn't the priestly type. She didn't need to feel guilt just because she wanted a family.

"I understand, Leila," he assured, because it was the truth. He'd lost most of his family, but he'd always had Rubin with him. Later, he'd been accepted by Ezekiel Fortunes and Zeke's two brothers, Malichai and Mordichai. They'd formed another family unit. Then he'd had Nonny, the grandmother of one of the GhostWalkers in his unit. He'd always had people surrounding him, caring for him, and yet he was a walking mess. What had it been like for her? She'd been alone.

"You don't though, Diego."

Those long lashes swept down and back up again. Wet. Spiky. Heartbreaking. If she kept it up, he was going to have to put her on his lap and just hold her. If the men hunting them found the trail, which he doubted would happen, he'd cross that bridge when he came to it. Right at that moment, the only thing that mattered to him was to stop her tears.

"Then tell me, sweetheart." He massaged the nape of her neck, trying to ease the tension out of her. Trying to convey to her that she wasn't alone and she'd never have to be again if she could just see the man right in front of her.

"I flirted with him. With Leon. I was so tired of being alone, and he seemed decent. I really thought if I got to know him, maybe I'd be attracted to him. I was the only one who lived in the dormitory, and he came there with his friends. I didn't see the others when he knocked on my door, and I opened it. He punched me so hard it nearly knocked me out. They dragged me inside and I was too groggy to fight him off. The others held me down . . ." She trailed off again, turning her head away from him. "If I hadn't drawn his attention, it never would have happened, and all of them would still be alive."

"How many other women would they have raped?" he asked gently. "You're not thinking about this clearly, Leila. If they were so willing to rape you, it was in them. They would have done the same to other women. More than likely they already had. The fact that he incapacitated you immediately leads me to believe it wasn't the first time and Leon had perfected his technique."

Leila fell silent, but she leaned into him. The tension slowly faded from her body. Diego remained silent, letting her work it out for herself. He knew he was right. He was good at reading human nature. He might not have met Leon and his friends face-to-face, but he'd met many men like them. Enhancements often brought out the worst traits in the soldiers. Introducing aggressive predators into the DNA was asking for disaster. He should know. For every good characteristic, there were two bad.

"I didn't think of it that way. Now that you've pointed it out, I believe you're right."

"Did those running the laboratory allow you to keep the baby?"

"They were excited when they found out." Her gaze met his. This time the green was as cool as ice. "They knew if they tried to take her from me, I'd declare war on them."

Diego waited for her to continue. He was beginning to feel a sense of urgency, and he reached for the owl, an automatic reaction he'd had since his childhood and all the years he'd practiced communicating with the birds in the forest. Now, despite long months away, he connected easily with the great horned owl. Once he had her attention, he sent out a command using the notes of a male owl calling to her.

They had developed their private language over time. The female owl was extremely intelligent, and she had caught on to his various call patterns and the meanings behind them very quickly until, over the years, they'd developed communication skills he hadn't believed possible. He needed her to find the intruders and let him know their exact position. He preferred to hunt them a good distance from Leila. No matter that he told her she could defend the den they were in, he didn't want her to have to.

The notes of the male owl were as close to the real thing as possible. Her eyebrow shot up. "You're telling an owl to do something."

He nodded. "I need her to let me know the location of those men hunting you."

"She can do that?"

"Don't tell me you aren't able to utilize animals, because I think you can."

"Not like that. I wish I could."

"It took me several years of working out patterns that would sound close enough to a male great horned owl calling to a female. She took less time to learn it than I did to develop it."

"That's amazing. Even just the fact that you persisted."

He gave her a faint smile. "You'll find I'm quite stubborn when I want to do something. I tend to persist until I get my way. I can work at something for years and never stop until I manage to attain my goal."

"That's not a bad trait to have. You sound like you think it is."

"It can be very bad. I got myself into a lot of trouble when I was young. If my commanding officer knew half the things I did, he'd most likely throw me in the brig."

"I doubt that. I think you're considered very valuable by everyone but you."

She could be right. He hadn't given it much thought. "Please continue telling me about what happened with your daughter and how you came to be separated."

Leila sighed. "Mistakes. Misjudging people. Not knowing who was an enemy and who wasn't. I was sent out a few times to help in situations with troops. While I was gone, they had a woman looking after the baby. She seemed okay at first, but after the second time, when I returned, I found I didn't trust her—or anyone else but Marcy, my commanding officer's wife. Not that I trusted him. The baby is highly intelligent. They didn't take that into consideration, or that I might have ways to communicate with her that they didn't."

She looked at him as if he might not believe her. He nodded, hoping to reassure her that he would always believe her. "There have been several GhostWalker babies born in the last few years," he told her, still massaging the knots in her neck. Each time she gave him more information, she tensed as if she expected him to condemn her. "Every single one shows remarkable intelligence and the ability to understand and communicate before they are able to speak."

Her eyes widened in shock. "Grace isn't the only one?"

She called her daughter Grace. Nonny, Wyatt's grandmother, was Grace Fontenot. She was the best woman Diego knew. If Leila's daughter was anything like Nonny, she would grow up to be an incredible human being. More and more, Diego believed he'd been born to be with this woman. Every sign seemed to point in that direction. They were even free of the taint of Whitney's pairing that had originally bothered so many of the GhostWalkers. Everything he felt for Leila was from getting to know her. Being in her mind. Seeing who she really was.

He admired her courage. He respected her as a soldier. The fact that she was so injured and yet ready to defend their position got to him. He hadn't expected the intense chemistry. She was injured. He was her doctor. He was caring for her in ways that forced an intimacy between them that should have been awkward. It wasn't.

"No, Grace is in good company. I love that you named her Grace. Wyatt, a member of my unit, has a grandmother and a daughter named Grace. We all call his grandmother Nonny. She's one of the most amazing women I've ever met."

"I liked the name. It's maybe a little old-fashioned, but it suited her."

There was love in her voice. Her face had gone soft. He'd never seen that look on his mother's face. Not even when she looked at Rubin, and he was her favorite.

"You're beautiful all the time, but when you talk about your daughter, you're even more so."

Faint color swept under her skin. "You always make me feel good about myself. Thank you for that, although I don't know how to handle it. It's a little embarrassing, but still makes me feel good."

He brushed a kiss on top of her head. "Why did the woman watching Grace make you feel as if you couldn't trust her?"

"Grace sent me impressions of a man in a white lab coat taking her blood. It hurt her. I realized that when I was gone, my commander would allow the lab to study Grace. I had no way to protect her when I was gone. I didn't want them experimenting on her. I'd heard such terrible things about Whitney and what he was doing. The other soldiers would talk sometimes. It was terrifying knowing Bridget was with Whitney."

He couldn't imagine how painful it must have been for her to know her sister was in the hands of a madman.

"What changed everything? How did you come to a place where you tracked Bridget down?" Even as he asked her, he listened for the great horned owl's response.

The large bird could elongate its body when sitting motionless on the branch of a tree. The coloration allowed it to blend into the bark, a perfect camouflage. Diego and Rubin had learned to mimic the owl, often sleeping in the branches of a tree when they were children out hunting for their families. They'd learned to camouflage and be still from the fierce predatory owl. They'd taken many lessons from the great horned owl. To strike fast and decisively, not giving opponents time for resistance. Mold their bodies to their background and go completely still, holding the position for hours. The owl was intelligent and fierce, protective and territorial. Diego had those traits in abundance.

"Marcy. She didn't allow anyone, not even the commander, to touch Grace while I was gone. She didn't approve of a lot of the things going on at the laboratory, or how I was raised as a soldier. She slipped a note to me when she handed me Grace. Grace was bundled up and sleeping. I could see that Marcy was extremely nervous. Her eyes kept darting around the room, and when she spoke to me, she turned her face into the blankets and tote filled with Gracie's things. I knew we were under observation, and she didn't want anyone watching to know she was conveying anything to me but how my daughter was in my absence. I went along with it and didn't even read the note until I was alone in the bathroom."

"The woman was an ally?"

"Her name is Marcy Chariot. She's a registered nurse and married to the commanding officer. She overhears quite a bit of what is going on when there are discussions about the genetic enhancements. She was appalled when she heard what Whitney was doing to some of the women. At first, she didn't believe what she was hearing. She thought if the rumors were true, Whitney would be stopped. She asked her husband about it, and he told her many factions in the government believed he would create the soldiers of the future. Her husband told her that Whitney had a program imprisoning the women and forcing them to give birth to babies he could experiment on."

Diego swore under his breath. He knew it was true. They'd actively hunted Whitney in the hopes of stopping him, but he had too many allies willing to shield him. They showed up at compounds known to be used by him, but he was always already gone.

"Marcy told me they were all disgusted with the way he had treated my sister and that she was in a bad way. They feared, because I had a baby, that he would force Bridget to have one and the experiments would continue on that child. Marcy had the last known location of Bridget. One of the officers had visited the compound and saw her. He said she looked as if she was very ill. Whitney was known to put cancer and bacterial and viral diseases into the women for his experiments. She worried that Bridget was being used that way."

"Marcy has Grace now?" Suddenly, it was extremely important to Diego that the child was safe.

Leila's nod was slow. "I had to trust her. I felt I had no choice. I had to get to Bridget if at all possible. The first place was already abandoned, but I tracked her to the next location used and was able to get her out. I needed a safe place to stash her while I went back for Gracie. Luther was the only one I could think of who might help us. Bridget needed care. She has no filters, and the assault on her brain is horrific. It feels to me as if she has a massive brain injury."

"Whitney removing Bridget's filters makes no sense. Whitney saw the results in his first unit of GhostWalkers. Brain bleeds. Seizures. Continuing to remove filters and experiment in that direction is an abomination. If you make a mistake, you do your best to rectify it, not double down and ruin the lives of other human beings," Diego declared. As far as he was concerned, Whitney was a sadist, especially when it came to women. Whitney didn't consider the things he did to them torture, but that was exactly what it was.

"The fact that the government protects him is mind-boggling," Leila agreed. "At least I was given a choice. No one just experimented on me. I was talked to several times by the head of the lab, and I could have turned them down."

Diego wasn't as certain as Leila. The experiments came under the heading of top secret. Few knew of the lab and the soldiers coming out of it. He hadn't even known, and he was a Ghost-Walker. Whitney piggybacked on the experiments done to the volunteer soldiers. If information had been disclosed to Leila, especially when she was a child, they would have leaned on her, broken her down psychologically, to get her to comply. Diego had been around those experimenting on the soldiers and women, and their fanaticism outweighed their morals. Betrayal and treachery were the norms.

"Why did you want to be enhanced?"

"I was shown footage of what the soldiers could do. Footage of Luther. I really wanted to meet him. My grandmother had talked about Luther often. I knew she regretted the things she'd said to him, but she couldn't find him to make things right. My father had tried while my grandmother was alive. I wanted to be able to do that for her and my father. I also thought if I could be as fast and as strong as the soldiers, I would have a better chance of getting Bridget back."

"That makes sense," Diego agreed. "I was given the same rhetoric, and they convinced me to sign up. I can't very well fault a child for choosing enhanced physical strength. I was choosing enhanced psychic talent." He flashed her a grin because sharing with her made all the problems easier. "Guess we both got screwed."

"Maybe." She rubbed her palm along his thigh. "And maybe they screwed themselves. Most of their soldiers implode, like Leon and his friends."

"And the ones taking you up the mountain to the site where they were going to land a helicopter." He knew the exact location of the only clearing available to set a helicopter down safely up the mountain. It was a good distance above their cabin. Rubin had used it on many occasions to practice diverting lightning strikes. "Whitney's supersoldiers are worse. And they never last long. Pumped up the way Whitney makes them, their bodies give out fast."

Leila tilted her head to look up at him. Her cheek rubbed against his shoulder. "If something happens to me, will you find Gracie and protect her? I need you to do that for me. I know what I'm asking, but it's important to me to know she's in safe hands."

His first reaction was to protest. To tell her everything would be fine and she would be the one to get her daughter back, but he knew the real world wasn't always accommodating. Things could change in seconds. It had for him already. He had come home to die, and yet dying was the furthest thing from his mind. He'd felt more alive in the last few days than he ever had.

"I give you my word, Leila." He rubbed his chin on top of her head. "I'd like you to make up your mind that you're going to live through this. No other outcome is acceptable." He turned fully to her and captured her face between his palms. "Do you hear me? No other outcome is acceptable."

Her green eyes searched his for what seemed an eternity. A slow smile curved her soft mouth. He found himself wanting to kiss her.

"I hear you. I want you to hear me. Your life is important. It is to me and, I'm certain, to a number of others. It isn't just your talents that make you worthwhile; it's who you are fundamentally. I want you to come back to me as soon as we're in the clear."

He brushed his lips over hers because the temptation was too much to resist. "I keep my promises, Leila. I don't make that many, but the ones I do make, even to myself, I consider that my bond. I'll come back for you. We'll get Gracie together. And then we'll find Bridget if Luther wasn't able to get to her before they took off with her."

"The tracking device. You shot me with one; you must have shot her as well."

"I did. A highly intelligent teammate of mine developed it, making it impossible to find in the body. Those who took her won't have a clue we have a way of finding her. As far as they know, only you and Luther were there. The others don't know about me. Even if they did, they wouldn't know who I am. Even then, if they realized who I am, it would never occur to them I would have such a sophisticated tracking device on me when I was simply coming home."

"Whoever invented your tracking device needs a better way to deliver it. It hurt worse than a bug bite and bled."

"You were stoic as hell," Diego pointed out. She had glared at him. Even then, in the middle of a firefight, she made him want to laugh. Now they were sitting in a makeshift den created out of dirt, branches and forest floor debris. She was severely injured, and they were being hunted by soldiers. None of that seemed to matter. She made him feel alive and happy. She made him want to laugh despite the grim situation. For him, she was the perfect woman, one who would stand at his side and cope with everything that came their way. Most importantly, she would love their children and stand in front of them.

"I didn't feel stoic," she said. "I was very, very angry. If I could have risked a shot at you, just to shave a little flesh off your arm, I probably would have done it. Luther warned me you were going to shoot a dart at me. I told him absolutely not."

He couldn't help the grin. "Yeah. I saw that little exchange. I took the shot just in case Luther decided to warn me off."

Her green eyes went cool, but there was a hint of laughter in them. "You're a little on the ruthless side, aren't you?"

He raised an eyebrow. "A little? Woman. That's insulting."

Her laughter melted something hard and stony inside him. He wasn't sure how she managed, but she turned the worst of conditions into fun. Women threw themselves at him. It wasn't as if he hadn't been with women, but he didn't enjoy their company. He could have spent a lifetime in Leila's company. She was just . . . easy to be with.

"Most men would think it was insulting if I called them ruthless. It isn't a compliment."

His grin widened and she reacted, tracing one of the indentations around his mouth with the pad of her finger.

"It is a compliment," he insisted.

"You have dimples."

He did his best to scowl at her. "I don't. Dimples aren't manly, Warrior Woman, and just being ruthless proves I'm all man."

She rolled her eyes and burst out laughing again. "Stop. It hurts when I laugh."

The owl settled on the top of their den, emitting a series of calls much like she would make to her young. That galvanized Diego into action. He pressed a kiss to her temple, and then made certain she had everything she needed to defend herself.

"Water and ammo on your right. More weapons on your left. I'll be back as fast as possible."

She didn't protest or cry. He had known she wouldn't. Her expression was one of utter resolve.

"I'll protect our happy little home." She flashed a smile at him, the last thing he saw when he left her. He took that someplace deep in his heart and, signaling the owl, headed up the mountain toward the place where he had left the bodies in a gorge.

6

Diego shed most of his humanity as he ran up the mountain, setting a fast pace as he swerved around the trees, ducked beneath branches, and leapt over the ribbons of water. Nearly every genetic enhancement he had was that of a predator. He utilized every one of the acute senses to aid him in his run toward the gorge where he'd left the bodies.

The owl had shown him there were five intruders on the mountain. She indicated her disdain for them by ruffling her feathers and sending a warning cry echoing through the trees. Her disdain grew when not a single man looked up to spot her as she sat in the tree right above their heads, her body elongated, frozen in place as she watched the men moving around, eyes to the ground, looking for tracks. She shared the impressions with Diego.

Diego continued his run without missing a stride, but he had the exact location of the five men. They were looking for signs, casting back and forth. One continually sniffed at the air and ground. The owl watched that man with some curiosity, showing

Diego the strange way he ran his nose through the leaves and brush around the site where Diego had shot and killed their fellow soldiers.

Diego expanded his senses to encompass the area just above where the men were searching. A field of rocks and boulders studded the mountain, jutting out and forming what Diego called a basking knoll for snakes. Two ribbons of water wound their way through the rocks, bubbling over smaller stones. Diego knew timber rattlers had a den in the caves concealed by the rocks. The knoll was the perfect place to curl up in the sun, out of the trees.

Timber rattlers were carnivores. They hunted voles, rabbits, mice, squirrels and any other small rodent. The water close by was a draw to the rodents and allowed them access as well. Often a den could hold several hundred snakes until the males left the pregnant females. Diego knew exactly where that den was.

As he ran up the side of the mountain, he took advantage of the owl's information, checking the exact position of each of the men hunting Leila. The man Diego targeted first was the "sniffer." He ran his nose along the ground, hunting for any evidence of Leila's passing. Diego had worked to rid the forest floor and adjacent area of any blood splatter, but the scent would be there. It might be faint, but most animals could ferret it out. A sniffer was a soldier who had an enhanced sense of smell.

As he continued his route along the narrow game trail that wound through trees and beds of rock, Diego used the owl's vision to study his opponent. The man continually ran his nose along the debris on the forest floor. Once he had the sniffer pinpointed, Diego expanded his mind to include several of the larger timber rattlers.

The rattlesnakes' scales were brown, with the zigzag bands running across the body being a dark black. The pattern was distinctive, identifying the timber rattlesnake. At the tip of the tail was a hollow rattle. Heads were triangular and bodies thick. It was easy to identify a timber rattler, but not always easy to see them, especially when they moved through the leaves and debris on the forest floor with its dappled light.

He nudged the larger ones, agitating them, before he took command of them. The smallest of the six that slithered beneath the leaves and twigs on the forest floor was a little over four feet long, but the others were much larger. The biggest snake was almost seven feet long and most likely weighed in at nine pounds. He directed the snakes toward the sniffer, who continued to run his nose through the leaves and dirt on the trail of blood Leila had left behind.

The timber rattlers were silent as they surrounded the man, the largest positioning himself directly in the path the sniffer was traveling. The moment the man's head went down to trail through the leaves, all six snakes struck, rearing back to deliver a full load of venom before heeding Diego's command to leave the area fast.

The sniffer screamed and rolled over and over, trying to cover his face, his chest, both thighs and arms all at the same time. The other men in his unit rushed to him, tried to hold him down to determine what happened. One brought up his rifle, aiming in the direction of the fleeing snakes. The owl launched herself into the air, flying straight at the shooter, talons extended, her powerful wings carrying her swiftly from the branches above them straight to the attackers.

The man trying to spray the ground with bullets shrieked in fear and pain as the owl raked her talons over his face, ripping skin and one eye. The force of her blow sent him tumbling backward. She pulled up at the last moment, flying toward the forest and the safety of the trees.

Diego urged the snakes to a faster pace, getting them out of harm's way. All the while he continued to run up the mountain, using the faint game trails that cut through the trees and brush. He had put the snakes and owl in jeopardy in order to slow down the five men. He didn't want them anywhere near Leila. If anything went wrong, he was determined to take all of them with him.

The owl continued to send images to Diego. The sniffer had stopped screaming, but he writhed around on the ground, moans and groans coming from his throat. Two of his fellow soldiers knelt beside him, attempting to assess the wounds. The fifth soldier crouched beside the man with the torn face.

Diego slowed as he approached the group of men. He stopped just inside the tree line, his gaze moving over the scene. Each snake had done its job, injecting a full load of venom into the sniffer. The neurotoxin was already spreading fast through his body. No matter what his friends did to try to save him, it wasn't going to work.

While the two men worked on the sniffer, the third was doing his best to bandage the face of the soldier the great horned owl had attacked.

"Hold still, Duncan," the soldier hissed. He looked warily around. "We must be close to her nest. They'll defend their territory fiercely."

"I didn't have time to shoot her," Duncan groused, clutching his weapon. He rocked back and forth. "I'm going to lose my eye, Terry."

"Yeah," Terry replied. "Not going to lie to you."

"I don't understand why they want that bitch so badly," Duncan said. "What can Leila do that we can't? They've always coddled her. If we catch up with her, I'm killing her. The commander isn't going to know how she died."

"I think she killed the entire team," one of the two men attending to the sniffer put in. "They were good at their job, but she's on a different level, whether you want to believe it or not."

Duncan snorted. "How good can she be? She had the same

training we did, and she's a female. She has no business being a soldier."

Terry was silent as he continued to clean up the wound from the owl's talons. Duncan swore over and over. Finally, Terry sighed. "I agree with Gerald, Duncan. That woman may be small, but she's got skills none of us have. She wiped out Leon and his friends, and that was after they bashed her in the head. It's more than possible she killed the team bringing her up the mountain."

The second man treating the sniffer turned to look at Terry. "How? You heard what they said on the radio. She was probably going to die from her wounds." He sank back on his heels, turning his attention to the sniffer once more. "You're not going to make it, bud." He pulled out a small revolver, pressed it to the sniffer's temple and pulled the trigger.

The act should have been shocking to Diego, but he was half expecting it. He was somewhat surprised that they didn't do the same thing to Duncan. He was going to slow them down.

"We don't have time for this crap," the soldier who had pulled the trigger snapped. "The helicopter isn't going to wait for us." He stood up. "We've got to run that bitch down and end her fast. That's the only solution to this. She's responsible for how many dead?"

Gerald stood, backing away from the sniffer's body. "Damn, Pete, you could've warned me." He flashed a scowl at his fellow soldier. "And yeah, I agree with you all that the bitch has to die. We need to find her fast and get rid of her. I'm just going to point out that you'd better not underestimate her."

"I don't think she's all that," Duncan snarled. "Damn, this hurts."

"You tried to get with her once," Pete said. "I remember she turned you down flat."

Terry and Gerald helped Duncan to stand. He shoved them

away. "Yeah, the little bitch thinks she's so much better than everyone else. I say she isn't."

"Then where's Harold and his men? All they had to do was haul her ass up the mountain to the rendezvous site," Terry said. "She was wounded. We know that much." He gestured around him. "This was their last known location. She isn't here and neither are they. You want to explain that?"

"It wasn't her," Duncan muttered mutinously.

Terry indicated the sniffer's body. "He said there was a bloodbath here, but the trail ended. How? If there was a bloodbath and Harold and his men were still alive, they'd be making their way to us. They've disappeared. That should tell you something."

"So you believe one wounded woman killed them all and disposed of their bodies?" Duncan demanded. He sounded heated, angry and even confrontational.

Diego wasn't surprised by the aggression in the men. Each of them had been enhanced with predatory genetics in order to make them faster and stronger. He didn't understand how those running the laboratory, which had been in existence since the Vietnam War, continued to make the same mistakes Whitney was making. Whitney enhanced psychically, something these soldiers didn't appear to have had done to them, but the animal genetics alone were enough to raise their aggression levels off the charts.

Diego knew from his talks with Luther that those recruiting soldiers to the enhancement program were proud of the fact that they didn't conduct the kinds of experiments Whitney did, yet they had to see that a good number of their soldiers were spiraling out of control, just as Whitney's often did. Psychiatric tests were imperative. By now they had to know that, yet they continued to make the same mistakes.

He believed that the soldiers volunteered in good faith. They had no idea what those altered genetics were going to do to them.

He hadn't known, and the predatory aggression was difficult to keep under control. He was surrounded by men who had a strict code. Many of the soldiers from the lab Leila came from seemed to be sent out alone or put with others who, as they became more aggressive, egged one another on.

Diego had many enhancements—some he'd developed into razor-sharp weapons and others he was good at, just not expert. What he was particularly good at was his affinity with the local wildlife. He sent out a call to those nearby. A male fox, two bobcats, a raccoon family, as well as several skunks in the vicinity.

The Appalachian Mountains had a certain reputation. Not just a reputation—they were, quite frankly, eerie. Diego's call was haunting and seemed to reverberate through the trees. He sent it several times, with a long silence in between so the soldiers couldn't fail to notice the sudden lack of droning insects.

He looked toward the sky and sent out a call for the turkey vultures and red-tailed hawks. Then he sent another call for beetles and bottle flies to join the feast. His next haunting call was to all scavengers in the area. When the last notes ended, echoing through the deeper forest, fog began to drift out of the trees into the clearing. The fog was low to the ground and resembled fingers extending toward the four remaining soldiers.

The men looked at one another uneasily. "I hate this place," Duncan declared. "Let's get on with it. The sooner we find her and kill her, the quicker we go home and I get medical treatment."

"We aren't killing her," Terry stated. His voice was low but firm.

Duncan spun around. "No one put you in charge," he sneered. "Majority rules, and we all say she dies if she isn't already dead."

Diego studied the soldier named Terry. He didn't change expression when Duncan confronted him, nor did he back down. He did wait for the others to begin moving in the general direction of the small ravine the sniffer had most likely pointed them toward. Terry didn't pull his weapon or aim the automatic slung around his neck, but his hand brushed both guns as he began to trail behind the others.

"Turkey vultures," Gerald announced, indicating the sky a short distance away. "A lot of them."

Pete scowled up at the circling birds. More and more joined those in the sky. Some sank down below the trees where they couldn't see them. "If we're lucky, it'll be Leila and we can get the hell out of here."

"I told you," Duncan said, his voice triumphant, despite the bandages covering one entire side of his face. "She's dead. The boys are probably nursing a few wounds, and their coms aren't working."

Terry shook his head, clearly not believing the way the others did. He let a few more feet separate them. When Gerald glanced back at him, Terry crouched in the dirt and studied the ground as if looking for tracks. Gerald relaxed visibly. Not too bright, Diego decided. Terry was the one decent man with the others. Diego could read his resolve. If they found Leila, she wasn't the one who was going to die. At last, evidence that there were soldiers like Luther, who had a strong moral code.

Pete was the first one to get to the top of the ridge. He simply went in the direction of the vultures. The birds were everywhere, on branches of trees, on the rocks and circling in the sky. There were several already on the ground, tearing at carcasses strewn around a few feet below the ridge. A moving carpet of beetles covered the ground and whatever dead carrion lay there. Bottle flies were everywhere, their bluish-green bodies flashing in the streaks of sunlight.

The fog hadn't made it into the ravine, but it was slowly moving that way. A red-tailed hawk dropped from the trees, passing through tendrils of the ghostly grayish mist, moving relentlessly toward the gorge, landing on the ground beside the beetles. An opossum ambled through the grass and rocks to sniff at the very edge of one of the mounds covered in insects.

The wind shifted slightly, carrying the smell of rotting flesh to those on the ridge. Duncan swore and turned his face away from the sight.

"It's not Leila," Pete said unnecessarily. "I think we just found Harold's team."

"She couldn't have done this," Duncan insisted. "She's not good enough that she could have killed all of them. How could she be? Have you seen her?" There was bitter distaste in his voice.

Gerald moved closer to the edge to peer down at the bodies. "Every damn one of them," he announced. He crouched down, one hand rubbing his jaw as he studied the scene below. The wind tugged at his hair, and the fog swirled around him.

Diego let loose another eerie cry that sounded as if it came from deep within the forest, much like the wail of a banshee, a heralding of death. The wind and fog rushed toward the soldiers in a sudden surge. A bobcat emerged from the trees, snarling, staring at Pete, malevolence in his yellow eyes. The cat was difficult to see with its coloring and the gray of the thickening mist.

Pete tried to bring up the rifle that was hanging by a strap around his neck. As he did so, the great horned owl shot out of the fog, striking the soldier with blunt force, talons piercing his hand and neck. The rifle dropped from the nerveless hand and would have fallen to the ground if it hadn't been for the strap.

Amid a flutter of wings, the sky darkening for a moment, Duncan, Pete and Terry could barely make out the bobcat spinning around after it snarled, showing its teeth. It faded into the swirling fog and then was gone into the forest. The great horned owl did the same, its coloring allowing it to disappear as if it had never been.

The only evidence that the owl had been there was the blood dripping steadily from Pete's broken hand.

Once again, the forest went totally silent. After the rush of strange activity, the silence was almost deafening. At first, it was the lack of insects droning and the absence of the scuttering of lizards and mice through the leaves. Then they became aware of the number of vultures sitting in the branches of the trees. The gleaming black feathers stood out as black shapes, not just on the tree limbs but on several of the larger boulders lining the ridge. The turkey vultures, and there easily could have been thirty or more, stared at them with round, beady eyes. The combination of ominous silence and the strange behavior of the birds created a creepy, almost supernatural atmosphere.

"Wait," Terry whispered. "Where's Gerald?"

Immediately the three men stared at the spot where Gerald had been crouching, looking down into the narrow, somewhat shallow gorge.

"Where'd he go?" Pete asked, his voice no more than a whisper.

Terry took a step toward the edge of the ridge and then halted abruptly, his hand going to the M4 strapped around his neck. "There's blood on the ground."

The men gripped their rifles and formed a loose circle, going back-to-back as they surveyed their surroundings.

"Moving to the ridgeline," Terry announced, taking slow, careful steps toward the spot where Gerald had last been seen.

Diego's respect for Terry went up another notch. Terry was determined to look out for his fellow teammate. Duncan desperately wanted to lead the others, but he was clearly reluctant to go near the gorge. His gaze was fixed on the forest. The vultures and the last appearance of the owl had traumatized him. His hands trembled so much that his rifle was visibly shaking. Pete moved in sync with Terry, covering his back, but Duncan stayed where he was, his head swiveling from one side to the other.

Diego was patient. He didn't like leaving Leila for too long, but she was safe. He had not received any indication from his wildlife spies that others were hunting her. He also trusted her abilities. Leila had already proved herself in battle. She might be injured, and he wasn't discounting how badly she was hurt, but she would fight if she had to. He believed her safe where she was. That gave him time to manage the soldiers hunting her.

Terry, his finger on the trigger, crouched low to examine the ground. "There's fresh blood here. It looks as if he fell off the edge." He peered down, stiffened and then rose. "It's hard to see with this fog. It seems to be getting thicker, but I'm sure his body is down there."

"What?" Pete said, whirling around. "Is he alive?"

"I don't think so. He's lying on top of the mass of beetles. Those are bodies down there for sure. It's no wonder the vultures took flight with Gerald falling on top of them," Terry reasoned. He continued to study the motionless body, trying to see through the swirling gray of the fog. "He isn't moving."

"We need to get out of here," Duncan proclaimed urgently, still not changing his position. "Right now."

"We have to check," Terry said. "We have to ensure he's really dead and doesn't need our help."

"Screw that," Duncan shouted, suddenly turning his weapon toward Terry.

"Think about it, Duncan," Pete said. "We can't just go back and tell the commander we left his body here. He's going to send someone to check on this site. If Gerald is still alive, and we've just left him to die, we're all going to be court-martialed."

Duncan swore, his voice harsh as he uttered one foul curse after another. "If you're going to go down there, get to it. I've got to get to a medic." He backed farther away from the ridge, separating himself from the other two.

If he were Pete and Terry, Diego wouldn't trust that Duncan wouldn't attempt to kill them. Neither of the two soldiers seemed to consider that Duncan might be that close to losing all courage.

Terry set his pack on the ground and rummaged through it, coming up with rope, which he securely anchored. "I'll go down."

"Make it fast," Duncan muttered and took a few more steps to put distance between him and the others. Twice his finger stroked the trigger of his rifle, his narrowed gaze on Terry.

Diego didn't want to shoot him. He preferred to add to the legend of the mountains, but he wasn't going to allow the man to murder the one decent soldier on the team. Keeping his eye on Duncan, Diego began to circle around to get behind him. Pete was concerned with protecting Terry from falling as he rappelled down the side of the gorge. It wasn't particularly deep, but it was steep. Diego didn't want either of the two men paying attention to the retreating Duncan.

To ensure Duncan didn't decide to shoot his fellow soldiers, Diego gave an order to the bobcat. He didn't want to spook Duncan into firing but did want his concentration to be on the eyes shining at him through the swirling fog. Bobcats were nocturnal creatures, and as a rule their various vocalizations added to the eerie reputation of the Appalachian Mountains.

The cat wasn't happy with Diego summoning him from his den during daylight hours. He answered the call reluctantly, made his appearance and was already retreating when Diego sent out another call for aid. Diego's summons sounded like a male challenging the other male for territory, but the notes were slightly off. Just enough for the bobcat to know Diego's call.

Duncan froze when he heard the unnerving snarl. It was impossible for him to tell where the frightening sound was coming

CHRISTINE FEEHAN

from. That meant he couldn't pinpoint where the cat was. The soldier began to turn in circles, his anxiety climbing.

Pete glanced up, looking toward the forest, but then, seeing nothing, turned his attention back to Terry, although he continued to glance toward the forest every few moments. The fog swirled in the air, growing heavier. Rising higher. Shadowy and murky, the mist diminished the ability to see clearly.

Pete called out, "Watch our backs, Duncan."

Duncan ignored him, moving even farther from the forest and the ridge, trying to get to the only spot that was relatively clear. The ground was clear, even of rocks, a large oak tree with low-hanging branches providing the only cover. Duncan inspected the tree.

Diego nudged the cat to not only give the soldier a low warning hiss of displeasure but also show himself briefly from a distance, assuring the animal through images that he would be grateful and the cat could go back to its den. The bobcat provided the distraction Diego needed, emerging from the fog, eyes shining evilly, fixed on Duncan as if he were prey.

Duncan whimpered and lifted the rifle to aim toward the bobcat. It had already slunk back into the forest, the fog dropping that shadowy veil. Diego took the opportunity to climb the tree. The moment he was in the branches, he froze, exactly the way the great horned owl did, his body appearing to be part of the tree should Duncan look up again.

Duncan retreated, step-by-step, until his back was against the solid trunk, his wary gaze fixed on the spot where the bobcat had disappeared. So close to him, Diego could see how badly the soldier was shaking. He had been the most aggressive, yet he was the one truly falling apart. He had no business being amped up. Diego couldn't imagine what his psychiatric evaluation had been like, but those in charge of the laboratory should have known better.

Duncan had easily shot his friend in the head because he didn't

112

want to be bothered to wait for him to die. He didn't want to expend any time trying to make him comfortable while he was dying. Duncan's life was all about Duncan. As a rule, the teams were a brotherhood, but Duncan didn't fit into that unless he was the leader and he could have all the attention.

Diego watched him for a few moments as Duncan switched his attention back and forth between where the bobcat had disappeared and Pete. Each time he put his attention on Pete, he stroked the trigger of his rifle. Diego would have bet a month's pay that he was considering shooting Pete and cutting the rope that would allow Terry to make his way back up to the ridge.

Diego inverted, moving like a lethal, hunting leopard down the trunk of the tree in complete silence. He didn't so much as disturb a leaf. Fear had a smell to it, and Duncan stunk of it. He was continually squirming, twitching, and turning his head from side to side in quick, jerky movements.

Diego found a pattern in the way Duncan's neck twisted and turned, moved forward and then back. Using the strength of his legs to hold him, he waited for Duncan's head to come toward him. Striking quickly, he wrapped one arm around Duncan's neck and placed his other hand on the back of the head, tilting it forward to control him as he applied pressure to the neck. The force was great enough that it instantly cut off the blood supply to the brain. It took nearly ten seconds for Duncan to go limp.

Diego eased him down to the ground and covered his mouth and nose with his hand, cutting off the air supply. Duncan's body reacted to the lack of blood to the brain and now the lack of air. Diego was relentless, waiting patiently, keeping his body in the shadow of the tree. The fog thickened. Silence reigned. Even after he was certain the life was gone from the soldier, Diego waited a few more moments, checked him and then disappeared into the fog, retreating to the edge of the trees, where he could watch Pete.

Diego had a decision to make. He didn't kill innocents. Not that he thought Terry was all that innocent. More than likely, he was a man similar to Diego. Still, Terry seemed to have a code. He knew Duncan had planned to kill him. Pete most likely knew it as well. They had plotted to kill Leila. Terry was the only voice of objection. Did Diego kill him simply because he was part of the unit under orders to retrieve Leila? That didn't sit well with him.

Movement caught his eye, and Diego watched as Terry pulled himself over the ridge and sat for a moment, catching his breath.

"I take it Gerald is dead," Pete greeted, sounding resigned.

"They're all dead, and so is Gerald. Someone cut him all to hell with a blade. Thighs, armpits, throat. If it was Leila, she had to be extremely fast. Gerald was no slouch."

"You sure she cut him to pieces? He was right there in front of us. I had my eyes on him. At least I thought I did." Pete rubbed at the bristles on his jaw. "Snake bites, owl attacks, what the hell is going on?"

"I don't know if it was Leila," Terry admitted. "But whoever killed Gerald did it right under our noses." He sat up straighter and looked around. "Where's Duncan?"

"Bobcat scared the piss out of him," Pete said, a sneer in his voice. "He would have run like a rabbit if he wasn't afraid of being alone." He jerked his head in the direction of the tiny clearing. "He made sure he was safe. I don't think either one of us is safe from him though."

"He knows I'm not going to allow him to kill Leila." Terry made it a statement. Daring Pete to contradict him.

Diego could see Terry was ready for action. Concealed from Pete, Terry had wrapped his fist around his knife and gently, stealthily drew it from the leather scabbard on his belt.

Pete sighed. "I knew that was going to be a problem for you. Damn it, Terry. She's bad news. If she did this"—he indicated the dead men in the gorge—"we're in trouble. If they all died trying to get her back, how do you think two of us have a chance to bring her in? Think about it. If we get her in our sights from a distance, shooting her would be a mercy for all of us. I need to get back to the lab and get my injuries taken care of as quickly as possible."

Diego found it interesting how Pete could sound so reasonable. Maybe he believed what he was saying. He didn't make a move against Terry. It was possible Pete's enhanced instincts allowed him to realize the danger he was in. He also didn't believe Pete. Pete wanted Leila dead. Why? What was it that made these men want to kill her? Did she know something about them they wanted to keep hidden?

Terry nodded slowly and glanced toward the tiny clearing. The fog continued to swirl through the trees and across the rocks. "I think it would be a good idea for you and Duncan to get back as soon as possible to rendezvous with the helicopter to get you out of here. I'll see if I can pick up any tracks. If I can't, I'll double-time it to catch up with you."

Pete nodded and rose. "I think that's a good plan. I'll see what Duncan has to say. He wants out of here, so I can't imagine him objecting."

It was Pete's voice, so reasonable and cooperative, that told Diego he planned to murder Terry. Pete sauntered over to the clearing, his large frame disappearing and reappearing in the swirling mist. Diego moved with him, circling around, never taking his gaze from his target. He was four feet from him when Pete stopped abruptly, his entire body stiffening.

"What is it?" Terry asked, letting Diego know the soldier hadn't taken his eyes off his companion.

"I think he's dead, Terry."

"Dead?" Terry echoed.

Diego didn't blame Terry for thinking it was a setup.

"Yeah," Pete snarled. "Dead."

Terry remained silent, a good tactic, Diego thought. He wasn't a man to make quick decisions. He assessed a situation thoroughly before he made a move.

Pete took a couple of steps toward Duncan's body. Duncan looked small, crumpled on the ground. There was no doubt he was dead. Pete looked around, looked up into the tree and then crouched down to examine the body.

"I'm not sure what killed him," Pete announced, "but he's still holding his gun."

Diego watched as Pete bent over Duncan's body and removed a revolver from his boot. He checked it and then reached behind him to shove the weapon into the back of his belt. Before he could stand, Diego was on him, plunging a knife into the back of his neck, severing the spinal cord. Pete went down face-first as Diego slipped into the shadows.

"He's dead as well," Diego announced calmly. "He planned to murder you with Duncan's holdout gun."

There was silence. Terry didn't bother to duck down in an effort to save himself. Instead, he stood up, facing the sound of Diego's voice.

"Who are you?"

"Name is Diego Campos."

Terry was silent. It was clear he knew the name. Most soldiers did. Diego had a reputation with his rifle.

"Your men tried to rape Leila while she was severely wounded and couldn't defend herself. I left their bodies in the gorge for the vultures."

"They weren't my men."

"And these men, the ones you're traveling with, planned to kill her."

"I'm aware." Terry didn't defend himself or try to explain that he would have protected Leila if he could.

"They planned to murder you."

"I'm aware," Terry repeated.

"You tell your commanding officer if he persists, he's going to have a war with the GhostWalkers on his hands. Won't be difficult to find me if he wants to pursue this."

"They want Leila back. Is she alive?"

"You tell them to leave it alone."

"And it's over?"

"I'm not making any promises." Diego left it at that. He slipped back into the forest and waited until Terry made up his mind to start back up the trail. Only then did he do cleanup, depositing the bodies with the others in the gorge.

7

Leila had never met a man like Diego Campos. If someone had told her about him, she would have laughed at them. Called them a dreamer. A believer in fairy tales. She'd been around men since she was ten and she'd never come across a single man like Diego.

How he managed to get her to his cabin, she had no idea. In a way, his strength was frightening. He had a will of iron. Having known him now for several days, she felt he was undefeatable. She knew he made a relentless, merciless enemy, but he was the sweetest, gentlest man she'd ever known.

She looked around the cabin. It was surprisingly neat—and homey.

"I hope you're hungry," Diego said, breaking the silence.

Leila thought that over. It wasn't exactly silent. There was music outside the cabin, the wind blowing through the trees, the continual buzz and call of insects. She found that her ability to hear was even better than it had been—and she'd always had excellent hearing.

Night had fallen by the time they made it to the cabin. Diego had to be exhausted. He'd carried her the entire way, insisting on taking the smoothest trails so he wouldn't jar her. He seemed to know each time she felt like she couldn't take the pain anymore, and he'd call a halt, acting as if he were the one who needed the break.

When they reached the cabin, he'd allowed her to rest, and then he took her into the shower. He didn't seem in the least embarrassed to strip down to his boxers while he washed every trace of blood and dirt from her. He took his time with her hair, shampooing it twice and conditioning it. She should have found the experience mortifying, but instead, she enjoyed every second of his care. She'd never had anyone treat her the way he did.

He wrapped her in towels and sat her in an extremely comfortable rocker while he dried her hair with a towel and then braided it for her. He seemed to have energy in reserve because after he found her a clean shirt from his pack, he started chopping vegetables for dinner.

Were there really men like Diego in the world? She didn't think so, but he was living proof. Watching him work in the kitchen was actually mortifying when showering with him wasn't. She could hunt down a target and kill them, but she had no real idea of how to cook a single thing. Just learning to heat up bottles for Grace had been challenging. She had no interest in cooking—until now. She wanted to be able to make Diego something so she'd have it ready when he got home after a long day.

Leila felt the color rising under her skin. What was she thinking? That the three of them, Gracie, Diego and her, were going to be a family? That was ludicrous. She was beginning to believe in fairy tales, and it had to stop.

At that precise moment, as if he had radar or was locked into her, Diego half turned, looking straight at her. "What is it, sweetheart?"

He did that. He called her "sweetheart." "Honey." Once or twice, it had been "baby" in a soft, velvety tone that kept her from telling him she was no baby. She liked it when he called her those things. She especially liked when he called her "Warrior Woman."

She shot him a faint smile because how could she not? He was so beautiful to her, standing there in the kitchen with the single light shining on him. His hair gleamed from the quick shower he'd taken. He wore soft jeans that clung to his narrow hips and butt quite lovingly. It was the thin tee stretched over his chest and abs that caught her attention. He had more muscle than she'd realized, yet she should have known. He'd carried her all that way without breaking a sweat.

Placing the tongs he'd been using on the stove, Diego turned to face her fully. "Leila? Tell me what's distressing you."

She couldn't help herself. He melted something inside her that just seemed to open the floodgates. She was certain it was his voice. He put some kind of compulsion on her to blurt out the truth, no matter how humiliating it was.

"I was thinking, like an idiot, how nice it would be to have Gracie with us. The three of us." She choked out the last admission.

He went to her immediately, crossing the short distance in the silent way he had. He gave the impression of a great jungle cat stalking prey, yet she felt comforted by his presence. She already had such faith in him that she wasn't in the least intimidated.

Diego bent to brush a kiss on the top of her head. Her heart slammed hard against her chest. Her mouth went dry. She rubbed her palms on her thighs, wondering how he could possibly look at her the way he was—so intensely. So focused. As if she were the only woman in the world. He seemed to do that a lot.

"Why like an idiot?" he asked, his voice low and mesmerizing. "The idea sounds perfect to me. This is a nice place to visit, but I want to take the two of you to my place in Louisiana. The house is empty right now. Lonely. I couldn't stand to be there, but you and Grace would make all the difference in the world. You'd turn that empty house into a home just by sharing it with me."

That sounded very much like he would want them to stay. Visit? Stay? Would she want that? Could she do it? "I don't know the first thing about making anything into a home."

"You did for Grace," he said.

"You don't know that." Just the fact that Diego believed he wanted her to make a home for him and said it with so much conviction warmed her.

"I do know it." He turned back to the stove.

That conviction in his voice got to her. Turned her to mush inside. "Are you real?" she had to ask, because if she ever allowed herself to believe and he wasn't—he would shatter her. She hadn't realized she could be so vulnerable or that she had the capability of falling for a man so fast. It was out of character.

"Unfortunately for you, sweetheart, I'm all too real. And I've made up my mind you're the one."

His tone was so mild, so matter-of-fact, that at first his declaration didn't sink in. When it did, the blossoming joy she felt was shocking. Too shocking. Why would a man like Diego look at someone like her? Especially now, when she had to rely on him for everything. The only reasonable explanation she could think of was that he had white knight syndrome. She wasn't a woman who needed to be rescued. Was she?

Leila wanted to leap up and pace. Go running. Do something physical to stimulate her brain. She had to figure things out before she allowed herself to get swallowed in the fairy tale. Maybe she could have the fairy tale for a few more days if she didn't push too hard and demand answers. Would that be so bad? She couldn't go anywhere. She couldn't get to her daughter. Why couldn't she have this fantasy just a little longer? But she knew better. If she stayed with him any longer, with his sweetness and the idea in her head that she had a chance, her heart would shatter when it all fell apart.

"Diego, you know I'm very independent. Once I'm back on my feet, you won't have to take care of me."

"I like taking care of you, but I'll like you being my partner even more. I'm not the kind of man who wants or needs a woman who can't defend our children. I need someone strong. Had a shit childhood, babe. Not going to have that for my children." He reached up into the cabinet and pulled out two plates.

There it was again, that low, velvety voice that seemed to brush along her skin, creating the most amazing reaction in her body. Just his voice alone was enough to give her fantasies. But she wanted the real thing, not a fantasy.

She watched him serve the mixture of vegetables and protein noodles onto the two plates while she considered the last possibility of why he was so interested in her.

"Do you think, and I don't know how it could have been done, that Whitney paired us together and we're reacting to that? Marcy told me about a rumored program he had to get children from those he's genetically altered."

"You were never around Whitney." He placed one of the plates on a small, hand-carved tray. "How could he pair us?"

"I don't know, but he had my sister."

He flashed another heart-stopping grin at her. "Then I'd be paired with your sister. I can assure you, while it might appeal to some men to be attracted to sisters, it holds no attraction for me in the least. In fact, it sounds like a recipe for disaster. And smacks of disloyalty."

She liked that he'd tacked that on, the part about being disloyal if he was attracted to her sister.

Diego handed her the tray and placed his dinner on the small table beside the chair that was opposite the rocker. "Do you want something to drink?"

"Just water."

"The spring water here is extraordinary." He brought her a glass filled with clear liquid before seating himself opposite her. "I thought we'd rest tonight and tomorrow start on your PT. We need to get serious about it."

"PT?" She carefully put a forkful of vegetables and noodles in her mouth and was a little shocked at the burst of flavors. He hadn't just chopped up the vegetables and heated them; he'd actually used spices to make them taste good.

"I allowed one of the men who came after you to live. The others were very much like the five who were rushing you up the mountains, but he was a decent man. I gave him a message to take back with him. They'll know you're alive, and it will depend on how seriously they take me whether they send a little army against us. Just in case, it will be best for you to be in good shape. They won't expect it."

"They know I have to go back," Leila reminded him. "They know I'll never give up my daughter."

"No matter what, we'll get Grace back. You don't have to sell your soul to have your own daughter given back to you. I made it very clear that I'm a GhostWalker and that the carnage belongs to me, not you. I also made it clear why those soldiers weren't going home. Terry recognized my name. He knows who I am, and I have no doubt his commanding officer will know my reputation as well."

"They lost a lot of their soldiers. They aren't going to be happy about it," she pointed out.

"They sent them against you, and they know how good you are in the field—they trained you. And they certainly know Luther's abilities and his experiences."

"But they didn't know about you," she pointed out.

He shrugged, sending her a quick, almost mischievous smile. That little grin lit up his eyes and softened the unrelenting, harsh beauty of his face. Her heart reacted in the now-familiar way it had, a curious wild thumping and then a weird melting sensation. He was potent—at least to her. She had been afraid of those physical reactions to him, but now they just seemed normal to her. She was fairly sure that in fifty years she would have those same reactions when he walked into a room.

"They do now. They also are aware the GhostWalker teams stick together. They go to war with you, me, and Luther, they'll be declaring war on the GhostWalkers. Those running that laboratory know the advantages we have."

"You're in the military. You can't just declare war on other branches."

His eyebrow shot up. "Are you in the military? Do you get a paycheck? Did you sign papers joining a branch of the service?"

She frowned. She'd never considered what he was pointing out. "My life has been the training my commanders gave me since I was ten years old. I lived in a small housing dorm by myself until I had Grace, but I never needed for anything. I honestly didn't need a lot and rarely asked for things. I have a board specifically for making a list of anything I need. I've always been provided with everything I needed as soon as it went on the list."

That little smile turned from his melting one to one of pure predator. "You aren't technically in the military and have free will to go anywhere you wish. The moment a GhostWalker claimed you as a partner, that put you in our sphere of protection, by all the teams."

His statement should have bolstered her spirits, but her heart crumbled. A GhostWalker claiming her could make her safe. Make Gracie safe. But that was, once again, white knight syndrome. She stared down at the food on her plate, refusing to react too fast to his statement.

"There you go again, Warrior Woman, thinking I have some redeeming qualities, which I don't. Stop thinking it, and you won't be so disappointed when you realize I'm not claiming you for you but for my own selfish reasons."

Leila couldn't help looking up at the amusement in his tone. There was that look again, the little grin that softened the crueler lines in his face. Once again, her heart accelerated, drumming out of control.

"Selfish reasons? Because you're getting such a great bargain with me. I come with a baby and zero skills as a cook."

"Very selfish reasons, woman."

"You don't make any sense."

His eyes met hers. Intense. Focused. She felt she could drown there if she wasn't careful. There was no looking away. No pretending she couldn't see the hunger there. She found herself blushing, the treacherous color sliding under her skin and creeping into her face.

"I make perfect sense. I'm looking at what I want. I am not looking for a cook. I'm looking for a partner. My life growing up was shit, Leila. My mother didn't want me and beat the hell out of me as often as possible with switches and whatever else she could find. She reminded me daily I wasn't worth anything but guarding my brother and hunting for food for the family. She didn't protect us, not even my sisters. I want a woman who will stand in front of my children. Who would fight at my side if necessary. Who would be willing to sacrifice everything for her family. I don't need a cook. I need you. You're that woman."

She had to blink back tears. No one had ever stated anything so amazing to her with the absolute conviction Diego did. He believed what he was saying. She despised that his own mother had told him he wasn't worth anything. She knew better. He was the best man she knew.

"You're making me emotional, and I'm not even pregnant."

His smile was back. "Were you emotional when you were pregnant?"

"It was mortifying. I once started crying because I couldn't find this silly bracelet Marcy had given me. I'd had it since I was sixteen. I mean, a bracelet? I don't wear jewelry, but when I misplaced the bracelet, I was devastated and just sobbed."

Instead of laughing at her as she expected, Diego frowned. "Did you find it?"

Leila nodded. "It was right there on my dresser, but I had accidentally pushed it toward the wall so it had nearly fallen off the back. Fortunately, one of the beads was larger than the others and it caught between the dresser and the wall, and I spotted it when I calmed down. It just felt ridiculous and out of proportion to fall apart over something so inconsequential."

"Your bracelet isn't inconsequential, sweetheart. How many times in your life have you been given a gift? That gift means something to you, and it should. When you pack up your things, make certain you bring that with you."

"You make it sound so easy, Diego. I doubt that my commanding officer is going to just let me go after all the work they put into my training."

"You aren't a member of the military. They may have trained you, but they failed to make you part of the military. Had you been captured on one of your missions, they would have denied you were any part of them."

"Naturally they told all of us that. Wouldn't the military do the same thing with the GhostWalkers?"

"They do when we're going on certain missions, but we have the backup of the other GhostWalker teams. We have certain advantages, and those advantages are growing. You'll be one of our advantages."

Diego stated the last with so much certainty she couldn't help the wave of exhilaration that raced through her. He just gave her so many compliments, although he didn't act in the least as if he had. He acted as if everything he said about her was a fact. Was it? If she could see herself through his eyes, maybe she would begin to have self-worth. She wanted to have a good image of herself in order to give Grace feelings of self-esteem. She wanted her daughter to be confident in every aspect of her life, not just as someone who knew how to hunt and kill.

"Nice to think I'll be an advantage. I hope you feel that way if you take me home and find out I'm not all that good with household things."

"Such as?"

"I'm organized, so I'm fairly neat. But I looked around and you're a neat freak. I might drive you crazy if I don't put everything in its place. I forget to add half the things I need to my list most of the time. Sometimes I can't stand to have the windows and doors closed. I feel like I can't breathe. That could make you crazy."

He burst out laughing. The sound was rich and had that underlying velvet tone that caught her every time.

"That's it? That's what you're worried about? I have a list of things longer than your arm that are going to drive you crazy. Hopefully, I can find ways to make my shortcomings up to you. I'm good with paperwork. Rubin despises paperwork, so I got very good at it. Lists are a specialty. You want all the doors and windows open; we'll make sure we have good screens. The swamp can be very humid, and insects seem to like to invade our homes there. I happen to like space, so it won't bother me to have the house as open as possible."

"Doesn't it bother you that you have an answer for everything?"

She set her plate down on the little table and picked up the water glass. It wasn't her smartest move because her hand trembled. She wanted to put it down to weakness, but she wasn't certain that was the reason. He was freaking her out just a little bit with his absolute certainty.

"No, does it bother you?"

"I don't know. I think you should have more concerns. You don't know me that well." That was honesty, not having low self-esteem. At least she thought it was a legitimate reaction. "No one can predict if a partnership will work out or not."

His eyebrow shot up, and that slow grin of his took her breath. "I learned from a very young age to be decisive. I'm fortunate in that I have a mind that works very fast and processes information at a rapid speed. You do as well, although you tend to take your time to think something through. I have a little experience on you, but that doesn't mean you aren't going to catch up with me rapidly, because you are. You just have to learn to trust yourself."

"Are you ever wrong?"

"Rarely, but it happens. No one is right one hundred percent of the time, and I'm well aware of it. The mistakes I've made have been monumental when I've made them. Hopefully, I never repeat them. I also am an excellent listener. I've had to be in order to better protect Rubin and the others in my unit. If I make mistakes with you, I'll want immediate communication so I can modify my behavior. I haven't really lived with anyone for a long while. I eat with Nonny often, but I try to fade into the background if possible. I don't interact as much with the others as I appear to. That means I'm bound to make mistakes in our relationship, but I can promise you I'll only make them once."

She didn't quite understand how asking him if he was ever wrong had led to him making assurances to her. She was doing her best to caution him about her shortcomings, but he kept turning the subject around to assure her.

"Diego, I have no doubt that you believe we can be good together if we both make that commitment and want it enough to work at it." How could she explain to him how confused she was feeling without pushing him away? She wanted to be with him, but it was disconcerting to her when she'd never had those kinds of affirmations in her life. How could she believe in him? She had Grace to think about. She knew no other way of life than the one she had.

She didn't like her life. The only bright spot in it was her daughter and Marcy Chariot, the commander's wife. Leila wanted to be with Diego, but she barely knew him. Her instincts had always been good, and the chemistry between them was explosive. She liked him. *But.* Wasn't there always a "but"?

He stood with his easy grace and took the plate she'd put on the table along with his and carried them to the sink. She caught a glimpse of his face, and he was back to that expressionless mask she knew he showed the world. Her heart sank. She'd most likely sabotaged the best thing that could have ever happened to her.

She wasn't a coward. She never had been. For the first time in her life, she wanted something solely for herself. She wanted Diego. She just wasn't certain how to go about it.

"You know, Leila, you're right. I shouldn't push you so hard. There are a lot of things to consider, especially since you're a mother." He glanced at her over his shoulder, his dark hair falling across his forehead.

"Diego, I don't feel pressured by you." He could make her heart stop with that one look. "I really don't. You're saying all the things I want to hear."

"You don't really see me, Leila. The truth is, no one sees me.

That's on me. I'm good at deception. I thought with you I could be different. I want to be seen by my partner. I doubt if anyone else will ever know me. I wanted that with you, but pushing you when you're not ready isn't a good idea." He gave her another faint grin that didn't reach his eyes. "I suppose that could be considered a form of bullying."

"I didn't feel bullied. Believe me, I'd tell you if I did. I felt as if someone—you—cared for me for the first time in my life. I feel that way every time you talk to me or do anything for me. It isn't because you saved my life; it's because I do see you."

"Maybe you only think you do."

She had to find a way to get him to be open with her again. He had closed himself off. He still had that low, gentle tone with her, but he wasn't using the voice—the one she instinctively knew he had reserved only for her.

"You mentioned your mother a couple of times. What was your father like?" She truly hoped he'd been a good man who loved his wife and children.

Diego leaned one hip against the sink, half turned to face her. Again, that dim light seemed to wash over him, putting shine in his hair and casting his face in a shadow. His eyes held a peculiar glow to them, almost as if he were a wolf or a large cat of some kind. Hunter's eyes. Eyes that could see in the dark. Eyes that could look inside you and expose your soul.

"My father was a very stern man. He and my mother were extremely religious, and just about everything was a sin. Telling my sisters stories of fairies and fantasy was a sin. Missing a deer with a single bullet was a sin. Pretty much everything was." He went silent.

Leila's heart sank. She had hoped for a good memory of his father. He had to get his code somewhere. It hadn't been from his mother.

"On the other hand, there was a lot more laughter in the house with my father around. He cushioned my mother all the time, although he was insistent on having children. He believed it was her fault that she had so many girls when they needed sons. Rubin tried to tell him he was responsible, but my father didn't take kindly to a very young child telling him anything about the reproductive system. He could never quite accept the fact that Rubin was brilliant. My mother, as sick as she was, recognized it."

Leila wondered why neither of his parents saw the genius in Diego. It was there for anyone with half a brain to see.

"My father may have been exacting, but he taught us how to survive. To fish, hunt, track, to live off the land. If we hadn't had him, Rubin and I wouldn't have made it."

She saw through the little he told her about his life. He'd lived under harsh conditions and simply accepted it. His childhood was where he'd learned that calm acceptance.

"Tell me something no one knows. Not even your brother."

He dried off the plates and returned them to the cupboard. "I've done a lot of things, sweetheart. Most of them aren't things to discuss with someone you're courting." He sent her another enigmatic smile. "Perhaps a year or two after we give Grace a brother or sister."

Leila allowed her gaze to drift over him. She couldn't help feeling a little possessive. And she liked the idea that he wanted more children. He seemed to accept Grace as much as he accepted her.

"Have you been around a lot of children?"

"A couple of the GhostWalkers in my unit have families. Wyatt and Pepper Fontenot have five little girls." His mischievous grin came back, this time lighting his eyes. "They have triplets and twins. Those little girls, the triplets, when they first came, were really intelligent, but just tiny toddlers. They're very venomous, and when they were teething, it was quite a circus. We had a few nicknames for them, 'the Little Vipers' being the most prevalent. That didn't go over well with Pepper." He laughed at the memory.

Leila loved that he'd shed that hard edge he usually wore. She didn't want him to have it around her.

"Then there's Trap and Cayenne Dawkins. They have twins, a boy and a girl. Trap is on the spectrum and so off-the-charts smart it's scary. Cayenne is as lethal as hell but is totally devoted to Trap. I have no idea how they work, but they do. You rarely see one without the other. Trap has even managed to be a good father. I suspect Wyatt works with him. The two of them have always been tight."

"Do they live close to you?"

He nodded. "Wyatt's grandmother has lived out there in the swamp for years. She welcomed every single one of us. Until I met her, the only other woman who had an impact on me was Lotty, Luther's wife. She was very much like Nonny, a woman who was a full partner with her man and very devoted to her family."

"I'm glad he had that," she murmured. She knew he heard the note of exhaustion in her voice because he immediately lifted her, cradling her close to take her to the bathroom.

"Let's get you in bed and we can continue the conversation. It's been a long day, and I think we both could use some sleep."

For some reason she liked that he admitted he was tired as well. She didn't feel quite so much of a burden. He had a spare toothbrush, which was especially nice, and once she was under the covers, she felt quite comfortable. He hadn't put her in the loft, instead choosing the room she knew he most likely used. Rather than leaving her alone, he tossed a sleeping bag on the floor and stretched out after extinguishing all the lights.

Out of the darkness, Diego's low, velvety voice brushed over her. "You really want to know something about me no one else knows?"

"Only if you're okay with telling me." She wrapped her arms around herself, holding her breath, hoping he would share a part of his life with her he'd never entrusted to anyone else—not even his brother.

"After my father died, my two older brothers, Caleb and Abel, left in search of work in order to provide for the family. When they didn't come back and things got tight, our mother insisted I go hunting for food. It was a particularly hard winter, and the snow just kept coming down. We were pretty damn young to go out in a blizzard, but I guess she was desperate. Rubin didn't say a word, he just caught up a rifle and stalked out. I followed him. I'm not sure either of us believed we'd be back. You couldn't see your hand in front of your face, and it was cold. Have you ever been so cold you honestly thought you'd freeze to death and someone would come months or years later and find your body perfectly intact because the cold preserved you?"

Leila could tell he was really asking. He wanted to know about her past as much as she wanted to know about his. "I was ordered to slip into Siberia during one of the worst cold spells they had. The information was that Akim Sokolov, a known arms dealer, was hiding out there. I was to eliminate him and get out of the country without being seen. Akim Sokolov was reputed to be best friends with Artem Kozlov, a known member of the Russian KGB. That explained why he was being protected, why he was allowed to hide from all the law enforcement hunting for him."

"You went in alone? No backup?"

Was there a thread of anger in his usually calm voice? She had a strange reaction to that note, her body suddenly completely aware of him. She was grateful for the darkness.

"Yes, that is how I work best. I have never been so cold before or since. It felt like my blood had turned to ice. It took time to locate Akim and then plan out what my course of action would be.

I would have preferred to do so in the warmth of a house, but I needed to do reconnaissance on Akim's residence if I was going to be successful."

"My little warrior woman. Unsurprisingly, you persevered no matter the circumstances."

She laughed softly, sharing that moment with him. The darkness made it so much easier to be natural with him. "I wasn't going back with a failed assignment hanging over my head. The men barely respected me, and falling down one time would have put me in a much more dangerous position."

There was a small silence. "Dangerous?" he echoed.

She shouldn't have used that word. It was the truth, but she should have known he would take exception to her being in any kind of danger from her fellow soldiers.

"I was able to get to my target and eliminate him," she assured. "And I made it out of the country with no one the wiser. What happened with you and your brother in the blizzard?" She blatantly changed the subject, although she genuinely wanted to know.

"Rubin and I were able to get meat for the household, but during the hunt, we discussed why our older brothers hadn't returned. The plan had been for them to get work in the nearest town and bring home supplies to the family. They'd been gone nearly two months. We both knew they would never have stayed away if they could help it. Rubin thought they were dead. I was sure our mother thought so as well."

"But you didn't?"

"I did, but I wanted to know for certain. I needed to know. At night I'd lay in bed and think about it. It seemed so wrong to me that we just assumed they were dead, and we left them as if they didn't matter. As if because they hadn't contributed the way she wanted, our mother thought it was no big deal to write them off."

Her heart went out to that little boy who struggled with the knowledge that his mother thought they were expendable. That *he* was expendable. She wanted to put her arms around him and hold him close.

"The longer I lost sleep over it, the more important it became to me to find out where they were and what happened to them."

He turned his head toward her. She imagined that little boy determined to find out what happened to his brothers in order to put things right. In the dark, his eyes appeared much like that of a large cat. Those eyes, glowing the way they were, sent chills skittering down her spine despite her heart going out to the child he had been.

Diego fell silent again, and she needed the sound of his voice to keep her grounded. "Tell me what happened." She whispered the plea because the night seemed to be taking on a sinister feel.

"I didn't want Rubin to know what I was doing, so I waited until he was doing his early morning chores and I snuck away. The snow was coming down heavy, and I knew it would fill in my tracks. I had an idea of the route Abel and Caleb would have taken toward town. I knew it would be impossible to actually track them after two months and a couple of blizzards, but I'd reached a point that I didn't always need physical tracks in order to follow someone."

Once again, his eyes found her in the inky dark, sending that same chill down her spine. It wasn't a threat, but his statement felt like one. She had a strange talent for finding her targets, one she couldn't explain, but she instinctively knew this man would be far superior at tracking. Once set on a course, he wouldn't stop until he succeeded. That was both good and bad for her, especially since he appeared to want her.

"Did you find them? Find out what happened to them?"

He turned away from her. "Yeah. I did. They were traveling the way I figured they would go when they suddenly veered off course and started up toward the old mine. After two months, there were no tracks and the snow was very deep, covering the ground so I couldn't tell what had caused them to leave the main track and head up toward the mine."

"Someone chasing them?"

"I think it was a something. And I think one of my brothers was injured. I believe they went to the mine for shelter."

Leila thought about what it would be like for the two young teens to hike through the forest, knowing their father had just died and they had to support their family. "What do you think happened to them, Diego?" She couldn't help the compassion in her voice. She felt terrible for those two boys. And worse for Diego. He had been so young.

"Sweetheart." His voice came out of the night, stroking over her skin like the touch of fingers. "I didn't tell you this to upset you. I wanted to share something with you I've never talked about to anyone, but I should have chosen some other experience, not that I had many in my childhood better than this one. And most of the time, Rubin was with me."

She understood what he was saying. Rubin knew most of the things that had happened to Diego as a child. "I want you to tell me. I asked you, remember? I do feel terrible for your brothers and for you, at least the child that was you. When Marcy first told me she had overheard her husband and some others talking about Whitney and what he'd done to my sister, I knew I had to find Bridget and get her away from that madman. You had two brothers you were looking for and you already knew they were dead. At least when I set off looking for Bridget, I knew she was alive. Please tell me the rest of what happened."

"There isn't too much more to tell. I found their skeletons just outside of the mine. Caleb clearly had injuries to his leg. It appeared as if he'd encountered a bear. At least I thought it was a bear. The break was severe, with obvious trauma to the bone. There were more signs on both of them of an attack by a large predator. It would be unusual for any bear to attack so viciously unless they had disturbed it in some way. It had clearly followed them."

She rubbed at her thighs. Her muscles didn't like her lying around in bed so much. "I've not heard about bears attacking people."

"As I said, it would have been highly unusual. The bear could have been injured. For all I know they could have shot it, thinking to bring back the meat for the family."

For the first time, Diego's voice wasn't so matter-of-fact. His tone gave away the fact that he felt a deep sorrow. She was very tuned to him and definitely reactive to him. Those notes in his voice sent the need whispering through her to hold him close. To comfort him. She doubted if Diego had experienced very much comfort in his life. That made it all the more important to her to be the one to give him the things he needed.

"In any case, I found their remains and buried them deep. I didn't feel my mother deserved to know what happened to them. That was wrong of me, but at the time I was still holding on to anger with the way she treated all of us. I knew if I told Rubin, he would tell her. He always did the right thing, no matter what his feelings were. I honestly wanted to be more like him and not Satan's apprentice, as my mother called me, but I had too many anger issues to always do the right thing. I didn't even want to. On my way home, I came across a doe who had broken her leg. I was able to bring that meat home to the family. I was still punished for leaving without permission, but I escaped the worst of her wrath. And it helped to conceal from Rubin what I'd really been doing."

"You feel guilty."

There was a small silence. "Perhaps a little. I laid them to rest and marked the grave site carefully so I would know any time of year exactly where their remains were. I wanted to be able to go get them and bring them home. I don't know why I never did. I think it was because I didn't want to admit to my brother what I'd done."

"Diego, I hate to admit this to you, but I probably would have done the same thing. I didn't experience the things you did, and I find myself angry with your mother. I wouldn't have wanted her to know I'd found my brothers and laid them to rest."

"I should have told Rubin. I didn't even leave him the information when I had all my affairs in order."

"You had your affairs in order? For what reason?" She didn't like the sound of that.

"I'm a soldier, Leila," he said, his voice gentle. "I always keep my affairs in order. But if I'm being honest, and because I want a real relationship with you, the truth is, I suffer from depression. It's a mental health issue I've been unable to overcome. It doesn't hit that often, but when it does, it drags me under deep and fast. I've always struggled to get back my equilibrium. It doesn't ever happen when I'm working, but once I'm on downtime, I can fall into a dark hole. Unfortunately, that's something you'll have to take into account when you're making up your mind whether you want to take a chance on me."

"Do you go to counseling?"

"Nope."

"Do you take meds for it?"

"Nope."

"Diego, you're a doctor. You know better."

"Yeah," he admitted, "I do."

8

Diego was a taskmaster. A dictator. A relentless, merciless tyrant. Yep, that was the only word that really described him—"tyrant." He transitioned overnight from a sweet, gentle caretaker to a ruthless, demanding sadist.

Leila glared at him. "Do you have a personality disorder?"

He raised an eyebrow but continued massaging her legs. It wasn't the easy, light massage she was certain she needed—at least she knew she preferred. No, he was doing deep tissue, working every muscle thoroughly. She could have sworn he smiled briefly, but if he did, it was faint and gone in less than a second, so she couldn't be certain. Had she been, she might have kicked him hard.

"Personality disorder?"

"Don't pretend you have no idea what I'm talking about. You went from sweet caretaker to sadistic masseuse. And you did it overnight."

"I'm keeping you from getting blood clots."

Definitely a trace of humor in his voice. She made a face at him. "I think you're being unnecessarily enthusiastic about it."

The deep tissue massage hurt, but it also felt good. He had indicated, at breakfast, that he wanted her up and walking, that they would go outside, where he had set up a target range. She was excited that she would be doing *something*. Anything. She wanted to be back in shape and on the move as fast as possible. She particularly liked that he included training in her recovery program. That showed he meant what he said when he indicated he wanted a partner. He "got" her. She was a fighter, and she would fight at his side, not hide away in a safe room if they were attacked. She had skills, and she wanted to continue to use those skills.

Leila had a love of her country. She even had great respect and sympathy for her fellow soldiers. Despite many of the soldiers she'd encountered in the program being overly aggressive, there were also some who were good men. Each of the soldiers had volunteered for the enhancement program with the idea that they could better serve their country. The soldiers couldn't possibly have predicted the unfortunate results. They had no way of knowing the enhancements would bring out just as many negative traits as positive ones. She believed her training and physical enhancements enabled her to keep other soldiers safe.

"Don't like you thinking about men."

She scowled at him, lifting her head from the mattress to pin him with her narrowed eyes. He should have withered, but he only lifted an eyebrow.

Diego moved from massaging her legs and thighs to her hips. She should have known lying in bed so much would compromise her hips. There were so many sore spots, some far more intense than others. She decided not to voice her opinion of his masseuse abilities. She was half joking and half serious. She didn't want him to think she whined during training.

"Babe, you don't have a poker face."

"I don't know how you can read what I'm thinking from an expression on my face," she grumbled. "I can't decide if you're the best masseuse in the world and what you're doing feels amazing or if it just hurts like hell."

That earned her one of his brief faint smiles. She'd do just about anything to get his smile.

"And what's with the comment about other men? I don't believe for one minute you're the jealous type. You're too laid-back for that." But he wasn't. He was intense beneath that calm façade, and she knew it. She saw into him, into places no one else did. He kept those traits hidden from the rest of the world. She shouldn't like knowing things about him that others didn't, but she secretly reveled in her knowledge.

"Not going to discuss this with you until I've put a ring on your finger and you and Grace are living with me." He sounded gruff.

His hands were magic. He might be targeting every sore muscle she had, but he was definitely easing the painful knots.

"Don't look at me like that, Leila. You see inside me, whether you want to admit it or not. I'm no hero. I never will be. I have something dark and ugly in me, and you're very aware of it."

"You aren't nearly as bad as you think you are." But she knew he was capable of terrible things. Horrific things. Whatever genetic material had been used to enhance him, she knew it wasn't brawn so much as cunning predator. A thinking predator. The way his mind worked, he was always hunting prey.

"Don't kid yourself, Leila. You have to know what you're getting. Who you're getting. I would protect you and Grace with my life. But I don't show mercy to my enemies. I hunt them down and make certain they can't come at us again."

"You aren't making a very good case for yourself."

"Turn over. Let's get this done so you can go outside."

His hands on her body, helping her roll over, were so gentle she melted inside. He might think he was a monster, but he was unfailingly gentle with her.

"I want you more than I've ever wanted anything in my life. The truth is I've never wanted anything for myself. I never thought about having a wife and children. I figured I'd make certain Rubin was taken care of and happy, and then I'd end it. Rid the world of the darkness in me."

His fingers found the knots in her neck and began to work them out. She forced herself to relax, to breathe through the pain.

"Diego." She whispered his name on an exhale. On a protest.

"The minute I saw you, Leila, I knew you were the one. Every single thing about you appeals to me. I know I'm asking a lot. I know what you'll have to live with. But I also know I would move heaven and earth to make you happy."

"By your own admission, women chase after you."

"But I don't chase women. I would never disrespect you."

He worked his way down her right arm, and it felt a little like heaven—or hell. She wondered if she decided to stay with him, if that would be her life—a mixture of heaven and hell. She was grateful she was on her stomach with her face turned away from him. He seemed to be able to read her every expression, and she wanted to be conflicted. She told herself she was. She had Grace to think about. But if she was honest with herself, she'd already made up her mind. As much as Diego seemed to want her, she wanted him.

"Having said that, Leila, I won't tolerate that kind of disrespect from you. There won't be any cheating. Not physically or emotionally. I'm not meeting your needs, you say so. You communicate that to me immediately. If I piss you off, don't sit on it for days, letting the wound fester—tell me so I can make it right."

"We're going to have disagreements," she pointed out.

"I don't want a yes woman. I want my warrior woman. I respect your opinions. I have no idea how to have a decent relationship or how to parent. I do know we don't need to hit our children or raise our voices to them."

She couldn't help turning her head to look at him. Her eyes met his. There was pain there. She'd known there would be. If his mother were still alive, Leila might consider doing her in. "I like that. I don't know how that will work when they're teenagers, but I'm okay with no hitting or yelling."

"There will be consequences," he said. He bent his head and brushed a kiss across her cheekbone. "I believe in consequences."

She did as well, but she had the feeling she'd be tempering his disciplines when it came to consequences for their children. Diego wasn't a man to let things slide. She let her lashes drift down as his hands moved across her back, finding every painful place.

"When you're looking inside me—which is very cool, by the way—can you tell if I'm healing the way I'm supposed to?" She wanted to change the subject. The intensity of their conversation was draining. If she wanted to have energy to go outside and shoot at targets, she needed to relax.

"I sped up the healing process as best I could. I also gave you my blood twice. The first time, it was to save your life, so I didn't feel I had much choice. I knew my blood would enhance your gifts, but your eyesight and hearing were already good. The second time, I felt giving you blood would help speed the healing process. You needed it, but it was marginal whether you could do without it or not. I chose to give you the blood."

She realized that someone else might consider him ruthless and arbitrary, making decisions for her when those decisions affected her hearing and eyesight. She liked that he was decisive. When she was alone on an assignment, she had to make life-or-death decisions, and there was no room for hesitation.

"Am I close to being healed yet?" she asked hopefully.

"Babe, I removed your spleen. You have other damage. The repairs are coming along nicely and are much further along than they would be if you'd had regular surgery. That doesn't mean you can leap up and go running around playing soldier."

"Is that what you do? Run around playing soldier?" There was no way to keep the amusement out of her voice. The way he put things was hilarious to her.

"I don't play soldier. I wish I did. I hunt using the skills of every predatory animal Whitney put in me. Soldiers have little chance against me."

She opened her eyes again and studied his face as he focused on her hips and buttocks. The lines in his face were carved deeper than one would think on first glance. He was an extremely handsome man, but not in the accepted sense of the word. There was a brutal, almost cruel, handsomeness to him. If she had any talent for drawing, she would want to draw his face over and over. It would take a million years to get it right.

"Do you know what kinds of animals he put in you?"

"Raptor and reptile, as well as wolf; leopard; two different kinds of tigers, Siberian and Bengal; as well as polar bear and wolverine. Do you see a recurring theme? Whitney enjoyed his little pleasures. He knew I was already too much of an alpha, renegade personality, and he did his best to amplify every aggressive trait I possessed."

She was silent for a moment, enjoying the feeling of his hands moving down the backs of her thighs. He wasn't exactly impersonal, but he was careful not to be inappropriate. She wasn't certain how he managed to feel possessive and detached at the same time. He was Diego. That was her answer.

"You ready to head outside?" he asked after he'd finished massaging both her legs and feet.

Elated, Leila tried to flip over quickly, but he laid a hand on the small of her back, fingers splayed wide, taking up most of her back, preventing movement.

She hissed her displeasure at him. "I'm more than ready, Diego. I despise being cooped up."

"You can't make any sudden movements. I know it doesn't feel as if you have a thousand stitches in your belly, but you have the equivalent. The repairs appear to be holding, but that doesn't mean if you decide to go dancing, they will."

She blew out her exasperation with a blast of air. "Seriously? I'm just turning over."

"Then you'll do it slow. I'm going to help you roll over and sit up. Once you're sitting, take a minute to make certain you don't get dizzy."

Leila tried not to roll her eyes at him. He was simply looking out for her, the doctor in him taking over, but seriously? She wanted to *move*. There was no getting away from his strength as he aided her in rolling over and sitting up. For a moment the room spun, but she was never going to admit that to him. She breathed her way through it, waited for her head to clear and looked triumphantly at him.

"I'm fine."

He handed her a bottle of water. "Hydrate."

Again, she resisted making faces at him. She thought living with Diego, the man, was going to be difficult, but she found the doctor annoying. She could argue with the man, but it would be silly to try to argue with the doctor. And she'd lose every time. She drank down half the bottle and looked at him over the top.

"I can walk. My legs feel strong."

He nodded, that slow, heart-stopping grin flashing for just one moment. "I've got a couple of trekking poles for you. I want you using them at first. I've got the gear for target practice. Are you hungry?"

Leila shook her head. "Nope. I just want to get outside. Out into the open."

He helped her to stand. Again, she felt dizzy and had to lean into him. Diego circled her waist with his arm. It felt like an iron bar, but it also felt safe. *He* felt safe. A solid wall holding her up. He was patient, waiting until the momentary weakness had passed.

She rubbed her face against the wall of his chest, inhaling deeply, taking him into her lungs before she stepped away from him. "I'm ready."

He handed her the trekking poles, indicating the door with the duffel bag he'd picked up.

The moment the cool breeze touched Leila's face, she felt so much better. The day was beautiful. Not too cold, certainly not overly hot. There was no fog swirling through the trees, just a million shades of green surrounding them. The house was in a very small clearing, the towering trees and thick brush several feet back from the cabin.

"Rubin and I like to see what's coming at us," he explained.

"What if you get trapped in the cabin?" She couldn't imagine, but if someone did sneak up on them, they would have a problem disappearing into the forest.

"Three escape routes, Warrior Woman. I'll show them to you when we go in this evening."

She liked that they were going to be outside for several hours. They walked slowly along a faint trail toward the destination Diego clearly had in mind.

"You said you mostly healed animals before you did surgery on me. Tell me about those animals and how you came about helping them." She not only loved the sound of his voice and wanted him talking to her, but she wanted to know everything there was to know about him. She knew he loved animals—probably more than he did humans.

He matched her pace. She was a little awkward using the trekking poles. It wasn't something she was used to, and she needed to establish a rhythm. More than anything, she was weak, and that made her cautious. She didn't want to fall on her face and have Diego decide it was too early for her to be outside. His voice would distract her and keep her moving even when she felt a little out of breath.

"The first time I ever healed an animal was my sister Lucy's pet rabbit. We weren't allowed pets, but she'd found some baby bunnies all alone. All of the babies in the nest were dead but one. Most likely we had eaten the mother, but none of us told her that. Lucy managed to keep that one alive. She really fought for that little thing."

He matched her steps for a couple of minutes in silence and then strode ahead of her. She could see two camp chairs placed side by side in a small opening facing the trees. He set the duffel bag down and came back to escort her.

"You were telling me about the baby bunny and your sister Lucy."

He took the trekking poles from her and helped to lower her slowly into one of the camp chairs. "My sister Lucy liked to sing. She was a ray of sunshine dancing around the house. Even when she did chores, and she did a ton of them, she danced and sang. She put that little baby rabbit in a sling around her chest to keep it warm. You have to understand our mother thought singing and dancing was a sin. A big dark, black, ugly sin. That meant Lucy would have to be subjected to an exorcism, according to our mother. She said Lucy had the devil in her and it needed to come out."

He paused and looked down at Leila. She hadn't considered that he was that much taller, but he seemed to tower over her. His features were once again hard, giving him that brutal edge. His mouth looked almost cruel. His look alone set her heart pounding, but she refused to look away. She looked beyond the intimidation to the rage inside him. And it was rage. Deep.

He didn't look away from her, even knowing what he was revealing to her. He let her see the killer in him. That was there in his eyes. She could have sworn she saw flames leaping behind those dark angry eyes.

"Tell me," she whispered, reaching out to place her hand gently over his wrist.

His first instinct was to jerk away from her, but he didn't. He continued looking down at her with the eyes of a savage predator. She refused to look away or be intimidated. She absolutely knew she was the safest person in the world from him.

"Tell me, honey," she encouraged.

"My sister was sunshine and light. She was one of the few bright spots in our home, and yet because she dared to sing or dance, our mother had to do her best to extinguish her light. I could barely stand by and watch the things our mother did to her, all in the name of what was holy. Lucy didn't utter a single word no matter what was done to her."

Leila found herself holding her breath. She knew something terrible was about to be revealed. Diego's expression didn't change. His voice remained low and without inflection. Still, she knew, and air caught in her lungs and burned.

"It wasn't enough for her that she hurt Lucy. Our mother ripped that little rabbit from the sling Lucy made, and she flung it across the room toward the fireplace. It hit the pipe and landed on the floor. Before our mother could stomp on it, I snatched it up and was gone. I was fast, really fast, and once in the forest, even Rubin wouldn't be able to find me if I didn't want to be found."

"You knew she would punish you."

"I'd stopped giving a damn what she did to me a couple of years earlier. In any case, Rubin blocked the doorway, giving me even more time to get under cover. The rabbit was in bad shape, with two broken bones. I wasn't going to allow it to die. I knew I could heal it. I felt a well of heat and energy rising when I put my hands over the little body. Weirdly, I could see inside the rabbit's body just by laying my palms over it. I could easily map out every bruise and every broken bone."

"Was it scary to realize you were seeing inside the rabbit? I think that would have both elated and horrified me." Leila couldn't imagine making that discovery or knowing what to do with it after she found out she was able to look inside a creature.

His gaze swept the trees and along the ground, then he took a seat next to her. She noticed he did that often. Searching for tracks, always alert to his surroundings. She had always thought she was wary, but Diego was clearly a cut above her when it came to vigilance.

"I can't say I was horrified. I was overcome with the need to fix everything wrong. I could feel heat rising in me, radiating through my palms. It was difficult to control the temperature, and I was fearful of killing the baby rabbit myself. It took time to figure out how to use that energy to heal the bruising and the broken bones."

She didn't understand the sorrow in his voice. It didn't show in his expression, but his dark eyes had taken on a haunted quality. She couldn't help herself. Uncaring that he might reject her, she stood, swayed only for a moment, and took the couple of steps to his side. She straddled him, sitting fully on his lap, half expecting him to push her off. It was just that there was too much pain in his eyes. Comforting him was a compulsion impossible to ignore.

Diego looked shocked. He hadn't expected her to notice his distress, let alone react to it. She had the feeling no one had ever made an effort to comfort him. Or no one had cared enough to see he needed it. She leaned into him and brushed a kiss over his lips.

"Did the rabbit die?" She nuzzled his throat and then laid her head against his chest. She wanted him to tell her what had happened next to cause that look in his eyes.

"No." He cleared his throat, and his arms circled her with unexpected fierceness. "No, the rabbit lived. It's just that Lucy . . ."

He trailed off and buried his face between her shoulder and neck, sending a million goose bumps rising on her skin. She shivered and burrowed closer. Diego's arms tightened to steel bands. He brushed a kiss on top of her head.

"I worry talking about my life will give you nightmares."

The way his tone stroked velvet caresses over her skin was a revelation in just how easily Diego could bring every nerve ending in her body to sizzling life. She hadn't known she could ever react to a man physically the way she did to him.

"I want to know every detail of your life, Diego. If it's something that causes nightmares, I want to share that with you. Hopefully, by telling me, it will lighten that burden in you."

He caught at her chin, forcing her head up until she had no choice but to meet the full intensity of his dark gaze. She felt color rising beneath her skin. She hadn't ever considered that she would flirt with a man or, in this case, be brazen enough to tell him the truth. Her truth. She was all but declaring her growing feelings for him.

"My sister was horrified that I had saved the rabbit. She was the only one I told. I showed her the little guy, and she backed away from it. She told me only the devil could have done such a thing and I had to get rid of it. She told me never to tell anyone I could do such a thing and not to do it again."

Was there shame in his voice? The hard lines in his handsome features remained exactly the same. She was staring into his eyes, and she couldn't see shame, but she still felt it in him. In his heart. In his soul. His own sister had said those things to him. An older sister. One he admired and thought of as practically the shining light in their home, yet his saintly sister copied his mother when it came down to it. She had all but destroyed her younger brother in that moment.

It was no wonder he never allowed anyone to know of his healing skills. He hadn't told Rubin or his GhostWalker unit for what he believed was a very good reason.

"When they found out Rubin was able to heal, did they view it as coming from the devil too?"

She felt his instant rejection. His body stiffened, and his hands clamped down on her hard enough that if she fought him, she would bruise. He didn't frighten her. Nothing about him did. She remained relaxed, leaning into him, sharing his personal space. It felt intimate and weirdly right.

"They never knew about Rubin. And if you knew him, you'd understand why no one could ever think that Rubin's incredible talent comes from the devil."

She caught the warning in his tone. She doubted if he even knew it was there. Instead of being put off, Leila liked him all the more for his intense loyalty to his brother. She wanted him to have that same allegiance directed toward her.

"What happened to the baby rabbit?" She dared to hope that he hadn't destroyed it as his sister had instructed. "Did you kill it?"

For the first time, he looked uncomfortable, his gaze sliding away from hers. "I couldn't do that. It was really tiny and helpless. I hid it, made a warm burrow for it and fed it myself. When I left the house, I'd carry it with me against my skin." Faint color actually crept under his skin. He not only sounded embarrassed but looked it as well.

She hugged him tighter. "You're so incredible, Diego. Truly wonderful. If I wasn't already falling hard for you, that right there would have done it for me."

His eyebrow shot up, and all trace of embarrassment disappeared. Once more, he looked the confident, commanding man she knew him to be. A trace of male amusement showed in his eyes, setting off a series of spinning roller coasters in her stomach. She just managed to avoid pressing her hand over the spot in an effort to still the chaos.

"For being my warrior woman, you certainly have more compassion in you than is good for you. It's a wonder you can function in the field."

She was aware of the underlying serious question. "It's different. The men I hunt aren't innocent. They aren't helpless. They have every chance to kill me."

Leila felt him wince. His arms tightened into the steel bands around her again as if he could shield her from the assignments she carried out.

"The idea of you facing them alone without backup doesn't sit well with me."

"When you're used to working within a team, that makes sense to you, Diego, but I've never worked with anyone else. I don't ever depend on someone else. I know if I get into trouble, no one is coming. I have to figure out how to get in and out of wherever I'm going without a hitch. I also don't have the responsibility of looking out for anyone else. It's just me, and I can just worry about myself."

She pushed back against his arms, signaling she was ready to get off his lap. She was all too aware of him and how vulnerable she'd made herself. He dropped his arms at that slight signal, and she slid off his thighs to stand in front of him, her hands on his shoulders to steady herself.

"Thank you, Diego. You have no idea how much I appreciate you."

He turned his head and brushed a kiss along the back of her hand. "I'm not sure what I've done to deserve a thanks."

"A million times you could have taken advantage of me or just misconstrued what I was doing, but you didn't."

His smile transformed his face, causing fireworks to detonate in the very center of her core. The sparkles radiated outward along every nerve ending and rushed through her bloodstream with little electrical sparks.

"Don't think you're out of the woods, sweetheart. I have every intention of taking advantage of you, just not until you're one hundred percent."

That should have made her happy, but she found herself wishing she was already one hundred percent or that he would put aside his gentlemanly behavior.

"Are we going to take bets with our little shooting match?"

She settled back in her chair and picked up the weapon of her choice, examining it carefully before loading it.

"That wouldn't be exactly fair," Diego pointed out.

"The arrogance of my man. You have no idea if you can outshoot me. Just because you have a big bad reputation and I don't, doesn't mean you're better than I am."

He laughed. Actually laughed. The sound was like music to her, playing over her skin and sinking deep, branding his name somewhere she knew she'd never get it out. She didn't want to. The truth was, she was already lost. Free-falling right off the cliff when she wasn't a risk-taker. She was a methodical huntress. She planned ahead for every contingency.

Falling so fast and so hard for a man hadn't been in her plans, but now that it had happened, she accepted it. She had made up her mind that she wasn't going to be a coward and pass up the opportunity to be with a man like Diego Campos.

"Let's do this." She lay completely prone on the ground, eyes on the series of targets he'd set up. "You go first."

Diego stretched out beside her on the ground. He wasn't super close to her, but she could feel the warmth of his body, and it was distracting. Apparently not for him. He didn't miss. Every single bullet fired was a kill shot. It gave her an incredible rush, knowing he hadn't gone easy on her. She didn't want easy. She wanted a partnership. She knew the reputation of Diego Campos. If you ever had the misfortune to get into the sight of his rifle, you were as good as dead.

She would like to see what he could do with a knife. He seemed to prefer to use knives, something she disliked. Killing with a knife was very personal. Up close. She could feel the blade enter the target and knew the damage she'd done. She could see her prey's eyes, feel their emotions. She didn't want to use a knife if she could avoid it. But she was excellent with one when the need arose.

She took her time with each shot, knowing her skills would surprise him, maybe even impress him. At least she hoped he would be impressed. She was an excellent shot, and like Diego, she didn't miss. Each bullet fired was a kill shot. When she'd hit the last target, she couldn't help but look over at him, anxiety uppermost. She knew most of the men she'd trained around despised that she was a better shot than they were. She wasn't Diego Campos good, but she was very close.

The look on his face was everything she could have wanted. Fantasized over. Needed. There was sheer pride in her. A slow grin swept up toward his eyes, lighting that darkness. It might have been brief, but it was there.

"You should have insisted on a bet."

That said it all. Was everything to her. Before she could reply, from somewhere in the forest, quite close, the great horned owl issued a challenge to any owl entering her territory. Diego reached over and gently curled his fingers around Leila's shoulder. She looked up at his face, and a shiver of fear slid down her spine. His entire demeanor had changed. She was no longer looking at her sweet companion; she was looking at a full-on predator. There was no mistaking the killer in his eyes.

He didn't speak, but his hand moved, signaling her toward the cover of the trees. She didn't argue. She was up and moving in a low crouch straight into the thicker forest. He moved with her, shadowing her every step, her smaller body dwarfed by his. She wanted to demand that he stop protecting her. She was his partner when it came to threats—and in this case, the threat was there most likely because of her.

Once both had been swallowed by the deeper foliage, Diego indicated a large tree with an extensive root system. "Crawl in there."

She frowned at him. She didn't hesitate because there were spiders, lizards and mice; she was used to dealing with insects, reptiles and even rodents. She took a few heartbeats, shaking her head at him. "How am I going to be helping you if I'm hiding like a coward in there?" She hissed the question, keeping her voice a mere thread of sound.

"You won't be hiding for long, Warrior Woman." He flashed her a grin. "I'm just going to scout out the enemy. I'll let you know how many."

"It could be your brother. Or Luther."

"The owl knows both men. She would have let me know they were on their way, but she wouldn't have raised an alarm."

Leila didn't argue with him. She crawled beneath the framework of roots. Diego placed several weapons as well as ammunition beside her right hand and a bottle of water beside her left.

"Won't be long, sweetheart. Catch a nap if you're so inclined."

"A nap?"

"Don't tell me you aren't a little tired. You've been working nearly nonstop after lying in bed. You're still not completely healed. A nap will do you good."

"Is that what you do when you're about to go into combat?"

"Yep. Keeps me sharp." He grinned at her, pressed a kiss to his fingertips and then placed the pads of his fingers on her lips. "Seriously, Leila, this won't take that long. I just need to know where they are, who they are and how many, and lead them back this way if they're lost."

"Well, if that's all, a nap sounds like a perfect choice."

9

t was a mistake to send anyone to hunt him in his own territory. Every commander should know that. Whitney occasionally sent his supersoldiers against a GhostWalker unit to test them. It never ended well for the soldiers. There were times when Diego speculated that Whitney wanted to rid himself of a group of troublesome soldiers, so he sent them against the GhostWalkers.

But the commander of the soldiers sanctioned by the government? He would know better than to send someone out once Diego had identified himself as a GhostWalker. Even if the commander didn't recognize his name, the fact that Diego was in the Ghost-Walker program should have been enough to deter him. If he wanted Leila back, he could apply through proper channels, although she was Diego's woman. He would never stop fighting for her, and neither would his fellow GhostWalkers. That was their code.

Sending anyone after her, knowing they were entering Diego's home turf, was just plain stupid. Diego was aware that Luther could arrive any minute if he hadn't succeeded in stopping the soldiers from taking Bridget. Rubin would be on his way as well. Diego didn't need them, but he did worry they would walk into a trap. He would have to leave signs to warn them.

Rubin would know the long vertical bear rubs on three trees in a row were made by Diego as a danger sign. It was possible Luther might see them and know that Diego, not a black bear, had created the bear rubs. He marked several trees on and off trails as he hurried down the mountain in the direction the owl indicated she had spotted intruders.

Rubin knew to be cautious in his approach to the cabin. They were always careful when they returned. The cabin was unoccupied for months on end. It was known throughout their part of the mountains that the land was owned by Rubin and Diego. They paid two neighbors to watch over their property in their absence. If an occasional hiker went off course and found the cabin, the two men took care of it immediately, escorting the intruders away.

The GhostWalker commanders had the information on the location of the cabin available to them. Being the commander of an experimental program most likely gave Leila's commander a very high security clearance. Diego was positive, depending on that clearance, that the commander could access the information.

Diego crouched low to the ground as he neared the location where the owl had spotted intruders. He laid both palms on the forest floor, going very still, allowing his enhanced senses to the forefront. At once, he connected with the underground network created by the forest of mushrooms. The network connected all the trees and even some of the larger shrubs and brush, creating a vast communications center.

He could hear the heartbeat of the earth. The rustle of lizards, mice, voles and a multitude of other creatures rushing through the vegetation on the forest floor. Insects buzzed around the mushrooms, ferns and other flowering plants seeking nectar and pollen. Diego was patient, allowing the natural flow of the forest to sink into him, to become part of him.

A fox den off to his right still had two kits in it. A quarter of a mile away, a bobcat lay curled up in a hollow tree, but it was alert. The cat was a male and had claimed a fairly large territory that intersected with two females' territory. The bobcat was aware of intruders. Diego had the impression of the cat grimacing, pulling back lips to silently show teeth. Several deer dipped velvety noses close to the water pooling at the bottom of a thin ribbon of water that was flowing out of the mountainside to collect in the rocks below.

He felt the shiver of a tree, one of the taller oaks, as something heavy moved along its branches. On the ground below the tree, he felt the tread of boots. Something large stretched out on the ground and wrapped itself around the large fern covering the roots of a red spruce tree.

Diego had the location now. He'd identified at least three intruders. In one spot, very close to the oak tree where he was certain a soldier rested in the branches, the ground was extremely hot. Too hot, as if a fire raged beneath the ground, disturbing the mycelium network. He concentrated, getting a feeling for that site. The size and shape of what was putting off that much heat. A fourth soldier? Would a soldier generate that high of a temperature? He knew one of the GhostWalkers from Team One was married to a woman who could use fire as a weapon. Was he dealing with someone similar?

He called to the female great gray owl. He needed eyes in the sky. The soldiers were still a distance from him. He pulled his hands from the ground and stood facing the interior. The men were just off the main trail. They were using the trail as a guide to make their way up the mountain, even as they hid their presence in the dense trees and brush.

The owl called to him five times. Each cry was that of a female calling to her mate, but she was indicating she had eyes on five soldiers. He called back to her to protect herself. If they were enhanced, it was possible one or more might become aware of her presence—of her spying. He didn't want her injured or killed on his behalf.

Diego set out jogging, using the faint game trails to make his way quickly to where the soldiers rested. At one point, he switched from the game trail to the habitual path the bobcat used to make his way through the denser foliage until he managed to get close enough to hear their conversation. Diego remained very still, becoming part of the trees and brush surrounding him. He rested his palms on the ground, better to read any warning. Mostly, he eavesdropped.

"What'sss wrong, Bobby? Can't talk?" The voice came from above, somewhere in the branches of the oak tree.

Diego narrowed his gaze, quartering the tree, looking for the soldier who had spoken.

Two of the men resting, sitting on the ground, laughed as if the soldier had said something hilarious.

One man had his arms wrapped around the branches of the large bush in what appeared to be a stranglehold. He hissed, narrowing his gaze at someone or something in the tree above him. "F-f-fuck you, Dean." His voice stuttered, and spit dripped from his mouth as he delivered the classic comeback. He twisted his body in an impossible coil around the plant, clearly agitated by the taunting.

Diego studied how the body seemed to elongate. The arms were stretched to impossible lengths. As Bobby coiled around the bush, he tightened his body and arms until he appeared to be crushing the plant.

"Don't get riled up yet, Bobby," the one Diego suspected of generating heat said.

Bobby turned yellow eyes on the man sitting calmly on the ground. His tongue darted out, long and forked. "Ssshut him up, Russss." He drew out the "s" of each word.

"You never could take it, Bobby," Dean snapped. "You dish it out, but anyone says anything to you, and you whine like a little baby."

Diego had to look with more than his own eyes. He had more than excellent vision, but he still was unable to spot Dean in the trees. The man seemed to have a cloaking device, a way to become part of his background. Diego knew there was a woman married to one of the men on Team Three who could cloak herself and even those around her. Diego tapped into the vision of one of the raptors Whitney had made a part of his genetic makeup.

He knew he shared the traits of an eagle, hawk and falcon as well as an owl. Whitney hadn't stinted on his genetic cocktail. He chose to use the sight of an eagle to find the soldier the others referred to as Dean.

"Leave him alone," Russ ordered. "We can't have him losing his temper when he doesn't have a target in sight."

The other man who had been sitting rose abruptly, his wary gaze fixed on Bobby. "Come on, Bobby, don't pay any mind to Dean. You know he's full of shit." There was a soothing quality to his voice. Not compelling, just soothing. He paced away from the others and then back. "We're all in this together."

"That'sss what you sssay, Billy," Bobby said, his spit falling from his mouth in two steady streams. "I don't think Dean agreesss." The last word was difficult to understand as Bobby sputtered and stuttered and hissed.

The fifth man slowly switched his penetrating, distinctly warning gaze from Bobby to Dean. Diego could easily follow his line of sight to the soldier in the tree. Even with the sight of an eagle and knowing where he was, Diego might have missed Dean, but the soldier moved, easing away from the trunk to step onto a thick branch. The tree looked as if it came to life, shimmering transparent so Diego had to blink rapidly to bring the apparition into focus.

"It was a joke, Jim. Bobby can't take a joke."

As a cloaking device, it was excellent, much more so than wearing clothes that reflected one's surroundings or changing the color of their skin to mirror the backgrounds they were in. Dean appeared to be part of the tree itself, and even staring straight at him didn't help to find him. The man seemed to fade until he couldn't be seen.

But Dean had been looking at the soldier he called Jim. All of them were. Diego had pegged Russ as the one running the unit, but there was genuine fear when they looked at Jim. Jim looked the most normal of all of them. When he spoke, his voice was mild. Even. Nonthreatening, yet the look he'd given Dean had been one that made every one of his fellow soldiers leery.

"Do we have a plan?" Billy asked Russ.

Russ shrugged. "Our intel says five soldiers brought the package up the mountain to rendezvous with a helicopter. They didn't show. She was severely injured. Whitney thinks they had to stop and work on her, maybe give her a blood transfusion. He's got Cooper's team parachuting into the meadow at the highest elevation on this side of the mountain. There's a clearing there. They'll be coming down to meet us. They also have a medic with them."

Russ turned his attention to Jim. "If she's bad, it will be up to you to pull her through. Whitney offered us big rewards. Money, women, promotions. It all depends on retrieving the woman and delivering her alive to Whitney."

"I heard those soldiers were no joke. They might not be Ghost-Walkers, but they have skills," Billy said.

"We were all briefed on their abilities," Russ said. "What we have going for us is far superior to them. Whitney had a lot of years to make us the best. We've got the benefit of all those who came before us, men and women. We know the GhostWalkers are fucked-up. They have skills, but they're flawed. We aren't."

"Russ." Dean's tone was cautionary. "I wouldn't say that."

Russ shrugged. "Together, we're unstoppable. We've got everything we need to succeed. Whitney has faith in us. Who's going to stop us? The soldiers running up the mountain before they make sure the old man is dead? One old man. They couldn't even kill him."

He signaled to the others. "Let's move out."

Diego shadowed them, a dark menace pacing along beside the men, unseen and unheard. He studied how each moved. Dean, the soldier in the tree, stayed cloaked, very difficult to see. Diego caught glimpses of the man, tall with lots of muscle, and that was only when the cloaking device seemed to glitch for the space of a microsecond. It took Diego several minutes to recognize a pattern. There was a slight malfunction in the cloaking device. Every fourth minute, the transparency shimmered, briefly revealing the man behind the strange camouflage.

After ten minutes of watching, Diego wondered if Dean could remove the transparent cloak. Was the thing permanent? Was the man forced to be an apparition at all times? What would that do to him over time? At first it would seem cool. He'd feel superior, able to conceal himself in any situation, like a phantom. But eventually Dean would want some normalcy. How could he be with a woman? How could he be around his friends without them wondering if he spied on them?

Then there was Bobby. He moved constantly, not really walking in a straight line but undulating his body, the muscles contracting as he propelled himself over the trail. He was mesmerizing in the way he wove a pattern in the dirt. If Diego had come along behind him and inspected the tracks, at first glance he would have thought a very large and heavy snake had made those marks on the trail.

On close examination, Bobby appeared misshapen. His muscles were overly bulging in places, and his head was bullet shaped. His mouth opened continually, his long, forked tongue emerging, twisting this way and that as if he could scent the air. His ears were smaller than normal, and his eyes were a strange, yellowish hue. Twice he nearly went to the ground, his body undulating in coils as if he couldn't stop himself.

Russ was the soldier who had been sitting on the ground, and the spot had been extremely hot. The ground had protested as if the man was burning through the layers of soil to the very heart of the earth. Even the mushrooms had recoiled from his presence. As he, by turns, jogged or walked up the trail, he set a steady, easy pace that would cover miles in a timely fashion. It took a few minutes of observation to notice that when he jogged, he seemed to leave blackened leaves and twigs behind. Twice, smoke curled up from the debris on the trail.

It took even longer for Diego to notice that Russ's skin would alter subtly from an even tan to spots of deep red and charcoal black. The change happened when he jogged. When he slowed to a walk, the effect would disappear.

Whitney had always tried to place armor under the skin of his soldiers, making it much more difficult to kill them. Bullets didn't work unless they managed to hit the precise spot where there was no armor, usually the throat. Armor made the soldiers slower and much stiffer, like a robot. These men were not at all like that. Diego doubted they had armor under their skin.

Jim definitely seemed the most normal of all the soldiers. He moved easily, gracefully, his boots barely skimming the ground. He didn't look in the least bit winded, almost as if he were taking a stroll through the park instead of moving stealthily through steep, difficult terrain.

The owl flew overhead, drawing Diego's attention. They were nearing the gorge where the bodies of the soldiers who had attempted to murder Leila lay. The owl called out to warn him of a disturbance in the trees above the gorge. Branches shook on the oak tree looming above the ravine. Because he was looking for him, Diego spotted Dean shimmering like a transparent veil as he balanced on the branch and peered down at the decomposing bodies.

Movement caught Diego's eye below the tree. It was Billy, or at least half of him. His upper body contorted and twisted as if trying to emerge from a ghostly egg. The bottom half of his body—hips, legs and feet—was invisible, hidden in that oval shell surrounding him. A teleporter? Diego knew they existed. A couple of the GhostWalkers could teleport, but not in the same way. As far as he knew, they didn't get stuck between. What had Whitney done?

Every single GhostWalker was flawed in some way. Some had worse defects than others, but all of them had strengths to make up for the problems they had. Was Whitney continuing to experiment with animal and reptilian DNA even when he knew how badly things could go wrong? Looking at the soldiers Whitney had sent, he was certain the man hadn't learned his lesson.

Dean stayed in the tree, and Billy managed to pull himself together by the time Russ, Bobby and Jim arrived to peer down into the gorge. Diego was still unsure of Jim and what gifts or drawbacks he had. The others seemed to give him a wide berth and a lot of respect. Even Russ, who was clearly in command, seemed leery of Jim.

Diego waited to hear what the others thought they were looking at.

"You'll have to go down there, Billy," Russ said. "We need to know who's dead and if the woman is there as well. It would be good to know how they died."

The soldiers stared down into the ravine and then looked carefully around them. Russ indicated to Bobby to fall back to protect them. He sent Jim ahead to scout for any tracks that might indicate what had taken place.

Billy didn't hesitate. One moment he was standing under the tree Dean was sheltering in, and the next, he appeared in the gorge. At least a part of him appeared. Once again, he seemed to have to fight to bring his entire body forward with him. Diego knew teleporters had to be precise when they moved from one location to another, or they could end up in the middle of a boulder or tree trunk. But to have to struggle to get your body to come together each time you teleported had to be terrifying. The idea that you would never be whole had to take its toll each time the man made a jump from one place to another.

Diego studied Billy as his body slowly appeared. The soldier was slumped over, unable to stay on his feet without support. Teleporting made him extremely weak. Diego had experience with weakness after healing. Depending on how much energy he used, the crash could be anywhere from mild to extremely dangerous, rendering him unconscious.

He still had no idea what kinds of gifts Jim had. He needed to know his strengths and weaknesses before he began his attacks. He had no problem using his rifle to kill them from a distance, but he had to know he *could* kill them that way. Whitney was notorious for protecting his soldiers with armor.

Below, in the gorge, Billy had begun to straighten up. He looked around him, carefully inspecting the dead. "Smells pretty bad. The vultures and beetles are having a field day. There are at least eight or nine bodies. Don't see a woman."

"Can you tell what killed them?" Russ asked, raising his voice to be heard.

Vultures circled above the gorge and stared down at the carnage below them. Diego noticed several of the birds looked warily toward the tree Dean was in. Not a single vulture took up residence in the branches overlooking the gorge. Did that mean they could see through the cloak to the man shielded behind it?

Diego blinked rapidly, calling up the raptor in him. Eagles had excellent vision, and he used the sight of the large bird to view Dean and his shimmering cloak. When he looked at the soldier through the eyes of the raptor, the outline of the man wavered repeatedly behind the blurring cloak.

The fact that birds were aware of the soldier's presence even when he was cloaked was very interesting to Diego. It was a major flaw. It wouldn't take soldiers with the enhanced vision Diego had very long to become aware of the enemy hiding in the trees. All it would take was one soldier very aware of his surroundings and nature to spot there was a problem if birds were reactive.

Diego slipped away from the site, becoming a shadow in the forest, following Jim. With Jim separating himself from the others, it was an opportunity to dispose of him before the soldiers reached Leila. It was imperative, before he struck, to know Jim's gifts. He'd prefer to stay silent so the others weren't aware they were being stalked.

Jim was thorough looking for tracks, but he stayed on the trail, resisting the lure of the deeper woods. He stopped occasionally and studied the forest on either side of him for long minutes, his eyes carefully searching the edges leading into the trees. He examined brush and fern, looking for twisted, bruised leaves.

Diego stayed in the trees, watching the man for signs of any talents that made him lethal. He couldn't forget the way Jim's fellow soldiers acted around him. None of them wanted to be close to him. There had to be a reason.

Jim suddenly crouched down, one palm sliding just above the ground while he looked around, his gaze going to the trees where Diego was concealed. Jim's head tilted first one way and then the other as if listening for something. Diego knew he couldn't be seen, and he wasn't making a sound, but there was no doubt in his mind Jim knew he was there. Had the soldier tapped into the mycelium network? Was he capable? Diego didn't think so. It was something else.

"If you need help, Leila, I can give that to you. There's no need to be afraid. Just come out where I can see you."

Diego was shocked to feel the compulsion embedded in the voice. The notes didn't affect him—compulsion rarely did—but he hadn't expected this man to have such a strong talent in that area. He should have, given the way his fellow soldiers regarded him.

He came out of the trees, ensuring Jim wouldn't see him until he was within throwing distance of his knife. He didn't want to use a gun and hoped his own voice would work on the soldier to keep him from attempting to shoot him. He would prefer for Jim's friends not to have a clue what happened to the man.

"I'm not the Leila you're apparently looking for," Diego greeted. "I live up here; you're actually on my property."

He kept his image somewhat blurred so it would be difficult for Jim to see his features. He'd been told he could look predatory, and that was the last thing he wanted his adversary to think.

Jim immediately gave him a friendly smile. "A local? Maybe you'll be able to help me." His voice was very amicable. He stood up slowly, taking several steps toward Diego. "My sister was hiking the trail, and she didn't check in with us. I was worried about her, so I came looking. It hasn't been long enough to call for search and rescue." As he spoke, he continued forward toward Diego, closing the gap between them, looking completely at ease.

As Jim approached, the hairs on Diego's body reacted, standing up. He'd had a similar reaction when he was close to his sister-in-law, Jonquille. She drew lightning to her, and the ensuing electrical storm was always life-threatening. But there was no storm overhead. Diego couldn't sense one brewing. No rain. No thunder. The clouds weren't right for an electrical event. It was Jim generating the electrical reaction in Diego's body but without the help of a storm. That was puzzling.

Jim's smile was friendly—and practiced. It didn't quite reach his eyes. The female owl screeched a warning. Deliberately, Diego took a step toward the enemy, coming straight to him at a casual, steady pace. He didn't look at the sky when the shadow of the owl moved over him. Instead, he took another step into his enemy's space.

Jim stretched his hand out in greeting. "Jim Volter. I'm glad to meet a local who knows the area."

Diego gripped his hand, taking care not to use strength. Jim didn't either. There was no bullshit vying to see who was stronger, yet the moment Diego came into physical contact with Jim, he knew he was in trouble. The touch might be light, but the man instantly connected with Diego's heartbeat by pressing one finger over the pulse point in his wrist.

Diego felt the mild disruption, so faint that it was only the healing well inside him that allowed detection of the electrical pulses moving toward his heart. He smiled, looking straight into the soldier's eyes, allowing Jim to see his true character, the one hidden from most people. The killer.

"Nice to meet you. Name's Diego. Diego Campos."

Healing energy could go both ways. Diego had discovered that as a child when he'd first been trying to learn how to help animals.

He could use that same energy to humanely kill a suffering animal. It wasn't that different from what Jim Volter was doing. He smiled as he introduced himself. His first step was to protect himself, to neutralize the electrical activity Jim pushed into his body.

"Whitney knows better than to send his soldiers after us, but he just can't help himself." He tightened his grip on Volter to hold him in place as he allowed the deep well inside him to open fully. "The dead bodies you and your friends found in the gorge? Those are my kills. Stupid to enter my terrain and challenge me."

At hearing Diego's name, Volter started to pull away, and then he relaxed, grinning, sure of himself and his ability to kill using his talent.

"None of them were friends of mine," Jim said. "Where's the woman? Did you kill her too?"

Diego's body was flooded with electrical pulses, but that healing well of energy slid through his veins and arteries, settling the activity until it was normal. He brought up his other hand, palm out, inches from Volter's chest as if he was showing him that he had no weapons—or he was about to push him away. They stared at each other, neither giving an inch. Volter was confident he could kill Diego and he remained relaxed, even when the heat pouring into one spot on his chest increased.

Diego shrugged casually as he continued to raise the temperature of Volter's heart. "Leila? You'll be happy to know she's alive and well. Why would Whitney want her when he has her sister? He knows if you take her, it's going to piss off some pretty important people."

"Whitney knows there's something special about her. He's been talking to someone in that lab for a long time and knows all about Leila. He says he needs her to create the perfect soldier." Volter's grin turned evil. "You know what that means, don't you? She'll be up for grabs. I intend to be her partner, so if you had any aspirations in that department, you can forget them." As he spoke, he sent a jolt of electricity arcing through Diego's veins.

The healing energy rushed to swarm around the snapping, crackling massive charge of electricity bent on short-circuiting Diego's heart. All the while, Diego continued to turn up the heat on the one location in Volter's chest, directly over his heart.

Diego never looked away from his enemy. The intensity of the heat grew quickly. He'd always found it difficult to control when there was so much energy, and it gathered fast and was centered in a precise spot. Repairing arteries and veins had been a huge learning curve when it was done with heat.

Killing was so much easier. A concentrated amount of heat he didn't have to control was all it took. With an animal, he euthanized as quickly and as humanely as possible. He had heated the body much slower than he normally would have to prevent Volter from realizing he was in trouble. Now, it was too late. By the time the soldier realized his chest felt as though it was on fire, his core temperature had risen too high and his organs were already shutting down. His heart couldn't take the elevated temperature. His brain faltered.

Jim Volter fell to his knees and then collapsed on the trail. Diego was relentless, following him down, ensuring the man died quickly. He left him on the edge of the trail. There would be no visible signs of injury. No bullet wound. No knife stab. Diego removed the few tracks he'd left in the dirt when he'd confronted the soldier.

It wasn't long before the others came looking. Russ and Bobby arrived together. Both rushed to Jim's side and crouched low. Russ examined the body while Bobby kept a lookout.

"It looks to me like he was alone when he bought it," Russ said.

At the uneasiness in Russ's voice, Bobby twisted his neck and hissed in agitation. His body undulated, contorting continually.

"Knock it off, Bobby," Russ snapped. "Get some control. We all have to learn control or we're going to end up like this. I think his own talent killed him from the inside."

Bobby cursed and put his hands on his hips. His arms were long and thick, the muscles moving incessantly.

Diego left them to it, taking to the trees to go back to the gorge. Dean would be looking out for Billy. Billy had to teleport back up to the main trail. He would be weak when he did so, and it would be Dean's job to protect him until the weakness passed. Diego moved through the trees as quickly as his cat DNA allowed. He needed to see to Dean before Billy was out of the gorge and completely recovered.

He called to the red-tailed hawk to find Dean's position, although he was certain the soldier hadn't left the tree overlooking the gorge. Sure enough, the hawk gave a confirming cry. Diego didn't hesitate. He moved with ease through the trees, using the abilities of a leopard. Fortune favored him in that the wind was picking up, going from a slight breeze to a stronger one. And it was blowing in the direction he was traveling. If foliage moved and caught Dean's eye, he would put it down to the wind.

Diego traveled fast, but rather than use the sight of the leopard as he approached the tree Dean was in, he switched to the eagle's vision. Instantly, he could see the man behind the cloaking device. Dean was on the branch overlooking the gorge, shouting to Billy to forget trying to see what killed the men. He was circling the branch with one arm as he leaned over to call out instructions.

Diego landed in the tree directly behind him just as Dean was straightening up, pulling himself into a less precarious position. He struck, catching Dean with one hand on the side of his face and jaw and the other around the back of his head. With no hesitation, he snapped Dean's head up and around. He used lethal force, breaking the neck and then, in one move, leaping to the ground, holding Dean's body in front of his.

Simultaneously, Billy transported from the gorge to the same exact location he'd started from. Again, his head and shoulders appeared and one leg partially. He slumped to the ground, clearly weak, not paying attention to his surroundings. Dean's body was only a few feet from him, but he was so disoriented Billy didn't spot him.

Cognizant of time passing, knowing soldiers had parachuted above Leila's location, Diego attacked Billy, rising up from the forest floor to shove a knife into his skull, severing the spinal cord. It didn't matter, with Russ and Bobby ahead on the trail, that Diego had left evidence that someone had been responsible for Billy's death. Dean might have fallen from the tree and broken his neck. Jim looked as if his own talent had killed him. Not that Diego minded if Whitney knew he was responsible.

He took to the trees again, traveling the arboreal highway, using the cat's speed and agility to leap from tree to tree to catch up to Russ and Bobby as quickly as possible. The two men were still hovering over Jim's body, discussing what had killed him and waiting impatiently for Dean and Billy to show up.

Russ moved restlessly from spot to spot, leaving behind blackened needles and vegetation, revealing to Diego that the more the soldier became agitated, the hotter his internal fire became. He was uncomfortable and paced, turning continually into the wind in an effort to cool his body temperature.

From the tree overlooking the two men, he called the hawk and the owl. He summoned the bobcat and two families of raccoons. Bobby smelled overwhelmingly like a snake, and once he took to the ground, writhing and undulating, he appeared to be one. He hissed continually, his long-forked tongue darting out of the notch in his lip to test the air for chemicals. The owl launched herself from the tree stump she'd been observing the "snake" from. Her talons raked over the face of the snake, one hooking in the tongue and yanking viciously.

The red-tailed hawk ripped at the throat of the "snake," tearing through flesh while six adult raccoons attacked the legs and feet. A bobcat snarled and clawed at one of the arms, crushing down with its bite. Bobby howled and thrashed, attempting to get to his feet, but the weight of the raccoons held him down. The raccoons paid particular attention to his feet, biting through his boots and tearing at his scaly skin.

Russ turned toward his downed companion, hurling small fireballs around the man in an effort to scare off the animals and raptors. That only seemed to incite them more, particularly the birds. Another owl arrived, the gray's mate, ripping open Bobby's face and tearing out one eye.

Russ yelled and threw more fireballs, this time attempting to hit the bobcat. The fiery sphere landed in the middle of Bobby's stomach, and instantly, flames began to lick over his clothing.

Diego took advantage of the chaos, using his favorite throwing knife to end Russ. The soldier never saw it coming. Never realized he was in danger. He was staring in horror at his companion, trying to find a way to help him, when the knife penetrated his chest, the blade embedding in his heart. The second knife took him in the throat, and the third severed an artery in his thigh.

Diego retrieved the knives and put Bobby out of his misery before he once more took to the trees to get back to Leila.

10

Leila heard them coming a good ten minutes before the intruders reached her location. She was lying prone, her belly stretched across the ground, allowing her to not only hear Whitney's soldiers coming but to feel them as they jogged along the trail. The path they took wasn't a common one. It was located on the Campos property and wasn't a proper road but a game trail used regularly by animals.

She counted five of them and she rechecked her weapons. A calm descended, the way it always did when she went into battle. She was used to fighting alone and relying only on herself. She wasn't counting on Diego to return, although she knew he would. She trusted him. He would never leave her alone unless it couldn't be helped. He was that kind of man.

A part of her was grateful Diego wasn't with her. She knew if he was, her attention would be divided, and that was always a risk. With just herself to look after, she felt more confident. She did wish she was a strong telepath. She knew Diego was, but she couldn't reach him. He had to initiate. She wanted to warn him so when he made his way back to her, he wouldn't run into an ambush. The thought made her more determined than ever to hunt and kill the approaching enemy.

She heard them when they were a mile out. They had stopped on the trail, presumably looking for tracks.

"Alex, you need to pick up the trail," one said. He had the voice of someone used to issuing orders.

"Devin is the sniffer, Cooper, not me," Alex protested.

She knew a sniffer had bear in him, and bears were the best at finding food, even miles away. Their sense of smell was up to three thousand times better than a human's. She knew he would find her. How could he not? She was a human being, and no matter how many times she showered, she would still smell like a human being.

"You're our tracker," Cooper snapped, impatience coming through. "You can't always leave everything up to Devin. You're so lazy, Alex. Pull it together."

"It's not my fault that my DNA causes me to tire easily. You try having sloth, lion and owl monkey in you. All of them need to sleep sixteen or seventeen hours a day." Alex sounded whiny.

Leila rolled her eyes. What had Whitney been thinking to put together a concoction like that? It was ridiculous.

"You were lazy before Whitney ever offered to have you in the program. They were going to toss your ass out because you couldn't complete the requirements no matter how many chances they gave you." Cooper's voice was filled with contempt. "Did you think I wouldn't read the evals on any soldier under me? I take my job seriously. You start looking for tracks, and you'd better find something that points us in the direction we need to go."

"Come on, Alex," another voice said. "We don't want Russ's team to find the girl before we do. They'll get all the rewards if they bring her in."

"All you think about is fucking some bitch," Alex said. "Sheesh, Dillan, you can't keep it in your pants for five minutes."

"At least he's thinking, not sleeping," Cooper said. "Get moving, Alex. And don't follow Devin. He wants to have access to those women as well."

"More than one," Dillan said. "Devin's like me."

"Lying, saying whatever you think the bitch wants to hear so you can fuck her," Alex said. "Yeah, you two are a real winning pair."

"Just because you can't get it up doesn't mean the rest of us aren't men," Dillan snapped.

Leila shook her head. They didn't sound like a cohesive unit. Conquer and divide. The sniffer would find her first. If he liked women, he might very well not tell the others he had found her. He might decide to take her for his own. She went over a bear's anatomy in her mind. The placement of her shot was important. Once she fired, she would have to move quickly. The others would hear the shot. She'd have to kill the sniffer with her first shot, even if it took him a little while to die.

"What are you implying?" Alex bristled. "I've been married and had a kid."

"That you abandoned," Cooper said. "Get the hell onto the trail and find the bitch. She's injured, so you should be able to handle it if you run across her."

Alex let out a roar, a fairly good mimic of a lion, proving he did have that DNA in him. There was a long silence, giving Leila the opportunity to check the whereabouts of Devin, the sniffer. He was much closer than she'd anticipated. Alex was heading into the forest, clearly attempting to follow Devin's tracks, but he was moving slow.

"I'm going to put a bullet in that moron's head someday," Cooper groused. "He's just about useless. I don't know why I got stuck with him."

"Whitney was pissed at you."

Leila noted immediately that the voice was calm, matter-of-fact. That man didn't seem to be someone who would rile easily. She found it interesting that Cooper was in charge, not the one who seemed the more logical choice.

"Yeah, he was, Kyle." Cooper immediately quieted talking to his friend. It was easy to hear that camaraderie in his tone. "Probably had good reason too." Now there was a shared amusement. "I capped his favorite ass-kisser."

"He's probably hoping you'll do the same to Alex so he doesn't have to," Kyle said. "You want to do it, we'll all be looking the other way."

"We'll need his gun to take out her guards. Whitney said she had at least five of Chariot's soldiers bringing her back to their compound. He wants them all dead."

Kyle laughed. "He's such a bloodthirsty asshole. He does like his petty revenges. He was mad that he got the flawed sister. That's what he called her. I'm betting Bridget was just like every other kid he fucked up. He doesn't ever want to take responsibility for what happens to them when he screws with them over and over. When he gets her sister, no matter how great she starts out, he'll turn her into a psychotic bitch no one can stand."

"Bridget is nearly catatonic. Can you imagine wanting to be paired with that?" Cooper asked.

"Alex would want her. He wouldn't have to fight too hard to get some." Kyle laughed again. "Maybe instead of capping him, we should persuade Whitney to pair him with Bridget, not Bridget with him."

"You're a mean son of a gun, Kyle," Cooper said, joining in the laughter.

Leila wished she had both men in her sights, but she had to turn her attention to Devin. She could see the man casting around on the ground and lifting his nose to scent the air. He was a big man, and rather than stand upright, he employed a strange crawl using feet and hands. His knees didn't touch the ground as he shuffled quickly over the forest floor. He stopped abruptly, remaining in that position as he looked around him.

"I know you're here." The voice was deep and had a rumble to it. "No one is going to harm you. Come out, and we'll see to your wounds."

Alex would be arriving in the next five to seven minutes. She didn't have time to engage with Devin. She took careful aim, going for a double lung shot rather than the heart. He wouldn't survive if she took out both lungs. She squeezed the trigger. The bullet flew true. She wasn't a woman who missed her target, and certainly not when he presented it to her rather close.

The sound of the gunshot would alert his team and they would come running. She couldn't remain caged in the roots of the tree. She hated giving it up when Diego had provided everything she might need for a prolonged stay, but she'd already slung her weapons around her neck and shoved the ammo into the small bag he'd left. Rolling out from the roots as soon as she fired the weapon, without even checking to see if Devin went down, she was on the move.

She could hear the labored breathing, the air escaping from the downed soldier's lungs. She leapt for the branch of a tree and nearly fell. The movement jarred her insides to the point of excruciating pain. Diego was not going to be happy with her.

Taking a deep breath, she pulled herself into the crotch of the tree and waited there until the crashing pain settled. She was surprised at how weak she was. Ordinarily, she wouldn't have exerted much energy pulling herself into a tree. She could leap high, although she had seen Diego jump at least ten feet into the air, and his forward leap was double that. He had done so effortlessly, and when he landed, he was silent, already running forward without breaking stride. She couldn't even come close to that.

Leila knew she didn't have a lot of time before every soldier— and Diego—would come after her. She climbed higher, where the foliage was much denser. The tree was sturdy, each branch strong, but she remained against the trunk. She used the thick bark as a backrest when she settled against it, arranging her weapons so she could use them in any direction. One of her greatest strengths was her ability to stay absolutely still if need be. She needed that skill now. She froze in place and, much like the great horned owl, blended into the trunk.

The sniffer was still making strange noises as if the air in his lungs was rushing out of a hole, but he had ceased rolling around on the ground. He was dying, each breath a strain. She found it heartbreaking and wished there had been a better way to ensure a kill. He had come after her like a bear would, so she had chosen the method she would use to slay a bear if it were attacking her.

She remained still as the tracker, Alex, parted the brush and peered around warily. He remained under cover for a few minutes, studying the scene. Finally, he crept slowly toward Devin, looking at the ground, studying every mark in the dirt and examining the nearby plants for signs of bruising.

"Dev." Alex kept his voice low and his finger over the trigger of his semiautomatic. "Dev, talk to me. What the hell happened? Who did this?"

Devin was on his side, his body shuddering, eyes wide open in a stare of fixed horror. His mouth gaped open as he tried to find air, but it was too late. He was already dead, his heart just hadn't realized it yet. It beat slowly and irregularly.

"Damn it, Dev." Alex got close enough to look for wounds.

The body shuddered again, and the death rattle was loud. Alex jumped back, swearing, turning in a full circle, pointing his weapon at everything.

The wind shifted minutely, sending the branches of the surrounding trees swaying. Leaves and needles fell to the forest floor. Bullfrogs set up a chorus of protests, and lizards skittered in the thick vegetation. Alex yelled and squeezed down on the trigger, a look of terror on his face as he spun around and around, shooting at the leaping shadows.

Bullets hit the tree where Leila remained motionless. He was aiming far too low to hit her, but movement might draw his eye. Several ugly thunks told her Alex had managed to hit the dead body of his friend with his wild shooting. As he fired his weapon, he yelled at the top of his lungs. There was nothing subtle about his fear. If he had gotten any paler, he would have been a ghost.

Leila followed his movements with her eyes only. The tree shivered several times as bullets hit the trunk. From somewhere above her, she heard the call of a hawk. She was certain the sound was real and not Diego, although he was so good at imitating the raptors, she wasn't sure why she thought he still wasn't close.

She couldn't feel his presence. Before she had known of Diego's existence, back when she was fighting off soldiers with Luther, she'd felt him. She'd known he was there. She hadn't known who he was, but she had felt him. Felt his energy. Everything in her reached for him. Knew him. The good in him and the darkness.

She had heard him signaling to Luther, using the birds to announce his presence. To let Luther know he was joining the battle. She'd known when he insisted on shooting all three of them with a tracking device. She'd made it clear she knew what he was up to, and she wanted no part of it. She'd also known he was ruthless enough to ignore what she wanted. That should have put her off him, but instead she found herself more intrigued than ever.

Leila didn't care for men that much. She didn't respect them. There were a few soldiers she thought were decent men who worked hard, but she stayed away from them, not trusting anyone. She had a built-in radar for the soldiers who were operating on the edge. There was a taint to them, an aura surrounding them that warned her off them. She'd known it when Leon had come to her door with his friends and forced their way in.

Diego was so certain he was dark and twisted. He thought of himself as a monster, but from the moment he'd come into her life, she had known he was different. He was a good man with a strict code of honor. Because she felt people, saw auras and could often see inside a person where no one else could, she knew the heart of him.

Since spending these few days and nights with him, not one thing he'd done or said had changed her opinion of him. He was thoughtful and kind. He listened to her and treated her with respect. He hadn't once taken advantage when he could have. Even when a part of her wanted him to. He was a gentleman, whether he thought so or not.

The raptor let out two rapid cries, alerting her to the soldiers rushing to the battle. This would be Kyle and Cooper. Deliberately she took a breath and remained very still. If she shot Alex, the two soldiers were experienced enough to follow the trajectory of a bullet. She couldn't move quickly through the trees as she would normally be able to. Her best bet would be to remain absolutely still and wait for a better opportunity to rid the world of Whitney's creations.

Where was the third soldier? What kinds of genetics did he have that might enable him to spot her? She had the precise location of Alex, who finally had gone quiet, finger off the trigger, retreating into the trees and brush to hide. The hawk had warned her that two soldiers were coming toward her fast. She had guessed

Kyle and Cooper, but it could be Dillan and one of the others. The bottom line was that the third man, whoever he was, was stalking her, and the hawk hadn't yet spotted him.

A chill slid down her spine. She was far too experienced to move, but now she had a very bad feeling. In the space of a few moments, she had gone from the hunter to the hunted. Strangely, she actually thought about trying to reach out to Diego. That stray thought was nearly as disturbing to her as the fact that there was a wild card somewhere stalking her.

When had she become dependent on Diego? Was it because she wasn't one hundred percent? A blowtorch seemed to be burning her insides. An ice pick pierced every internal organ she had, stabbing over and over. Truthfully, she felt weak and lightheaded. Diego wanted her lying prone on the ground. She realized there had been a reason for it.

Had she been operated on in the conventional way, her recovery would have taken much longer. As it was, Diego, twice a day, promoted healing. She knew it cost him in strength, but he still did it. For her. Everything he did seemed to be for her. He was a strong man, a good partner, and here she was, cowering in a tree waiting for him to come and rescue her.

The fronds of a large fern just behind the body of Devin parted to reveal a soldier. He surveyed the scene in front of him, his features impassive until his gaze settled on Alex. His jaw hardened and he glanced over his shoulder to speak to someone she couldn't see.

"Devin's dead, Cooper. I don't know if Alex killed him, but it's likely with all the bullets he wasted."

"I didn't kill him, Kyle," Alex denied, clutching his semiautomatic to his chest, his eyes wild. "He was dying when I got here."

"How?"

Alex gestured around him. "How the hell should I know?

Something out there. It sounded like he was having trouble breathing."

"Did you try CPR?" Kyle stepped out of the bed of ferns into the open. "Did you do anything at all to try to save him?"

"He was *dying*," Alex emphasized. "I didn't know what killed him. I tried to hold them off to give him a chance just in case they were still around."

Kyle gave a snort of derision. "You didn't even get close enough to see what killed him."

Cooper stepped to the very edge of the foliage. His weapon was pointed in Alex's general direction. "Unless you killed him, Alex. You better not have." He nodded toward Kyle, and the other soldier jogged across the uneven ground to crouch down beside Devin.

Leila realized Cooper was covering Kyle. Neither man trusted Alex. They really were considering that Alex might have shot Devin. Where was the loyalty with these men? Or was it just Alex they were suspicious of? She remained very still, letting the air slip silently in and out of her lungs. She couldn't afford to become distracted and caught up in the drama happening below her. She had to always be on full alert for the missing soldier.

"He was shot multiple times," Kyle reported, turning to glare at Alex. "Semiautomatic. If he wasn't dead already, you sealed the deal, Alex."

Alex shook his head frantically, fear in his expression. He was aware the other two soldiers were willing to kill him. "You should have heard the death rattles. I'm telling you, he was dying. I fired in a sweeping circle because I was certain whoever had tried to kill him was still out there, waiting to finish him off."

"Yet you didn't examine him," Kyle said. "You didn't try to help him."

"I couldn't," Alex insisted. "I had to protect him."

Cooper's eyebrow shot up. "By shooting him multiple times?"

Alex swore and stepped closer to the cover of the forest. "You're getting this all wrong. What did kill him, Kyle?" he added, clearly hoping to distract the other two.

Kyle took his time before answering. "A very well-placed bullet. The shot was a double lung hit. Best chance of killing a bear. His heart and lungs were in the same place a bear's might be. Whoever shot him knew he was bear."

He straightened slowly and took a step back. "Alex knew Devin was bear, but I don't think he's had any experience killing a bear. He wouldn't have known to take that particular shot, nor do I think he's a good enough marksman to make it."

He began casting around for signs on the ground and then looked toward the tree with the huge root system. "The bullet was fired from that direction. Shooter was low to the ground. My guess is he was hidden in the roots of that tree."

"Or she," Cooper corrected. "It could have been Bridget's sister."

"Not if she was really in as bad a shape as the radio chatter implied," Kyle said. "They made it sound as if she was at death's door. In fact, they said they thought she wasn't going to make it and to be prepared. They were ordered to bring her body back no matter what."

Fine tremors began internally in Leila's body. That wasn't a good sign. It hadn't occurred to her that weakness was going to be a factor. She'd always been in top physical condition and relied on her conditioning on any assignment she took. She couldn't do that now. She was beginning to sweat, another bad sign. Even if she could hold out, she didn't know what kinds of genetics these men had in them. Sweating could give her away just as easily as movement.

Cooper cursed and stalked over to the tree. "Alex, get the hell over here. You're supposed to be the tracker. Read the tracks. Tell me who was here and where they went."

Alex sent him a wary look and shuffled forward until he was near the tree Leila had been hiding in. She hadn't left anything behind, but the impression of her body had to be pressed into the soft ground. If the man could read tracks at all, he should be able to find her, or at least know approximately where she was.

Her heart accelerated just a little as she watched Alex cast around on the ground and even crawl partially between the roots.

"You have to see this, Kyle, or you're not going to believe it," Alex eventually called out. He sounded intrigued. Something had captured his attention.

Kyle crossed over to crouch beside him. He let out a low whistle and then threw a look over his shoulder to Cooper. "There are no tracks, just a carpet of beetles. Thousands of them. They're not only beneath the tree but surrounding it, obliterating any tracks that might have been in the dirt."

He stood up slowly and turned to the other soldier. "We're dealing with someone who is enhanced. We have to be. No way did these beetles just coincidentally show up in this exact spot. Why aren't they swarming over Devin's carcass if they're looking for food? Someone arranged this, and that person is powerful enough to take command of insects."

Kyle's voice was leery. For the first time he appeared shaken, and both Cooper and Alex recognized the shift in his demeanor.

"What are you thinking, Kyle?" Cooper demanded. "Spit it out."

Kyle sighed. "Whitney has a bad habit of sending out his soldiers to pit them against GhostWalker teams. He doesn't tell anyone what they're going up against; he just sends them. As soon as we were given this assignment, even though we were going up against Chariot's soldiers, it occurred to me to do a little research so we didn't walk into a trap."

Cooper cursed under his breath. "Are you telling me you think

Whitney sent us up against the GhostWalkers *and* Chariot's soldiers?"

"I think he should have been a little more forthcoming about who owns the land we're traveling through. You ever hear of the Campos brothers? Rubin and Diego Campos?"

There was silence after Kyle's question. Leila could have sworn Alex looked pale enough to faint.

"Don't know much about Rubin," Cooper finally conceded, "but even though he supposedly flies under the radar, rumors have turned Diego into a legend."

"Rumors aren't always true," Alex contributed.

"I think in this case," Kyle said, "we'd better treat them as if they're gospel. Rubin and Diego Campos were born right here. They still maintain the property and come up a couple of times a year to help out the locals."

"I'm going to kill Whitney myself," Cooper declared. "He sent us here to get us killed."

Kyle shook his head. "Maybe not. I checked how often and when the brothers come to this area, and they aren't scheduled for a few weeks." He pushed his hand through his hair, another display of nerves. "Having said that, it doesn't mean they haven't arrived early. Something or someone took charge of those insects. I believe it has to be a GhostWalker."

Cooper swore again. "One of them could easily have made that shot."

"Rubin plays doctor to his neighbors. He's a doctor in their unit, and they send him out on rescue missions. Diego goes along as the big gun protecting his brother and the rest of the crew," Kyle said. "If I had to guess who made that shot, I think it would have to be Diego."

Alex backed away from the tree, realized he was getting closer to the fallen Devin, and swung around and hurried across the small clearing, putting distance between the other two soldiers and himself. "We should leave. Get the hell out of here. I heard he was a damn ghost in the woods."

"Rumor, Alex, remember?" Kyle taunted.

"Don't be such an ass, Alex," Cooper added. "This is all speculation. We just have to find Bridget's sister and bring her back with us. We'll avoid any confrontation with GhostWalkers. If we're not a threat to them, they won't hunt us." There was the tiniest sneer in his voice, as if he looked down on the GhostWalkers for having a code.

Off to the left, in deeper forest, the sound of a twig snapping was muted but loud enough that all three soldiers froze. Cooper reacted first, indicating with silent hand signals for the other two to separate by several feet and enter the forest. He took up a position several feet from Kyle, so Kyle was in the middle between the two other soldiers.

Leila watched them until they were swallowed by the dense trees. The wind touched her face with wet drops. Mist. The fog that often appeared in the Appalachian Mountains was creeping in. It would provide more cover for both sides. It muffled sound and distorted sight. Diego had cautioned her about getting lost in the mountains due to the heavy forest and the shroud of dense fog.

She had a good sense of direction, and she didn't panic. It didn't occur to her that she could get turned around as many hikers had. The myths surrounding frequent disappearances usually had to do with legendary creatures, not the complexity of the land or the debilitating fog, the real reason for those disappearances. She didn't believe she would become a statistic. But she was weak.

It was necessary to decide if she was going to climb down and try to make her way back to the cabin. She'd torn something when she'd made the leap for the tree branch. All along, Diego had said she was fragile. She hadn't felt that fragile in comparison to what she had been, so she'd overestimated her abilities. She had to ask herself if she was bleeding internally. That would definitely contribute to her feeling of severe weakness.

Unease slid through her. Her body reacted to the unknown threat with a surge of adrenaline, providing the necessary strength to steady herself. The internal tremors ceased, and she very slowly slipped her knife from the scabbard at her waist. Keeping the blade tight against her wrist, she held the hilt concealed in her fist.

Listening with her acute sense of hearing, she detected something large sliding along the tree trunk above her. The tree shivered ever so slightly, alerting her, letting her know she wasn't alone in that tree. Her attacker was above her, making his way down. Slithering like a snake. This was a soldier, and he had snake in him, enough that his sense of smell had been alerted. Why hadn't he called back the others?

Leila remained still, as if frozen in place, hoping to portray a woman too frightened to move. This was the missing Dillan. Probably her sweat and heat, if he saw through heat sensors, had drawn him to her hiding place. She waited, breathing steadily. Ready.

He dropped down to the same branch, his arm circling her neck with tremendous force, pulling her sideways, away from the tree trunk. The knotted muscles in his arm locked against her throat, cutting off air.

"You stay quiet, girl. Don't make a sound. Don't fight me. Do you understand?"

She tried to nod, but he kept her immobile. She tapped his arm with her fist and let out a muffled choking sound as she slumped back into him.

"I said stay quiet," he reiterated. "We don't want company, do we?" As he reminded her, Dillan loosened his hold the tiniest bit, allowing her to draw air into her lungs. "Are you injured?"

Again, she started to answer, muffled a cough and reached up to tap his arm with her closed fist, alerting him to the fact that she was hurt.

"Can you walk?"

Once again, she raised her fist to tap his arm, only this time, her fist rose fast from his forearm. She drove her fist straight to his neck, the blade of the knife penetrating deep, severing the artery. Slamming her other elbow into his ribs, she continued the motion with her knife, stabbing deep under the armpit, cutting that artery. His arm dropped away from her, and she leapt from the tree to the forest floor. Blood poured from his wounds, and he tried to shout, to warn his companions.

The sound was somewhat muffled by the fog, but she was certain Dillan's voice carried through the trees. They would come to check on him, and she had to be ready.

Ignoring the agony radiating through her body, she ran deeper into the forest, the fog a thick gray cover. As she ran, she shoved the bloody knife back into the leather sheath. She would need it soon enough, but she wasn't taking chances. She was weaker than she liked, and she wasn't about to fall on her own blade. The soldiers would be coming, and she wasn't going to be taken to Whitney. The man was mad. Totally insane. She saw what he did to her sister, and going to Whitney's compound as a prisoner wasn't going to happen.

The moment the forest swallowed her completely, she stopped moving. Movement produced sounds. If she was going to ensure those men didn't take her to Whitney, she would have to hunt them. One at a time. There was no way, in her condition, that she could take on all three at once.

Leila considered her options. If she waited, hoping Diego would show up so she didn't have to move around, she feared the three soldiers would eventually find her. No, it was far better to hunt them. Once she made up her mind, she didn't hesitate. Ignoring her protesting body, she hurried toward the tree where Dillan's body was sprawled in the branches.

The sight was macabre, blood running in rivers down the trunk of the tree. The body hung partially upside down, swaying, caught only by one arm and one leg. The fog concealed the hideous sight one moment and then revealed it the next when the wind drew the veil of gray back.

Cooper burst from the trees, swearing loudly, spinning around in a circle and then staring up at his teammate. "Kyle, that son of a bitch killed Dillan."

Leila could see Kyle crouched close to the ground, examining the dirt and plants for tracks, for anything that might tell him who or what had managed to kill Dillan.

"If I didn't know better, Cooper," Kyle said, straightening, "I'd say the woman did this. If it was Campos, he's got the smallest feet imaginable. But no woman would get the drop on Dillan. It just wouldn't happen."

Leila rolled her eyes, but her attention was on Alex. The man hadn't gone near the body. He was still in the forest, not setting foot into the clearing. She circled around to get behind him, working slowly and carefully through the brush. A thousand ice picks stabbed at her insides with every step she took. Her body felt a little like lead. She was going to have to end this fast if she was going to prevail.

She smelled fear when she came up behind Alex. The wind blew steadily now, taking the fog with it, spreading that gray veil through the trees. She went to the ground, propelling herself forward using toes and elbows to get close to Alex. The noises he made were annoying, a whining hiccup as he rocked himself and stroked his finger over the trigger of his semiautomatic.

Leila rose up behind him fast, slamming the blade of her knife, all the way to the hilt, into the back of his neck, severing the spinal cord. She didn't bother to retrieve the knife; she didn't have that kind of time. She turned and sprinted into deeper forest. Kyle had already shown he was adept at reading tracks. She didn't want to give him an easy trail to her. There was no running a distance, not when her strength was fading. She took to the trees, turning back, circling around, using the branches to move from one tree to the next until she found one close to Alex's body that was dense with foliage.

"He fuckin' killed Alex right under our noses," Cooper snapped. "Which way did he go?"

Kyle nodded toward the interior. "Took off running to the west."

Cooper knelt beside Alex, removing his weapon and ammo belt before slinging it around his neck. "You still think it was the woman?"

"I said no woman could have done this," Kyle corrected. Already, he was following the tracks leading him deeper into the forest.

Cooper stayed beside Alex's body, going through his pockets. He even took money from the wallet Alex had on him. He pocketed the cell phone and one bracelet and then sat back, holding his head in his hands as if grieving. Leila knew he disliked Alex, but he must have felt responsible for him. He looked stricken—and he wasn't paying attention to his surroundings.

She waited, once more completely still, fading into the tree, not moving a muscle. Time ticked by—time she didn't have. Kyle would discover she'd taken to the trees. She hadn't laid too long of a trail on the ground. Cooper finally sighed and stood up, facing her, presenting several targets. She was fast and accurate with a knife, and she didn't hesitate. She threw one into his heart, burying the blade deep. A second followed to sink into his lower abdomen. As he turned, the third knife severed the carotid artery.

Cooper went to his knees, blood pouring from the three wounds, the rifle hitting the ground as he dropped it.

"Not bad." Kyle's voice came out of the fog. "I knew you wouldn't be able to resist the bait." He stayed hidden, not taking chances. "You may as well show yourself, Campos."

He had set up his friend to die so he could double back and catch his opponent.

She wasn't the best at throwing her voice, but with the fog and dense foliage, she decided to take the chance. She wouldn't be using a knife. This required a gun, and if there was one thing she was very skilled in, it was hitting a target, close up or far away.

"Not Diego," she said, keeping her voice low. Still, it carried on the wind to him.

His head jerked up and he narrowed his eyes. "You want me to believe you bested Dillan? And then Cooper?"

"And your bear and the coward. Four of the five of you. Little old me. A woman." She poured a taunt into her voice. Contempt. Amusement. Kyle was the type of man she'd run across so many times. He believed men were far superior to women. He couldn't conceive of Leila wiping out his entire team.

She studied her target carefully. He had an idea of where she was and was careful to turn sideways, presenting the least amount of targets to her. She took aim. Gave a slow exhale. She pulled the trigger. One shot. One. The bullet flew true, just as she'd known it would. She'd practiced enough. When she aimed at something, she hit it.

Leila jumped from the branch to the ground, inhaling sharply as her insides jarred her. For a moment, darkness swirled around her, but she fought it off and made her way to where Kyle lay on the ground, writhing, desperate for air. The sucking sound was audible.

She kicked his rifle away and squatted beside him. "I killed the bear with this shot. You saw it for yourself and yet were so certain you didn't have to be afraid of a woman. You should have been. You had the evidence right in front of your eyes, but you refused to believe."

She didn't end him mercifully. She walked away, leaving him fighting for every breath, knowing he wouldn't last long, but he'd have time to think about sacrificing his friend and colleague just to die himself.

She put as much distance between them as possible, heading in the direction of the cabin. She knew she wasn't going to make it back to the safety of Diego's home, but she tried.

11

Don't you die on me," Diego whispered. "Use that stubborn nature of yours to stay alive." His heart pounded and he tasted fear. Real fear. He hadn't known fear since he was a child. When a man didn't care if he lived or not, he didn't fear death. But now . . . now there was Leila.

He examined her quickly, right there on the trail with night falling and the fog thickening. She had torn loose three of the repairs and was bleeding internally. He had to make a quick choice—treat her there and stop the bleeding or take her back to the cabin and hope she didn't lose too much blood before he could work on her.

Diego was a decisive man. He always had been. Performing surgery psychically would take a huge toll on him. He wouldn't be able to get them back to the cabin. And she needed blood, a transfusion. He couldn't give that to her without setting everything up for him to crash afterward. They needed the safety of a shelter.

"Damn it, woman." He lifted her and began to run up the trail toward his cabin. Each step jarred her. He knew he could be hurting her worse, but he had to sacrifice smoothness for speed.

She made no sound. He wasn't even certain if she was fully aware of everything around her. The evening was wet and gloomy after a beautiful day. That boded ill, an ominous warning that everything could go wrong in a single heartbeat. Diego knew all about wrong. All about having anything worthwhile ripped away from him.

Not you, sweetheart. Fuckin' universe doesn't get to take you away from me. He picked up his pace. *Don't leave me, woman. You're strong. Fight for us.*

Diego figured he should have told her to fight for her baby. Her daughter. Little Grace. That was more likely a bigger incentive. But he wanted to be the reason she chose to stay.

There was a faint stirring in his mind. She poured in, but slowly, filling his mind with her. It was an astonishing feat when she wasn't naturally telepathic.

Not going anywhere. Just super tired.

She sounded tired. She felt tired to him. The strength of how worn she was terrified him. She was bleeding internally, and that so easily could be the death of her. He increased his speed, staying to the wider trail he rarely used when he traveled up the mountain. He had always preferred the game trails to the rough road where he might encounter others. There were times when hikers or neighbors were on the road, forcing him to interact with them. He always did so in a cultivated, easy manner when he didn't feel any of those things.

You have a right to be tired after hunting the enemy the way you did. He wanted to keep her alert. Tied to him. The more they spoke intimately, mind to mind, the closer they became. It was impossible to be in someone's mind and not see the heart of them. Not know what they were truly like as a human being. Or what enhancement did to them.

Reading Leila simply caused him to want to be with her more than ever. He doubted if that closeness would have the same effect on her once she could see into him.

Amusement burst through his mind. He found himself, despite the circumstances, reacting to her sense of humor. *The Leila effect*, he told her. *Lightening the load.*

Well, you are rather silly sometimes, Diego. You always want to think the worst of yourself. You crack me up. You're running up the mountain, carrying me on your shoulder, intending to save my life for the second time, and you want me to think the worst of you.

Put like that, it did sound a little whacked. *Selfish reasons, woman. I want you for myself. Think of it as the big bad mountain man claiming the sweet little innocent woman and carrying her off to his lair.*

Just as he knew it would, her soft laughter poured into his mind again. He loved the way she viewed life. She could have been bitter and resentful, but instead, she looked for good. She found humor in things others wouldn't. She made him see the humor in situations he would never have found amusing.

Sweet? Innocent? I just hunted and dispatched five strangers. In anyone else's book, I wouldn't be referred to as sweet and innocent.

Let's remember they were assholes.

The cabin came into sight, and relief flooded him instantly. He had the door to his house open and took her straight through to the bedroom to put her on the bed in record time. Shrugging out of the various packs and weapons he carried, he hurried through the cabin, gathering everything they would need once he crashed. And he was going to crash big-time.

"Okay, babe, I'm going to set us up for the transfusion. Don't expend any energy until I've had a chance to assess the situation with you and then repair any damage. Once I do that, I'll transfuse you, but again, remember, I'm going to go down hard."

Her long lashes fluttered and then lifted. He found himself

looking into her vivid green eyes. There was censure there. Apprehension. There was also a nameless emotion he wasn't used to seeing when anyone looked at him.

"I don't like you doing this, Diego." Her voice was a low murmur.

He peeled off his jacket and began to insert needles into the arm that would be closest to him. "Babe, really? You're bleeding internally."

"But you take on those same injuries when you're healing me, don't you?" Her gaze remained steady on him. "You're risking too much."

"I'd risk anything to save your life, Leila." He was absolute. Firm. Decisive. "You just relax and let me see what we're facing."

He had the needles in his arm and hers. He removed his boots and sat on the bed, facing her. "I've put everything you need, including weapons, on your side of the bed, just like last time. You have lights and anything else you might need while I'm out."

Diego placed his palms just above her abdomen and reached for the well of healing energy inside him. The moment his hands were in place, he felt the shifting, the heating inside him. The heat imaging mapped out the bleeding and the areas where the jarring of her body had damaged those sites all over again.

There was no use wasting time on cursing. Leila had done what she had to do to stay alive. He had to do whatever was necessary to keep her alive. For him, there was no alternative.

"It's going to get hot, to the point of being uncomfortable, sweetheart," he warned. He despised hurting her when he knew she was already in pain. "If you pass out, it's all to the good. Just saying I'm sorry before it gets too bad."

Again, her eyelashes fluttered and rose, and he was looking at all that vivid green. "I'm sorry for putting you in this position. And if anything goes wrong for either of us, just know I wouldn't trade my time with you for anything."

Clever little demon one-upped him. He wasn't good at the hearts-and-flowers thing. She needed him to kill a man for her, he was all over that. He could show his love for her that way, but finding the right poetic words wasn't going to happen.

He didn't reply, turning his focus inward, mapping out every torn and bleeding wound. He had one fleeting thought that his brother could have done a much better job, but he pushed the moment of doubt away and began to work. He was all she had, and that meant he had to be enough.

For the next two hours, he was lost in a world of blood and damaged organs, operating with skills he didn't believe he had until he had no choice. He was meticulous about every touch of heat he applied, welding over the rips and tears until her veins and arteries were smooth and holding. Until every organ was once again functioning properly. Only then did he come back to himself, swaying, his body in agony. His insides felt as if he'd taken a blowtorch to them.

Careful not to move around too much—he feared he was now bleeding internally—he stretched out beside Leila, took a long drink of water and began the transfusion between the two of them. He closed his eyes and breathed through the pain.

How had Rubin done this over and over? Diego had watched his brother do surgery on some of the worst wounds possible, and yet he'd survived. A few times it had been close, but never once had Rubin complained. Jonquille, his wife, had once saved Rubin's life by taking on the terrible wounds he'd suffered. He'd seen this scenario play out multiple times over the years, but he hadn't felt what Rubin had. He'd set himself up as Rubin's protector, not his aide, when it came to healing.

He wished he'd learned from his brother. Rubin was an incredible psychic surgeon, risking his life without hesitation to save others. Diego guarded him carefully and ensured that those around him wanted to do the same. Rubin detested that he was surrounded by a unit of men willing to take a bullet for him. He would have been furious had he known Diego had added to the men's need to protect him. He used his voice to influence subtly whenever possible. He felt he could have used Rubin's help right at that moment. He was going down and was fairly desperate for someone to watch over Leila for him.

～

Rubin drove the four-wheel-drive pickup up the mountain as fast as the vehicle would allow him to travel. Using four-wheel drive slowed everything down going up the rugged terrain. He did push it to the maximum speed on any of the straighter stretches, but those were few and far between.

First, he'd gone over everything Diego had said before he left, and Rubin had gotten a bad feeling. He found Diego's parked truck in the space below Luther's home, where they often left a vehicle. He'd gone to check with Luther, knowing the old man would have a finger on Diego's mental state. Instead of Luther, he found dead bodies strewn all over the vast acreage.

Going up the mountain, he stuck to the road until he saw vultures circling near the gorge. He found more dead bodies. Alarmed, he continued. There was another problem area with more bodies. It looked as if his mountain was a war zone.

Pulling the truck up to the cabin, he was instantly aware it was occupied. He'd seen the tracks of his brother running up the road. He was carrying someone. Ordinarily, his tracks were light or nonexistent. He hadn't even tried to hide them. Instead, he ran fast, uncaring that someone might be able to track him. That was out-of-character behavior and meant someone was in need of medical assistance.

He opened the cabin door and found himself looking down the

barrel of a gun. The woman aiming the weapon at him was pale, weak and slumped in the bed beside Diego. She also wore an expression that told him she would pull the trigger if he presented a threat to them. Diego was transfusing her, but he looked out of it.

As a rule, if someone were to enter their cabin, it would be Diego guarding everyone. The fact that he'd barely stirred was more alarming than ever. Ignoring the gun aimed at him, he crossed the room to his brother's side.

"What's happening here, Diego?" Rubin asked, removing the needle from his brother's arm. "There are dead bodies strewn all over the mountain. I called for cleanup, but it's going to take a miracle."

Diego barely opened his eyes to acknowledge he knew who was beside him. Alarm spread. There were no visible injuries on Diego, but something was really wrong.

Rubin helped Diego lie back against the pillows. "I need to look you over. Are you wounded?"

"Help Leila first." Diego didn't open his eyes. He knew he was in a precarious position. He'd never once indicated to Rubin that he was capable of psychic surgery. When Rubin examined Leila, he would know. "She was shot. Lost her spleen. Had to try to repair several organs, veins and an artery. She was running around today, fighting off soldiers. Ripped things open. Did the best I could for her, but she needs an expert."

Diego didn't want anyone else helping Leila. He wanted her to view him as the one man who would sacrifice anything for her, but the truth was, Rubin was unbelievable as a surgeon. Whether hands-on or psychic, Diego didn't know anyone better. He had instincts that never seemed to fail. Sure hands. That well of healing in him was unbelievably strong. Diego wanted what was best for Leila, and sadly, it wasn't him.

"I take it Leila is the name of the woman aiming a gun at me."

There was a low note of amusement in Rubin's voice despite the situation.

"Rubin is my brother, Leila. He's an amazing doctor. His skills as a surgeon are legendary. He's going to examine you and fix anything I may have missed."

Fingers stroked featherlight caresses over his hand. Tentatively. Barely there. He managed to turn his head, although it took tremendous effort. Leila lay beside him, eyes closed, breathing a little labored, but her fingers were moving over the back of his hand. He turned his hand to capture hers, threading them together, needing her touch as much as he needed Rubin to fix everything that could possibly be wrong.

You didn't miss anything. I don't want anyone else. You saved me the first time, and I know you did just as well this time.

They were connected so closely that it didn't shock him that despite the fact that she wasn't telepathic, she had found the pathway without his aid. The only problem was that pathway included Rubin.

"You performed surgery on this woman, Diego?"

Diego deliberately kept his eyes closed. He knew Rubin thought he had cut her open and performed surgery in the accepted sense of the word.

"She was going to die if I didn't," Diego explained. "And stop calling her 'this woman.' Her name is Leila, and she's *my* woman."

A long silence ensued, but Diego didn't take the bait. He didn't open his eyes. He was too exhausted. He simply shifted just a little closer to Leila until the heat of his body seeped into the coolness of hers. He wanted to put his arm around her, but his body felt like lead. After the run up the mountain, a difficult healing session and giving blood, he had crashed.

"Diego." Rubin's tone was cautionary. "You're certain you aren't wounded? This is unlike you."

"Just tired, Rubin," he assured.

Again, there was a silence. He heard Rubin moving around the room, shifting positions so he was kneeling on the other side of Leila.

"If I didn't know better, I'd think you crashed after using a psychic talent."

That tone was one Rubin used when he wanted to throw his opponent off the track and make it seem as if he had no real interest in the subject. What it really meant was that his extremely intelligent brain was computing information at a rapid rate, and he would puzzle out exactly what was truth and what wasn't.

"You're going to find out as soon as you examine her. I did my best, but I'm not you." He made the admission because he truly had no choice.

Again, there was silence. Diego pried his eyes open just enough to see his brother bending over Leila, his palms inches from her body as he examined her. Rubin was thorough, moving carefully from the top of her head to her toes, and then his hands moved back to her middle. His palms remained over her abdomen for so long Diego couldn't keep his eyes open.

I don't think I can do this. Leila sounded shaky.

All his body wanted to do was sleep, but he couldn't leave Leila alone with Rubin while he allowed himself to drift off. She'd gone through hell and was nervous having another man show up when she was so vulnerable.

Rubin is my brother, sweetheart. He's the best man I know. You're safe with him.

He's married. You said he was married. If something goes wrong, just with him healing me, he could be in trouble. I'm worried enough about you. I don't want him on my conscience.

She was telling him the truth, and yet there was more to it than that. She didn't trust Rubin. She had reason not to trust men, and she was in a very vulnerable position. What he couldn't understand was why she didn't feel Rubin's true character. His absolute goodness.

I'm right here, sweetheart, he soothed. *I won't pass out. You're safe, I give you my word on that. And there truly isn't anyone better at this.*

He felt her clinging to him, her mind solidly in his. This was a woman who single-handedly destroyed her enemies when she was injured. The fact that she turned to him, trusted him, sent him soaring when he wasn't a man who soared. She'd introduced quite a few firsts in his life. Just the fact that she was counting on him gave him the added strength to stay alert.

What can he do that you didn't do?

Diego recognized that she was distracting herself, still clinging to him, needing him to talk to her so she didn't think about a stranger invading her privacy. She would be humiliated when she realized Rubin could hear her. Rubin was a strong telepath, every bit as strong as Diego. The two had been using telepathy since they were children. The more they'd talked to each other mind to mind, the more their abilities grew in strength. Now they did so without thought.

I don't have his expertise, Leila. The repairs he makes will hold up far better than what I did.

He felt her instant protest, and again, there was a visceral reaction of joy. He hadn't experienced joy in his life. Not ever that he could remember. She'd given that to him. She believed in him. He knew, because she was in his mind, that she could see who he truly was—not the white knight she persisted in calling him but the predator stalking enemies. She had to know that when he hunted, he was more animal than man, yet she accepted those traits in him.

Rubin lifted his hands away from Leila and sank back, his face pale. It was the first time Diego wasn't able to help him, although he tried to force his leaden body to work. Rubin needed care.

"Don't move," Rubin ordered. "She was in good shape. You did an extraordinary job, Diego. We'll be talking about that later when I'm not so tired."

Diego wasn't looking forward to that talk. He sent his brother a half grin. "Thanks for taking care of her for me."

"Didn't want a major lawsuit on our hands," Rubin said, giving him that same grin.

It was a relief to know they were in sync. Rubin might have a few hard questions for him, but he was Rubin. He rarely lost his temper.

"You take a bullet or knife?" The question was asked casually.

Leila gasped and turned her head toward Diego. "Did you? You've been hauling me around, doing surgery, taking care of me, protecting me, and you didn't say anything. How could I not know?"

"Babe, he was just asking the question. He intends to examine me next and is seeking information. That's all."

I notice you didn't answer the question. This time, Rubin was careful to send his statement only to Diego.

I don't want her agitated. She's in very fragile health, as you well know.

Who is she to you?

Diego made the effort to turn his head and look his brother directly in the eyes. *She's my Jonquille.* By stating Leila was to him what Jonquille was to Rubin, he knew his brother would understand exactly what she meant to him.

If she's yours, Diego, take it from someone who has made a million mistakes already: Don't keep anything from her. Not anything. It isn't worth the misunderstandings that can occur.

Diego had never witnessed any discord between Jonquille and Rubin, but Rubin was sincerely imparting advice. Diego had nothing to base relationship behavior on other than the few observations he'd made with his fellow GhostWalkers and their wives.

"Had a couple of close calls earlier," he admitted reluctantly. "During the fight at Luther's place. Burned my shoulder and biceps. Took some flesh wounds, nothing to write home about."

"Diego." Leila just said his name. Whispered it.

It was the way she said his name that got to him. As if she could barely breathe at the thought that he might have gotten hurt. His heart clenched painfully in his chest. In all the years he'd been alive, he had never heard that particular tone. Not once. Not even when he was a child.

"Told you, sweetheart, I'm perfectly fine."

"You're not," she protested. "You can't move. Your brother just performed surgery, and yet he's more alert than you are."

"Diego performed the surgery first and took on the damages," Rubin explained. "I reinforced what he did, but there wasn't damage for me to take on. Using this particular gift takes a toll, mostly because we expend a tremendous amount of energy. I suspect Diego was running on empty even before he used his healing abilities."

Leila turned her head to meet Rubin's eyes. "What does that mean?"

"It just means he's extremely tired. I'm going to take a look at him to ensure that physically he's fine. I may want to strangle him with my bare hands every now and then, but he's my brother, so he's safe."

"From you," she muttered and turned back to Diego. Her fingers tightened in his.

Rubin laughed. "She's got your number, Diego. A smart woman. He will make you crazy," he cautioned.

"You're supposed to be on my side, Rubin," Diego said. He closed his eyes and leaned his head all the way back. Now that his warrior woman was settling, he felt he could rest. "Tell her all the good things about me so she doesn't want to run off."

All the teasing went out of Rubin's voice. "You'll never find a better man than Diego, Leila, and that's the truth. He's loyal and protective, and he'll stand with you no matter what. You'll always be able to count on him. But he will drive you absolutely insane."

Leila's soft laughter played along Diego's nerve endings.

"You could have left that last part out, Rubin." Diego brought Leila's hand to his chest, right over his heart.

"Didn't want her to think I was lying about you."

His brother. Diego felt a smile well up. Leila had given him that gift. He loved Rubin but never acknowledged to himself what that emotion really was. He'd always called it protective. Loyalty, just as Rubin had described him. He wouldn't have said he was genuinely capable of love. Maybe he shied away from that emotion because once acknowledged, his heart could be ripped out.

"He was, baby," Diego said. "Not about me driving you insane. I'll be doing that. Can't help it."

"I know you will because you're a teensy bit bossy, and so am I." There was that sweet note of humor, almost a little girlish giggle. Everything about Leila was unexpected.

"Got a daughter to protect," Diego informed Rubin as his brother made his way around the bed to Diego's side. "You're going to be an uncle as soon as we make things official."

He felt Rubin's shock. Leila had to as well. Her fingers tightened in his again, and he pressed her palm against his heart.

"A daughter?"

"Name's Grace," Diego continued. "Leila is Luther's niece. Technically great-niece. I prefer 'great' because that makes Luther great, Rubin. He always wanted that title."

Leila laughed softly. "I can't wait to tell Luther your theory. I wasn't certain how he was going to take finding out he had two great-nieces, and we were bringing a war to his doorstep." The laughter faded, and there was guilt in her mind. "He didn't hesitate.

Not for one second. He didn't even question the relationship. Bridget looks like his sister, apparently. He took one look at her and immediately took us in."

"Luther's a good man," Rubin said. "Let me take care of Diego, Leila, and then I'd like to hear about your daughter and this war you brought to Luther."

"She didn't bring it," Diego corrected. "That was the choice of Commander Chariot. He sent his soldiers after her. They were seriously fucked-up, Rubin. Willing to rape her when she was shot all to hell. Chariot is having the same problems Whitney has. Too many enhancements shoved into the men, and they can't handle the aggression."

His voice was a low whip of sound. He couldn't help the sudden animosity welling up. He could be every bit as aggressive as or more so than the soldiers who had come after Leila. The difference was he had Rubin and the code of honor they lived by. It didn't matter how many predatory animals vied for supremacy in him. A part of him always clung to his humanity.

"Is Chariot aware you put his soldiers in the ground?" Rubin used his casual tone, the one that always alerted Diego to trouble. Rubin knew him, knew he would send a hard message to the commander and mean every word.

Rubin knelt beside Diego, his palms moving over him, starting at the top of his head. Diego took the opportunity to catalogue everything his brother did. He needed to learn as much as possible from him while he could. He had no intentions of having a career as a psychic surgeon, but he was going to be a family man. As such, he wanted to be able to supply his family with whatever they needed—including medical care.

"The sisters were taken by the government before Luther was ever aware of their existence," Diego said.

Leila nodded. "They took Bridget and gave her to Whitney. I would hear things, mostly through Marcy Chariot, the commander's wife. She knew I needed to know Bridget was alive, and she kept track of her as best she could."

"When Chariot sent his soldiers after Leila, he must have made a deal with Whitney to return Bridget to him, because those taking Leila were bringing her up the mountain to a helicopter that would take her back to the compound in Maryland."

Diego once again caught up Leila's hand to link their fingers. He needed the closeness with her but, more importantly, found he needed the intimacy between them. He felt protective of her and wanted her to feel his presence at all times, particularly when they were discussing difficult subjects like the kidnapping of her sister. She needed to feel that he was always on her side, that he would always have her back. She'd never had that, and he wanted to be the one to give her that confidence.

"Bridget was taken down the mountain to trucks waiting to transport her to Whitney." Diego continued the explanation. "When the second wave of soldiers came to take Leila, it was Whitney's soldiers attacking, not Chariot's."

Rubin frowned. "Chariot and Whitney conspired to take Leila and her sister?"

Diego nodded. "I wanted to make it very clear to Chariot that he would be dealing with me. That Leila isn't going back, and we're coming for Grace."

Leila shook her head. "It will be an all-out war, Diego. You know I don't want to be responsible for that. I can go back, bide my time, and when I'm ready, take Grace with me and run."

"Not happening, Leila," Diego said. "If Chariot is so brainless that he'd continue to pit his soldiers against GhostWalkers, that's on him, not you. In any case, that doesn't get us Bridget back. We have to find out what's happening with her. Hopefully, Luther managed to get her back, but if he didn't, we'll have to track her to wherever Whitney has her."

"There is another way, Diego," Rubin said. Finished with the exam, he stretched out on the floor on top of his sleeping bag. "One that might avoid bloodshed."

"Leila is staying with me, and we're taking the baby back," Diego said firmly.

"There's no other outcome," Rubin agreed. "The baby is family. She belongs with us. With the GhostWalkers, just as Leila does."

"Did you see the number of soldiers they sent after me?" Leila asked. She poured into Diego's mind. *He doesn't understand that they'll do anything to keep Grace and me. Chariot made it clear through his men that I had to come back if I wanted to have Gracie in my life.*

"Leila," Rubin said, "I've been sharing space in my brother's head since he was three. Maybe before that. I can hear every word you say."

Leila's green eyes blazed fire at Diego. "You could have said."

"Babe, seriously? Rubin's giving you the heads-up, but you would have figured it out soon enough. You weren't paying attention."

"That's not an excuse or an explanation. I'm your partner. You don't leave me hanging like that. It just makes me feel more vulnerable than I already do."

He liked that she explained her emotions to him. He wasn't a man to guess. He liked things clear and direct. He brought her knuckles to his mouth and brushed a kiss over them. "Understood. It won't happen again." He leaned over and brushed another kiss on the top of her head.

She flashed him a tentative smile. "I can see you're never going to stay in trouble for long."

"That will be a first," Diego assured. He turned to Rubin. "You have a better idea to keep my family together?"

Rubin nodded. "I believe I do. Diplomacy sometimes works far better than violence, Diego. In this case, I think it would be best if we pursued that avenue first."

"Diplomatic channels?" Diego echoed. "Seriously? When has that ever gotten us anywhere? The powers that be want to sweep our existence under the table."

"True, they'd rather forget how we got the way we are. But they also know each team backs up the others. We stick together. If every general running a team, as well as our team leader, shows up and confronts Chariot and his people, do you think they'll turn us down? They'll see the underlying threat, and they won't want any part of it."

Diego turned the idea over and over in his mind. "My fear is they'll stall before they'll consent to see us, Rubin. We need to get Grace as soon as possible. For all we know, they could be enhancing her. I wouldn't put it past them."

"I think we can rely on Major General Tennessee Milton to ensure the meeting takes place immediately."

"And Bridget, if Luther hasn't been able to get her back from Whitney?"

"We cross one bridge at a time. Let's secure little Grace and ensure no one can get to her. Once we know she's safe, we can concentrate our efforts on finding Bridget. Leila is going to need a few days anyway to recover before she can safely go into action. We could try the diplomatic approach, at least set it in motion while she's recovering," Rubin suggested.

Diego turned his head to look straight into Leila's eyes. He wasn't making the decision for her. If she wanted to go after Grace the moment she was able, he would be right there with her. He wanted her to know that.

12

Diego wasn't in the least surprised that Rubin waited several hours until Leila fell asleep before signaling him to go outside. There was no putting it off or getting around it: Diego knew he owed his brother explanations. He wasn't looking forward to it though.

Rubin had spent the time unloading supplies from his truck and putting everything away neatly, as was their way. They were both used to keeping the cabin clean and neat. They preferred outdoors and open spaces. The cabin was on the small side, so in order to be comfortable, they'd learned to keep everything in its place.

Diego followed Rubin outside to one of their favorite spots. They had carved out two downed tree trunks years earlier, making comfortable seats so they could view the night sky. Stars were abundant when they were lucky and there was no fog. The building site for the cabin had been carefully selected to get the most sun for growing vegetables. The forest had often tried to reclaim the area, but they kept the trees and brush from growing too close. They were always cognizant of escape routes, but they wanted an unob-structed view.

Rubin was silent for a long time, looking up at the sky and the drifting clouds. Twice he cast a furtive glance at Diego but re-frained from speaking. Diego had been reading Rubin all his life. Rubin had been his closest ally and his best friend. As much as Diego protected him, Rubin reciprocated. For many years, it had been the two of them against the rest of the world.

Diego was aware he'd hurt Rubin by not disclosing his ability as a psychic surgeon. Rubin would look at it as a matter of trust. It wasn't that, and Diego had to find the right words to explain, even knowing Rubin would reject the explanation.

"Before we get into anything else, we're going to address your mental health, Diego," Rubin said. "I know you're going to tell me you're fine now, especially because you found Leila, but you aren't. You're a doctor. You're intelligent. Depression is a real illness and has to be acknowledged and addressed. You have to remain vigi-lant the rest of your life if you're going to survive. And I need you to survive."

Diego stared up at the stars, knowing everything his brother said was the truth. He would have times when he had to fight the destructive thoughts in his head in order to stay alive.

"Just because I have Jonquille doesn't mean you get to leave me. I have as many issues from our childhood as you do," Rubin con-tinued. "Maybe they aren't the same, but I have them. It's always been the two of us. You don't get to decide you're not going to be here because you think I'll be fine. You don't get to make that de-cision."

Diego wisely didn't argue with his brother. Rubin needed to state what was on his mind, and Diego had always listened to him. He detested that he'd hurt Rubin—and he had. He hadn't meant to. He should have gone to his brother and talked things over with him. He hadn't because he knew Rubin would insist on him getting help. How? Diego had never been able to figure that one out.

Who did a man like him talk to? Would he be pulled off the team? When he was working, he was perfectly fine. It was the downtime that was the danger zone. He wasn't about to go to a therapist and have them declare him psychotic. Given his lack of emotion when he pulled the trigger, he knew that very well could be a diagnosis.

He'd trained himself from early childhood not to feel anything—at least, he believed he'd done that. His mother thought he'd been born psychotic, but he wanted to believe Luther—that she'd programmed him to think the worst of himself.

"Having Leila isn't going to make it easier in the long run. This is something you have to address head-on, Diego. Especially if you're going to allow this woman and any children to rely on you. You can't suddenly take yourself out of their lives because you're having a bad time."

Diego waited, but Rubin had fallen silent and was regarding him expectantly. Diego shoved his hand through his hair. "You're right, Rubin. Absolutely right. I've known I needed help with this, but I wasn't certain what to do. If I take medication, Joe could easily pull me off the team."

Joe Spagnola, their commanding officer, was a fair man, but he had to follow protocol. If he knew one of his men was suicidal, he would have no choice but to pull him from the team.

"If I talk to a therapist, I'm in the same boat," Diego said. "They'd report me, and Joe would have to act. Working is what keeps me going. When I'm working, I feel I have purpose. When I have no one to look after or protect, that's when the demons start talking in my head."

"What do your demons say, Diego?" Rubin asked quietly.

Diego shrugged, but he knew Rubin wasn't going to let him off the hook. And he didn't want his brother to just let it go. He wanted to survive for Leila. For Grace. He wanted to have Leila keep looking at him as if he were someone worthwhile.

Rubin didn't push him. He waited in silence, but Diego could feel the weight of his eyes. That penetrating stare. Rubin knew what he was going to say, but he didn't relent; he made Diego admit it aloud.

"I'm worthless. I'm a killer, born that way. My only use is to protect you from harm. That when Whitney enhanced me, he enhanced every killer trait I had and added to them. That I'm a danger to others."

Rubin nodded. "So, essentially, everything our mother programmed you to believe, and then Whitney took over her bullshit to reinforce every bullshit thing she said to you."

Diego knew that was the truth. He'd like to believe he'd overcome the things his mother had drilled into him daily—not only verbally, but she'd used a switch and a belt to try to beat the devil out of him. She hadn't managed to do so, no matter how hard she tried. She prayed constantly around him. She did her best to convince his sisters he was a "bad seed."

Diego nodded his assent. "Her voice is forever in my mind."

Rubin leaned toward him. "She was as mad as a hatter. I tried to tell you when we were kids, but she was so focused on you, and the moment my back was turned, she was on you."

Diego was shocked at the guilt in Rubin's voice. His brother was only ten months older, yet it was clear he felt responsible for the things his mother had done to Diego.

"You stood for me when no one else would," Diego pointed out. "I've always been grateful."

"You shouldn't have to be grateful. I know she convinced you that, somehow, I was so much better than you, but it isn't true. It was never true." Rubin regarded him for a moment and then swore, something he rarely did. "Stop looking at me like that. Do you have any idea how difficult it was for me to know she was beating you and blaming you for everything that went wrong? Especially when it was her fault. Do you hear me, Diego? The reason we didn't have enough food most of the time was her crappy decisions. She was good at pushing the blame onto your shoulders, and after a while, you just gave in. You believed her."

There was truth in what Rubin said. Even Luther had pointed it out. It wasn't that Diego couldn't see the truth—his mind didn't accept it. He'd been the outsider in his own family. The devil using magic even when he brought home food. Somewhere along the line, he'd stopped fighting and just accepted. It had been the only way he could survive.

"You became my purpose for living, Rubin," Diego admitted. "You stood for me. You interfered when she took the skin off me. You were my hero, and I wasn't ever going to allow anything to happen to you."

"She fuckin' programmed you to believe you were a dangerous psychopath. She was always delusional, as far back as I can remember. Toward the end, she hallucinated. Her hallucinations were always about demons and angels. She needed someone to be the devil, and she assigned you to that role."

Rubin didn't use the word "fuck." Not ever. It was an indication that he was really upset. Diego was good at feeling and reading energy, and rage was pouring off Rubin in waves. Looking at him, one would never know. Rubin looked perfectly calm, but Diego was in his mind, and there was that dark energy swirling around him, ready to swallow them both.

Diego realized Rubin wasn't angry with him. He was angry with their mother. Rubin had always been the voice of reason, even at a very young age. He could get their mother to listen to his logic when no one else could.

Rubin pushed his hand through his hair, and that nearly made Diego smile. He had the same mannerisms when he was agitated. He'd hero-worshiped Rubin from the moment he was born, and time had reinforced the way he felt about his brother. He hadn't realized for a long time just how many of Rubin's mannerisms he had.

"The demon in your head is our mother, Diego. She's that voice. The one telling you that you're worthless. You aren't. When Jonquille came into my life, you must have felt pushed aside. I didn't mean for that to happen. You're every bit as important to me. I believe we both have a codependency, and that's okay. That's how we survived. When I was adding Jonquille to my life, I assumed she was enriching your life as well. I should have talked with you."

"I love Jonquille. I'm happy you found her, Rubin. I don't want you to think for a minute that she's not family to me. She's been wonderful and makes a point of including me."

Rubin remained silent. Waiting. He wasn't going to allow Diego to get away with his simple statement. He wanted more. That was Rubin. Anyone else Diego would have walked away from, but his brother deserved answers. And Diego wanted to find a solution. He trusted Rubin implicitly. Whatever Rubin said to him would be exactly what was truth.

"I believed you would be all right because you had her. She's sunshine. She's amazing. You need her in your life."

The moment the words were said aloud, Diego realized what it sounded like. What it was. In his mind, Jonquille had taken his place in Rubin's life. She provided him with fun and laughter, but she was also a warrior woman, much like Leila. Not quite as much of a warrior, but she would defend Rubin to the death. She would stand beside him.

"In your mind, now that Jonquille was with me, you believed you had outlived your usefulness. You were no longer needed," Rubin interpreted.

"Something like that. Yes," Diego admitted. "It was all very logical at the time."

Rubin leaned toward him. "You have to work through this, Diego. We can find a therapist in one of the GhostWalker units. Joe wouldn't toss you out if you were seeing someone; in fact, he'd encourage it. If you need to take meds, that wouldn't necessarily exclude you from work either. The GhostWalkers don't work the way other units do. We're held to a different standard."

"Higher," Diego said. "Much higher. You know someone is always looking to get rid of us—permanently. I don't want to be the downfall of the GhostWalkers."

"Do you hear yourself?" Rubin glared at him. "You're practically quoting Whitney. And our mother. Everything bad that happens is your fault. You brought in more meat than I did, more food, and half the time, when we were all starving, she threw it out because she was certain you'd used magical means. The devil had helped you. She would let the girls starve before she'd feed them the meat, and then she'd send you out again in the middle of a blizzard."

Diego sent him a faint grin. "We started outsmarting her by telling her you brought the meat. Of course, I got the hell beat out of me for being lazy and not helping out, but the girls had food."

"Yeah, we outsmarted her, but she set you up to believe you weren't worth anything. You have to realize it all stems from her. From the shit childhood you had."

"You had the same shit childhood," Diego pointed out.

"You persist in believing I'm perfectly fine. You've seen me when I can't contain my temper. The rage I have inside me that I keep locked down tight because it's like a nuclear bomb going off when it escapes. I rely on you. Just as you rely on me. It's always been the two of us, Diego. It doesn't matter if I have Jonquille and you have Leila, it's still the two of us."

It was true that Diego thought of Rubin as perfect. Rubin had stepped in hundreds of times to shield him from their mother's wrath. He was the white knight. The true hero. Diego would do anything to protect him and keep him safe. He had devoted his life to that end.

But it made sense that Rubin would have just as many issues stemming from their traumatic childhood as Diego did. It wasn't just the mental illness of their mother; it was the loss of every sibling, as well as their parents, most of them in violent circumstances.

"We both have triggers, Diego," Rubin said. "We need to identify those triggers and learn to cope with them."

"Sounds easy enough, but it isn't," Diego said. "Can't take religious talk. It isn't that I'm not a believer, but it seems to me so many religions are twisted from what they should be. They're means of power and judging others. I have to walk out when people get talking religion."

"What about Leila? Have you discussed that with her? If she's very religious, that could be a problem."

Diego hadn't considered that Leila would be all about a particular belief. It was something he did need to talk to her about. He couldn't imagine that she was a fanatic, but it was always possible. That was a hard no for him. It always would be. No child of his would ever be raised to believe he wasn't good enough or had a devil in him.

"I haven't," he admitted. "I'll do that. You're right. Total trigger for me. Tends to make me feel murderous before depression sets in."

"Acupuncture can be a good treatment," Rubin said. "In lieu of medication, that might be a help."

Diego hadn't considered acupuncture, but it was a far more appealing treatment to him than a pharmaceutical. He wouldn't mind trying it. More than anything, he wanted to be a good partner for Leila and a reliable, worthy father. He knew a part of him would be overprotective, but he was also aware he felt things deeply. He would feel love for his children and want to find the best ways to instill confidence and a code of honor. Looking to his brother was one of those ways. He was willing to learn from the best, and Rubin, to him, was the best.

"We can fight this together, Diego," Rubin said. "Establish every trigger you have and find a way to cope with it. I'll be doing the same thing for me."

That was Rubin, making certain Diego didn't feel alone. He'd been looking out for Diego all his life, just as Diego looked after him. What had he been thinking? He hadn't been. He'd been in such a dark place, certain there was no more use for him. And he had to be useful. That was important.

"I have to be looking after someone, Rubin. That's part of my identity. I need to know that what I do is important and could save lives."

Rubin nodded. "I can see that. Again, she programmed you to believe your only reason for being born was to protect me. That's probably set in stone with you."

There was no "probably" about it. If Diego was anywhere near Rubin, he would step in front of him every time. He would do the same with Leila and Grace. He felt the same about the men he served with and called brothers. And there was Ezekiel, Mordichai and Malichai. And Luther. When he broke it down, he realized just how lucky he was. Many people didn't have the relationships that he did.

"I'll address the problems," he assured. "I will, Rubin. You know me when I make up my mind."

"They aren't going away because you've identified them," Rubin cautioned. "You need to follow up. We'll find a decent therapist within our program, and we can try acupuncture before medications."

Diego nodded. "Agreed."

"And you talk to your woman. You make certain she's right for you before you leap in with both feet."

"It's a little late for that," Diego admitted.

"That fast? How?"

Diego shrugged. "Honestly? I have no idea. Only that she feels like a ray of sunshine. She suits me. The woman can shoot."

Rubin regarded him with a raised eyebrow. "She can shoot?" he echoed.

Diego gave his brother a faint grin. "Nearly as good as me. You should see her. And she doesn't hesitate. I wasn't happy that she hunted down the men coming after her. Tore those repairs lose. She could have bled out, but she isn't the type to wait for her man to rescue her."

Rubin scrubbed a hand down his face. "Let me get this straight. You fell hard for a woman because she shoots nearly as good as you."

Diego's grin got a little wider. "Yeah, essentially, that's exactly what I did."

"You could give an aspirin a headache, Diego," Rubin said. "Sometimes I don't have a clue what to say to you."

"That's a first. You always have something to say, even if I don't want to hear it."

"This woman feels the same about you?"

"You were in her mind. Does she?" Diego meant it as a challenge, but he found he wanted to know what Rubin thought. Rubin was astute. Quick. More than once, when Diego had hooked up with a woman, his brother had informed him that her corn bread wasn't done in the middle. At the time, Diego hadn't cared that she wasn't the smartest woman on the block; he was in a bar and had picked her up for the night.

Rubin wasn't a man to pick up women in bars. It wasn't his style. Diego hadn't believed he would ever find the right woman.

If he did find her, he also believed she wouldn't be able to live with him.

"I was only there briefly and tried not to intrude, but yeah, I could feel her emotions for you were very strong."

"We done?" Diego asked hopefully.

Rubin scowled. "Not by a long shot. Did you really think you could get away with performing psychic surgery on that woman and I wouldn't notice?"

"I didn't have time or help or even the instruments to do the medical surgery. We were in the field, and she was dying. Either it worked or it didn't. I felt as if I had no choice," Diego defended himself.

Rubin crossed his arms over his chest and regarded him coolly. "I'm not upset that you performed the surgery, Diego—that isn't the issue. When a healer has the ability, he often has no choice when someone is dying right in front of him. How often have you done it?"

"Psychic surgery? On a human being? This was my first time. I know it wasn't perfect. I had to take her spleen, and I detested that, but . . ." He trailed off. What could he say? He'd done his best, using his skills as a surgeon and applying them psychically. "She needed blood desperately. I also knew from observing you that I was going to crash big-time. The fact that I'd never done it before and my stress was through the roof, I figured that crash was going to be bad."

"You do know you risked your life."

"I knew the risks. I've been around you my entire life, and I've seen the effects on you. More than once I had to save your life." He was matter-of-fact. He couldn't have walked away from Leila and her injuries for anything. The need to save her life had been one of the strongest compulsions he'd ever experienced.

"You said it was the first time you performed psychic surgery on a human being. What does that mean?"

Diego tried to sound casual. "You know me with animals. I can't take them being hurt. I might have to hunt them for food, but I also look after them the best I can."

Rubin again frowned. "Diego, what you did was actual surgery. It wasn't a healing session. Joe is a psychic healer. Each Ghost-Walker unit has a psychic healer. It isn't the same thing. A psychic surgeon is rare. Very, very rare. You must have realized you had such a gift, yet you didn't come forward. You didn't even tell me."

Diego could hear the underlying hurt in his brother's voice. "It wasn't that I was trying to hide anything from you, Rubin. I didn't believe I could ever perform surgery on a human being success-fully. I learned with animals, but I have such an affinity for them. I don't with humans. I never felt as if that particular talent was strong enough or developed enough to take a chance. I watched you and listened each time you performed a surgery, and your skill always left me in awe. I was never going to work at that level, and I knew it."

Rubin leapt out of the seat carved into the log and paced across the clearing. He stood with his back to Diego, his hands pressed to his temples, a clear sign of agitation. Diego knew his brother enough to know that he was fighting back anger. Maybe disap-pointment. But Diego had watched Rubin for years and knew how adept he was. How amazing. Even if there were others around with his ability, Rubin would stand out.

Diego rose as well. The ground trembled beneath his feet, and he could see the trees closest to his brother shivering. A few lizards and two mice raced out from under the leaves and grasses, running away from Rubin. Ants poured out of a small hill along with two brightly colored salamanders. Several frogs hopped through the grass toward the forest.

Diego was always amazed that his easygoing brother could stir up enough dark energy to send wildlife running. He produced a wave of calming energy to counter Rubin's mood. Then he waited. It was never a good idea to disturb Rubin in a rage. That would be worse than poking a bear with a stick. Like Diego, Rubin had been enhanced with predatory animals. They both had to fight the aggression the DNA produced in them.

Diego? Is everything all right? I can get to you.

Stay there, Warrior Woman. Everything is under control. I think I pissed off my brother, or rather our past has. He'll pull it together in another few minutes.

He didn't know about your ability to perform surgery, did he? He must be so hurt. I could tell the two of you are very close.

Yeah, he's upset. I'm just going to let him calm down.

I find it interesting that you both feel the same. Everything about you.

Not sure I like hearing that. The last thing he wanted was for Leila to compare the two of them. He was certain he would come up wanting if she did that. And what if she was attracted to Rubin?

Her soft laughter poured into his mind, filling all the lonely places with something bright and beautiful. Instantly he found himself relaxing even before her reassurance.

I definitely don't find him attractive the way I do you. Nor do I trust him the way I do you. I know he's your brother, and he risked himself as well to help me, but honestly, Diego? There is only you. I see only you. I would never allow myself to rely on anyone else.

She humbled him with her trust. He still didn't feel he deserved her, but he had no intention of being a martyr and giving her up. He intended to do everything possible to make her happy for the rest of her life. She'd had a terrible start and had every reason not to trust, yet he'd been granted that privilege. He intended to make sure she was never sorry.

Rubin rarely loses his temper. He felt compelled to defend his brother even though she hadn't said one word against him. *When he does, it's best to leave him alone until he calms down. Believe me, you'll like Rubin. He's worried about me.*

I got that he was. Even when he was working on me, I could feel the weight of his anxiety. It wasn't centered on me. He actually admired your work, but he was truly worried about you.

There was a question in her carefully worded statement.

Diego sighed. *Didn't want to discuss this until I have a ring on your finger.*

Pushy much? Are we really talking rings when we barely know each other?

You know me.

Her soft laughter filled his mind with joy. *Seriously, Diego? You're totally reluctant to tell me whatever it is your brother was anxious over, and yet you tell me I know you.*

Some things are best left out until a woman is well and truly hooked.

She laughed again, just as he'd known she would. That was one of the many things he loved so much about her. She had a sense of humor that swept him along, made him feel that same sense of play.

So, you're hiding something big from me. Lay it on me, honey. We may as well figure it out now.

Would it be easier to admit he suffered from depression at times when he was speaking telepathically? When he wasn't facing her? Or was that cowardly?

I know we're joking around, Leila, but I do suffer from depression at times. I can be moody, and I definitely have triggers.

He came out with it. He had to know if she was going to stick. That meant telling her the strict truth.

She seemed to know he was being absolutely serious, and she went quiet, the humor slipping away.

You have to know I can have a problem at any time. I'm discussing ways of coping when I feel like I'm not good enough, but it won't just go away magically.

He waited. Holding his breath. Not able to think about losing her before he'd even had the chance to show her he would be that man for her. Leila didn't hastily reassure him. He wanted her to, but he would have known she truly didn't understand the extent of the problem if she had.

Rubin was very upset when he arrived. I thought it was because he didn't know you were capable of performing surgery the way you did, but it wasn't that, was it?

No. He was cautious. Careful. She was too intelligent and already figuring it out.

You had so many weapons with you. You brought them all.

Not all. Just my favorites. The ones that mattered to me. He waited again, suddenly becoming aware the ground had settled, and Rubin was moving slowly back to him. There was concern on his face. He had to have caught parts of Diego's conversation with Leila. She wasn't adept enough to keep Rubin from hearing her. Like Diego, Rubin waited to hear what her verdict would be.

He needed to warn Leila just as he promised. *You're spilling over, connecting to both of us.*

Rubin moved closer to Diego as if he could shield him from the coming blow. His features were unreadable, but his eyes were filled with compassion and love. Diego had always had that. No matter how brutal the circumstances of his childhood, he'd always had that unconditional love from Rubin. He'd learned to love the same way. Rubin had given him that.

Honey. The voice was soft, gentle, filling his mind with what felt like love. At least the beginnings. It was different from the way Rubin felt to him, but he recognized the emotion. He'd never thought he'd feel it from anyone other than Rubin. He knew his brother had to feel it as well. Diego had warned Leila that Rubin could hear her, but she'd still opted to give him that, to expose her vulnerability to his brother in order to let him know she wasn't running away.

I think the best we can do for us, Diego, is ensure we have good communication at all times. Once you teach me your coping methods, I can be vigilant for signs to help you. We'll have to make sure we always have strategies in place for you.

Could she be any more perfect? She recognized there was no cure. She knew she would be facing a lifetime of Diego fighting off demons, yet she was willing to stay. She didn't immediately think she could fix him. She knew mental health issues were serious. She recognized why he had returned to his cabin, and she poured steel into her voice right along with that same beginning love. She was as determined as he was to face the illness head-on.

I believe that is a good idea. He didn't know what else to tell her. It was a little overwhelming to think he could have ended his life in that one bleak moment of despair. Had he succeeded, he would have missed not only recognizing his brother's needs and emotional support but also knowing Leila.

"We need to discuss your ability to perform surgery, Diego," Rubin said aloud.

Diego was uneasy that Rubin deliberately didn't break the connection with Leila. He had no idea what Rubin was going to say to him. He'd seen Diego's work. Rubin had to do mop-up to fix any mistakes Diego made. Yes, he'd saved Leila's life, but having Rubin dissect his work on the woman Diego wanted for his partner was humiliating. He'd never ever felt that way from anything Rubin had ever said or done, yet he already felt he was looking in a bad light.

"What you believe to be an absolute truth is actually another lie our mother beat into you," Rubin said. His voice was back to his calm, matter-of-fact tone. The one that said he knew what he was talking about, and he expected others to listen. "She told you everything you were able to do came from a place of evil. How many times did she say that to you? At least twice daily, sometimes over and over when she beat you. You were a child, Diego. You may think you know she was out of her mind, but how could the things she said and did not leave a lasting impression on you? They did me, and she didn't beat me. She didn't tell me I was a child of the devil."

Diego frowned, for the first time not following Rubin's reasoning. Yes, of course, he knew the things their mother had said and done were the ravings of a sick woman. But that didn't have anything to do with his level of ability. His confusion must have been evident to his brother, because Rubin sighed and shook his head.

"A psychic healer is rare, you know that. To have the ability to do psychic surgery is almost unheard-of. There are a handful of us, Diego. Do you really think such a gift—a gift of saving lives, of healing others—came from the devil? The surgeon risks his life each time he performs surgery. It isn't as if it's easy or can be done thoughtlessly or without repercussions to the surgeon. You've experienced the crash. The pain. You're operating on them and keeping them from feeling what you're doing, but you can feel everything. That exchange is a choice we make to save the life of the person in need. There's nothing demonic about that. Can you at least admit that?"

Diego still didn't understand where Rubin was going with his statements. "I don't believe psychic surgery is an instrument of the underworld. You have to admit everyone who has psychic talents has them in varying degrees. I can do a lot more with animals than you can, but you have that same ability."

"I would have that same high level, Diego, had I taken the time to develop it," Rubin objected. "When we were kids, we had to divide everything so carefully. We were *children*, Diego. We assumed the roles of adults, but we weren't adults. We had extraordinary gifts, yes, and we're both extremely intelligent, but we were still children trying to keep our family members alive."

"I'm well aware."

"We have the same gifts, Diego. We always have. You didn't have any real interest in lightning or diverting it, so you ignored that talent completely. I was intrigued, so I studied it carefully. Everything we did, everything we learned, we did to survive, and we got damn good at the things that kept us alive. You're hell on wheels in the forest. I doubt that Gino or Draden could keep up with you if you wanted to show off your skills. Gino is an elite tracker, but you have that same ability. You don't show it, but you developed it. I didn't. I'm good. I get by, but I had you to lead the way. Same with shooting. I'm good, but you never miss."

"Where are you going with this, Rubin?"

"You may not have worked on humans, Diego, but you're a damn good surgeon when you're wielding a knife in an operating room. You know human anatomy and your way around it. You practiced for years on animals with psychic surgery. I'm telling you that you're every bit as skilled as I am."

Diego was already shaking his head. "You had to go in after me and shore up the repairs. They weren't holding."

"They held when they shouldn't have," Rubin corrected. "You're that good. She shouldn't have been racing around the forest, leaping in and out of trees, not a week and a half after having her spleen removed. If I had done the surgery, the same thing would have happened."

Diego kept shaking his head. He couldn't comprehend what Rubin was saying.

"Keep in mind whenever I've done these surgeries, I have you or others with me to give me aid. Water, rest, blood. I have assistants. Even out in the field, I've got others, usually you, to ensure

I'm okay. You had no one with you. You had to give blood to the patient several times. On top of that, you were exerting tremendous physical strength in carrying her up the mountain and hunting the enemy."

"Rubin . . ." Diego trailed off. What could he dispute? Everything Rubin said was the truth. He never allowed Rubin to be alone when he was performing surgery because it was too risky.

"I'm telling you the surgery was superb. Every bit as good as what I can do, and you did it under very trying circumstances. I'm afraid you're going to have to let go of the notion that somehow my work comes from heaven and yours from hell."

13

~

Rubin insisted that both Diego and Leila rest the entire next day. For the most part, he left them alone while he put away the rest of the supplies he'd brought to the cabin. He cooked meals for them, but most of his time was spent talking to his Jonquille. He stayed outside so he wouldn't bother the two of them, decreeing they should sleep as much as possible. Diego had no dispute with that. His body wanted to shut down, craving sleep.

Leila stayed close to him, cuddling against him. She hadn't seemed like a woman who would want to be cuddled or touched, but she leaned into Diego, and when he'd reach for her hand, which was nearly all the time, she readily threaded her fingers through his. She didn't object when he fell asleep with one arm curved around her waist.

Diego had no idea what to think of the revelations his brother had given him. He respected Rubin and his opinions but didn't think he could possibly be right. Rather than dwell on it, he chose to sleep. He would need to be at full strength to bring Grace home.

He woke to the smell of stew. He recognized that particular aroma instantly. Rubin was making a favorite meal. The smell of fresh-baked bread filled the house. Diego untangled himself from Leila as smoothly and as quietly as possible and went to join his brother in the kitchen.

Rubin sent him a quick grin over one shoulder. "Knew you'd smell stew and bread no matter how tired you were, and you'd get up. Thought I'd make something healthy for you."

"Appreciate it." Diego sank into a chair facing the kitchen to watch his brother very efficiently take down bowls from the cupboard and gather silverware. "Rubin, you just took out four bowls."

"Yeah. We've got company."

Diego frowned. He should have known immediately, the moment he opened his eyes, if someone was close. Rubin couldn't be wrong. He was alert and, in Diego's opinion, extremely savvy in the woods. He should know if someone was close. He froze. What was he thinking? He was a GhostWalker, capable of slipping in and out of houses, moving through forest or desert unseen, unheard, leaving no trace behind.

"Zeke is here." He looked around the cabin, half expecting to find Ezekiel Fortunes lounging against the wall in plain sight, yet no one would see him.

Ezekiel was a big man, spoke rarely, but he didn't need to. He sometimes had extremely light amber-colored eyes, cool, like a fine whiskey. Other times his eyes could darken into an old gold, devoid of feeling. He was street-smart and had kept his two beloved brothers, Mordichai and Malichai, alive in harsh conditions that would have eaten them alive when they were just little boys living on the streets.

Zeke had saved Diego and Rubin from most likely going to jail. They didn't allow anyone to take their things or put their hands on them. The two boys had a tendency to permanently end any enemies, something police frowned on. They had hopped a train and ended up in the same city, looking for work and desperate for food. Surviving in the city wasn't the same thing as living off the land. Ezekiel found them, took them in and treated them as brothers.

"Where is he?" Diego asked Rubin. "It has to be Ezekiel. How did he know something was wrong?"

"I texted him. You know Ezekiel. If he found out through the grapevine that you had a woman and she was in jeopardy, he might cut our throats. I thought it best to keep him informed."

"Like you should have done, Diego."

The voice came from behind him. Low. Intense. That was Ezekiel. Diego turned in his chair to regard the man who was lounging against the doorjamb leading to the bedroom. He'd clearly already been inside the room. Diego was furious with himself because that meant Leila had been vulnerable in her sleep. Not that Zeke would harm her, not in a million years.

Ezekiel was a big man with heavy muscle throughout his chest and arms. His hair was black and always a bit on the wild side. He rarely trimmed it, so it fell in an unruly manner around his head. One would have thought it might soften his appearance, but there was nothing soft about Ezekiel.

"You're right, Zeke," Diego affirmed instantly. "I should have texted you."

"You didn't text me," Rubin pointed out. He brought his brother a bowl of stew and placed a plate of bread on the table to one side of him.

"I didn't have to text you," Diego said, leveling his gaze on his brother. "Don't try to sound hurt. You always know what's going on with me."

"Maybe so." Rubin sounded pious. "But it would be nice to get a text."

"Dang it, Rubin, you aren't fit for shootin' since you got married,"

Diego informed his brother. "Your feelings are hurt over every little thing."

"You saying I'm too sensitive?" Rubin demanded.

"That's exactly what I'm saying."

"He's not fit for shootin'?" Ezekiel echoed. "Is that a thing?"

He made his way to the kitchen, not making a single sound, boots whispering across the floor. For such a big man, it was an incredible feat. Diego had always admired the easy way he moved, so fluid. He was a first-class fighter, his skills honed on the streets. He'd certainly been instrumental in teaching both Rubin and Diego how to fight.

"Fair" wasn't a word used in a fight. Someone came for you, someone put their hands on you or yours, all bets were off. Ezekiel taught them to strike hard and fast, making it count immediately. He believed in ending a fight before it had a chance to begin.

"It's a thing," Diego confirmed. "Where's Bellisia?"

Bellisia was Ezekiel's wife. One was never far from the other. She was a tiny little thing, lethal as hell in the water.

"If we're going to war, and it looks that way, she's staying back with Nonny and all the kids to help protect them." As always, Ezekiel spoke matter-of-factly. Accepting the bowl of stew, he sprawled out in the chair across from Diego.

"You came because you think we're going to war?" Diego asked.

Ezekiel waved his spoon around. "You claimed a woman, and from what I understand—and I'll admit, I don't know the entire story yet—her commander is going to insist she go back to them."

Diego filled him in on Leila's history. "She isn't really under Chariot's command because she never legally joined the service."

"It wouldn't matter," Ezekiel said. "She's a GhostWalker if she's yours. That makes her ours." He shrugged as he took a bite of stew. "You're not in this fight alone, Diego."

"Thanks, Ezekiel." Diego was surprised at how surprised and

grateful he was that Ezekiel felt so strongly about backing him up. He wasn't used to relying on others, not even his fellow Ghost-Walkers. He tended to be the one they relied on for backup.

"You're not just a GhostWalker, Diego," Ezekiel said. "You're family."

That hit him hard. Zeke had always treated Rubin and him as family. Sometimes, most times, that wasn't a good thing. Ezekiel was exacting about everything. Education. Training. Code of honor. He backed up his edicts with his fists. If you didn't want a lesson in hand-to-hand combat or street fighting, you toed the line.

"Leila has a daughter, Grace. And a sister, Bridget. Even if they release Leila to us, we're still going to have to fight for the baby. If Luther hasn't managed to get Bridget back, she's most likely with Whitney. So it won't end with keeping Leila and getting Grace." Diego gave the warning.

Who is this man? Are you safe?

Ezekiel lifted his head, his peculiar-colored eyes giving Diego his penetrating stare. It was never easy to take the man's intense look. Diego always had the feeling he could see right through a man. In his case, he had a lot to hide.

He's family. Big brother, adopted, so to speak. Don't get out of bed and crawl out here with a gun. Ezekiel is most likely not alone.

Ezekiel wouldn't be happy that he wasn't being given important information, such as Diego being capable of psychic surgery. Diego had no intention of living his life the way his brother had to live—with guards around him nearly all the time. If Diego was being strictly honest, he was responsible for the intensity with which the other members of their unit watched over Rubin. Diego had used his voice to influence them every chance he got.

"Do you think that matters, Diego? I've got your back. The boys have your back. The rest of the team does. If I'm not mistaken, the other GhostWalker teams will say the same thing. We've all reached the point, between Whitney sending his soldiers to test us and trying to take our women and children from us, as well as our enemies in the White House, that everyone is fed up. We've established fortresses and escape routes. We have private satellites and our own helicopters and planes. We have more weapons than we know what to do with. Mostly, we have the ability to disappear. The faction in the government wanting us dead believes we're too big of a threat to them—and we are. We just haven't shown we're willing to fight back."

Diego thought about Ezekiel's assessment of the situation. The GhostWalkers would stand together, but the circumstances were explosive any way one looked at it.

I don't feel anyone else in the house.

Leila was being extra careful not to allow Rubin to hear the communication between her and Diego. He found having her make that effort felt all the more intimate between them.

Someone else is here, more than likely two more. Diego hadn't bothered to search for Ezekiel's two birth brothers, but if Ezekiel had felt it necessary to come to Diego's aid, his younger brothers would as well. They were tight-knit.

"Rubin believes we should try a diplomatic approach," he ventured aloud to Ezekiel.

Ezekiel shrugged. "There's always that. I'm sure when Joe hears what's going on, he'll want to pursue that avenue."

As usual, it was impossible to read Ezekiel's expressionless mask or his lack of tone. Diego could never tell if Zeke agreed with Joe or not. He rarely went against him; only Trap, their resident genius, on-the-spectrum billionaire—and he was probably certifiable—clashed on a regular basis with Joe. And everyone else if he bothered to speak at all. Which, most of the time, he didn't. Trap was more like a mad scientist, but he always got the job done. Always.

"I just think it's about time we assert ourselves," Rubin said. "I've had a few conversations with Joe. He's of the same mind."

"I thought the idea was to fly under the radar," Diego said.

"As if the massacre that took place on this mountain wouldn't be noticed," Rubin said, an edge to his voice. "You risked your life, Diego, and you had no business doing it." The floor trembled, and for a moment, the walls seemed to expand and contract.

Ezekiel turned his cool, penetrating gaze first on Rubin and then on Diego with far too much speculation. "Seems to me, Rubin, you're a bit upset at Diego. At first glance, it doesn't make sense, not when he was defending his woman. You have a closer call than it appears, Diego? You hurt and haven't said anything?"

A direct question from Ezekiel. He was family. He'd saved their lives numerous times. Diego felt intensely loyal to Ezekiel, but more than that, he respected him. Just the fact that he asked Diego, not Rubin, made Diego admire him all the more. He wasn't putting Rubin in the position of having to choose between snitching on Diego or lying to Ezekiel.

"Had a couple of minor wounds, but nothing I couldn't handle," Diego said.

The floor trembled again, and the walls contracted. He was pissing off Rubin again. He knew his brother's anger wasn't about the couple of near misses. It was the fact that he'd risked his life when he had such a rare and valuable gift. Diego had always insisted Rubin be guarded, to the point that Rubin rebelled. All that time, Diego had known he was capable of psychic surgery, but he hadn't volunteered the information, and worse, he'd put himself in dangerous situations time after time.

He has the right to be angry with you, Diego, Leila said. The feel of her was gentle in his mind. Not accusing, simply pointing out that he hadn't been fair to his brother.

I'm aware. Rubin deserved better. He couldn't bring his mind to believe the things his brother had said to him. No matter how long he contemplated Rubin's declaration, his mind rejected every word.

"You have something you need to tell me, Diego?" Ezekiel didn't take those amber-colored eyes from Diego's face.

Rubin's voice always got lower, softer, when he was at his most lethal. Ezekiel's soft voice developed a low growl in it. That alone could shake a grown man.

He can reduce me to a fourteen-year-old, he explained to Leila. *That voice and that stare of his used to not only keep us safe from outsiders trying to mess with us, but it heralded a beatdown because we'd screwed up.*

Diego had a sense of humor about it. He was grown. A lethal predator, and yet there he was, with his two older brothers trying to reduce him to a kid again—and succeeding.

Actually, you haven't caved, Diego. They might be attempting to intimidate you into revealing things you would rather not, but they haven't succeeded.

Ezekiel didn't let up for a moment. Those strangely colored eyes never left Diego's.

I think he's attempting to melt off your face, Leila whispered into his mind.

Diego had to work to keep from laughing. That wouldn't do at all in the face of Ezekiel's clear threat.

The door leading from the mudroom banged loudly, and a man sauntered in, his arms filled with canvas bags Diego recognized as the ones Wyatt Fontenot's grandmother, Nonny, used. Instantly, the familiar aroma of Cajun fare filled the house.

Mordichai Fortunes turned his head directly toward Diego as he moved past him to enter the space that was the kitchen. Their eyes met, and Mordichai winked at him. It was all Diego could do not to burst into laughter.

Who is that?

Mordichai, one of Ezekiel's brothers. He just saved my ass from his brother's wrath, just the way we used to when we were kids. We would divert Ezekiel's attention with distraction.

So he heard the entire conversation? Is that what you're saying?

Yep, he was somewhere in the house. His brother Malichai is bound to be around as well.

Rubin was on his feet, following Mordichai into the kitchen. "What did you bring?"

"Nonny worried I'd starve," Mordichai announced. "She sent everything you can imagine."

Malichai and Mordichai are always starving, Diego told Leila. *Mordichai still puts away the food. Nothing is safe around him. We all give him a hard time. And he doesn't have an ounce of fat on him. How he manages that, I have no idea.*

Mordichai was an inch shorter than Ezekiel, had extremely thick dark hair and the same golden eyes as his older brother. That trait ran in the family. He was very muscular, his arms and chest carrying heavy muscle, tapering to narrow hips and strong legs. Mordichai was the Fortunes brother who smiled the most and had a great sense of humor. The problem was, when he smiled, he showed his perfect teeth, but the smile had never once, that Diego could remember, reached his eyes.

Over the years, Diego and Rubin had noticed that Ezekiel took more care in how he spoke to Mordichai. And Nonny, who was welcoming and good to all of them, seemed to take special care with Mordichai. Diego was extremely fond of the man, but that didn't mean he knew him. Mordichai had his secrets, just like they all did.

"I'm sure Nonny meant for you to share," Rubin said. "She wouldn't have sent so much if she didn't."

Mordichai pulled the various containers out of the canvas bags to set them on the counter. There were so many there was barely room. He peered into the pot of stew Rubin had on the stove. "Did you make this, Rubin? It smells good." He reached for the freshly baked bread.

Rubin glared at him. "You don't get anything if you don't share."

"You wouldn't want me faintin' from hunger. I think my blood sugar drops fast if I don't eat all the time. You know that, Rubin."

Ezekiel heaved a sigh. "All you think about is food." He sounded resigned.

Leila's soft laughter moved through Diego's mind. *You all are definitely family. Rubin has forgotten all about being mad at you, and Ezekiel is totally distracted by his brother's appearance.*

Diego was caught by Mordichai's playful statement. It wasn't the first time he'd cracked jokes about low blood sugar. Was it possible Mordichai was diabetic? Diego glanced at Ezekiel. He would know. And diabetics couldn't serve in the military if they were diagnosed before joining.

Diego reached back into his memories of the boys growing up on the streets. There was never enough food to eat. Never. They were always hungry. He recalled Mordichai curled up on a mat in the tunnels beneath the city, beads of sweat covering his body. Shaking. Eyes unfocused. It had happened on more than one occasion. Often, he would limp, fall behind the others, even though he was tough as nails. It would happen unexpectedly, without any warning. Ezekiel would leave for a time, commanding the others to look after Mordichai. When he returned, he would give his younger brother medication.

Rubin, is it possible that Mordichai is diabetic?

It seemed impossible that they wouldn't have known. They were all doctors. It had taken longer for some to complete their studies. Mordichai had taken his sweet time, but in the end, he became a doctor just as the others in their unit had. Diego couldn't fault him;

he hadn't been eager to complete his studies either. He wasn't a man to stay indoors the way he needed to when studying and completing his residency.

Rubin's assessing gaze slid over Mordichai. The man looked fitter than any of them. He ran daily. He boxed, did martial arts, several different practices. He wielded weapons like a master. One would never look at him and think he had a physical ailment of any kind.

Not diabetes.

Diego trusted Rubin's assessment. Rubin might say, and even believe, that Diego had the same gifts, but Diego had been watching Rubin save lives for years. He knew how powerful Rubin's gift of healing was. It had started when they were children, that need Rubin had to help anyone sick. Diego hadn't had the same need.

There was a time when they had come across one of their neighbors. He lived miles away and was as mean as a snake, not only to outsiders but to his wife and children. Old man Kingsley had been out hunting, and he'd fallen down a rocky ravine. The two boys were barely twelve, but when they spotted the tracks of a man weaving and tripping, they followed.

It was clear Kingsley had been drinking, which wasn't unusual. Each time they'd come across him, he was drunk and belligerent, even at church. Diego wanted to leave him to his fate. He had no compulsion to climb down the steep ravine, which was a very dangerous climb, and see to the man's injuries. As far as he was concerned, Kingsley had gotten what he deserved. So many times, his wife and children had visible injuries on them.

Rubin had been adamant that they get down to the man and help him. Even then, Diego had realized his brother didn't have much of a choice. The compulsion to heal was so strong he couldn't walk away. Having many of those experiences with his brother gave him the insight that Rubin truly was different from him—and so was that well of healing energy inside him.

He knew his mother had influenced him to believe that anything he was able to do came from something dark and ugly, and everything Rubin did came from a pure place. He'd always thought of the two of them as light and dark, opposites.

Dang it, Diego. Rubin's ire filled his mind. *You persist in thinking you have something evil in you.*

Just memories coming up, Rubin. Trying to get past them. I know something is off about Mordichai. I've always known it, but I can't figure it out. That's unlike me. He wasn't above distracting his brother. And he really was concerned. He always had been. Mordichai had been a good kid and was an even better man.

Rubin moved up next to Mordichai, deliberately bumping him with his hip. "Don't you touch that stew if you're not sharing Nonny's food."

Mordichai heaved a pretend sigh of resignation. "Fine, I'll share." He slathered more butter onto the bread and stuffed nearly the entire thing into his mouth.

Rubin shifted his weight onto one leg, turning fully toward Mordichai. Rubin had seen him use that particular maneuver to place his body wholly toward a potential patient. It gave him more of an ability to assess any illnesses.

"Try to show some restraint," Ezekiel said. "You won't get me to believe Nonny didn't pack a lunch for you to drive up here with."

"Had to share with Malichai. You never get annoyed when he's eating all the food."

It didn't surprise Diego in the least to confirm that Malichai was somewhere in the house. Of course he was. He would feel the same way as Ezekiel and Mordichai. They were a family, and if there was trouble, they showed up. That was their code.

"There isn't enough stew for the two of us," Mordichai pointed out. "And as usual, he's taking a nap."

I take it Malichai is another brother, Leila asked.

Malichai is the youngest brother. He is married to Amaryllis, and just so you're aware, he lost his leg after an assignment. He's handled it well, and of course the government didn't want to lose him as an asset, so they've provided the best prosthetic available.

How terrible for him. His wife stuck by him, I hope.

She did. She's good for him. You'll like Malichai. When you meet him, you can feel what kind of man he is, Diego assured. Because he was in her mind, he felt her uneasiness with so many strangers close to her when she was still so vulnerable.

Rubin dished up the last of the stew and handed the bowl to Mordichai. "I always said you were the spoiled one."

He has some kind of shield, Diego. He masks the illness, but there is one. Not diabetes, but he's autoimmune.

How did he pass the strict physical requirements in order to join the GhostWalkers? And why would Whitney enhance him, knowing he was autoimmune? With his supersoldiers, Whitney doesn't expect them to live long, and he doesn't care what shape they're in, physically or mentally, but he does with the GhostWalkers. He prides himself on the teams and what they can accomplish. Why would he enhance Mordichai?

Rubin didn't have an answer. Leila did. *One of his gifts is masking. If Rubin is a powerful healer and can't find what's wrong with him, a man like Whitney, with no ability, might miss it.*

How? Rubin asked. *He has to run tests the entire time he's working with a patient. Blood tests, you name it. It would show up if he was autoimmune.*

They fell silent, each of them puzzling how Mordichai could have gotten into the GhostWalker program.

My best guess would be that someone found a way to alter the results of the lab tests. That was Leila.

That made more sense to Diego than any other answer. He glanced at Ezekiel. He would keep his family together at any cost. He'd never leave Mordichai behind. Ezekiel had been enhanced before any of them. He was an amazing doctor, and he would know exactly how to alter lab results.

Leila might be on to something, Diego told Rubin.

Ezekiel is capable, Rubin agreed.

"You know I'm just giving you a hard time," Mordichai said as he sank onto the floor, back to the wall, the bowl of stew in his hand. "Nonny sent enough food for an army. I'm not the only one bringing it in. Draden is outside setting up a camp. We knew the cabin would be too small for all of us. We're setting up a perimeter for safety. They'll bring the supplies and more of Nonny's food in as soon as they have the tents set up."

When you meet Draden Freeman for the first time, there is no fainting. No flirting. In fact, don't even look at him.

Why would you say that? Is something wrong with him?

Rubin gave a little snort of derision. Diego ignored him and continued. *He's a pretty boy. Used to be a model. Just to tell you, looks aren't everything. The man can be moody as hell. I don't think he sleeps. He runs all the time, and you know anyone who runs isn't running on all cylinders.*

Leila gave him her little laugh, the one that sent heat rushing through his entire system. Diego's eyes met Rubin's. His brother was smiling too. That was the effect that soft sound had on them. There had been too little laughter in their lives, not the real kind, and Leila had a way about her that made little things humorous.

Don't listen to him, Leila, Rubin said. *Draden was one of those really big deals in the modeling world, that much is true.*

What isn't true? He runs like a maniac, is moody, doesn't like talking much, and, Leila, just so you're warned, his wife is a straight-up assassin.

That produced another fresh round of laughter. *What am I, you goof?*

Rubin burst out laughing. Ezekiel and Mordichai both looked

at him expectantly. Rubin flashed a grin. "Can't help it. Leila just called Diego a goof. What could be more appropriate?"

"I'm so glad you're getting a kick out of our conversation," Diego groused.

"There are far worse things for a woman to be calling a man," Mordichai said very solemnly. "I ought to know."

"Women call you names?" Rubin asked.

"Does that shock you?" Ezekiel asked. "He's still writing his ridiculous profile for a dating app he saw. He's been working on it for a year, and he has three lines."

"You can't hurry these things," Mordichai said to Diego. "That poor woman of yours most likely feels you knocked her over the head with a club like in the old days."

"It's called sweeping her off her feet," Diego corrected.

"Actually," Rubin corrected helpfully, "she was shot and couldn't go anywhere. He had a captive audience and pretended to be a white knight."

"You took advantage of that woman," Mordichai said. "That's not right. You should have spent time courting her."

"I did spend time courting her," Diego defended. "I just didn't wait a year writing poetry on paper and never sending it."

Mordichai shook his head mournfully. "If you want a woman to stay, Diego, you're going to have to do more than dazzle her while she's bedridden."

"Since when are you the leading expert on courting women, Mordichai?" Ezekiel asked.

"I read books. You can learn a lot from books."

"I caught him reading romances," Gino Mazza announced as he entered the kitchen carrying canvas totes filled with more food. He put the bags on the counter and in the sink since there was little room left. "He has an entire library of romances."

Ezekiel raised an eyebrow. "That true, Mordichai?"

"Absolutely. And keep it up, Gino. I'll kick your ass."

"Just letting the others know you are the leading authority for a reason. Not sure if it's a good reason, but you still have one when the rest of us don't."

That man might have a few brains, Leila said. *Who is he?*

Gino is difficult to explain. Hard as nails. Only looks at one woman, his wife, Zara Hightower. He's an elite tracker, a hell of a doctor and impossible to spot when he doesn't want to be seen.

You admire him.

Diego hadn't thought much about admiring Gino, but "respect" was a good word to characterize how he felt about Gino. Gino was the man he would most like to have with him if they were facing a large number of enemies in difficult terrain. He was that good and that dependable.

You think he's the most like you out of all the men in your unit, Leila observed.

Diego frowned. Did he think he was like Gino? Gino didn't bother to hide his dark side from them. Before joining the military and the GhostWalker program, he had worked for Joe Spagnola's father, a man with a history of violent criminal activity. Joe was their commanding officer and leader of their team. He had helped save Gino's life when his family had been murdered. His family had taken Gino in, and from that moment, Gino looked after Joe in the same way Diego looked after Rubin.

To the outside world, Diego appeared to be the easygoing Campos brother. He took care of talking with others, whereas Rubin was more reserved. He had developed that persona, one that seemed outgoing and calm. One that did the necessary paperwork. He faded into the background easily, yet took center stage to divert attention from his brother. He wasn't any of those things. He was as dark as Gino. As willing to be violent as Gino. Now that Leila had pointed it out to him, he was much more like Gino than any of the others.

Maybe Ezekiel, Rubin said. *He has that same power in him that I feel in you and Gino. You persist in believing it's a bad thing. The three of you have done more good with your abilities than all the rest of us.*

That was definitely not true, but it was nice that his brother thought that. Diego felt he was learning quite a bit about himself and relationships. He just had to take it in. Accept that the things he'd believed about himself weren't necessarily true. Or at least try to view them in a different light.

"Are you really reading romance books?" Ezekiel asked his brother.

"Bellisia and Zara told me it was the best way to learn about women," Mordichai stated in between bites of stew. "So, Zeke, you want to make fun of me, I'll just let your wife know how you feel about her giving me advice."

Leila's laughter moved through Diego's mind. *Your friends are a little insane.*

They'll go on like this for hours.

14

Leila leaned on the railing of the porch surveying the grounds around the cabin. One would never know that an entire camp had been set up anywhere in the vicinity. She'd pictured the tents right outside the cabin, maybe surrounding them, but they were unseen, just like the GhostWalkers seemed to be when they wanted.

Diego stood close to her. Very close. She wasn't a woman who had ever felt the need to be protected, but she found herself liking the way Diego had such a protective vibe when he was near her. He liked physical contact. She would never have thought she'd want to be affectionate around others or have Diego hold her hand or put his arm around her waist, pulling her close in front of his friends, but she did like it. She wanted it. Maybe needed that closeness with him.

"I can disappear in a wilderness," she admitted, "but I couldn't hide an entire camp the way your friends have."

"Does it bother you to have them all here?"

When he asked the question in that low, velvety voice, his palm slid up her back to curve around the nape of her neck. The movement was a slow caress that sent little flames flickering over her nerve endings. She decided it was Diego, not Mordichai, who was the leading authority on women, but she wasn't going to give him more of an advantage than he already had.

She thought his question over before she answered. "It isn't that they bother me. How could it? They came here to help. They're willing to put their lives on the line for us. I'm just not used to being in such close proximity to so many men. I trained alone for the most part. The men who did come near me were usually those who were having trouble with the enhancements, and their aggression and dominant levels were out of control."

Diego's fingers moved on her neck, a slow massage that sent that burn flickering through her veins. At the same time, she felt tension she hadn't known she had easing.

"These men are all enhanced," he said, bending his head close so his lips whispered over her ear. "They are aggressive and dominant. Each of them. Some admittedly more than others, but they are. They consider you family, Leila. They would never hurt you or Grace, and they would fight to the death for you."

She pressed her lips together, leaning back into his massage. She knew he was trying to reassure her, but her experience with many of the enhanced soldiers hadn't been positive.

"Why do you suppose these men have been able to live with the enhancements when some of the other soldiers from Chariot's lab have been affected so negatively? It doesn't make sense. Chariot's people were careful in their selections. The men they chose were good men. I don't think any of them have the number of enhancements you and your friends do, and yet often they can't handle it."

"Whitney does a pretty thorough mental evaluation before he selects soldiers for the GhostWalker program. He prides himself on finding the men who can deal with the genetic enhancements. We weren't told that would be in the works. All of us had tested for strong psychic abilities, and we were on board for enhancing those abilities. But Whitney was looking for men he could enhance genetically as well. I think the evaluations played a large part in finding those of us who could take the levels of aggression in the predatory DNA he put into us."

"It's scary to think that every one of these men have such predatory traits."

He turned her to face him, tipping up her chin so her eyes met his. "I do, Leila. I have so many aggressive predators in me it isn't funny. In certain situations, I feel more animal than human. I can't say to you that aggression and dominance aren't a huge part of me. I need to hunt. I don't have to kill, but it is entirely too easy for me under the right circumstances. Most of us are that way. We have a code we strictly adhere to. And we help each other. We realized that there were no advocates for us, so if we wanted to survive, we would have to form close bonds between all the GhostWalker teams and back each other up."

Leila wasn't sure why she found it reassuring that Diego was so honest about the dominant traits in him, but because he shared with her so openly, she felt more comfortable with him. Trusted him more. It didn't make sense, but there it was.

One of Diego's more dominant traits was his protective nature. She wanted that for Grace and any future children she had. She wanted the stability of a home. Many of these GhostWalkers were married. According to Diego, they were devoted to their wives. She had paid close attention to the way they harassed one another, and it was always with affection. Each man had been introduced to her, and they had treated her with care and respect. Not one of the men had acted as if they were interested in her sexually. They didn't make her skin crawl or raise alarms. They treated her more as if she were a sister than anything else.

One of the things that stood out the most when she was introduced that morning at breakfast was the way Rubin and Ezekiel stayed close to her. Rubin had actually stood on the other side of her, one hand on her shoulder. Ezekiel had come up behind her for the introductions. She should have felt very vulnerable with him behind her, but she didn't. She felt safe. She could feel the waves of protection coming off the three men—Ezekiel, Rubin and Diego—and it felt good. She was very aware she wasn't one hundred percent physically fit. These men she was being introduced to were elite soldiers. More than soldiers.

"You must think Chariot isn't going to let me go. All of you must think that." Her stomach knotted, and the tension came right back.

"I doubt he would allow it without persuasion of some sort."

Her heart slammed hard against her chest. She pressed her fist over it in the hopes of quieting it. "I left Gracie with Marcy. She might be married to Commander Chariot, but she has always been a friend and advocate. If there is one person on this earth aside from you, Diego, that I trust, it's her. But Chariot knows she's watching Gracie. When I'm away, she always does. He probably has my baby in his home right this minute. Sometimes Marcy will stay at my little apartment in the dorm building, but there are times when she takes Grace to their home."

"You're worried that he'll hold the baby hostage and insist that if you want her, you have to return to them."

She nodded. "I think he will, yes."

"You do know how fucked-up that is, using a baby to force her mother to continue working for them. You don't even get paid, Leila. He's not treating you with the respect he gives his soldiers.

He sends you out on assignments that can get you killed with no backup. I doubt he was responsible for the decision to send your sister to Whitney, but he certainly knows about it. Just the fact that some of the soldiers were bringing you up the mountain to rendezvous with a helicopter to take you back to Chariot and the others were taking your sister down the mountain to return her to Whitney tells you how much Chariot is concerned with your well-being."

"It really doesn't matter if he's a complete bastard, Diego. If he holds Grace back and won't allow me to take her with me, I won't go. I won't leave her."

Diego swept his hand down the back of her head in a soothing caress that allowed her heart to stop pounding. It wasn't just a caress; it was a gesture of solidarity. He spoke volumes without saying a word. She loved that about him. She also believed in him. It made no sense. They weren't paired by some strange phenomenon. She had only been with him a couple of weeks, but those days had been intense. They had focused completely on each other, and more, they could each see into the other using telepathic communication.

"I think someone else has arrived," she whispered to Diego.

Diego circled her waist with one arm and tucked her into his side. "We've got two men coming toward us, just now emerging from the forest. The one hanging back a little is Trap Dawkins. Don't take offense at anything he says or doesn't say. He's probably one of the brightest men on the planet. I don't say that lightly. He's a self-made billionaire, married to Cayenne, one of Whitney's rejects, and he's neurodivergent. He doesn't like to engage in conversation, but Draden and Wyatt are working with him on social cues. He's a father now and knows it's going to be important to make those kinds of efforts."

"He looks uncomfortable. He doesn't have to be introduced."

She wasn't certain she could go through too many more introductions without wanting to make a run for it.

"Trap has abilities we may need to retrieve Grace. He was the one who managed to free Wyatt's daughters from a holding cell. They were scheduled for termination. Cayenne was as well. Without Trap, we never would have gotten to those children or Cayenne."

Leila could tell it was important to Diego that she try to understand his friend Trap. The man walking with Trap had wavy dark hair and a muscular build. He wasn't as tall as his friend, but he walked with confidence.

"Wyatt Fontenot is with Trap. Wyatt brought us all home to his grandmother, Nonny, a few at a time. We've made that area our home ever since. None of us can do without Nonny."

"Judging by the food she sent and how delicious it was this morning, all of you probably settled there because she's such a good cook. I'm beginning to believe you all think with your stomachs."

Diego's soft laughter was more in her mind than aloud, but it warmed her. She knew he didn't laugh often, and she took it as a gift every time she heard it.

As they got closer, she could see that Wyatt's wavy hair was extremely thick and unruly. It helped to give him an approachable appearance. He sent her a grin and gave her an old-fashioned bow.

"You don' know how happy I am to meet you, ma'am," he greeted before Diego could make the introductions.

Your friend Wyatt is quite charming.

He's Cajun. Don't fall for it. There's nothing charming about that man.

She laughed aloud. She couldn't help it. "Nice to meet you too. I'm Leila. Diego tells me your grandmother's name is Grace. My little daughter is named Grace."

His smile widened and actually reached his eyes. He definitely had charm. Diego's arm tightened around her. He bent his head and brushed a kiss onto the top of her head.

"Nonny will love that," Wyatt said. "Pepper and I have triplets and a set of twins. One of the twins is named Grace after Nonny. She'll love having another child with her first name."

"Five?" Leila was a little shocked. She had heard this before but hadn't really processed the information. These men didn't seem to be family men, yet they were.

"Five," Wyatt admitted. "We both want a large family." He indicated the man hanging just two steps back. "This is Trap Dawkins. He has twins as well."

"Twins?" Her voice came out as a squeak. "There seems to be a theme. Does anyone have just single births?"

"Be very cautious how you answer," Diego warned the other men. "We were discussing having children, and I don't want her running for the woods."

"We had twin sisters," Rubin announced helpfully as he came up behind them.

Trap's eyebrow went up. "Twins run in your family? And you're enhanced? I'll have to figure the odds."

To Leila's shock, he winked at her, indicating he was teasing Diego. This was the man they'd said was neurodivergent and would ignore her. Yet he had a sense of humor. The men were surprising her. Clearly, they were all trying to put her at ease.

Diego groaned. "Seriously, Rubin? You had to tell her that?" He kissed the top of her head again. "And you aren't helping, Trap. Sweetheart, they're in some kind of conspiracy. They probably rehearsed."

"Are you saying there aren't twins in your family?" She put a hopeful note in her voice.

"Well, yeah, there are." Diego sounded reluctant to answer. "I can't lie."

Leila found herself laughing again. "I don't know what to think about the twin thing."

"Wyatt has triplets and twins," Trap put in helpfully. "I've been considering conducting a study for a little while now, calculating the odds." His voice had turned speculative.

Leila knew immediately that he was actually contemplating doing exactly what he said. He might have started out teasing his friend, but the subject caught his attention, and he was already calculating and analyzing.

"We just lost Trap," Wyatt said as his friend turned away from them, back in the direction of the forest.

"He didn't bring the lab with him, did he?" Rubin asked.

"I wouldn't put it past him," Wyatt said. He flashed Leila another grin. "He was polite for several minutes."

He wasn't apologizing for Trap. She could see that right away. Trap was accepted exactly as he was.

"He's been doing a fast analysis of the men under Chariot's command," Wyatt continued, speaking directly to Diego. "Luther's with Joe. They'll be here any minute. We stopped off at Luther's place to ask a few questions."

"He answered you?" Diego asked.

"Luther wasn't very forthcoming about his life when I first arrived with Bridget. My sister," she clarified. "I asked all kinds of questions, but he didn't answer."

It seemed as though more and more men were arriving. That definitely boded ill for the easy recovery of her daughter. These men didn't believe for a moment that Chariot would give her up or they wouldn't have all come running. She tried not to show that she was becoming upset, but Diego seemed to be in her mind and caught her alarm.

What is it, sweetheart?

That voice of his was molten fire pouring into her mind, branding his name there. Filling all those places where she was terrified of having to leave him but so convinced she had no other choice.

You already know Chariot isn't going to let me go, don't you? That's why so many have shown up.

The chances are very low that he's going to listen to reason. We moved a satellite over his compound and are using it to catch any activity, such as his soldiers coming our way. We also have other ways of getting information. We'll know if he's sending another wave of soldiers to retrieve you.

Leila knew Diego was attempting to reassure her, but the news that his commanding officer and Luther were consulting together filled her with dread. Using a satellite cost millions of dollars. *Millions.* She couldn't even conceive of the kind of money it would take to put a satellite in the air and move it where one wanted it to go. There had to be a protocol in place for moving satellites. Without a doubt they knew very powerful people, but she didn't like the way the entire mess was shaping up.

Chariot works for the government. He has the backing of the United States military. Her heart was pounding too hard, and she couldn't seem to slow it down. Never in her life had she been close to panicking. What was wrong with her? She was going to get these men killed. They had families. Wives and children. They were good men. She could usually detect a taint on a person, something that instantly put her off. None of the men she'd been introduced to had that strange off-putting aura about them.

"Joe's here," Wyatt announced, turning away from the cabin to look toward the forest.

"Do you need to at least greet him?" Leila tried to step away from Diego. She was going to have to leave. It was the only way to keep a war from brewing.

"Sweetheart," Diego said, using his soft, mesmerizing tone. "I know you think this is happening because of you, but it's been shaping up for some time. Get it out of your mind that if you go back, this is all going to go away. It isn't. It won't. It's bad enough that we have Whitney harming young girls and women and turning us into . . . I don't even know what to call us. But we aren't entirely human anymore. We don't need another fully sanctioned lab doing the same thing."

"The soldiers volunteer." Leila couldn't get her voice to go above a whisper. How did he know what she was thinking? It wasn't as if she wanted to leave him.

"You didn't volunteer. They gave your sister to Whitney. That right there condemns them in our eyes. Why would they be in league with a madman? Why take the two of you from Luther, your only relative? And after they kidnap you, going against your parents' wishes, they train you to be an assassin and force you to work for them without the protection even the soldiers have."

She felt the floor of the porch tremble. Wyatt turned back, a frown on his face. Rubin and Ezekiel, who both had stepped off the porch to follow Wyatt back toward the forest encampment, stopped abruptly to face Diego.

Diego's arm still circled her waist, locking her to him. There didn't appear to be tension in him. One would never know looking at him that he was angry, but she touched his mind and found rage. The trembling of the porch floor was an indication, and his energy was powerful enough that three men felt it and turned back. She immediately stroked gentle, soothing caresses in his mind, giving him those images and the feeling of her touching him mind to mind.

"Diego, what is it?"

"These men think so little of our women they're willing to sacrifice them to further their own gains. When we were boys, we lost our sisters one by one. It was horrific to be unable to save them. We did our best to watch over them. To keep them fed, to brighten their lives. Don't get me wrong, our sisters did their part, but we valued them. We knew what they were. These men destroy the lives of women and children and don't seem to give a damn about them or what happens to them. Look at what Whitney did to Bridget. She has no filter and is wide open, so every noise, everything around her, hurts her. She's in constant pain. Chariot might say he didn't do that, but he did. He conspired to send a little girl to a madman, knowing Whitney was considered insane. Knowing his reputation. Hell, it was his wife who told you Bridget was in trouble."

His voice never rose from that low rumbling sound, but the edge to it let her know fury on her sister's behalf, on hers, burned through him. She fell a little bit more in love with him. His anger on her behalf was very real.

"Everything okay, Diego?" Wyatt called.

She felt Diego take a cleansing breath and release it. He nuzzled the top of her head before answering.

"Yeah, we're good here." He gestured for the three men to go on their way.

Leila noted that Rubin studied his brother carefully before finally turning and following the others.

The moment they were alone, she turned her face up to his. "I don't want these men to have to fight other soldiers, Diego, not on my behalf. I don't want to be responsible if even one of them doesn't make it home to his family. No matter what you say, they wouldn't all be here if it wasn't for what is happening to Bridget and me."

Diego urged her toward one of the rocking chairs on the porch. "That's true, but a showdown has been brewing for a long time. Our teams are always in the shadows. Very few people know of our existence, and that makes it easy for other factions to conspire against us and hunt us down. We've been sent on assignments that ultimately were designed to be suicide runs. I can't tell you how many times one or more of our teams were sabotaged by those sending us out. We serve our country. We save lives. As long as we're completely in the shadows and the things Whitney has done never comes to light, all of us will always have to question who's against us even though they're our commanders."

"That's all true," Leila agreed. She sank into the rocking chair and was a little surprised at how comfortable it was. Just like the chairs in his home, these were hand carved. "But you aren't looking at the entire picture, Diego. If the world knew that Whitney had introduced animal and reptilian DNA into you, the backlash would be horrendous. People don't like anything different. The prejudice against you would skyrocket. Those of you with various types of genetic differences would face unimaginable discrimination. Your kind wouldn't be tolerated."

"We're aware." Diego didn't look at her. In fact, he stepped back, his hand dropping away from hers, his mind abruptly retreating from hers.

Leila looked up at him. As with most occasions, his features were expressionless, but there was something in his eyes— disappointment? Hurt? What had she said that triggered that kind of reaction in him? He had to know what she said was the truth. He had to have been aware of the reaction people would have to them. He said he was aware, so why the withdrawal?

"Diego, what's going on?"

He turned back to her, his eyes hard. "'Your kind wouldn't be tolerated'?" His voice was low, sounding like the lash of a whip.

Instantly, she heard what he'd heard. "I'm so sorry for wording it that way," she apologized. "I'm the same as you when it comes to genetic engineering. I sometimes, when I'm trying to understand other points of view, put myself in their place to try to get out of my own head. I don't like forming arguments until I've listened and actually heard what the other person is saying to me. In this case, I was trying to make a case from someone else's point of view. But you have to know if there is a 'your kind,' I'm part of that with you."

As apologies went, it wasn't the best explanation. She had a bad habit of stepping outside herself when she was discussing anything controversial. It had always been important to her to hear the other side of something, even if it ended up making no sense to her.

"You just saw one of my flaws, Diego. I have a lot of them."

He paced away from her and came back, the restless movements of a caged tiger. She recognized that he had far too many predatory traits to be able to stay indoors long. She had no idea how he'd managed to stay with her in the little den he'd set up for her before he could bring her to the cabin. She admired him all the more for that.

Diego crossed the porch twice and then returned to stand in front of her. "There is a faction already looking to wipe us out. They've sent soldiers after our women and children. Joe was nearly killed. I can't tell you how many times they tried to kill Pepper and the children just because they're different."

"I worry for Grace. I know that I've passed some of my traits to her. I can see them in her already. But I never meant to imply that I felt any different from you. I identify with you and your Ghost-Walkers. Truthfully, a good percentage of the soldiers under Chariot's command are good men. Part of the reason I detest that we might go to war with them is because, like your friends, they didn't do anything wrong. They joined the program with the best of intentions. They honestly aren't any different from you or me."

Diego crouched down in front of her, his palms shaping her knees. Looking into his eyes immediately flooded her with warmth. He was always focused when he looked at her, as if she were the only woman in the universe. She shouldn't have trusted an attraction that hit so hard, so fast, and maybe she didn't, but she didn't want to lose him. The thought of not being with Diego was extremely upsetting.

She didn't need a man. She never had. She didn't want to be taken care of. She wasn't that kind of woman. Still. She looked at Diego's very masculine features. She couldn't conceive of leaving him behind, even if she knew it was the right thing to do to avoid a war.

"Sweetheart, I know you do your best to hear whoever is talking to you, and I should have taken that into consideration before I reacted like a hothead."

She didn't think he reacted like a hothead. He hadn't yelled at her or even condemned her. He'd withdrawn. She was going to have to remember that was his first reaction. She even understood. No matter what his mother had said or done to him, he had never reacted. He withdrew, internalized everything. It was a habit that would be difficult to break.

"I want you to hear me now. I know you're probably thinking we barely know each other. I'm absolutely certain Whitney couldn't have paired us, and even if he had, I would be grateful that he got you to notice me. I believe you are the one woman for me. I want to take that chance with you. Whatever is happening around us, whatever the GhostWalkers or Chariot's men choose to do, doesn't negate the fact that I believe we should be together."

"I feel the same way," she felt compelled to admit. "But it's weird that it happened so fast. Don't you suspect something isn't right?"

"Or it could be exactly what it's supposed to be. Why are two people attracted to each other? I may want you physically, but we haven't gone there. I know we can't right now, and I'm okay with that. I'd rather spend time with you than anyone else. Even Rubin, and that's saying something. I've never felt this way for anyone else, and I doubt if I ever will again. When I make a commitment, Leila, I follow through. That's who I am."

"You saw what happened just now. I worded my thoughts wrong and hurt you."

"That was my issue, not yours. We're getting to know one another. There will be things coming up we have to work through. Any long-term relationship has its ups and downs. We're bound to fall in and out of love, but if the commitment is there, and we only focus on each other, we'll make it."

"I have no idea how to have a relationship, Diego," she warned.

"We have Nonny. She was in a very good marriage. It wasn't always easy, but they were determined to make it work, and they did. We can go to her and ask questions if we need to."

"You'd do that?" She was a little shocked. Diego didn't seem the type of man to consult anyone over something so personal. She liked that he would care enough to do so.

"I think we should give ourselves every opportunity for success." He sighed and once more stood. "I'm a predator, Leila. I may have the protective instincts of all those animals and the ones I was born with, but I also have some very unfortunate traits."

"Do they keep you alive?"

He frowned. "Yes."

"Do those traits help you to save lives?"

He nodded slowly, his eyes softening from that hard, scary look to something she was beginning to crave.

"And those same traits help you to guard every man on your team." She made that a statement because she knew the truth of it.

His answering smile lit her up until she was so ridiculously happy that she could make him smile after he'd been upset. They had a long way to go to understand each other, but she felt if they could keep talking things out, they had a good chance of making it.

Diego's smile faded, and he suddenly turned his head, lifting his face toward the breeze. "Joe's coming this way, Leila. He's got Luther with him."

"Luther will be able to tell us what happened with Bridget," she said.

"He doesn't have her with him, so be prepared for that," he warned.

He hesitated, and she found herself tensing up. Waiting. He had something important to say and was finding the right words. That was a bit alarming to her. She looked past him to see Luther and another man striding toward them. It was easy to see the man's Italian heritage in his good looks. It was also very easy to see he was supremely confident. He moved with a fluid power, one that surrounded him.

Joe Spagnola wasn't particularly tall. He didn't have the bulk that some of the other men under his command had, but he had presence. She found a little shiver moving through her body.

"He knows things," Diego said. "It's one of his many gifts. When I say that, it's nearly impossible to hide much from him. We aren't trying to."

"Other than the fact that you are capable of doing the same kind of psychic surgery as your brother."

"He'll find out. I would like to keep that from all of them, but he's going to ask questions, and when he does, you can't lie to him. I'm asking you not to volunteer the information, but we can't lie to him. For one thing, he deserves our respect, and for another, he would know. He's got some kind of built-in lie detector."

"Is he a fair man?"

"I wouldn't follow him if he wasn't," Diego confirmed.

Leila was used to being around soldiers who were enhanced genetically. But she didn't have the experience with those who had psychic abilities. She believed most people had capabilities they hadn't developed but sometimes felt or even acted on in a limited manner. She certainly had moments when she knew things. She'd tried very hard to develop those traits, but she had the advantage of hearing about the GhostWalkers and their extraordinary abilities.

Diego's commanding officer approached the porch, Luther pacing easily at his side, showing that his wounds were healed, and despite his age, he could easily keep up with the younger man.

Leila tried to remain relaxed when Joe and Luther came straight up onto the porch. Luther awkwardly patted her shoulder.

"I was worried about you, girl. I didn't make it to your sister in time. I'm sorry. Luckily, we'll be able to track her. It was good to hear Diego had gotten to you before those men took you to a helicopter."

She glanced at Diego. She thought Luther would have been told the men had no intention of getting her to the helicopter.

"Those men had decided not to get her to the helicopter, Luther," Joe said. "Unfortunately, some of the soldiers who are enhanced physically can't handle the aggressive traits."

Luther didn't have to have it spelled out for him. His entire demeanor changed. He took a step back and turned his attention to Diego. "You took care of this?"

"I did. I'm sure that's what is putting Joe in an impossible situation," Diego acknowledged.

"Not impossible," Joe murmured and flashed Leila a charming smile. "I'm Joe Spagnola. It's nice to meet you, ma'am."

She could see how easily others would succumb to his charisma. "Just Leila, please," she said, hoping he wouldn't ask her questions.

Joe perched on the railing across from her. "Luther gave me a few details, and Rubin has provided a few more, but Diego, there are gaps. Big ones. I'll need everything, no surprises when I take this to the general and demand a meeting with Chariot."

"I'll do my best," Diego said.

It was all Leila could do not to look at him. She had the feeling this was going to be bad. Diego had been adamant that no one could find out about his surgical abilities, but instinctively she knew that this man would never stop until he uncovered every secret. Luther wouldn't have told him a thing. She had no intentions of revealing anything Diego had done for her, but she had the feeling Diego's loyalty to the man would be his downfall.

15

understand Leila had been shot when they carried her up the mountain." Joe made it a statement. "Let's start with that. She went down. What did you do?"

Diego felt the presence of his brother. Rubin always knew when there might be trouble. He'd had all those years of their mother abusing Diego. He'd developed an instinct for knowing when Diego was in trouble, just as Diego had that same instinct when Rubin needed him.

Joe scowled and turned slightly so he was able to spot Rubin's approach. Ezekiel moved onto the porch and stood at the farthest end from them. Joe sent him a long look before turning a thoughtful gaze on Diego. He remained silent, but Diego had the feeling just having Rubin and Ezekiel move close tipped Joe off that there was quite a bit he didn't know. That wasn't a good thing.

"I saw Luther had taken a hit. There appeared to be two different factions there. There were the ones that took Bridget and the ones that went after Leila. I had no idea who they were or what they wanted. They were already shooting at the women and Luther when I arrived. I needed to know and understand as much as I could, and it was necessary to ensure Luther wasn't in a bad way. I noted the direction of the teams taking the women. I had placed a tracking device into each of them, so I was certain we would be able to find them if the teams managed to get them away before I could go after them."

Joe nodded and continued looking directly at him. "I take it you caught up to Luther."

"Rubin and I had been with Luther over the years and knew some of his bolt-holes. I tracked him to one of them, and he told me that Leila and Bridget were his nieces. Well, great-nieces. When his nephew died, the girls were supposed to go to him, but they were taken by General Pillar. Bridget was given to Whitney, and Chariot retained custody of Leila."

At that point, Joe turned his attention to Leila. "Were you enhanced and trained as a soldier?"

"I was enhanced and trained as an assassin. I was never part of the teams. I lived in a separate building."

"You never volunteered at any point or signed papers?" Joe prompted.

She shook her head.

Joe turned his attention back to Diego. "Luther had been shot." He made it a statement. "You were able to patch him up enough that you sent him after Bridget?"

"He is a doctor," Rubin said. "You don't need to sound so skeptical. He went through med school the same as we all did."

"If you can't keep quiet, Rubin, you should leave," Joe said. "It isn't like I don't know you two have been covering for each other all the years I've known you."

Diego felt the instant reaction, that well of molten heat that could consume him if he ever allowed it. "Best not to talk to him that way, Joe."

Joe's gaze never once moved from his, a penetrating piercing laser. "Right now, I'm acting as your commanding officer, not your friend. Shocks me a little that I have to point that out when I'm getting the facts." The tone was mild enough, but Joe was at his most lethal when he sounded mild.

Leila unexpectedly reached out to thread her fingers through Diego's hand and pressed the back of her hand against his thigh. That touch, featherlight but all-consuming, instantly sent a wave of peace through him. She had that low energy, exuding calm.

So what if he knows you can heal in a pinch. Is it really that big of a deal?

The moment she sent the images into his mind, Joe's piercing gaze locked on her. "You have something to say, Leila, I would prefer you speak it aloud."

Her chin went up. "If I wanted everyone to hear it, I would have spoken aloud."

Joe burst out laughing. That was one of his gifts, Diego decided. He could defuse a situation easily. It was impossible to tell if his laughter was genuine. It felt and looked as if it was, but Diego was well aware Joe had many gifts.

"I suppose you have me there. Let's get on with this, Diego. You were telling me about Luther's injuries. Were they severe?"

That was a direct question requiring a direct answer. Leila's finger slid over his knuckles in a caress. Support. Encouragement. He'd never had that. Well, he had—he'd had Rubin, Ezekiel, Mordichai and Malichai, and he supposed he could count Luther, but it wasn't the same. It didn't feel the same. Leila was a woman he was falling in love with. He didn't expect her to reciprocate, at least not to the extent that he knew he was capable of loving her.

"Diego?" Joe prompted. "Is there a reason you're reluctant to tell me about Luther's injuries? I have a very high clearance."

Diego sighed. "It isn't that, sir." He decided if Joe was going to pull rank on him, he would be formal. "I have some small healing ability, and I had no choice but to use it. I didn't have the time or equipment to operate on him. I'd never used the ability on a human being and was very reluctant, but given his injuries and the fact that I couldn't be in two places at one time, I did my best with what I had."

Silence met his revelation. Joe slowly turned his head, first to look at Rubin and then Ezekiel.

"News to me," Ezekiel said. "I had no idea."

"I didn't either until yesterday," Rubin admitted.

Joe turned back to Diego. "Why wouldn't you let us know you were capable? Healing is a rare gift and can be used in the field when there's an emergency."

Diego sighed again. "I've seen you heal. And Rubin. It's incredible work. I've used it on animals but never had the confidence to use it on a human. I felt it didn't come from a good place and the ability wasn't . . ." He trailed off, searching for the correct word. He didn't want to say "pure."

Rubin had always been his example. When Rubin healed a patient, he gave everything he had selflessly. There was no motive other than to make that patient better. That would never be so with Diego. He might heal those he loved or respected, but he would never be like Rubin. He didn't have the ability to feel empathy for a great deal of the population.

"You have always used your gift of healing exclusively for animals?" Joe clarified.

Diego nodded. "I have many other enhancements that I work at either controlling or strengthening. We have two healers in our unit. And now Jonquille. So, three. I contribute in other ways."

"Did it occur to you to ask to be mentored?"

Diego shook his head. "Again, I felt as if I had a very mild talent."

"You healed Luther and then what?" Joe persisted.

"We thought it best to separate. I know that part of the mountain like the back of my hand. I grew up there. I knew I could outrun the ones who had taken Leila. There is only one place to safely land a helicopter, so I knew their destination."

"Luther went after Bridget, and you went up the mountain after Leila," Joe confirmed.

"Yes. I was a little less than a mile from them when I went up a tree to check how many and what they were doing. Leila was in very bad shape, and the men had decided to finish her off and just tell Chariot she didn't make it."

"They were going to rape me," Leila interrupted. She wasn't about to allow Diego to get in any trouble for killing Chariot's soldiers. "He saved me."

Joe's shoulders straightened, his mask falling into place. Ezekiel stood, moving restlessly in the corner of the porch. Diego could feel that pent-up dark energy from where he was.

"I made the decision to take them out. They had weapons drawn, and it was only a matter of time before one of them shot her." There was no apology in his voice. At the time, Diego believed he had no other choice if he had any chance at all to save her life.

Joe nodded his approval. "I expect that took all of thirty seconds."

Leila's little laugh warmed him. Diego settled his palm around the nape of her neck.

"You really do know him," Leila said. There was respect, admiration even, in her voice. "I had managed to keep a knife. The idiots hadn't really searched me. But I'd lost so much blood and was very weak. They'd dropped me coming up the mountain, and I felt something tear away inside."

That was far too much information to hand to Joe. It was all Diego could do to keep from groaning aloud. He had been certain, after confessing to a small ability to heal, he could glide right over aiding Leila, given that she had defended herself against several soldiers.

Joe's penetrating stare was once more a laser seeing right into Diego. Inwardly, he cursed. He didn't mind giving up the fact that he had a small healing talent. It wasn't unreasonable that he hadn't developed it. Each of the GhostWalkers had multiple gifts. Some were far more advanced than others.

"Luther told me you'd been shot. He didn't know how bad the injury was. By the sound of it, you were in bad shape."

Oh no, Diego. Leila realized immediately she'd put him in a terrible position.

Diego didn't like the waves of distress coming from her. She had hunched in on herself, turning her head to face him. Looking at him through eyes far too big, almost as if she were going into shock. Her lashes were wet. Her lips trembled. But it was the sudden panic in her mind that was the worst.

Uncertainty. Guilt. Fear even, that she'd betrayed him when she was only trying to get his commanding officer to realize the situation for her had been dire, and Diego had saved her life. She didn't want Joe to hold Diego responsible for the deaths of those soldiers when there had been a good reason for him to take their lives.

She'd been defending him. Championing him. Now, she was terrified that she'd put him in a very bad position with Joe. And she feared she'd lost him through her perceived betrayal.

Protecting his secret didn't seem as important as making her understand she mattered more. He was a grown man and should have let Joe and Ezekiel know the moment he had used his ability to perform surgery. He wasn't as good at it as Rubin and never would be, but neither was anyone else. He had his reasons for not giving up his secrets, and if Joe thought those reasons weren't good, that was on Diego, not Leila.

He leaned into Leila, resting his forehead against hers. "Leila, you're tired. Cut yourself some slack. You need to rest, not get upset because you told Joe the truth. You were slipping away, baby. That's the truth. I would have done anything to save you. Given anything. I'm a grown man, not some child hiding things from the insanity that was my mother."

"But I shouldn't have . . ." She trailed off. Her long lashes were wet, making his heart stutter. "I don't blurt things out without thinking. I wanted him to know you saved my life. Not just my life. If those men had been able to do what they intended, and that was the last thing I knew, along with the excruciating pain, before I died . . ." Again, she trailed off.

"I like that you're proud of me, Leila. And I like that you stand up for me." He brushed kisses along her forehead and trailed them down her wet cheek to the side of her mouth. "Do you want to lie down for a little while?"

"I'd rather stay with you."

He felt her uncertainty. A part of her thought he would reject her. She wasn't entirely convinced he no longer cared if his unit knew. They would be protective to the point he might shoot one of them, but silence wasn't worth Leila believing he would be angry with her over telling the truth.

"What is the truth, Diego?" Joe asked, his tone very soft, almost soothing.

Diego knew that particular voice. It didn't sound to outsiders who didn't know Joe as if it was a warning, but Diego had known

Joe a long time. He didn't like to see Leila's distress any more than Diego did. Joe was a man who stood for women and children. He stood for those not strong enough to stand up for themselves. He might look charming and easygoing, but that was deceptive.

"I had no choice. Leila was bleeding internally, and she'd lost far too much blood. I didn't have a team, or any real way of saving her life in a conventional manner. Along with healing animals, I had performed surgery on them if it was warranted. Again, I had never done so on a human, so I was very reluctant to try, but she was already slipping away."

There was total silence meeting his revelation. He didn't look at Joe or Ezekiel, or even Rubin. He brought Leila's hand to his mouth and pressed kisses into her palm.

Joe cleared his throat. "I want to be very clear on this, Diego."

That was a command to look at him. Diego did so, keeping his expression blank. The many predators in him reacted to any challenge. Learning to control the roaring voices, the adrenaline and testosterone, hadn't been easy, but he had done so.

"Are you saying you were able to perform psychic surgery on Leila?"

"I had no choice. As it was, I had to remove her spleen. She had massive damage, but the trajectory of the bullet was what really saved her."

Again, there was a brief silence. Joe continued to stare him down, triggering the predators in Diego. He breathed evenly. In and out. Counting his breaths.

"Did you know he could do that, Rubin? Ezekiel?" Again, Joe's voice was very quiet.

"I didn't have a clue," Rubin admitted. "Not in all these years."

"I didn't either," Ezekiel said. "But now that I know, I'm not surprised. Rubin and Diego are very much like twins. I should have realized what talent one has, so does the other."

"Diego," Joe said, a note in his voice that Diego didn't recognize. It was almost a hesitation, something Diego had never known Joe to do. "You do realize there are most likely under ten people on this earth who can perform psychic surgery."

Diego hadn't thought in terms of numbers. He didn't want to think of the repercussions. He had guarded his brother on the pretense of ensuring his brother's gift survived, but in reality, for Diego, it wasn't about his brother's ability to execute psychic surgery. He did know, for his team and every other GhostWalker team, that was the reason the surgeon was guarded so carefully. He didn't want the restrictions he knew his brother lived with.

"You know I'm capable of healing, but I can't perform surgery. I wouldn't even attempt such a thing, knowing the outcome would be disastrous," Joe continued. "You can tell us you felt you had no choice, but the fact that you could do actual surgery under the conditions you had, when you were alone and most likely giving blood as well, attests to the fact that you have a very strong talent."

Diego didn't want to hear that and was already shaking his head in denial before he could think how to react.

Joe leaned closer. "You can't deny it, Diego. You know if you were able to do those things, it's a miracle. Nothing less. You removed her spleen and fixed the damage . . ."

"Rubin had to reinforce my work. It didn't hold up," Diego said.

Joe turned his gaze on Rubin. "I thought you didn't know about Diego's ability."

Diego had to restrain himself from defending Rubin. Rubin wouldn't have welcomed his interference, and he had the feeling he was already skating on thin ice with Joe.

"I didn't know about Diego's ability until I arrived at the cabin and found him in a total crash situation. It was only when I went to examine Leila that I realized what he'd done. Diego, I'd like to agree with you that you don't have a strong talent because I know where that's coming from, but if I'm to be truthful, your talent is every bit as powerful as mine. I may have more experience, but you're every bit as capable."

Diego shook his head again.

Joe studied his face, making Diego more uncomfortable than ever. "What is it, Diego? Why do you feel you aren't capable?"

Inadvertently, his grip tightened on the nape of Leila's neck. She relaxed against him, moving into him despite the arms on the chairs creating a space.

"I don't feel the compulsion to heal in the way you do or Rubin does. It was a little shocking to feel it with Leila."

"And Luther?"

Diego shrugged. "It was a matter of necessity to heal him. That's what I did, but I wouldn't call it a compulsion."

"Is it possible that you trained yourself not to feel the need to heal because Rubin's talent was strong?" Ezekiel asked.

Diego despised the conversation. He knew it had to take place and that none of the men present would give his secrets away unless Joe decided he had to be as guarded as Rubin. He needed to convince Joe that he couldn't do surgery on just anyone.

Diego, you know that's more than possible, Rubin whispered into his mind. *From the time you were a child, our mother would tell you anything you were capable of came from a dark, evil place.*

I'm an adult, not that child. I should know what I feel. But he wasn't certain if that was true. Sadly, it was very possible that he had trained himself not to feel the need to heal a human. The need was extremely strong around animals. Over the years, he had convinced himself that healing animals, not humans, was his calling.

Joe's gaze moved from Rubin to Diego, but this time he didn't ask either of them to voice their conversation aloud.

Diego, think about it. Our mother drilled it into you from the time you were a toddler that anything you did came from a dark place. She even got our sisters believing it, or maybe half believing. She was insane. I tried to shield you, but there was no convincing you when you were a kid because we didn't talk about it. We never discussed it. We were trying to survive and keep everyone else alive.

Surprisingly, Rubin had included Leila in the communication. Her fingers pressed into his thigh. *You can't dismiss what he's saying out of hand, Diego. You're mortal, just like everyone else, and you have triggers. You have built-in beliefs that are so skewed you're having an impossible time accepting who you really are.*

Was he? He trusted Rubin more than any other person on the face of the earth. Rubin wouldn't lie to him. He had always put Rubin first because he believed in him, and his brother had never let him down. He wanted to develop that same trust with Leila. When she used the more intimate path of telepathy, it was much easier to spot a lie. As far as he knew, she had never lied to him.

"I don't know, Zeke," Diego finally said. "We told you a little of our childhood. What we didn't tell you was that our mother considered me to be a child of the devil."

Silence followed his admission, both Joe and Ezekiel waiting for more of an explanation. It was Rubin who answered.

"She beat the shit out of Diego, even when he provided us with food in the winter. She was certain he had used magic to lure animals to him. She persuaded him that anything he did, no matter the good of the outcome, came from the devil. She was relentless, telling him day and night, refusing to allow him to sleep at times. It was the cruelest form of child abuse, but it was his normal. He accepted it in order to help me keep our sisters alive. It stands to reason that Diego might have trained himself not to feel the need to heal. I was always the saint, and he was always a sinner. Worse than a sinner. He was a child of demons."

I don't want their sympathy. Or their pity. That was all a long time ago.

Once again, he felt Leila move in his mind. This time she seemed to stroke a caress there. It was an intimate feeling, and soothing, as if they were already a solid couple and she had his back.

They have sympathy for a young boy, Diego. They're just learning these things, and they care about you. You're so lucky to have people who care.

His fingers tightened on the nape of her neck in a brief acknowledgment that she was right. He was extremely lucky. He had held parts of himself away from his brother, his sister-in-law and Ezekiel, the man who had kept him alive on the streets of Detroit. Malichai and Mordichai had always treated him like a brother. The way Joe ran his team of GhostWalkers, it had always felt like an extended family. And there was Nonny. And Luther.

I am extremely lucky. I appreciate your helping me see it.

Diego didn't understand why he'd never realized just how lucky he truly was. He was a man who turned a spotlight on himself every day to check his behavior. He knew he was loaded with aggressive genetics. It was important to him that he didn't turn into a bully—or worse, a killer.

"Let me say this, Diego. To operate in the conditions you did and save her life, your talent, without question, is powerful," Joe said. "And there is no way it comes from a place of evil. You do an exchange, risk your life to save another. You knew that going in. We can discuss this at a later date. For the moment, I need you to continue with your report on what transpired after you did surgery on Leila."

To move on was a relief. Diego didn't want to think too much about how Joe and Ezekiel would treat him knowing he had some measure of psychic surgical ability. He would never be able to take the others hovering around him or the restrictions put on him. He needed solitude. It was the only way he found peace.

Leila's fingertips dug into his thigh. *You have me now. I can be a buffer when you need it. I won't mind. In fact, it would make me happy.*

The sincerity in her kept the knots in his gut from forming. She was willing, like Rubin, to stand for him. Or even in front of him if necessary. That revelation was earth-shattering to him. In answer, he stroked his hand down the back of her head and once more curled his palm around her nape. Physical connection with Leila was fast becoming a necessity.

"We both needed rest for a couple of days. I wanted to have time to heal her before I moved her. I'd put together a little den for us and erased all tracks leading to it. It was necessary to get rid of the scent of blood to keep any tracker with sniffing abilities from locating us. I knew that wasn't going to last, but I just wanted to buy us a little time," Diego explained. "I knew Rubin would be coming up that mountain after me, and I hoped Luther would be able to. I didn't count on either one of them, but in the back of my mind, if something were to happen to me, I knew either one of them would be able to find Leila."

He glanced at his brother. "Rubin knows me. He knows every sign of mine in the woods. I knew if I went down hard while I was working on her, he'd find us and protect her. As it was, she didn't need protection." He couldn't help the pride in his voice or the growing love in his gaze as he looked at her. He leaned into her and brushed a kiss along her temple, noting color had swept into her face.

He continued his report, letting Joe know about how four out of five of the soldiers were like the first ones, unable to control the aggression and dominance they felt. "Those men seemed certain they were superior to anyone else and were entitled to have whatever they wanted. The fifth man, Terry, was very decent. It was clear he would have put his life in jeopardy to save Leila. He had every intention to interfere with their plans. I let him go and told him to report back to Chariot that Leila had nothing to do with the kills. I identified myself so Chariot knew who he was dealing with."

"You thought this was a good idea?" Joe asked.

Diego nodded. "I did. I didn't want him trying to hold dead soldiers over Leila's head. She didn't kill them; that was my decision."

Leila cleared her throat. "Diego."

Her voice was very low, but Diego knew Joe, Rubin and Ezekiel had excellent hearing.

"I hunted those other soldiers," she admitted. "Every last one of them." She looked up at Joe. "That's how I tore myself up again."

"We had a cleanup crew see to the bodies. They were soldiers. They started out with good intentions," Ezekiel said. "They deserve to be buried decently. Their families have the right to know they died on an assignment."

"You can go to your grave before you admit that you were involved, Leila," Joe said. "Your injuries were enough to stop anyone from moving around, let alone hunt seasoned soldiers. I doubt the subject will come up, but if it does, when we go into a meeting, you stay quiet. If they ask you a direct question, you don't answer unless Logan Maxwell with GhostWalker Team Two allows you to speak. He's an excellent lawyer."

"That's very important, Leila," Ezekiel reiterated. "No matter what is said, who says it, or if things look as if they're going south, you stay very quiet and allow us to handle it. Logan is exceptional and will be your biggest protection."

"You know they aren't going to release me."

She pressed her fingertips into Diego's thigh, betraying her agitation. It didn't show on her face, but Diego could feel the waves of distress pouring off her. He leaned into her again.

"You aren't going back there, and we're bringing Grace home."

He said it with complete conviction because, for him, there was no other outcome.

She gave him a sad smile. "I really don't want all of your friends to risk their lives—or their careers—because of me. We talked about war between two factions of covert operatives, but what we didn't discuss is the likelihood of General Pillar pulling rank on everyone."

"Pillar isn't the only general in the game," Joe said. "This is about right and wrong. What was done to you was wrong. What they did to your sister was unconscionable. It was completely unethical. Immoral. Pillar is directly responsible for that decision. If he tries to double down, he's going to hit a brick wall. He has to answer to those above him, and they won't like publicity. Before they took you and your sister, the lab in Maryland was aboveboard in that they recruited men who wanted to join their program. They were told ahead of time what to expect, and Chariot never went beyond those parameters. Pillar forced him to take you into the program."

"How do you know so much about Chariot's work? It's classified," Leila asked.

Joe shrugged. "We're all classified. We have several resident geniuses. They can get their hands on anything they want. I don't condone it, and I try not to know about it if that's possible. But being a complete hypocrite, I use the information if I need it to keep my men safe and to have a favorable outcome on an assignment."

"In what way?" Leila asked.

"The GhostWalkers have enemies, factions who would like to see them wiped out. There have been times when our teams have been set up. We've been stranded, without a way home from a very bad situation. We've been ambushed. We've had men from other countries infiltrate teams we were training, just to assassinate us.

It's necessary for our backup plans to have backup plans. We rely on ourselves. On one another's teams. We can only trust one another, and we know that. I use information to keep our families safe as well as ensuring our teams come home alive and well."

Diego kept the pathway open between Leila and him. He needed to know if she would stand with them, even if things took a bad turn and the general refused to cooperate. There was a child involved, and a mother's instincts were strong. Right now, she felt Grace was safe and secure with Marcy Chariot, but if the general decided to play hardball and hold Grace hostage to get Leila to return, she could so easily cave.

As if reading his mind, Joe brought up the possibility. "I know you have to be worried that they'll hide Grace from you to force you to return. Trap and Wyatt calculated the odds, and both believe that's exactly what they'll do. They'll try to scare you into complying. Before we go into this meeting with the general, we have to know you'll stand with us no matter what they say or do."

Diego felt Leila's swift intake of breath. She held her air trapped in her lungs until Diego could feel her burning with the need to breathe.

He wrapped his arms around her to lend her his strength. "We would never leave without Grace, Leila. Never. Before we enter the meeting, we'll know exactly where she is, and if we have to take her from them, we'll do it. Someone will be on her at all times, ready to take her back."

Leila shook her head, nearly choking with the inability to take a breath. Diego couldn't blame her. The thought of losing her daughter was too much.

"Just breathe, sweetheart. Take a breath. In and out. You know how," he encouraged. "First, know they won't hurt her. Commander Chariot's wife is looking after her, and you've indicated to me that you don't worry when Grace is with her. She isn't going to allow anyone else with your daughter. She'll most likely be feeling as protective as you always do. You have to trust your instincts. They've always indicated the woman is on your side."

Leila drew in a shuddering breath and clung to him, her fingers digging into his arm. "You might not be able to get to her. They'll hide her from us, and she'll be guarded if the general is going to use her to get me to come back."

Joe leaned toward her, forcing her gaze his way. "I swear to you, Leila, before we go into the meeting, we'll know exactly where she is and have a plan to get her out if, at the end of the meeting, there is no resolution, or at least one not to our satisfaction."

"You've already set up a meeting?" Diego asked.

"We have," Ezekiel said. "We have the satellite in place, not just watching to see if the general sends more men to acquire you but to keep an eye on Grace. At the moment she is in Marcy and Phil Chariot's home. They do have soldiers watching the place, presumably in case we show up to take Grace from them, but we know their exact locations and how many. There is no doubt in our minds we can take her back without bloodshed."

Leila pressed her lips together. *Diego, I want to agree. But what if I panic?*

You won't panic. When push comes to shove, there isn't any backup in you. Especially when it comes to Grace. If you know there's a solid plan in place, you're going to carry out the orders, believing, like me, that we'll get her back.

You believe they can do it? Even if General Pillar insists they will keep her?

I know we can get her back. Diego poured absolute confidence into his voice and into her mind. *You have to decide whether or not you have faith in me. In the two of us and in our GhostWalker teams.*

I haven't been around the teams, Diego. You're asking me to put my daughter's life in their hands when I haven't seen them in action.

Diego chose to take their conversation out of the privacy of telepathy. She needed to know he had complete confidence in his team members. "You've seen me in action. My teammates are every bit as capable, and some of them more so."

She either believed him or she didn't. He knew it was asking a lot when she really didn't know him that well, but they'd run out of time. If she couldn't give her word, they wouldn't be taking her with them.

Leila's eyes searched his for a long time, and then she turned her attention, first on Joe, then Ezekiel and last on Rubin. Slowly she nodded her head. "I'm with you."

16

Diego had never seen so many generals gathered in one place. They wore their uniforms with stars and medals, looking as if each was trying to outdo the others. The meeting had been set up in Maryland, close to the compound where General Chariot, the commanding officer, oversaw the laboratory where the experiments were done.

The GhostWalkers had counted on General Pillar giving himself the advantage. The moment the venue for the meeting was chosen, they moved to secure Chariot's home, knowing little Grace was being held there. Guards were surrounding the home. The estate was behind locked gates. They had plenty of time to study the guards' movements as well as the position of all security cameras. Joe was certain Pillar had already made up his mind to hold Grace back in order to force Leila's compliance.

There had been several meetings with Logan Maxwell, leader of GhostWalker Team Two. He was a brilliant lawyer, had worked for NCIS and had a reputation in the military as a man who won his cases. Like all the GhostWalkers, Logan was enhanced, and Diego suspected his psychic gifts were a good part of the lawyer's success, along with his intelligence and knowledge of the law.

Frank Henderson had recently been promoted to vice admiral. He had been overseeing Team Two since that GhostWalker team had been formed. He was a rear admiral at the time, and he'd never relinquished his leadership over the team. They trusted him, and when he walked in with Logan, he did so with great authority.

General Theodore "Ted" Ranier oversaw Team One. He had been looking out for the first team of GhostWalkers since they had broken out of Whitney's lab after several had already succumbed to the experiments he was doing on them. With him was Ryland Miller, the commanding officer leading the team. Team One had the most problems, but Miller was married to Whitney's daughter, and she worked hard at helping the GhostWalkers overcome the lack of filters in their brains and other debilitating problems.

The two men entered the large meeting room together, exuding the same confidence Vice Admiral Henderson had. Technically, Ranier outranked General Pillar. Pillar eyed him with wariness but made no comment as the men took their seats at the large conference table.

Theodore Griffen was a phenomenon in the Marine Corps. He attributed his fast movement up the ranks to sergeant major of the Marine Corps in a few short years to his handling of GhostWalker Team Three. He was senior listed adviser to the commandant of Marines. He had worked tirelessly in Washington with the president and was extremely skilled in planning covert operations. His name and reputation were very well-known—especially the fact that he didn't back down when he believed he was in the right. And he always fought for his GhostWalkers. With him entering the meeting was Mack McKinley, the commanding officer leading Team Three. They were very skilled in urban warfare. McKinley had a reputation, along with Sergeant Major Griffen, for getting the job done no matter the odds.

Diego and Leila entered with Joe, Ezekiel, Rubin and Major General Tennessee Milton. Milton had been in charge of their team since it was formed. The Pararescue Team had originally been kept secret even from the other teams, but Major General Milton didn't believe they were safer completely alone, without backup. The GhostWalker teams had too many enemies. Milton wanted all the teams to be united. More than once, in the worst of times, he had come through for Team Four.

Leila was seated beside Logan, with Diego on the other side of her. Deliberately, when they walked in, Diego held her hand. Pillar scowled as if they were doing something wrong. Aside from showing they were a couple, Diego was making a point that Leila wasn't in the military. She wasn't under anyone's command and could show public affection even in a military setting. He was making a blatant statement.

Chairs scraped as they were pulled out and everyone was seated. Pillar took up a position at the head of the table, with Chariot on his right.

"I believe we have a problem, gentlemen," Pillar greeted.

"I believe you're correct," Logan answered.

Pillar scowled at him, staring, his shaggy brows drawn together. It was clear to Diego that Pillar was doing his best to intimidate Logan. That wasn't going to happen. Logan returned his gaze steadily.

"Leila Fenton belongs here with us, and she must return," Pillar stated.

"Leila Fenton and her sister, Bridget, were supposed to have been given to Luther Gunthrie on the death of their parents. He was never told that he was to take guardianship of them, nor was he told their parents were deceased," Logan said. "Perhaps you were unaware of this detail, sir, but it was illegal for anyone to ignore the wishes of the parents and kidnap these two young girls. Someone made the decision. The moment they did, they put the entire program here in Maryland in jeopardy. Kidnapping young girls, giving one of them to Dr. Whitney, a known madman, was illegal as hell, not to mention immoral. If this information were to get out to the public, that our military kidnapped young girls and forced them into a program that potentially could harm them without any compensation whatsoever, without any guardian looking out for their well-being, the repercussions to our military and our country would be enormous."

Pillar's face reddened with anger. "This is a classified program. Anyone discussing it would be held accountable, thrown into the brig, and would never see the light of day again." His voice was harsh with authority.

Logan raised an eyebrow. "Leila has every right to discuss her and her sister's position with the press and anyone else she would like. She isn't in the military. She never signed up for the program that she was put into as a child. She had no say in what happened to her. Neither did Bridget. As citizens of the United States, they have every right to bring a lawsuit against the government and the people who perpetrated this horrifying abduction and experiments on these girls. They were children with no one to protect them."

There was a short silence while Pillar consulted with Chariot, who shook his head several times. Pillar shuffled through paperwork and then turned his glare on Diego.

"There is evidence that several of our soldiers were murdered by a member of GhostWalker Team Four. I believe that GhostWalker is under your command, Major General." It was an accusation and a promise of retaliation if Leila didn't return to the fold.

Diego tightened his fingers around Leila's and pressed their joined hands against his thigh beneath the table to give her courage.

What if they arrest you?

They won't. We knew he would play this card. Don't respond, and don't look at all as if you're bothered by the accusations he's making, he cautioned.

Leila looked up at him, her face soft, her eyes loving. She looked devoted to him. His heart contracted. The woman was amazing. She was scared out of her mind, both for Grace and for him, yet she managed to look calm as well as loving toward him.

"Murdered? With all due respect, sir, 'murder' is a word to be careful throwing around. Diego Campos saved the life of a woman *your* soldiers were attempting to rape while she was dying of bullet wounds they inflicted. There is recorded evidence of this fact. The flaws in these men you continue to enhance are apparent. Worse, you know of the problems and still allow them to go out into the world as potential threats to the civilian population." Logan was relentless.

"Be very careful you aren't court-martialed," Pillar warned.

General Ranier responded before Logan could. "You had better be careful, Bradley," he interrupted, calling the general by his first name. "Don't threaten my men when they are recounting events that can be proven. You're in the wrong, and you know you are. Diego Campos saved this woman's life when your soldiers would have taken it in a violent and brutal way."

"I deserve to be treated with respect," Pillar snapped.

"You are being given the utmost respect," General Ranier pointed out. "You aren't in a court of law; you're here in this room, where we're talking this out. No charges have been filed against you or Chariot on Miss Fenton's behalf. We're here, attempting to make things right."

"Charges?" Pillar sputtered. "What the hell, Ted? No one can bring charges against me. I'm doing my job."

"Sir, with all due respect," Logan said, "your job wasn't to give an order to kidnap two young girls, give one to a man we all know is insane and enhance the other the way you do soldiers, grown men, who volunteer."

Diego nearly smirked. It took effort to keep his expression blank. Logan was implacable. He wasn't going to stop attacking, because it was clear to everyone in the room that Pillar wasn't going to relent and allow Leila to leave without a fight.

It makes no sense when he knows he's in the wrong. Diego sent the message not only to Leila but to all his fellow GhostWalkers. It was important that she saw that advantage. They could communicate with one another, all of them, without anyone else knowing. *What does he think he's going to get out of this?*

His ego is involved for sure, Ezekiel replied. *He has a reputation for insisting he's always right.*

If that's so, Ryland said, *how is it he's in command? How did he make general?*

Logan answered. *He's arrogant, yes, but he gets the job done. He has friends in high places, but he earned where he is. He's a brilliant strategist. You can't underestimate him. We've got a couple of people researching him now. They'll feed us any pertinent information we need. I do know he's a patriot through and through.*

"Respect." Pillar spat the word. "Ted, do you even hear what that upstart is saying to me? Who does he think he is? He isn't speaking to me with respect. Far from it. Put a muzzle on him or we're done here."

Diego thought over what Logan had said about the general. The man hadn't gotten where he was by being arrogant and overbearing—and stupid. The general wasn't stupid. He was deliberately coming off that way.

He's trying to provoke a response. But from whom? Diego mused.

He accused you of murder, Diego, Rubin said. *No general sends out soldiers they know are flawed in dominant and aggressive ways and then calls those dealing with them a murderer. He's misdirecting.*

Rubin was most likely right.

Keep him engaged for a few minutes, Logan, Diego said. *Let me give this some thought.*

No problem. I'm in my element. There was a note of amusement in Logan's voice. He could argue with a deity and win. He always claimed the practice was good for him. His fellow teammates deemed it impossible for him to find a woman willing to put up with his ability to debate anyone, anytime. Diego was thankful for that trait in him though. It gave them all the time needed to puzzle out what the general was up to.

Diego tuned out the arguing going back and forth between the general and Logan. He felt Rubin moving in his mind. Then Ezekiel. They were used to discussing strategy and passing information back and forth. Ezekiel was a strong telepath and often aided others in their unit who weren't quite as strong. Ezekiel brought in the others so they all could contribute to the discussion.

If the general is deflecting, it's because he doesn't want to answer specific questions. Like why he would take two young girls and force them into a program for soldiers, Diego pointed out. *Why would he give one of the girls to Whitney?*

Information coming in now, Ezekiel said. *Jesse Calhoun from Team Two has been gathering data on the general. According to what he's found, Bradley Pillar goes way back with Whitney, far before Whitney was ever accused of the crimes against the orphan girls he bought to experiment on.*

That shouldn't be a little shocking, Rubin said, *but it is. I find it crazy that a man like the general, who has spent an entire career standing for his soldiers, would be associated with Whitney.*

Diego considered the repercussions of backing Whitney and the reasons why a patriotic man who had dedicated his life to serving his country would associate with Whitney. He posed the question to the others.

Ryland was leader of the first team. When the men had begun to have problems, Whitney put them in cages, and some were mysteriously killed. Whitney claimed another man was responsible, but when the team members broke out of the cages, with the help of Whitney's daughter, it was discovered that the scientist had been experimenting on young female orphans before he ever tried his experiments on soldiers.

Whitney considers himself a patriot, Ryland explained. *He has that in common with General Pillar. Leila was taken when she was ten. It hadn't yet come out that Whitney was doing illegal experiments with children.*

But Pillar took my sister and me. He gave Bridget to Whitney, Leila protested. *He had to have known even then what Whitney was doing.*

She has a point, Diego agreed. *Pillar wouldn't have given Bridget to Whitney if he was unaware of what Whitney was doing.*

Logan fell silent, allowing the general to talk sternly to the room while he digested the revelation that Pillar had to have known what Whitney was doing all these years. The fact that he sent his soldiers after Leila, knowing they were flawed, spoke volumes. He didn't want Whitney's experiments or his culpable actions to come to light.

Logan cleared his throat. "Sir, I think it's necessary to cut through the bullshit. We need to focus on the real reason we're here. We aren't going away. Leila is prepared to go to the press and expose the experiments you've done here and the ones you conspired to aid Whitney with."

Pillar turned bright red, sputtering with anger. "You can't possibly condone such a thing. Every one of these soldiers and the GhostWalkers are classified. So is Leila."

"Again, I reiterate, Leila is not in the military. She never signed up for any of this. She was abducted along with her sister," Logan insisted.

"Ted, these threats are outrageous. Your GhostWalker teams

cannot be made public." His fierce gaze swept the room, taking them in. "Do you have any idea the prejudice people would have if they found out you have animal DNA in you? Reptilian? Snake? You would be hunted to the ends of the earth. Every foreign country would want a piece of you. If you think you could keep your identities secret, with the kind of scrutiny you would be under, you're wrong and you would be found."

"And are our lives more important than Leila's and Bridget's?" Logan asked, his tone very low. Those who knew Logan knew that when he spoke in that particular tone, it was never a good thing. He was about to go in for the kill.

Diego admired the way he led the general right into the noose. It was the old adage of "give the man enough rope."

"Yes," General Pillar thundered. He smashed his fist on the table. "Absolutely, without a doubt, the answer is yes. I've had a career of sending soldiers into combat situations. Do you know how many men I've lost? Do you know how many died in the First World War? Over a hundred thousand. Do you know how many were wounded? Over two hundred thousand. What if we could have prevented those deaths? What if we could have saved those lives and kept two hundred thousand men from having their lives torn apart due to terrible wounds?"

"I understand what you're saying, sir—" Logan began.

The general cut him off. "In the Second World War, we lost over four hundred thousand men, and over six hundred thousand more were wounded. The losses were pure insanity. If you can prevent such a terrible thing, why wouldn't you?"

"I agree one hundred percent with you that we should try to find ways to prevent a repeat of history. Everyone in this room agrees with you," Logan said. "But we're soldiers. We volunteered with the idea that we could save lives. But it isn't right to take young girls and experiment on them. To make their lives a living hell."

The general snorted his derision. "Leila Fenton's life was not a living hell. She was afforded every courtesy and every advantage the soldiers had. More so. She was treated with respect. When she got herself pregnant, her child was accepted and cared for."

"'Got herself pregnant'?" Diego nearly came out of his chair. Fortunately, from early childhood, he had trained himself to speak in a low, calm voice. He took a deep breath when Joe turned his penetrating gaze on him. He made every effort to keep anger out of his tone. "Leila didn't get herself pregnant. She was raped by one of your soldiers."

Diego turned his attention to Chariot. "I believe it was documented."

"That is correct," Chariot said immediately. He avoided Pillar's gaze. "There was evidence, including video and witnesses, those looking at the security tapes as it was happening."

By the deep scowl he wore, the general was clearly trying to intimidate Chariot into either staying silent or lying. Diego respected Chariot for telling the truth. If the general later decided to retaliate, it could be Chariot's career, yet the man refused to give in to the warning.

Before the general could respond, Ranier did. "Let's not get off topic here, Diego. I would very much like to hear what the general has to say. There is no question that he has dedicated his life to our country and our soldiers. Many times, when we thought soldiers lost, he was the one to bring them home safely. I, for one, want to know his opinion and his reasoning."

Diego heard the respect in the voice. General Pillar had to hear it as well. The difference was that most of the GhostWalkers in the room had certain talents. Every human being gave off energy, and

GhostWalkers were adept at reading that energy. Many of them had been genetically and psychically altered years earlier, giving them time to cope with the changes as well as be able to develop and use their talents. Reading energy allowed them to see true intent and to know if someone was lying to them.

General Ranier had respect for General Pillar, but like the GhostWalkers in the room, he didn't believe one sacrificed civilians, especially children. He didn't believe one took children and experimented on them. Those beliefs were very strong in him. He might sound as if he wanted to hear Pillar's opinions because he was leaning toward agreeing with the man, but General Ranier was far from agreeing. He felt very strongly that children and civilians should be protected.

The general had seen the results on his soldiers after they were enhanced. He had seen brain bleeds and the fight to maintain a code when their bodies turned against them, causing them to be aggressive and far too dominant. He had read report after report, studied the video evidence of them going into battles or carrying out a covert mission. He also dedicated his life in service to his country and his soldiers.

He believed in the GhostWalker premise, enhancing soldiers to save lives. He believed the strongest and finest should be chosen, and he'd helped implement the psychological studies given to the men before acceptance into the program. Nowhere had there been a reference to first experimenting on children.

Diego—and his fellow GhostWalkers—could feel the escalating anger in the general, but he appeared to be very interested, relaxed and confident. In no way did he betray his true emotions.

"Please continue, Bradley," General Ranier encouraged. "I think everyone in this room needs to hear what you have to say."

Pillar nodded. "What none of you seem to understand is that there is a price tag for everything in the military. A price tag for our computers, our paper products—you name it, it has to be paid for, right down to the most mundane thing possible. How are these things paid for? Quite simply put, gentlemen, they are paid for with our men's lives. Our soldiers. Our bravest men. I have had to send so many men to their deaths when it all could have been prevented."

Diego did his best to listen with an open mind, if for no other reason than to try to understand Pillar and his way of thinking. There was no possible way to agree with him, but it was worth listening to him in order to figure out how a man as intelligent as Pillar would find a way to justify the experiments on children. Not just any experiments—many of them were totally horrific, such as introducing cancer over and over to the child and operating without anesthesia, as well as so many other heinous and unconscionable practices.

Leila pressed her fingers deeper into his thigh, drawing his attention. She leaned closer to him, her gaze sweeping over his face, feature by feature, as if assessing his condition. *The floor is trembling. Is that you?*

That would be Rubin. My calm, reliable brother. Everyone will think it's me because Rubin always has it together. He very rarely loses control, but when he does, it is complete devastation. He included Rubin so his brother would hear the amusement in his voice and feel it in his mind. It always made him laugh when his brother turned hothead.

Poor Jonquille learned the hard way that Mr. Calm, Cool and Collected isn't any of those things and her brother-in-law with the badass rep is.

Rubin gave a snort of derision, but the floor ceased the mild movement and amusement immediately filled Diego's mind. *Don't let him fool you, Leila. He's furious with Pillar. I think he'd take out a gun and shoot him if he thought he'd get away with it. The reason I have such a foul temper is because my brother feeds me his anger and I have to get rid of it for the two of us.*

Leila stifled a giggle against Diego's arm.

That's the first time he's ever told that whopper, Diego told her. *It's a good thing he can direct lightning, otherwise it would strike him in the head for that lie.*

Can you really direct a lightning strike? Leila sounded awed.

Diego squeezed her hand and pressed it harder into his thigh. He loved that she was seeing a small part of his brother—how truly powerful he was. He wanted Leila to see Rubin the way he did.

He turned his attention to Pillar, trying to understand the man and how he believed.

"The soldiers in this room"—Pillar paused and looked around the room, including Diego, Rubin and Ezekiel in his slow, thorough perusal—"all volunteered for a program they believed in. That program had been in the works for years. Whitney believes in saving lives just as I do. We met many times to discuss how best to protect our soldiers and the young men of the nation."

"And women," Logan interrupted.

"What did you say?" Pillar demanded.

"And women." Logan raised his voice. "There are women in our military, and one would presume when you were speaking with Whitney about protecting the male soldiers, you would include the female soldiers as well."

Logan used just the right note of sarcasm to provoke Pillar. Before Pillar could speak, General Ranier did. "Logan, please stop interrupting."

Logan raised an eyebrow, turning toward the general. "Really, sir? You didn't think the women should be included? I feel it's a very pertinent point that they weren't included, considering that Whitney was already experimenting on female children. We know he acquired these girls as infants and toddlers."

"They were *unwanted,*" Pillar burst out. "Throwaways. Their own families got rid of them. Whitney gave them a purpose. He fed and clothed them. He provided an education for them. These girls had more training and education than most females in this country have ever gotten," he defended. "Let's circle back to the real problem. The needless death of soldiers. We knew, thanks to Luther Gunthrie, that one soldier of his caliber could be worth a battalion. He, alone, saved many lives and continued to do so throughout the years."

Diego knew that was very true. He knew Luther, and the man was nearly unstoppable.

"Once it was established that a genetically altered soldier could be sent out with specific orders to take out the enemy without being seen, we knew we had to create more. We were excited."

"We?" Ranier prompted. "You and Whitney?"

"There were others. The idea was taken to the vice president and two senators. We kept the circle small. I had asked permission to share with Whitney. He was our top go-to man and got things done. There is no doubt of his patriotism. Once he knew about Luther, he immediately went to work figuring out how to improve on our odds of creating a supersoldier. Too many hadn't measured up, and we couldn't figure out why. Whitney spent several years developing a protocol for the two laboratories to follow. While there have been things that have gone wrong, and I'll admit that, having Luther and all of the GhostWalkers proving we save soldier's lives every time they are sent out on a mission balances the negative."

"When did you realize Whitney was experimenting on young girls?" Logan asked.

Pillar threw his arms into the air and then slammed his fist on the table again. "You refuse to hear a word I say."

"I hear you," Logan said. "Are you aware Whitney gave some of these girls cancer repeatedly? That he operated without anesthesia several times on the same little girl, causing her heart to stop numerous times? Were you aware that he removed filters from their brains so they are unable to function properly because they can't drown out the noises around them? Did you condone his practices when you gave a little girl to him? Bridget Fenton, a child who should have gone to the very soldier you claim has saved multiple lives. Instead of Luther getting custody of his nieces, you made certain he knew nothing about them, and you experimented on them. Had he known, Luther would have come after you. You know that, or you would have consulted with him."

Again, Pillar waved Logan's accusations away. "Luther Gunthrie had no contact with his family whatsoever. He knew nothing of the girls. They would have been a burden to him."

"You mean he might not have gone at the drop of a hat to do your bidding if he had two little girls—girls grieving for their parents—to look after."

Pillar's features hardened. "Kids get over death much faster than you think. In any case, I am telling you that Leila Fenton was trained as a soldier. She will face charges if she doesn't return."

"You can charge her with anything you want to make up, sir," Logan said, "but the bottom line is Leila isn't in the military. You need to give the order to bring her daughter here so we can take the child with us when we leave."

"Leila Fenton abandoned her daughter. She's been gone several weeks. The child is in protective custody. The last thing we're going to do is hand her over to a mother who leaves her to spend time with a man and then shows up when she feels like it to reclaim her."

Diego pressed Leila's clenched fist to his chest, right over his heart. *Joe, now would be a good time to give the order to get the baby. We'll want to know the moment she's clear and safe.* He included all the GhostWalkers in the telepathic communication.

I did the moment the windbag proclaimed that Leila was going to be charged. The team has begun Operation Night-Night. They'll inform me the moment all guards are asleep and they can move on the house safely without bloodshed.

Marcy, Chariot's wife, has been my friend, Leila hastily told the others. *She might try to protect Grace. Please don't hurt her.*

Diego felt her anxiety. It wasn't for herself. She'd heard the threats Pillar made, the accusations and the remarks designed to make everyone think Leila was a negligent mother. With all of that, her thought was for the commander's wife.

"Out of curiosity, do you condone the breeding program Whitney has devised for the women he continues to hold prisoner?" Logan asked. "Is there justification for that program?" His tone had gone mild once more, a soft, compelling inquiry that invited a real answer.

Gifts. Psychic gifts that had been developed until they were razor-sharp. Pillar talked about the soldiers saving lives, but he didn't understand how powerful they were. The program he oversaw dealt only with physical genetics. He had no understanding of what someone with enhanced psychic abilities could really do.

"Obviously, Dr. Whitney is a brilliant man. He's a genius beyond compare. I fear, with all of his success, the constant pressure to produce more, and the continual persecution he faces every day despite his contributions, Whitney's mental state may have deteriorated. He has so many enemies. He oversees several labs, and twice now the men he trusted violated that trust and tried to build their own army for their own gain. A woman he trusted sold out the program to a monster. He's under tremendous pressure, and yet he continues to find ways to aid our soldiers."

"He's sacrificing children, and now he's forcing women into cages where men rape them in order to produce the babies he wants," Logan said. "You know that is true. I can't imagine that you're not keeping your eye on him."

For the first time, Pillar looked disconcerted, the lines in his face deep. "I tried to talk to him, but he's become extremely reclusive. He believes he has a massive target on him, and he's not wrong. He moves around all the time, which makes it more difficult for him to continue with his brilliant work. That frustrates him and adds to his paranoia."

"Knowing what he's doing, you still aided him in getting Bridget back," Joe said. "You sent her back knowing her fate."

Pillar's head went up. A muscle jerked in his jaw. "The woman has problems, and he needed to ensure she was looked after properly."

Leila's breath hissed out in a slow show of pure anger. "The reason my sister has problems is because that man experimented on her and removed the filters from her brain. He created the problem."

"And he's doing his best to rectify it. Who else will be able to help her?" Pillar demanded. "I suggest that you stop your drama and return to your unit."

Operation Night-Night is a success. Package safe and secure.

The absent members of Diego's GhostWalker team checked in, allowing those confronting General Pillar to carry out their mission.

"Leila will be going with us," Joe said. "So will Grace. There will be no charges brought against her or any GhostWalker. When you choose to create soldiers such as those of us in this room, men and women with altered DNA and enhanced psychic gifts, you are risking far more than you know. We are patriots. We joined the service and volunteered to be enhanced. We worked at learning to control the DNA in us and strengthen our abilities so we could better serve. Again, we are patriots, but we have a strict code we live by. That code is one of honor, and we take it very seriously. We believe in protecting those who can't protect themselves. We don't condone or allow men to rape women or experiment on children or adults. We weren't created for those purposes. We were created to ensure it doesn't happen. We're sent into the field to stop atrocities. We certainly aren't going to condone them here in our own country."

Pillar looked around the room. "Are you threatening me? Because it sounded very much like you were."

"We are ghosts, General. We can walk unseen through walls. You watched us come into this room, and you believe your eyes. You believe that those seated at the table with you are the only ones here. I'm telling you that you're wrong. There are GhostWalkers unseen in this room. Every soldier you brought with you that you ordered concealed has been incapacitated. Your men aren't lying there with rifles aimed at our heads. My men are aiming at yours."

Pillar sent a wild look around the room and then, tellingly, looked up toward the ceiling and across toward the upper-story mezzanine. "Ted?" He appealed to General Ranier.

Joe continued relentlessly. "Grace has been recovered and will go with us. Leila will go with us. In return, she won't go to the press, and we won't make public the experiments being carried out by our government. And you won't receive a visit in the middle of the night. You can retire with your career and reputation intact."

"You can't do this. You're a soldier, and I order you to stand down. To turn Leila Fenton over to me."

"You cannot give me orders, General," Joe stated. "As far as I'm concerned, you're a disgrace to your uniform. You condone the kinds of horrific experiments that the United States condemned in other countries. You've stated in no uncertain terms that you believe it is perfectly reasonable for children to be experimented on. Logan recounted a small number of the atrocities your friend Whitney carried out, and you stated those were necessary. It is on record, but I can assure you that record won't see the light of day. Resign. Do it immediately. We're done here."

For the first time, Chariot stood. "My wife? She was with Gracie."

"Your wife is perfectly fine. We don't make a habit of going after innocents. If you have any influence over General Pillar, now would be a good time to use it."

"Bradley," General Ranier said. "Resign. These men are lethal, and you don't ever want to be in their sights. You're getting off easy."

Pillar sagged. Sat down.

He realizes he helped create us, and he doesn't stand a chance against us. He got what he wished for, he just didn't realize he would suffer the consequences, Diego told Leila as they stood to leave.

17

Other than the heat and humidity reminding her she didn't need to be pinched, Leila felt as if she were in fantasyland. A fairy tale. Gracie was excited to meet other children, and Wyatt's triplets instantly adored her. Ginger, Cannelle and Thym hovered over Gracie, seeing to her every want.

"That child is going to be spoiled in no time," she observed, happiness blossoming. Tears burned behind her eyes. This was exactly what she wanted for her daughter. People who accepted her. Would love her. Friends she could play with.

Diego had warned her that the triplets carried venom in their bite, but they all knew better than to bite. Trap and Wyatt had developed an antidote. She admitted to herself she was a little anxious and watched them carefully, but so far, the three little girls had been loving and protective.

"No need to worry about spoilin' a child with too much love," Grace "Nonny" Fontenot assured, a smile on her face as she watched the interaction of the children in the play yard. "There really is no such thing. Lovin' them and at the same time givin' firm boundaries will see to it that your child will grow up healthy and responsible."

Diego laughed. "Seriously, Nonny? You're going to say that with a straight face? You have those boys to raise, and I can tell you, they're wild as hell."

Leila gasped and nudged him. *Don't say "hell" to her.*

"Sweetheart," Diego said aloud, "she has four grandsons. Raoul is just plain psycho and she knows it. He goes by 'Gator' and thinks he's funny. She had no idea what he was doing half the time when he was growing up. There's Wyatt. You've met him."

"He seemed very nice." Leila eyed Nonny warily. She really liked the woman. Nonny exuded warmth and had welcomed Leila and Grace into her home immediately. She had taken Grace onto her lap and talked to her softly, exclaiming over having the same name. Grace had taken to her instantly. The last thing Leila wanted to do was upset her by calling her grandsons wild.

The entire house was a monument to family. Going up the stairs were photographs of the boys as they grew. At the bottom of the stairs were two hand-carved chests containing handmade quilts and other precious things for her grandsons' wives. Diego had explained what a hope chest was. Traditionally, a woman had a hope chest to collect linens and other items in preparation for marriage. Nonny had longed for great-grandchildren, so she'd had each grandson carve a hope chest for his future wife. Nonny then filled each with handmade quilts and other things she thought their brides might want. Leila loved the idea and silently vowed she would have one for Grace.

Nonny sighed and gave Leila a resigned grin. The expression made her look like a very young woman. "Unfortunately, Diego is tellin' the truth. My grandsons are a wild bunch. Good, steady boys, but tryin' to get them to go to school and stay out of fights was impossible."

"But they take their responsibilities seriously," Diego said. "And they are the best with children. The absolute best. I hope to parent Grace the way Wyatt does his girls."

Nonny beamed. "He is a good dad, but we have a lot of help here. Remember that, Leila. I know the boys can be intimidatin', but each of them helps with the children. They contribute knowledge and various other needed skills. They're all good with the girls."

Leila had met many of the men on Diego's team. She was used to being around enhanced soldiers, and she wasn't exactly intimidated. Still, trusting her daughter to strangers was not in her nature. That would have to come with time.

"It's quite beautiful here," Leila told Nonny. She had never been to Louisiana before. She'd trained in a multitude of environments, but this swamp wasn't one of them. No one was going to send a soldier into known GhostWalker territory and risk losing them just for training.

Nonny preferred to sit outside on her porch where she could look at the river and forest, as well as watch the children in the play yard the men had constructed for them. If Leila had such a view, she might live on her porch. The breeze came off the river, cooling the heat of the swamp. At night, a million stars were on display. There were no lights to outshine them. The sounds of branches and leaves whispering in the wind added natural music to the character of the swamp. The sunsets and sunrises had to be spectacular.

"I'm envious of this spot, Nonny," she admitted.

Diego leaned into her and brushed a kiss along her cheekbone. He did that often. He liked touching her. Holding her hand. Kissing the top of her head or giving her a more intimate but chaste kiss on her lips. Each time he did, her heart reacted. Her nerve endings rushed to life. Her entire being seemed to reach for him.

Leila sat in the rocking chair beside Nonny, switching her gaze from the play yard to the river to the forest and back to Nonny. Diego stood just to the right of her chair and a little behind her. His hand was on her shoulder. Occasionally, his fingers would do a slow massage, easing knots she hadn't known she had. He did that without fanfare, yet she was very aware of the flow of energy between them.

Support. It was silent, but he was there, standing with her, his touch a solid commitment, a promise that he would be there for her in the difficult times. This was all new to her. She had taken a giant leap of faith, not only for herself but for her daughter. It was a risk, but love sometimes required risks.

She couldn't call her decision a sacrifice, but it felt a little like one simply because she was so scared of the unknown. Love required sacrifice. In many ways, the sacrifice was his. He was taking on her daughter as well, and doing so without hesitation. Already, he had spent a great deal of time wooing Grace. He was unfailingly gentle and soft-spoken with her daughter. He carried her close to his body, relaxed but protective. Grace had taken to him right away.

Contentment. Peace settled into Leila. This was what she'd always longed for but hadn't been aware of. She hadn't even known it could exist, but she wanted this kind of life, not just for herself but especially for Grace. For any future children.

"You haven't had a chance to see Diego's home yet," Nonny said. "It's beautiful, built of cypress and treated to last, even with all the insects and weather."

"You have a house?" She turned her head to look up at Diego. The look on his face caught at her, made her reach up and cover his hand with hers. No one had ever looked at her that way, with that focused intensity, with something very close to love etched into his hard, masculine features.

"I told you I had a house," Diego said. "But until you and Grace are in it, that's what it is. A house. We'll make it a home together."

"It's really beautiful," Nonny said. "Rubin and Diego took me there to see it. Their houses are next door to each other, just set back far enough from the river, like this one is."

"Swamp and waterway exits in an emergency," Diego said. "Plenty of cover for us, but at the same time, we'll see anything coming at us."

She had to smile. How many women would want to be reassured they had emergency exits if they were attacked? Her first thought hadn't been the river might flood and they'd need to evacuate, it had been, *What if soldiers come to try to take Grace?* Soldiers from Pillar or Whitney. Before she could voice her concerns, Diego had already indicated the house could be protected, and they could get out several different ways should they need to.

"Drawback," Diego said. "Living next door to my brother."

She felt his amusement and knew he was teasing. "That could be a problem," she agreed soberly. "But he is married, and you said his wife is sweet."

Nonny lifted her unlit pipe to her mouth, chewed on the stem for a moment and then indicated Diego with it. "That boy is a tease, Leila. He keeps that straight face of his, so you don' always know what he's up to, but half the time he's full of . . ." She broke off with a laugh.

Diego's eyebrow shot up. "Full of what? Really, Nonny, I can't believe you just told my woman that."

"On your side, boy, always," Nonny assured. "Your woman has a good sense of humor. You need that when you make a life with someone. Long-term relationships are full of compromise and sacrifice. Berengere, my man, and I had a few ups and downs, but humor and commitment always got us through those tough times. We turned to each other, never to anyone else, for emotional support. Always look to each other just as you are now. Times will get rough, but you both have what it takes for the long run. At the end of the day, it will be well worth it." Nonny stuck the stem of the pipe back in her mouth and bit down, as if adding an exclamation point to her brief words of wisdom.

Diego's fingers brushed through Leila's hair. "She definitely has a sense of humor. We were in some fairly sticky situations, and she always managed to make me laugh. It didn't matter how dicey the situation, she found humor in it somewhere."

The way the pads of his fingers moved in her hair, barely there but skimming down the back of her head, somehow massaging her scalp, sent a rush of heat through her. A rush of awareness. She wanted that connection with Diego for the rest of her life. In that moment, sitting on Nonny's porch with the wind skipping over the river water, turning the surface to diamonds and ruffling the leaves in the trees, she knew it was always going to be Diego. She knew it with absolute certainty.

"Relationships can be hard, but if you rely on each other, don't turn to others for emotional support but to each other, if you're willin' to hash things out, even if that means being upset, you'll do just fine." Nonny continued her advice. "Watched these boys and their women struggle at first to become good at a relationship when they really had no road map. But they are committed." She leaned toward Leila. "If there's one thing I can guarantee about my boys, they know what absolute commitment is."

Everything in her settled. Leila knew herself very well. She was the type of woman who needed and wanted certain things in her life. In her man. Everything was right here. In this place with this man. She nodded toward Nonny, but her attention was centered on Diego.

I am falling in love with you, she admitted. She turned her head to look up at him. The look on his face sent a million butterfly wings brushing along the walls of her stomach.

Grateful you're finally catching up, Warrior Woman. He smiled, that slow, sweet, real smile that transformed him if only briefly, but the warmth remained. *I fell like a ton of bricks before I ever got near you. Watching you defend your sister and Luther did it for me. I could barely take my eyes off you long enough to back you up.*

She knew it was true because when they spoke with a telepathic intimate connection between them, he couldn't hide any emotion from her. He certainly couldn't hide a lie. He actually had felt that way about her when she had a gun in her hand. Many men wouldn't.

My feelings for you have grown stronger every single day, even when I didn't believe they could get deeper, he continued. *But seeing you in every capacity, as a woman, as a mother, it's impossible not to love you more.*

He could melt any woman's heart. She was grateful it was hers he was after. *I didn't know I could trust a man the way I trust you. I didn't think it was possible. And I never believed I would ever want to give a man the chance to prove himself.*

Again, his fingers stroked through her hair, and he leaned down to kiss the top of her head. It was those little touches that made her feel so much a part of him. Other women might not like their men to connect physically when others were around, but she realized that was a huge part of the attraction to Diego.

"I haven't been the most trusting woman in the world, Nonny," Leila revealed. "Diego changed that for me. He makes me feel like the most important person in his world. It really is all him. Just the fact that he finds my atrocious sense of humor funny shows you he's meant for me."

"She's never going to keep a straight face when little Gracie acts up," Nonny informed Diego. "Berengere could never keep a straight face at our boys' antics. I had to learn to do that, although the ridiculous things my grandsons got up to were so hysterical I'd have to go into my room and smother my laughter with a pillow."

Leila could picture Nonny doing just that. She seemed so at peace with herself. She had a pipe in one hand and a shotgun leaning against the wall close to her other hand. She appeared serene and perfectly content. Being close to someone who gave off those low waves of energy, so low it was soothing . . . she wanted that not just for her daughter but for her sister.

"Did your grandson tell you about my sister, Bridget?" she asked. Her voice sounded strangled.

It was difficult to know she was in such a good, safe place while Bridget could be enduring the worst of Whitney. The man was a sadist as far as she was concerned. She had to get to her sister as soon as possible. They had to settle Grace in a safe place before they went after Bridget. The planning was already in motion. Ezekiel and Joe would be holding a meeting as soon as they worked out the mission. In the meantime, Diego was ensuring Leila and Grace felt safe as he introduced them to what would be their new home.

"Yes, he did. Ezekiel told me most of it, including that you had a good woman lookin' after Grace for you."

"Marcy Chariot. She looked after me before I ever had Grace. When Gracie came, she acted like a grandmother. I'm sure she's missing her."

Nonny turned those all-seeing eyes on her. "And you, Leila. She must be missing you and wondering if you're all right."

Leila smiled at the thought. Marcy had been in her life since she was ten and terrified out of her mind. Her parents had died, and they took her sister away from her. There was only Marcy to comfort her. It was Marcy who, despite shifts at a hospital, would see to her every need. If she could have, Leila knew Marcy would have taken her into her home.

In all honesty, Leila missed Marcy and wanted to check in with her. She understood why she needed to wait to contact her, especially since they were going to launch an attack against the elusive Whitney. He seemed to escape unscathed each time anyone hunted him. This time, the GhostWalkers weren't involving anyone higher up. They weren't about to reveal their plans to anyone, although Luther guessed and wanted to go along. Someone always tipped Whitney off, and he would leave before he could be captured or killed.

Leila believed that Marcy knew her well enough to know she would never leave her sister with Whitney. No one other than Diego's team and Luther knew Bridget had a tracking device in her that Whitney wouldn't be able to detect. The tracking device would lead them straight to Bridget's location. There was no way Whitney wouldn't be with her. He would want to "debrief" her. That was what he called his sadistic interrogations, according to Bridget.

Whitney had several laboratories, some hidden within the military system. Others were private labs he appeared not to have an association with until, after much digging, the connection was found. By that time, he was long gone. He moved from place to place, overseeing others doing his experiments. It sucked that he had her sister.

"I can't wait to bring Bridget here," Leila said. Her gaze swung to the play yard, where the little girls were helping her toddler on a small slide. There was a tall slide, but the three little girls had avoided it, directing Grace to the short one. Grace threw back her head and laughed, a baby sound of pure joy, holding out her arms to one of the girls, who picked her up.

"Ginger," Nonny cautioned. "I know you're very strong, but it would be best if you didn't pick Grace up. Her weight might hurt your back."

For a moment, Ginger looked mutinous, but then she kissed Grace on the forehead and gently deposited her on the ground. Both hands went to her hips, and she glared at Nonny. "I'm superstrong. She won't hurt me."

Thym and Cannelle spun around with shocked looks on their faces at the tone of their sister's voice. They looked like exact replicas of Ginger, yet neither appeared to agree with the way Ginger spoke.

The screen door opened behind Leila, and the most beautiful woman she'd ever seen stepped outside. She was small but had real curves. Her hair was dark and glossy. She wore it in an intricate braid that was extremely thick. Strange dark patterns were stamped through the mass of blue-black hair. Her eyes were large, framed with very heavy black lashes. They had the same blue tint as her hair. Her eyes were even more unusual than her hair—nearly a purple violet but with a diamond starburst through the dark center.

"Ginger, do you think it's okay to talk in a disrespectful manner to Nonny like that? Do you talk to anyone you love in that tone of voice?" Her voice was low and sultry. Enthralling. There was no hint of anger in it or in the energy she gave off. She gave the explanation patiently.

Oh my God, I've never seen anyone so beautiful. Who is she? Leila asked.

Pepper, Wyatt's wife. She can't be touched by anyone but Wyatt unless she's pregnant. She recently gave birth to twins. An experiment was done on her, and she has some kind of biochemical that makes her very, very alluring.

Leila didn't like the sound of that. She didn't want to know Diego might find another woman beguiling, even if she couldn't help it and neither could he.

She is not my warrior woman. She doesn't meet a single one of my needs. I don't look at other women. For one, she belongs with Wyatt, and he's a good friend. I wouldn't do that to a friend. Two, I am in love with the woman sitting right here. She's all I can see.

Ginger raised her chin. Leila tried not to smile at the defiance written on the little girl's face. She had a mop of dark wavy hair that fell in whorls and ringlets around her face.

How awful for Pepper that she has to worry all the time that someone will want her if she just touches them. That's so isolating. His reassurance was very sincere. She felt his warmth surrounding her. That made her a little ashamed when the other woman had so much to contend with.

She and Wyatt are good together. He's managed to find a way to live with men ogling his wife. Not so certain I'm going to be as tame.

"She was being disrespectful to *me*." Ginger snapped it belligerently, but the moment the words came out of her mouth, she looked as if she wished she could take them back.

Her sisters gasped again and took a step back from her, shaking their dark spiraling curls. "Ginger," one protested.

"I think it's a good thing that your father is not here at the moment, young lady. In fact, not just your father, Uncle Zeke as well. You know what being disrespectful is. You don't talk to Nonny like that. Not ever." Now that sweet, soft voice had turned to pure steel. Pepper Fontenot was no pushover, and she clearly wasn't going to rely on Wyatt or Ezekiel to deal with her errant daughter.

"She said I had to put Grace down, or I could get hurt." Ginger's lower lip trembled.

"She's an adult looking out for you," Pepper said. "But that shouldn't matter, not when it comes to Nonny. We all treat Nonny the way she treats us, with love and respect."

Tame? Leila couldn't hide her smile as she looked up at Diego. Her heart gave that strange stutter when her eyes met his. *You think it's tame being a man who controls his jealousy?*

Tame. I used that word because my reactions can be more animal than man. I do have violent tendencies when you're threatened.

Men looking at me doesn't constitute a threat, silly.

Ginger kept one hand on her hip, but she didn't look quite as defiant. "I'm strong, Mama. Really strong. Stronger than kids twice my age."

"That doesn't mean your back is fully developed, Ginger. You just had your third birthday, and you're still growing. That isn't the point. Tell me what the point is."

Leila turned her attention back to the conversation between Ginger and her mother. It was an interesting question to ask a child just turning three. The question seemed far too complex, and yet Leila could see the child turn to her sisters.

They're talking telepathically, aren't they? she asked Diego.

Unfortunately for all of us, they've been able to do that since they were barely able to walk. Or run. They are incredibly fast. We used to have to watch them like hawks.

The three girls crowded close, and one put her arm around Ginger as they bent their heads together.

What are they doing?

Leila couldn't help thinking those little girls were super close, just as she had been with Bridget before Whitney and Pillar had ripped them apart. Her hand crept up to find Diego's. She threaded her fingers through his but kept her gaze fixed on the triplets. Little Grace toddled over to them, and instantly, the three girls drew her into the middle, where she was protected. Leila glanced up at Pepper, wanting to convey she thought the girls were sweet.

Pepper caught her gaze and winked. The woman had fantastic eyes. Very different. The vivid violet color surrounded by dark lashes.

Ginger is a handful, Diego supplied. *She's the little ringleader. The other two are more cautious, but she has to know everything yesterday.*

The three of them are little geniuses, and sometimes, because they're so young, we forget that.

Genius or not, Ginger is in the wrong. Leila wanted Diego to know she was firm about that. Gracie was not getting away with ever talking to Nonny that way. *Pepper is right in reprimanding her.*

"The point is, I shouldn't have spoken to Nonny that way," Ginger said painfully. She gripped her sisters' hands and looked straight at Nonny, remorse stamped into her little features. "I'm very sorry, Nonny." She ducked her head when tears shimmered in her eyes. "I don't know why I got upset. But I love you, and I shouldn't ever say mean words to anyone I love."

"I love you too, Ginger," Nonny said and held out her arms.

Ginger ran to her and threw herself onto Nonny's lap, burying her face against Grand-mere's shoulder. She hugged the older woman very tight.

Nonny tilted Ginger's face up toward hers and kissed her. "Your momma hasn't met Grace yet." She lowered her voice to a conspiratorial whisper. "You'll have to tell her about Grace having the same name as me and your baby sister. I'm not sure your mama knows my given name is Grace because she always calls me Nonny."

Leila was absolutely certain Pepper knew Grace was Nonny's name, but she pretended not to hear, willing to let Ginger be very important, having knowledge her mother might not.

A smile broke out on the little girl's face, lighting it up instantly. After hugging Nonny tight around the neck, she scooted off her lap and went to her mother, solemnly holding out her hand. "You have to meet Gracie. She's just a little baby."

Pepper took her hand and moved down the steps with her. "Where did she come from?"

"She's Uncle Diego and Leila's little girl," Ginger said. "She's so cute, Mama. Isn't she, Thym?"

Thym nodded enthusiastically. She and Cannelle were on either side of Grace, ensuring she didn't leave the play yard and head toward the river. There was a fence surrounding the play yard, but the gate was wide open. Leila found it rather amazing that the little triplets were so careful of her daughter. They weren't very old, and yet they were very focused on Grace's safety.

She also found it sweet the way Nonny and Pepper handled Ginger after she showed remorse. The incident wasn't brought up again. Her guilt wasn't hammered home. She was forgiven the moment she showed real remorse and that she understood why she shouldn't have done what she did. Leila liked that. She liked watching as Ginger took her mother down the steps and across the grass to the play yard, where Pepper crouched down in front of the toddler as her triplets happily introduced her, all three talking at once.

"I love this for Grace," Leila said. "She only had Marcy and me before this. I'm surprised she isn't too shy to interact."

"She doesn't seem in the least afraid," Nonny agreed. "You're raisin' a very confident young lady. She'll be pure steel, just like Ginger. You want that, Leila. A woman can be soft when she wants to be and steel when she needs to be." She laughed softly. "The goal is to let a child have their own personality, their own goals, dreams and beliefs. You want that for them. You want them to be able to stand up for what they want or need. You want them to stand up for those less fortunate who can't do it for themselves. But . . ." She laughed again.

The sound of Nonny's laughter brought warmth and closeness, as if she were sharing a secret world with Leila.

"But?" Diego encouraged.

"You raise them right, you're goin' to have them standin' up to you. Arguin'. Going against your rules. Decidin' for themselves what they want, long before it's good for them."

Leila sighed. "I was that child. Bridget was always the rule follower. I think it's so funny when I see things on the Internet indicating the firstborn is the angel child and the second a little demon. I was always the one driving my parents crazy with questions. I questioned everything. It had to make sense to me, or I wasn't going to listen. I was lucky in that my parents were very much science-based and didn't mind explaining everything to me. Ginger definitely reminds me of me when I was a child."

"And you've grown out of that?" Diego teased. He bent down to nuzzle the space between her neck and shoulder. "Just remember, I'm excellent at hearing lies."

Leila burst out laughing. "I'm not sure I'll ever grow out of needing explanations. And I fully admit to being stubborn. I'm not proud of that trait, but it's there."

"There's nothin' wrong with holdin' your own opinion if you can honestly say you listened and did your research," Nonny said. "You have the right and sometimes the duty to stay strong in the face of everyone else tellin' you different."

Leila sent Diego a teasing grin. "I think your grand-mere is a very wise woman."

"I think Grand-mere has found a way that sounds logical to allow you to get your way."

"Diego," Nonny said, pinning him with her laughing gaze. "I believe Miss Leila is goin' to get her way, even more than that adorable child you're already so in love with."

Leila's breath caught in her throat as Diego's gaze swung to Grace. The toddler was fully engaged in a conversation with Pepper. It was the look on Diego's face, the hard lines, soft now, his features filled with warmth, and his eyes . . . his eyes. Those dark eyes, looking like velvet, were soft with love. There was no other word for it. Diego had fallen for Grace. He'd claimed her fully just as he'd claimed Leila. He was all in, happy to be her father.

"You makin' it legal?" Nonny asked. Her tone was mild.

Diego nodded. "Just as soon as we bring Bridget home. I've

already got the necessary paperwork going for the marriage and adoption."

They had talked marriage. She hadn't brought up adoption, a part of her fearing he would have a wrong answer. She wouldn't be with someone, no matter how much she wanted to, if he didn't embrace her daughter.

"Adoption?" she echoed, trying to keep her tone neutral.

"She's ours, isn't she?" Diego asked. His intent gaze didn't leave her face. Waiting.

Leila nodded slowly. "Yes, she's ours. I just thought you would wait."

"For what?" He sounded genuinely puzzled. "You're going to marry me. Spend your life with me. That means that little girl will spend her life with me as her father. I never want her to think she wasn't wanted. I want her to grow up knowing exactly who her father is and that she was wanted from the first moment you told me about her."

He could melt her heart in seconds. He always seemed to say the exact thing she needed to hear. "How can you be so certain?"

"Sweetheart, you committed your life to mine when you left Chariot and took a leap of faith. I'm not doing any less." He flashed her that slow, beautiful smile that sent butterflies winging through her stomach. "Truth is, Leila, I know. In my heart. In my soul. I know we belong together."

She knew it as well; she just didn't understand how it had happened so fast. How it was so intense. She couldn't look at him without her heart skipping a beat.

Pepper made her way back to the porch. There were four rocking chairs set out, and Pepper took the one positioned at an angle so she could face Nonny and yet still keep an eye on her children. "They're so happy little Grace is here." She fanned herself, and Nonny reached into a small cooler that sat by her chair and handed

Pepper a bottle of water from it. "I'm glad. I was a little afraid they would be jealous when the babies first came." She smiled serenely. "You can see how they are with Grace. They're very much the same, maybe more so, with the twins. From the moment the twins were born, the three of them wanted to take care of them."

"Are you feeling okay, Pepper?" Diego asked.

Leila really looked at the other woman, trying to see beyond her natural beauty. It was difficult, but Diego wouldn't have asked if he hadn't seen—or felt—something worrisome.

"I've been really tired," Pepper admitted.

"You may be anemic."

Pepper nodded. "Wyatt said I was, but I don't seem to be responding to the iron supplements."

"Does he know why you're anemic?" Diego persisted. "Have you had Rubin take a look at you?"

"Not yet. Wyatt was going to talk to him today." She gestured toward the swamp. "It isn't life-threatening, but Wyatt said he wanted Rubin to take a look. They're at Trap and Cayenne's, doing something in the laboratory. Trap wanted Joe, Wyatt and Rubin to look at something important he's working on. I just got a text from Wyatt. They'll be home soon."

What laboratory? Leila tried to keep anxiety out of her mind, but she'd brought Grace to this place believing no one would ever experiment on her. Leila had gifts, and she was enhanced genetically, just as Grace's biological father had been. She could already see how advanced Grace was physically. There was almost an animal quality to the way she moved, fluid like a cat, sure-footed when she was only seventeen months and should be off-balance occasionally. And she could climb anything.

Diego brushed his palm soothingly down the back of her head before settling his fingers against her scalp. "Trap spends a great deal of his time in his lab. Wyatt is like he is."

"The girls would bite when they were teething or afraid," Pepper said, lowering her voice. "Trap and Wyatt developed antivenom specifically so that no one here could be harmed if there was an accident. They've removed tracking devices Whitney put in a few of the women. They're pretty remarkable."

"Did they take the girls to the lab?" Leila challenged.

"Not Trap's lab. The one here." Pepper indicated the locked garage. "We talked to them first and explained what we were doing so they wouldn't be afraid. It was hardest on Thym, but she does whatever her two sisters do. The best thing is always to convince Ginger first, and the other two will follow her lead. By the time we made that decision, they trusted Trap and Wyatt. They adore Zeke. Actually, all the men on the team."

Nonny smiled and shook her head. "They get a little jealous when one of their uncles finds his woman. In particular, Bellisia, Ezekiel's wife. They did their best to run her off, but it only lasted a day or two."

"Zeke sings to them," Pepper said. "And tells them stories. If Grace is having a difficult time sleeping or she's sick, call Uncle Zeke. He has a gift for soothing a baby, although he'd never admit it."

Diego's finger and thumb found Leila's chin, and he tilted her head back, forcing her to meet his gaze. *No one will ever touch our children without our permission. You have my word, Warrior Woman.*

It was impossible not to fall in love with him.

18

~

Leila clung to Diego's hand as he pushed open the door to her new home. Diego held Grace against his chest, her booty tucked in tight against his arm. She was sleepy and cuddled against him, her eyelids drooping and her wealth of thick red-gold hair gleaming in the last light of the day.

The sight of her daughter held so protectively made Leila's eyes burn with tears and her heart flutter. She involuntarily tightened her grip on Diego's hand. This man. Handing her the world. She'd never thought she could be so happy. And it was all so unexpected.

The house was large and positioned back from the river, but where she could hear and see the water, just as Nonny could from her front porch. The covered wraparound deck added another dimension to the outside, expanding the house by quite a bit. Just as the Fontenot home had hand-carved rockers on the porch, so did this one. All cypress wood, the planks fit tightly into one another, matching the exterior of the house. She loved it, and she hadn't even seen the inside.

The wind ruffled the surface of the river, turning the water into dark, shimmering jewels. Overhead, the sun had already dropped so that layers of deep purple, blue and orange streaked the sky. The beauty of the surrounding swamp matched the river as the wind set the branches swaying. Moss lace, looking like intricate shawls, swayed and danced, hanging from the twisting outstretched boughs of trees. To Leila, it looked like a scene out of a movie.

"Baby's already falling asleep," Diego said as he indicated for her to open the door. "Long day for her. Meeting new friends, Nonny especially, who loved to have her on her lap." He stopped and looked down at Leila, meeting her eyes. "If Grace had been uncomfortable with her, I would have intervened."

It was impossible not to see the sincerity in him. She didn't say aloud that she would have stopped anyone from holding her daughter had Gracie objected; she didn't need to. Diego had shown time and again that he understood her nature. Just like Grace, everything was new and a little overwhelming, but she was exactly what he'd named her—Warrior Woman.

"I know you would have, Diego." And she did know. She'd known it the entire time they were with Nonny, and his teammates were moving furniture and stocking the house with food and other items.

She had been surprised when there was only Nonny and Pepper at the Fontenot home. At least, the only visible ones. She knew they always had guards on the property, keeping Wyatt's family safe. Diego told her the others were ensuring their home was comfortable and had whatever was needed.

That had made her laugh. "Like towels? Blankets? A bed? What did you do in that house? Sleep on the floor?"

He'd given her his lazy grin, the one that could melt her so easily, and he'd shrugged. "Slept on the floor. Ate at Rubin's. Told you, sweetheart, it was just a house. Now that you and Grace are going to be there, it will be home."

That had gotten to her. Diego didn't think he had a romantic bone in his body. He often told her he was no poet, the way Rubin was. She didn't need a flowery speech. His abrupt words, always spoken in that low voice, enthralled her. That was poetry enough for her.

Leila stepped inside, and the interior took her breath away. High vaulted ceilings were built with cedar planking. Space. So much space. She could breathe in that massive room. It was sparsely furnished, but what was there was solid and nice. She had always appreciated craftsmanship and recognized that whoever had designed and built this home had done so to last. To fit in with the landscape and to keep it safe from the river, the swamp and invasive insects for generations. This was the house Diego was offering to her.

For some unexplained reason, her heart beat out of control and her mouth went dry. She hadn't believed she would ever have her own home. Not ever. She was certain she would spend her life in the dorm apartment that had been her living quarters for so long.

"How many bedrooms did you say this house has?" She wanted to ensure her sister would have a place to stay until the healers and doctors had helped her enough that Bridget could choose where she wanted to live. Leila hoped Bridget would want to stay with her, but just because she felt that way didn't mean her sister would. They didn't know each other. Their relationship was one of the many things Pillar had ripped away from them.

Diego stopped in the middle of the great room and turned fully to her. "Why do you suddenly feel sad to me?"

That voice of his was enough to turn her inside out. "I was just thinking about Bridget. I don't even know if she's going to want to stay with me. We hadn't had contact since they separated us."

He stepped closer to her, warming her with his body heat. "Sweetheart, I guarantee Bridget is going to want to be with you. Did you see the way she readily sacrificed herself for Luther and you? She has no filters, and the violent energy had to be excruciatingly painful. She had to be terrified to be taken back to Whitney, but she still tried to draw attention to herself and away from you and Luther. She might not have your capabilities because of the things Whitney did to her, but she has your fighting spirit. She has your protective instincts and sense of family. When you were able to find her and got her out, she went willingly."

Leila couldn't help reaching up to touch his face. "You always seem to know the right thing to say to me."

"And we have four bedrooms in this house and two bathrooms. If Bridget decides to settle here, we can either add her own bathroom or build her a house close to us."

"You won't mind her living with us?" She found herself holding her breath.

"I expect her to live with us. She needs an anchor. She needs you and Grace. She'll need a safe haven while she's learning to navigate the outside world. We need to be close to her to help her. And you'll want to reinforce that you're family, that she has us to lean on."

Relief swept through her. She hadn't realized she was so worried about Bridget accepting. "I know this sounds crazy, but I've felt guilty for years for allowing us to be separated. I've been so afraid she blamed me, especially when I found out how terrible a man Whitney is. It was awful to think she was left in his hands and I was responsible."

"Babe, you were ten. Grown men came and took her."

"My parents always told me to look out for her from the first moment she was born. I adored her. We were so close. And then they came right after we lost Mom and Dad. She was hysterical. I was hysterical and combative. I raged for weeks, but I had no idea where they took her, and they wouldn't tell me."

The guilt, fear and anger had been overwhelming. She had been grieving for her parents and suddenly was grieving for the loss of her sister as well. There had been no one to talk to her. There wasn't anyone who would give her answers. She was scared for herself, not understanding why doctors were poking and prodding and constantly taking blood. Weeks went by. Months. There was no word of her sister.

"Months turned into years. I had no idea if my sister even lived. I paid attention when I was in the laboratory. The men wore white coats and gloves on their hands and would compare notes in quiet voices, mostly ignoring me once they took blood and tissue samples. I realized if they forgot I was there, they would talk among themselves. I was seventeen when I learned Bridget was alive and in the hands of Dr. Peter Whitney. That was seven long years of guilt and suppressed anger, anxiety and fear, before I even knew my sister lived."

"I can't imagine what you went through not knowing if Bridget was alive or dead," Diego said. "If I'd lost Rubin that way, it would have driven me insane."

Some people might just give her platitudes, but she knew he meant it. He was aware of the enormity of what she'd suffered and could relate.

"I'm a survivor. I learned to stop fighting the men who would come to take me to the laboratory. I kept as quiet as possible, saying very little, and observed, listened and eventually realized I couldn't escape. That's when I began to cooperate with my captors so I could learn everything I could. My end goal always was to find Bridget."

Diego's gaze was wholly focused on her as he shifted the sleeping toddler in his arms to hold her closer to him, ensuring Grace was secure.

"Fortunately, you found her. She knows you're going to come for her. We're already planning. We have tonight to settle you and little Gracie in. We're making a night jump to get to Bridget."

"I should be going with you," Leila said. "She's my sister. I'm the one responsible for getting her away from that horrible man."

"I understand that way of thinking because I would be exactly the same." He took one hand from the baby and cupped her cheek. His touch was gentle beyond measure. His gaze drifted over her face. "But we both know when we go into a combat situation, which this will be, we have to go with those familiar with one another."

Diego turned away from her, and she followed him through the house to one of the bedrooms. She was becoming agitated thinking about the men going into combat, risking their lives in order to rescue her sister while she stayed home safe. That didn't sit well with her at all.

Leila barely took in the beauty of the house as she trailed after him through the archways and wide hall to the room his sister-in-law, with the help of some of the other women, had set up as a nursery for the toddler.

The room was spacious and held a white crib and matching dresser. There was a changing table and cupboard high enough on the wall that a child couldn't access it. Someone had painted a mural on one wall. She stopped in the middle of the room to stare at it in wonder.

"Who's the artist?"

"That would be Ezekiel," Diego said as he gently deposited the sleeping toddler in the crib. "You should see the one he painted for Bellisia when she was recuperating from a stab wound. Bellisia needs to be in or near the water to feel okay, and she was unable to get in the river. He brought the ocean to her. He painted the mural on wood, covering the wall at Nonny's, so he could take it with them when they moved into their home. They have it in their sitting room."

"I can't wait to see it. This is absolutely gorgeous." The theme was Beatrix Potter. Many of the stuffed animals were Beatrix Potter. The entire collection of the Potter books stood between two themed bookends on a shelf. There were two full shelves of children's stories. "I can't believe they did this for her."

Once again, she felt the burn of tears. How was it possible that she'd gone from her stark, lonely existence to this? It seemed unreal. A fairy tale. Her gaze fell on Diego.

He raised an eyebrow as he turned on the baby monitor. "What?"

"It's you. You're magical." She leaned over the crib and kissed her daughter before pulling the railing up. She had to do something to distract herself before she began to cry. She hadn't thought a person could cry so many tears of joy.

Diego swept an arm around her shoulders. "I hear my brother and Jonquille on the porch, sweetheart. They're bringing food."

"I think we're being spoiled."

"Everyone wants you to know you're welcome here. They're glad you're here." He urged her to walk out of the room, pausing to close the door on their way out.

"They don't know me," she pointed out.

"They know me. If I tell my friends and family you're the one, the only one for me, they trust that I would never bring someone here that won't fit. You fit."

That was a good feeling. He seemed to create quite a few in her. She wanted to bring up the mission to recover her sister, but Rubin and Jonquille were already knocking and pushing open the front door.

Jonquille was petite and delicate looking with short, platinum-blond hair, very striking in her appearance, especially beside Rubin. Rubin, like Diego, was a handsome man, with his bronzed skin and dark hair. The aroma of roast and gravy rose from the tote Rubin carried.

Rubin gave Leila a smile, one very reminiscent of Diego. She hadn't noticed before how much they looked alike, but now that they were in a different environment, she could see how closely they resembled each other.

"Brought my wife to meet you, Leila. This is Jonquille, the love of my life."

I told you he was the romantic one. He writes poetry about her.

Diego sounded as if he might be mocking his brother, but in her mind, he *felt* proud of him. Admiring. Even a bit envious.

She looks as if she might need a man who can write flowery words. They must be well suited, just the way we are. She didn't need poetry. She needed what Diego gave her. Peace. Contentment. Protection. Loyalty.

Diego tightened his arm around her shoulders. "Best sister ever," he greeted and bent to brush a kiss on Jonquille's cheek. He didn't loosen his hold on Leila to do it.

"I'm so pleased to meet you," Leila said. "Thank you for putting Gracie's room together. It's amazing and far better than I could ever have done."

Rubin indicated that they should keep walking toward the kitchen. Jonquille went with him, but she flashed Leila a smile. "I'm so glad you like it. I did research on various children's rooms and loved that look. I had never read the Beatrix Potter books, so I did before I chose that theme. Fortunately, I'm good on a computer and I'm a fast reader. I loved the stories and envisioned reading them to her."

"I love the variety of children's books you chose," Leila said. "I read quite a bit and want Grace to develop a love of reading as well." Involuntarily, she pressed tighter to Diego. "I'm looking forward to reading all the children's books at every age level. When I was little, my mother read to me. When Bridget came along, she read all the same books to her, and I got to hear them all over again. I want to experience that with Gracie."

"I want to do the same with our children," Jonquille agreed. "Rubin and I talk about the way we want to raise our children so we can work out the kinks ahead of time."

Rubin placed the tote on the middle island in the kitchen and began to pull out the warmers. "Bottom line, we aren't going to physically punish our child or yell." He glanced at Diego, who exchanged a very sober look with him. "We're raising them with praise and encouragement."

Leila tried to read the brothers. She knew a good deal about Diego's childhood. Those things were the exact opposite of what he had experienced.

"I like that," Leila said. "I can't imagine anyone raising their voice to Gracie or striking her."

The moment she used the word "striking," Diego stiffened beside her. She had the feeling anyone daring to hit their daughter would find themselves on the wrong end of his predatory wrath.

"I was very impressed when I heard Pepper reprimanding her daughter for talking back disrespectfully to Nonny. She handled it quietly but sternly. At the time, I thought: That's the way I hope to talk to Gracie when she gets too far out of line."

"That must have been Ginger," Rubin said, humor in his voice. He exchanged another look with Diego, and this time, she felt the laughter in them both.

Jonquille must have as well, because she bumped her hip against Rubin's. "Being disrespectful, especially to Nonny, is *not* funny."

"Everything that child does is funny," Diego contradicted.

"She's a little spitfire. While I'm glad she's Wyatt's naughtiness to raise, I anticipate we might have similar experiences."

"For sure, Trap will," Rubin said, sounding far too pleased. "His twins not only inherited a combination of crazy genetics, but they are extremely intelligent."

"The worst combo," Diego agreed, sounding just as pleased as Rubin.

The tone of their voices and the humor in Diego made Leila laugh. "You don't sound in the least sympathetic," she pointed out. "Just saying, karma can be a bitch. What you're wishing on your friend could just as easily happen to the two of you."

Jonquille nodded her agreement. "And you both would deserve it."

"Just remember, baby"—Rubin kissed Jonquille's ear—"whatever happens to me, happens to you, and the same goes for Diego and Leila."

"And still, you're wishing this on your friend Trap," Leila said.

The two brothers looked at each other and burst out laughing. The sound filled the kitchen and warmed Leila even more. She couldn't help exchanging a raised eyebrow with Jonquille, and they both burst out laughing. It felt—right. Perfect. A perfect moment. Diego just kept giving them to her.

"Trap deserves to have his little twins giving him heck," Rubin said as he casually reached into the cupboard and pulled out four plates.

Leila found it strange that Rubin knew where the dishes were in her home and she didn't. She also immediately caught on to the very close relationship between the brothers. Diego would never expect Rubin to knock and not enter their home immediately. That meant the brothers would have the code to each other's homes. Diego would expect his brother and sister-in-law to be welcome to any meal. It was a statement of their family dynamic.

She took a moment to think about how she really felt. Did she consider it an intrusion? Did that kind of closeness appeal to her? She would be expected to welcome Rubin and Jonquille anytime, day or night. Most likely, with any child they had it would be the same. But Gracie would have that closeness. They would treat her like their own, just as she knew Diego would treat Rubin's child as his. The way he embraced Grace. It was the way Nonny became a grandmother to all of them. She accepted them into her family without reservation. She would be giving that legacy to Grace and any other children she and Diego had together.

It wasn't that they didn't have their own lives or their secrets. She certainly knew Diego did. But there was such beauty in the closeness of the brothers. They showed each other unconditional love. Diego was giving her that gift.

She looked at him and knew her heart was in her eyes. "What does Trap do that you both are certain he needs his children to be like Ginger?"

"*Worse* than Ginger," Diego corrected. "Ginger is an escape artist, but there isn't anyone better than Pepper at it, and she's their mother. She had to have passed her genetics to those kids."

"Already the dynamic in the household has changed," Rubin said. "And for the better. Before, Trap said and did just about anything he wanted, and Cayenne went along with it. He would disappear into the lab for days, sometimes weeks on end. Cayenne brought him food and took care of any of his other needs, but he ignored her and the outside world. That had to change after the twins were born."

Jonquille nodded. "Cayenne had never so much as held a baby. She was terrified of being a mother and still is. She's always relied on Trap to show her the way. I think he thought Nonny would do all the teaching, but Cayenne became super protective of the babies and wouldn't take them out of the house for a long time. That meant Trap had to deal with them instead of hiding himself away in his laboratory."

Again, Leila heard the underlying laughter, this time in Jonquille's voice. Diego had told her that Trap could be abrupt and rude, and if he was, not to take offense. She was beginning to get the feeling that the three of them had great affection for Trap but wanted him to work a little harder at social interaction. She thought he had made an effort when he was introduced to her.

Leila found herself enjoying dinner with Rubin and Jonquille even though she wanted to be alone with Diego. She wanted to explore the house and sit on her front porch as well as check on Grace repeatedly.

Diego sat beside her rather than across from her, his hand on her thigh when he wasn't cutting up his food. "One of Trap's best traits is his absolute loyalty and love of Cayenne. If she needs him, he's going to be there. There's no question about it. And he would never yell at his children. If he did, Cayenne would take them to the basement and weave spiderwebs around them and in every doorway. When Trap first was enticing Cayenne to stay with him, he remodeled the basement and told her that part of the house was hers and he wouldn't invade it. She's held him to that."

The conversation was informative, giving her a picture of the various members of Team Four and their spouses. She wanted their dinner to go on for a long time, yet she wanted it to be over. She felt as if she'd waited a lifetime for Diego. She was grateful when Rubin and Jonquille said their goodbyes and finally left her alone with Diego.

"I really want to take a hot bath before bed," she managed to say.

"Good idea, sweetheart. You do that while I get our kitchen clean and check on Grace, and then I'll hit the shower."

Of course he was going to do all that while she soaked in a hot bath. That was so Diego. Truthfully, the hot bath relaxed her.

Through the window, she could see so many stars, a vast array lighting up the sky. The stars looked like points of fire, a scattering of brilliant multifaceted diamonds. When one fell, she made a wish as she slowly dried herself off, all the while staring out the window. The only thing she had that might be comfortable to sleep in was a T-shirt that fell to her thighs. She put that on and nothing else before making her way to the master bedroom.

Leila stood uncertainly just inside the door, holding on to the frame with one hand. This was their first real night together, and she wanted it to be good for Diego. She didn't want to let him down. He was sitting up, already in bed, his hair still damp from his shower. His chest was naked and on display in all its muscular glory. The sheet was pulled up to his hips. He looked up the moment she appeared in the doorway as if he were tuned to her presence.

"Come here, sweetheart," Diego encouraged.

She felt the color sweeping up her neck into her face. "I don't have anything nice for tonight."

"I don't need lingerie, Leila. I need you."

"But don't men like to see their women in lingerie so they can unwrap them, kind of like a Christmas present?"

"Where did you get that idea?" There was a touch of masculine amusement in his voice that should have put her off, but the way his voice could turn velvet soft, stroking over her skin in a caress, prevented her from taking offense.

She sent him a smile, trying for calm, for confident, when her insides had become a roller coaster. She pressed a hand to her stomach to keep the butterflies at bay. She believed in honesty, and she wasn't in the least embarrassed by her reasoning.

"I read a lot of books. The heroes in the books seemed to like their women to wear really sexy lingerie to bed so they can take it off."

She half expected him to laugh, but she should have known better. This was Diego. He didn't make fun of her lack of knowledge or her reading habits. Instead, he tilted his head to the side, his dark eyes drifting over her with utter focus and intensity, heating her everywhere his gaze touched.

"I think those books are going to give us valuable information, Leila. At the same time"—he held out his hand—"we're us. You and me. No one else is in our bedroom, and we can do anything we want. Right now, this minute, if you're not ready, I want you to know we can sleep together the way we've been sleeping. Close." There was reassurance and honesty in his tone.

She *wanted* him. She wasn't afraid. Nervous, yes, but not afraid. She wasn't going to leave him thinking she didn't want to be with him in every way.

Leila crossed the room to him. Diego flipped back the sheet to allow her to slide in beside him. She nuzzled his shoulder with her chin. "I don't care that I'm not in lingerie for myself. I wanted this night to be special for you."

"Lingerie doesn't make our night special, sweetheart. *You* do." He turned her face toward his with two fingers under her chin, and then his lips were on hers.

Gentle. So gentle. Barely there. His touch burned like a brand despite being so featherlight. There was no demand for entrance. No demand on her at all, but the need was urgent. Hunger blossomed, and she parted her lips. Fire poured into her mouth, down her throat, rushed through her veins and settled low. Burning. Demanding. Growing into a full firestorm.

His fingers tightened in her hair, so she felt that same burn in her scalp. Little flicks of electricity seemed to snap and spark over her skin. Heat rushed through her veins to pool low with an urgent demand. She had never felt so alive. Every nerve ending flared and sizzled. He kissed her over and over, deepening the kiss, but never once was he rough. He turned her heart over with his gentleness.

I had no idea a man like you could exist, Diego. I'm so past falling. I'm already there. I love you so much I ache with it.

Diego pulled back just far enough to look into her eyes. Something powerful and reassuring moved behind the dark velvet color. He made her heart skip a beat just looking at him.

"I'm going to love you forever, sweetheart. *Forever*. Days will pass, weeks, months and years. The world is going to keep turning, and life might get hard. I'll love you through that. Always. When we grow old and sit on our porch the way Nonny does, loving our grandkids, you're going to feel my love more than ever. I can promise you that."

The lump in her throat and the burn behind her eyes threatened to derail her, but she needed him to hear her. "I'm not always the best at expressing emotion, Diego, but I know you're the man for me. I want you for the father of my children. I want them to be like you. I want to wake up every morning to your face and go to bed every night feeling exactly the way I do right at this moment."

"How do you feel, sweetheart?" His lips brushed her forehead. Both eyes. Traveled down the side of her left cheek to the corner of her mouth. "What are you feeling?"

"How much you love me." She whispered the truth to him. "Beautiful. Feminine." He made her feel sexy, but she was going to skip telling him that. It was the way he looked at her, so focused. He could have been a feral predator fixed on his prey with the intensity with which he regarded her.

His face was carved with deep lines of lust, but raw love shone through so clearly in his dark velvet eyes. She needed him to want her exactly the way she was. She needed the look on his face and the possessive hunger in his eyes.

He lowered his head to hers and once more took her mouth. Lightning seemed to arc between them, igniting a firestorm of absolute need. Her stomach clenched, and deep inside her core she went hot and liquid.

This time, when he lifted his head, it was to take little nips over her chin, along her neck and throat. Each time his teeth gave a tiny sting, his tongue followed, easing that ache and sending heat spiraling down her spine. Then his mouth was on her left breast, his tongue stroking and teasing her nipple. Only then did she realize he had somehow managed to strip off her shirt, leaving her completely naked. She didn't have time to be embarrassed or think too much about her lack of clothing in front of him. It was impossible to think clearly when his very clever mouth was wreaking havoc with all her senses.

Then he shifted. It was a subtle movement. Very gentle. Not in the least raising alarms. She was so focused on the sensations he was inducing with the heat of his mouth, his stroking tongue and his nipping teeth, that she failed to notice at first that they had changed positions. She was lying on her back, Diego blanketing her, yet the weight of his body was mostly off her.

She wanted to feel him. All of him. Every inch of his naked body. She took the opportunity to run her palms down his back, shaping his subtly defined muscles. She loved the feel of him. She felt as if she were melting into him. Merging with him. And maybe she was. He was kissing her again, and she was lost to her surroundings, her head spinning. Little colorful lights burst behind her eyes.

Then he was kissing his way down to her chin, her throat, her breasts. There seemed to be a direct line between her nipples and her core. Seeing his focused expression, his need, those lines of sensuality carved deep into his face, brought her to even more of a fever pitch. She knew great sex started in the mind, and Diego filled her mind with love, with erotic images, with his own stark hunger for her. Those things were definitely as much of a turn-on as what he was doing to her body.

"Diego." She whispered his name. Her talisman. The only time she'd experienced sex, it hadn't been good. She trusted Diego, she did, but there was a small part of her ready to panic, to fight the moment he got rough. The moment he showed he was out of control.

He gave her gentleness. So very gentle, almost worshiping, as his tongue and hands moved over her body, sending flames flickering through her.

Diego. This time, she flooded his mind with adoration. With her hunger. Her need. Mostly with overwhelming love. She hadn't known she was capable of loving a man so deeply.

The angles and planes of his face were stamped with pure sensuality. His tongue felt like a hot brand sweeping over her. He was so incredibly gentle. She could barely catch her breath as he built the need and hunger in her body. Each time his tongue moved in her, a firestorm erupted through her body, and colors burst behind her eyes like so many stars. Her heart beat too loud, sounding like thunder in her ears. A glittering pleasure rushed through her, detonating like dynamite.

The entire time waves of pleasure rolled through her, she stared into his eyes as he blanketed her body with his once again. With her fingertips, she traced the lines in his beloved face. She loved the hard angles and planes of his features. His dark velvet eyes, so brown at times they appeared black. She could stare at him for the rest of her life. The love shining in his eyes and carved into his face always took her by surprise.

She felt him hard and thick against the slick heat of her body. She ached for him. Ached to share the same skin with him. To be one instead of two. He wrapped one fist around his heavy cock and lodged the crown in her. She expected to be scared, not excited. He began to slowly sink his body into hers, and the exquisite burn consumed her.

Her blood thundered and roared in her ears with her pounding pulse. She felt his heartbeat in the thick cock pushing against the sensitive walls of her channel. He thrust gently with his hips, slowly filling her. She touched his mind to ensure he was feeling the same kind of pleasure she was. She surrounded him with her— with fiery silk and the intensity of her love.

He gripped her hips and surged deeper until he was buried completely, locking them together. The fire was scorching, threatening to consume her.

I had no idea it would be this good, she admitted, concentrating on the mixture of sensuality and love etched into his masculine features. Her head tossed helplessly from side to side, but she never lost eye contact with him. It was the most intense thing she'd ever experienced. *Diego.* She breathed his name into his mind on their intimate path.

His body moved in hers, making the earth tremble and the stars in the midnight sky stream in little comets while the firestorm burned out of control. It felt like flames roared through them both, the intensity of his thrusts driving them higher. Deep inside, the tension coiled tighter, building, always building. Then his fingers dug deep into her hips, and she gave herself up to him. To the fire. To the storm. To that molten intensity that the two of them created.

"Love you so much, Warrior Woman," he said while her body clenched hard around his.

"Love you beyond anything, Diego," she whispered, meaning it.

19

~

The insertion into the Congo was by HAHO—high-altitude, high-opening jump—from a good twenty-seven thousand feet air to ground level. Entry wasn't going to be a picnic. It never was when they went into a jungle, in the dark, in unfriendly territory. The glide would take them nearly forty miles, using their compass and land features map for their directional reference.

The Congo rainforest was the second largest in the world. The forest was spread over six countries. The trees were taller than in other rainforests because the elephants, gorillas and other animals limited the density of smaller trees, which could be found in other rainforests throughout the world. That was both good and bad for the team.

The fact that Bridget was in the Congo was shocking to everyone. It was the last place anyone thought Whitney would take her, which was probably why she was there. They had monitored General Pillar's secure line, and he had warned his good friend Whitney that the GhostWalkers had threatened him and he was resigning his position for health reasons. That warning was enough to get Whitney moving, as he often did when he felt threatened. Not one GhostWalker had ever considered that he would establish a laboratory in the Congo.

That warning was also enough to get the general killed. A week after the meeting with him and two days after he warned Whitney, Pillar was dead. His death appeared to be suicide, but as the GhostWalkers had a satellite in the air monitoring his house specifically, they were able to see the assassin enter and leave the house. The assassin was a supersoldier, a man who supposedly had been killed in action several years earlier. It was clear he was part of Whitney's army.

The GhostWalkers were loaded down with a list of claymore mines, C-4, blasting caps, time-delay igniters and forty feet of det cord explosive. They had ten minutes of fuse time, frag grenades, and red, green and white smoke grenades. They each had three hundred and thirty-five rifle rounds and three magazine pistols, and the snipers were bringing several rounds for the SVDs. They each carried two extra battery sets for the radios issued to them. They also carried a UV water purification device and a trauma kit. All pretty standard.

It was also very standard that if they were compromised, they would be on their own. Normally, they were sent out on a mission. Even then, the government would deny all knowledge of their existence. This mission was not approved by their government, nor did anyone know about it. The GhostWalker teams had initiated, planned and were carrying out this covert operation on their own.

GhostWalker Teams One and Four were parachuting into the Congo to retrieve Bridget and destroy the laboratory. If possible, they would locate and kill Whitney. GhostWalker Team Two was their extraction team. They would be flying a CV-22 Osprey, a tilt-rotor aircraft designed for low-level penetration into hostile enemy territory day or night. The Osprey would be accompanied by two AH-6 gunships for cover. The light craft carried formidable artillery.

The third team was their backup in case of an emergency. They were ready to engage in battle, work to retrieve or supply any possible support needed. Every single GhostWalker was on board, ready to help.

Joe gave the order at 02:00. "Suit up. We're thirty minutes out. Check oxygen. Double-check one another's gear." Gino checked Joe's gear.

Joe signaled the men at 02:20. "Final in-oxygen check. Five minutes, we depressurize."

Diego glanced at his brother. As always, he wasn't comfortable with having Rubin accompany them on such a dangerous mission. Just the jump alone could be disastrous. A high-altitude jump in the dark into a dense rainforest was extremely dicey.

He knew Rubin was uncomfortable with the others protecting him. Before, Diego hadn't cared that his brother didn't like it. He had encouraged those on the team to protect Rubin. Now, he had a taste of his own medicine. He was the man who set up to guard the backs of his team. He should have jumped first and set the specialty night strobe for the others. The moment he indicated he would make the HAHO jump first, Joe, Ezekiel and Rubin simultaneously and adamantly said no.

Joe gave him his cold, piercing stare when he would have protested the decision. There had been instant silence among the team members seated around the oval table where they were planning the mission. He had been with those men for several years, Mordichai and Malichai even longer. Now they were looking at him with a mixture of alarm and speculation. Diego hadn't liked it at all. He'd always managed to fade into the background while remaining in plain sight. He knew that was going to be impossible.

Joe, Rubin and Ezekiel hadn't told the others he was capable of performing psychic surgery, but they weren't going to allow him to put himself in harm's way when someone else could assume that role.

He'd ventured a quiet argument that Bridget was going to be his sister-in-law and that none of them would be there if it weren't for his decisions, but Joe kept his stone face and Ezekiel leveled his icy gaze at him. That only brought more undue attention. He was grateful his brother didn't rub it in his face that he was now in the same boat with him. Most of his team members had no idea why Joe had nixed the obvious choice to protect them, but they didn't weigh in on the decision.

"One minute . . . thirty seconds. First jumper in the door," Joe said.

Mordichai stood at the door with Diego directly behind him. That strange alarm he had was building and building.

"Go!"

Mordichai dove before Diego had a chance to assess the blaring alarm. It was overwhelming.

Something's wrong, Joe. I have to follow him right now. I need clearance for the jump.

Diego didn't look at Joe; instead, he stepped up to the door and stared out into the night. It was dark, just a sliver of a moon, so small there might as well not have been a moon. The wind whipped at him, clawing at him in an attempt to drag him from the plane. The engines roared. Adrenaline rushed through his veins. Usually, on a jump like this one, fear was familiar, but now that fear was for Mordichai, not himself.

You certain?

Absolutely, no time to waste. The feeling was growing in strength, and it was all he could do not to hurl himself out into the night after the man he considered a brother.

The temperature at this elevation was around minus fifteen. The vicious cold snapped and bit, and the wind stung every exposed part of his skin. He could smell the jet fuel as the plane traveled close to a hundred and fifty knots.

Joe double-checked his gear. Diego took a deep breath, grateful his friend knew him so well and didn't question that feeling that had saved them so many times.

"Go."

At the command, Diego dove without hesitation. The wind hit hard, jerking and tugging, pulling at him. He fought to control two hundred pounds of gear. The rucksack hung between his legs was a hindrance to his movement. Then the roar of the engines ceased and he was free-falling. In that moment, as he soared alone through the dark sky, the feeling was euphoric. Exhilarating. He loved the jump. The sky was a place of absolute peace.

Diego pulled his chute abruptly, putting on the brakes. His speed went from one hundred and twenty miles an hour to about twenty. The force jerked his body hard. The wind rushed by. His helmet muffled all sound, leaving him soaring in a peaceful, dreamlike world. In those moments, there was freedom. Euphoria. Contentment. He dropped through a dark world in silence, basking in the cocoon of peace.

Still, in the back of his mind, he was aware he was suspended by a sheet of silk in a commercial air traffic space. There was always the possibility of splattering like a squashed bug on a passing jet. That knowledge didn't deter his happiness when flying in and out of the clouds as the dark enfolded him.

Fog surrounded him just as he caught sight of the ground rushing at him with alarming speed. The jungle spread out in front of him, a macabre grayish-green sea. There was no strobe to guide him down, and jumping without a clear destination was always dangerous. He'd followed Mordichai quickly, and perhaps his fellow

GhostWalker hadn't had time to set up the strobe, but the urgency in his gut told Diego something else had stopped him.

The trees and grass were various shades of green, even with the gray veil of fog, allowing him to judge where he needed to set down. He flared his chute thirty feet out, slowing down. When he landed, there was the familiar light jolt, and without hesitation he reeled his chute in fast. The others would be on their way down. His first course of action was to find Mordichai and determine what the problem was—because there was one. The sense of urgency was overwhelming.

Diego blocked out everything but the night itself, allowing the animal in him to move to the forefront. He found it somewhat ironic that he'd spent years learning to suppress what was now his natural nature, but in times of an emergency, when he was needed to find his brethren, he used every bit of his energy to bring forth every animal trait that could benefit him.

At once, he could see clearly into the foggy interior of the rainforest. The wind brought him scents and sounds of small rodents and reptiles scurrying in the debris on the forest floor. Immediately, he pinpointed Mordichai's location. Near him were two other individuals murmuring to each other as they warmed themselves on a small heat device. Mordichai was located in the tree above them and he wasn't moving.

Coming to you. He sent the telepathic call to his brother. Ezekiel had taken Rubin and Diego in and raised them along with his younger brothers, Malichai and Mordichai. Long ago, they'd established telepathic communication.

There was no answer. Nothing at all. The silence ratcheted up Diego's sense of alarm and urgency tenfold. He knew Mordichai was alive, but there was no response, not even a stirring in his mind.

He moved through the trees in silence, utilizing the cat in him, moving with fluid stealth, the hairs on his body acting like radar, allowing him to recognize what was around him and how close it was. He smelled the enemy before he came up on them. He had to remove them before the rest of his team came looking for Mordichai.

By now all the men in his unit would have made the jump, even without the night strobe to guide them that only the Ghost-Walkers would have been able to see. If these men were roving guards for Whitney's compound, they couldn't be allowed to radio to warn those inside they were coming.

He caught Mordichai's scent. The cat in him snarled, lifting lips, exposing teeth. The image was strong in his mind as he took to the arboreal highway, leaping into the trees and landing softly on a branch. He began to run. It was suddenly more imperative to get to Mordichai than to take out the two guards.

Beneath him, as he flashed by, he noted the men warming drinks over the small device they were using for heat. They were both big men with a lot of bulky muscles, particularly around their necks and shoulders, making their necks appear wide but very short. That raised an immediate alarm. He identified them as supersoldiers, men who had failed the psych evaluations but whom Whitney had accepted into his program.

Those men wanted to be souped up and gladly "died" on some mission in order to become what they considered superior to every other soldier. Sadly, they didn't realize their lives would be very short. Whitney treated the men as disposable because they didn't meet his strict regulations. He needed a private army, and creating them allowed him to continue with his experiments.

Nearly all of Whitney's supersoldiers had far too much bulk, their bodies distorted. As they continued mutating, in quite a few cases, so did their bodies. Whatever Whitney was trying for lately, most of the time it didn't work for long. That hadn't deterred him from continuing with his experiments.

The forest, even at night, was a vast, seemingly endless wall, undulating with colors of green, emerald, moss, teal, lime, fern and so many others. Liana, a rainforest creeper, fell to the ground from great heights like dangling ropes. It was a beautiful, alluring world, and one Diego, with his numerous animal traits—especially his cat traits—appreciated.

He leapt from branch to branch until he was beside the tree directly above the heads of the two soldiers. Mordichai was hanging from his chute in the canopy of that tree. Fortunately, the tree was an afrormosia, one of the largest canopy-topping trees in the rainforest. The fire-resistant bark glowed silver in the night or in shade. During the day, the trunk appeared auburn.

The lower part of the tree was bare of branches, making it impossible for Diego to simply continue as he had been doing. That sense of urgency grew, and he knew Mordichai was in trouble. He quickly removed his boots and socks to free his feet. He had enough leopard DNA in him to go up the side of the trunk. He would have to do so silently without alerting the soldiers on the ground.

Two of Whitney's supersoldiers, he reported to the others. *Going after Mordichai now. He's caught in the canopy of an afrormosia.*

As he approached his fellow GhostWalker, he saw instantly what the problem was. Blood wasn't getting to his brain properly.

His chute is pressed across his neck and chest. Bad positioning. I can see his toes are barely on the branch, keeping complete pressure off his chest and neck, but it's dicey. He's not really responding.

Even as he informed the others of the dire situation, he was supporting Mordichai and cutting through the straps. Mordichai was nearly unconscious. He'd slowed his heart and lungs, but the strap pressed tight, cutting off his blood supply.

You with me, brother? You can't make a sound. Enemy close.

There was a tentative stirring in his mind. *Knew you'd come for me.* Mordichai sounded weak. Exhaustion flooded Diego's mind. *Just had to hold out.* Faint humor followed the words. *You took your sweet time. My toes didn't want to stretch that far. They were cramping like mad.*

You did a good job staying alive. Zeke would have followed you to hell and pulled you back. You never would have heard the end of it.

He reined in the chute. They were very high up in the canopy. There was too much foliage for the soldiers below to see them, even if they caught a sound or two. Those sounds wouldn't be easily identifiable, but he would prefer there was no warning whatsoever, especially with his other team members close.

Diego was thankful for the strength given to him by his animal DNA. He had to support Mordichai to keep him from falling. In the end, he lowered him to sit on the branch and hang on to the trunk while Diego dealt with the errant chute.

Status on Mordichai, Ezekiel snapped. He sounded calm, but Diego knew him. There was an underlying note that could spell disaster if his brother was in a very bad way.

Hanging in there, Diego assured. *He'll rest while I take care of the two soldiers below the tree. I have to get rid of them to bring Mordichai down.*

Doing great, Zeke, Mordichai reassured. *Just thought I'd take a little snooze while the rest of you set up our fallback.*

He sounded stronger. Diego dropped a hand on his shoulder and allowed the well of healing energy to rise. He did his best to keep the heat on the cool side so he wasn't giving away the fact that he had any talent, but Mordichai was his brother, and it seemed the more he used his ability, the more adept he became at it.

Mordichai stirred, looking up at him, speculation in his gaze, but he didn't say anything.

Joe gave the coordinates for the place they had chosen as their base. *Setting up for a run. If you need help, now's the time to say so.*

I can take care of these two souped-up soldiers, Diego said. *Too many of us may tip one of them off. I don't know their talents as of yet.* He didn't intend to stick around long enough to find out either. He intended to kill them both before either could become suspicious and use their radios to warn the compound.

Need help with Mordichai?

Diego sent Mordichai a quick grin. *He'll be carrying me out of here.*

Don't take all day, Joe ordered. *We're on a tight schedule.*

The rainforest was hot and very humid. Made up of several layers, the emergent level was anywhere from seventy to two hundred and fifty feet high. Diego and Mordichai were concealed in the canopy where most of the birds and wildlife resided. They had to stay very still and move slowly when they did move in order to keep from startling any of the birds or monkeys.

There were no flowers winding their way up the trunk of the afrormosa to the light. No moss or lichen hanging over the branches or crawling up the bark. The tree did have ropes of tough vines hanging in tangled twists or dropping straight down from the branches in the canopy. None were long enough to reach the forest floor.

You okay for me to leave you? They couldn't linger in the canopy. Their mission required them to act that night. If they waited too long, they would have to abort.

I'm good. Just catching my breath. Whatever you did helped me quite a bit.

Even though they were talking telepathically, Diego knew the others on their team were looped in. He frowned at Mordichai and gave a slight shake of his head, indicating they weren't discussing anything to do with his healing ability any further.

Abruptly, Diego turned away from his foster brother, and leaving his pack wedged in the crook of the trunk and two branches, he shifted around to the back of the tree, away from the soldiers, and began his descent.

In the surrounding trees, monkeys watched as he silently descended. The steady drone of crickets and cicadas filled the night. Tree frogs called back and forth, and various other species chimed in to make the night a cacophony of jarring noise. Diego kept his energy low so that he didn't appear to be a predator on the hunt. That would send the animals into a chaotic and noisy frenzy.

As Diego descended into the inky blackness, his night vision adjusted. He could see easily with the sight of the leopard. The hair on his body allowed him to assess exactly where his enemies were. Leopards were stealthy creatures, and the DNA allowed him to move with that same fluidity in silence. He made his way down the trunk of the tree and stood quietly directly behind the two men. He blended into the night so that even if they turned their heads, it would be very difficult for either of the men to spot him.

It wasn't difficult to pick up what they were saying, both grousing at having to spend the night in the jungle. It wasn't what they'd signed up for. One did the complaining while the other listened.

"Don't know why we're always the ones on roving patrol when the big man shows up, Peyton," the one with dark hair cut very close to his scalp said.

The other soldier, Peyton, shrugged. "We got the short straw this time, Bertram. He never stays long. Things will go back to normal in a couple of days."

Bertram scowled as he extended his hands over the small heating device between them. "This entire assignment sucks. I thought we'd end up in the States or Europe. He's got those women locked up, and they all need servicing." He smirked. "I've been waiting for that assignment. We're just rotting out here."

"You get plenty of women. You spend half your time raiding the locals."

"Not the kind of fun I'm looking for," Bertram said.

"I put in for both the States and Europe at any of his labs," Peyton said. "Just like you. I know they give us shit assignments before he determines that we're going to be loyal to him. That's what he's looking for, Bertram. You talk too much. You can't talk about him or anything going on in the labs."

"Who the hell do I talk to?"

"Everyone. You complain constantly, and when you complain, you talk about Whitney and the experiments taking place. You talk about handling dead bodies and how they look like mutated insects. You just can't keep your mouth shut."

"Who the hell is going to tell anyone else? We're all in the same boat, and everyone here knows what's happening in the laboratory."

"And every single one of the guards here wants the same thing we do. They want a different assignment. They're going to repeat everything negative they can about you, me and one another. It isn't like they're loyal to us. The minute Whitney arrived, you can bet he had a full report on every guard. He probably had it long before he arrived."

"That sucks."

Peyton shrugged and moved several feet away, turning his back on his fellow soldier to relieve himself.

Bertram swore under his breath, crouched down and once more held out his hands to the small glowing heater.

Diego didn't wait. He came up behind Bertram like a ghost, absolutely silent. One hand went around the soldier's head, palm slamming over his mouth while his blade severed the spinal cord at the back of the neck. He eased the body to the ground and immediately crossed the short distance to the second soldier.

Leopards were efficient predators, making Diego one as well. He'd honed his skills in the Appalachian Mountains and perfected them thousands of times working in the field in various terrains.

He had his human brain to plan for any contingency. He was able to keep his energy low rather than projecting the energy of a predator.

Ordinarily, when a leopard was on the hunt, the monkeys and other wildlife noticed and went into a frenzy. By keeping his energy low, Diego wasn't detected. Even so, Peyton began to slowly turn his head toward Diego, looking over his shoulder. Diego was on him before he could react, slamming the knife into the base of his skull, dropping him to the ground. He ensured both men were dead before going up the tree to get Mordichai.

Enemy down, bringing our brother home.

Feeling fully recovered. Diego is getting me out of this tree, but I'm not sure how.

I'm carrying your ass, Diego informed him, as well as the others. *Recommend if you're going to be playing around with your chute, you lay off Nonny's food.*

Yeah, that's not going to happen. And just for the record, Malichai eats far more than I do.

That's called deflecting, Ezekiel chimed in. There was relief in his voice. It was clear his younger brother was feeling a lot better.

Diego hefted Mordichai onto his back. *Hang on. I'm climbing down now and won't be able to hold on to you this way. It's faster going down.*

Yeah, I'm hanging on but closing my eyes. Just to say, Diego, you're totally insane.

Diego found himself laughing. Leila had given that gift to him, the ability to genuinely laugh when he'd forgotten how. If he considered what he was doing, going down a bare tree trunk with a full-grown man on his back, Mordichai was most likely right.

Once on the ground, Diego left Mordichai to rest while he retrieved his gear from where he'd stored it in the jungle. It didn't take long for them to join the others in preparation for their attack on Whitney's laboratory. The battle plan was already being discussed.

"It's imperative, before we engage in battle, that we know where Bridget is and if there are any other innocents in that lab. We're taking it down. That means if Bridget isn't the only woman held there, we will have to rescue others, and we'll need to know how many," Joe reminded. "Trap has the ability to see through walls. You take the south and west sides and sweep the entire building from that direction, Trap. Wyatt, you're Trap's partner. Relay everything to the rest of us."

"Ian has the ability to see through buildings as well," Ryland reported. He flashed a small smile when most of the others on the team turned to stare at Ian McGillicuddy. "He'll take the north and east sides, sending to all of us the information so we'll know if there are other hostages and where they are. Diego, you're his backup."

Ian shrugged and exchanged a long look with Trap. "No problem," he agreed.

"Each of you has your assignment and where to set up," Joe continued. "Hold position until Trap and Ian report. If ever we were going to prove GhostWalkers own the night, now's the time."

"We know Whitney is present. He's our secondary mission. We secure Bridget and any other captives, and then we take out Whitney if it is at all possible," Ezekiel added. "Malichai and Gino, you're together making the try for Whitney. If nothing else, take down his house when the all clear comes."

"Nico and Mordichai are sitting back on the north side, covering all of us," Ryland said. "On the south, it will be Rubin and Tucker. They'll have our backs in that direction."

"Zeke, Ryland and Kadan will take the dorms with the soldiers," Joe said.

"Kyle and Gator are the resident bomb experts. You're on the vehicles and maintenance buildings. Set them to blow on clearance," Ezekiel said. "You'll be able to utilize their mortar shells and any explosives they have."

"Once inside, Sam and Jeff, you're on the communication room," Joe said. "Every means of communication must be down. Wire the shit out of that room and everything around it. When it blows, I don't want so much as a stick left intact."

Sam and Jeff exchanged a quick smirk.

"The rest of you know your partners and the entry points to breach the lab. Be ready to get into the laboratory when we're given the information from Trap and Ian. No one makes a move until then," Ryland said. "When we do go in, every enemy goes down. The buildings are flattened, so they can't use them again. All equipment, computers, anything with Whitney's data, goes. Everything has to come down."

"Let's do this, gentlemen," Joe said. "If anyone gets in trouble, give us a heads-up and your backup will pull you out."

Moving through the oppressive jungle in single file to keep from disturbing wildlife or tripping any alarms the laboratory had set took time. The compound, as with most of the camps they encountered, was set in rows, with the troop barracks the first three long buildings to the north of the actual laboratory.

The command center with communications was located in the center of the laboratory. Those working as lead scientists were housed in the right wing, and their assistants had dorm rooms in the left wing, with the communications in the center between them. Vehicle and maintenance buildings were on the north side. Whitney's apartment was approximately forty feet from the laboratory on the east side.

They had the positioning of the buildings but needed to know where Bridget was and what shape she was in before they attacked. They also needed to know if there were any other innocents inside before they made their move.

Nico and Mordichai broke off from the others to make their way through the jungle to the taller trees to the north of them. Rubin and Tucker did the same, circling to the south. They would split up and find the trees that would allow them to cover the teams' retreat with Bridget.

The remainder of the GhostWalkers, in their designated two-man teams, sprinted silently through the thick vegetation to work their way in close, to be ready for the go signal.

Kyle and Gator crouched low to the ground, blending in with the night, running toward their destination, the vehicles and maintenance buildings. With his night vision, Diego was able to see Kyle roll under a large tank while Gator went for the roof of one of the buildings.

Diego and Ian made their way to the north wall of the laboratory. There were two guards patrolling. Diego disposed of both, allowing Ian to get right up to the outside wall. Despite Whitney being in residence, the compound wasn't on high alert. Clearly, no one expected an attack. That gave the GhostWalkers a decided advantage.

Charges set, Kyle said, *in vehicles and maintenance buildings. Gator is on the lab roof. I'm hitting the foundation.*

Charges set on all three dorms, Ryland reported. *Ready to breach.*

Diego's job was to guard Ian's back as he used his gift to see through the walls of the laboratory to find Bridget and send images to the waiting team members. Once they knew where she was, Joe would give the order to take down the entire compound.

Whitney's not home. His apartment is wired to blow sky-high, Malichai reported.

He's in the laboratory, north side. Last room. Bridget is with him. Ian's voice was tight. He sent the images of the various rooms, most empty. *There's a guard at the door and another man in with them. He appears to be a tech. Guards at every entrance door.*

Trap gave the same data. Guards on the entrances and exits. Otherwise, the building appeared to be mostly empty. It was easy to see the Congo lab was run on a skeleton crew.

Ian's entire demeanor changed, the telepathic connection he shared with every team member became tinged with crimson red. He had been sharing images and data with the others just as Trap was, his manner calm, and suddenly, he was in a stone-cold fury. *Didn't find anyone else innocent on this side. Going in. He's hurting her.*

Diego had been facing the jungle, guarding Ian's back as he walked up and down the length of the building. He swung around, feeling Ian's outrage. Matching it. Before his fury could manifest in ground-shaking ways, Ian had taken off and was already entering the building through a side door.

Ian's in. Going after him, Diego declared.

Drop thermite and get to the lab, Joe ordered.

Swearing under his breath, Diego went through the closest door. He knew a guard was on the other side from the images Ian had sent them all. He went in hot, cutting arteries as he swept through, sprinting down the hall toward the room where Whitney held Bridget. As Diego flashed past the door Ian had entered through, he caught sight of a guard on the floor in a pool of blood where Ian had dropped him.

In comms room, Sam reported. *Guards down, techs down, setting charges.*

Engaging with remaining soldiers in barracks. Barracks wired, Kadan said.

Even as he ran down the hall, Diego registered the various teams checking in. The door to the laboratory was wide open, and he somersaulted in. Ian had the guard on the floor, and the two men fought viciously.

Time slowed down. Seemed to tunnel. Gun in his fist, Whitney turned toward Ian and the guard in macabre slow motion. Diego used blurring speed, inserted his body between Ian and Whitney as he whipped out the KA-BAR knife he kept between his shoulder blades. Using the strength of a fully grown tiger, he slashed the honed blade through skin, muscle, and bone, nearly severing Whitney's arm. Blood shot into the air and poured from the wound. The gun hit the floor and skittered toward the table Bridget was strapped to.

The thermite triggered throughout the compound. Explosions killed numerous guards as the charges on the vehicles and in the munitions dump detonated simultaneously. Explosions rocked Whitney's apartment, reducing it to nothing but splinters on the ground, with orange and red flames igniting everywhere.

At the same time, the explosives planted on all three of the guard's dormitories ignited, lighting up the surrounding jungle and shaking the earth. The world turned orange and red as flames shot into the sky and raced through the shattered remains of buildings.

Inside the laboratory was instant hell as the charges in the communications center tore the building apart and lifted the roof. The walls blew outward, and fire raged in every corner. The force of the explosion threw Diego against the steel legs of the table Bridget was strapped to. Beams from the ceiling rained down along with drywall and boards, all on fire. Ian flung his body over Bridget's as Diego staggered to his feet, looking for Whitney. The heavy beams, debris, flames and smoke made it impossible to see much. Already, the air was clogged with deadly smoke.

Diego used the knife he still gripped in his fist to slice through the straps holding Bridget prisoner. "Taking you home to Leila, kid," he announced softly, fearing she might be so disoriented she would fight. They didn't have time for that.

Bridget nodded and didn't protest, even though it appeared to hurt her when Ian shifted her weight onto his shoulder in a fireman's carry. Diego tossed the blanket from her gurney over the lowest mound of flames and both men leapt through the fierce red and orange wall to the fiery outside.

"Do you need medical?" Joe demanded as they made it to the rendezvous point.

Ian gently lowered Bridget but kept his arm around her. "Do you?" he asked.

Bridget gave them a wan smile. "I need my sister."

"Then let's get the hell out of here," Joe declared.

20

uther," Leila whispered. "I can't do this. I really can't." She
backed away from her uncle toward the door leading outside.
Escape. She was more than good at escape. She'd proven that many
times over.

"I thought that man was your world, girl." There was no repri-
mand. No judgment. Luther was stating facts as he saw them.
"Was I wrong?"

"No. Yes. Meaning you aren't wrong. I am in love with him. I
want this more than he does, although he'd never believe it, but there
are too many people. Where did they all come from? Who are they?
I don't know any of them, Luther." She wasn't in the least confused
about loving Diego—or wanting to be his wife. She knew that with
total certainty, but their wedding was supposed to be private. Small.

"You're scared of a crowd? You're a badass, Leila. He calls you
'Warrior Woman.' You can't be afraid of those people out there."
He indicated the other door, the one he was supposed to walk
through with her on his arm.

"I don't like people staring at me. I stay in the shadows, Luther. This is too much. Nonny said small."

"This is small in comparison to many of the Cajun weddings, Leila," Luther said patiently. "From what I gathered, these celebrations can go on for days. Any excuse to party."

"Days?" She knew her voice sounded faint because she felt that way. She absolutely couldn't be in that crowd for days. "Go get him, Luther. I have to tell him."

Luther studied her face. She hoped he could look beyond the perfect makeup Pepper had applied to see her very real distress. She needed Diego to understand she wanted to be his wife. She wanted to spend the rest of her life with him, but she couldn't make herself walk out of the little room and face so many strangers.

And then he was there, pouring into her mind with his strength. With love. With absolute command. Her rock. *What is it, sweetheart? I can feel your distress.*

The moment she felt his touch, the instant he filled the empty places she hadn't known she had until she'd been with him, the terrible knots in her stomach began to loosen. Her lungs began to work the way they were supposed to.

I'm having a panic attack. She was honest with him. She was always honest with him. No matter how difficult it was, they'd promised each other they'd tell the truth. *I don't mean to hurt you, Diego. This is about me. Facing so many strangers. All of them staring at me.*

She felt him move through her mind, a careful assessment. *I get it, Leila. I understand completely. We've been programmed to stay in the shadows, even if we're in plain sight. I do know these people. They're the men who went with me to bring your sister back to you. They're the ones who took back Gracie for us. They're the ones who backed our team when we needed to get out of the Congo. And yes, there are a lot of them.*

His voice was low and velvet soft. The images and words he

used could have been designed to make her feel guilt, but she could feel his sincerity. He was giving her the information because it was the truth.

The knots in her stomach tightened all over again. She wasn't a coward. She'd never allowed fear to stop her from doing anything she wanted or needed to do. Those men had risked their lives without questioning why they should. Diego's team members and men from the other teams had done night jumps into the Congo. They had defied General Pillar, going so far as to threaten him. The threat had been subtle, but it was there. The repercussions could have been immense.

I am not telling you who the guests are to get you to walk down that aisle, sweetheart. I wanted to reassure you that I wouldn't let just anyone come to our wedding. If you want me to cancel it, we can do that.

Did she want that? Had Luther brought him to the room, that was exactly what she would have told him she wanted. Now, thinking about it, she wasn't so certain. Those men had displayed tremendous courage going into enemy territory. They'd faced Whitney's personal army of supersoldiers in order to get her sister to freedom.

What were they asking of her? A chance to celebrate. To see their friend Diego married. A chance to have a party. Laugh. Eat. Dance with their women. They'd brought their children with them, and even Gracie was having a good time playing with the other GhostWalker children.

No, we can't cancel, Diego. She made the decision, and she meant it, but he couldn't fail to read her trepidation.

Do you want me to walk you down the aisle?

She leaned on him too much. Ever since he'd performed the operation removing her spleen, she'd felt vulnerable. Intellectually, she knew it was because she wasn't one hundred percent physically fit. She'd always been strong and agile. She hadn't ever considered that she would be injured so badly that she couldn't defend herself. She hadn't realized what effect that had had on her mentally.

Leila looked at her uncle, patiently waiting. "I'm talking to Diego. He always seems to know when I'm upset about something."

"He's a good man," Luther said. "And I was sure you were discussing the crisis with him."

"He didn't even get upset with me," she admitted. "Right away, he said he would cancel the wedding if I didn't want to walk out in front of all those people."

"Do you still want to cancel?"

She pressed her hand to her stomach. A small roller coaster. A few knots still tangled tight. She shook her head.

Luther broke into a smile. "Never thought I'd have the privilege of walking my girl down the aisle, but like most men, I thought about it. Lotty couldn't have children. I didn't mind. I loved her with every breath I took. Every cell in my body. She was enough for me, and I've never regretted a single moment with her. I want that for you and Diego."

Leila made up her mind instantly. *Luther will walk me down the aisle. That way, you'll get the full effect of all the work Pepper and Nonny did.*

Amusement filled her mind. *I doubt they had to work too hard, woman. You're so beautiful, I ache inside whenever I see you.*

"Diego always tells me he isn't a poet or romantic in the least. He claims he doesn't have words to give me, but he says the most beautiful things to me." She hugged herself and smiled at Luther. "Words don't mean nearly as much to me as actions do."

"That's the way it should be, honey," Luther said.

"He shows me in a million ways, every single day, how much he loves me," Leila told her uncle. "He always puts me first. Not just me, but little Gracie as well. You should see him with Grace."

Luther held out his hand to her. "I have seen him. Believe me, honey, I watched him carefully with you and the baby. I want only the best for my nieces. I think Diego is the best, and it's very clear to me that he loves you."

There was absolutely no way she would take away Luther's moment. She knew since his wife died, he'd found very little in the way of happiness. "Thank you for being here with us today, Luther. I'm aware that, like me, you don't like crowds. This can't be easy on you."

"I'm more than honored to escort you down the aisle, honey," Luther assured.

They approached the door, and it was immediately opened by Joe. He gave Luther a grin.

"Glad to see you coming through, Leila. We had a little bet going whether you'd come to your senses and head for the hills or continue with this lunatic idea of Diego's. The others thought you would have some form of self-preservation, but I saw that gone look on your face and bet you'd stick around."

Luther threw his head back and laughed. "Even if she did run, that boy would chase her to the ends of the earth. He knows a good thing when he has it."

Joe nodded his assent. "I believe you're right, Luther."

Music played. It didn't sound like any wedding march Leila had ever heard, but it was upbeat and fun. Bridget moved up the aisle to stand opposite Rubin, who was acting as Diego's best man, just as Bridget was Leila's maid of honor. Luckily, there were enough anchors in the crowd that her sister wasn't feeling any pain at all in spite of the fact that Whitney had stripped her brain of most filters.

Leila took a moment to take in her sister. She still looked drawn and pale, but her face was relaxed, and her smile was huge. Her eyes were bright. She met Leila's gaze, and instantly, Leila felt the love Bridget projected.

At Luther's urging, she started down the aisle, following Wyatt's triplets and Gracie as they threw the petals of flowers in front of her. Gracie was very enthusiastic with the tossing of petals. They went into the air, showering the four girls with colorful flowers. She threw them at the people seated in the rows of chairs on either side of the aisle. She ate one just to see what it tasted like. All the while, Ginger, Thym and Cannelle kept her moving when she tried to do a little dance and got distracted by a purse on the floor by a chair.

Luther and Leila exchanged an amused look, and then she looked toward the archway that had been set up where Diego stood. He had that smile, the one she loved so much, his gaze on Gracie. He looked so proud of her. It was easy to forget he wasn't her biological father.

Diego's gaze lifted to her. She felt his swift intake of breath. The surge of love pouring into her mind. So Diego. So her man. She concentrated on him. How handsome he looked in his suit. How he made her heart skip a beat the moment their gazes connected. How focused he was on her. It was easy to block out everything around her once she was falling into his gaze.

She tightened her hold on Luther's arm, blinking back tears of joy. *This could be the best day of my life.*

I'm with you, sweetheart. I can't say for certain because we've had several incredible times together. I know I'll treasure every memory I ever have with you.

I'm going to love you like you never expected to be loved, she vowed.

I never thought any woman would ever love me, Leila. Not ever. You're a miracle to me. I swear to you, no matter what happens in the future, you're always going to be safe with me. Things aren't always going to be perfect. Life can be tough, but I believe we'll do fine as long as we're together.

Diego took several steps to meet them, and Luther put Leila's hand in his before leaning down to brush a kiss on her cheek. Luther answered the preacher when asked who was giving the bride to the groom. When he answered, his voice was firm.

Diego led her to the archway, which was covered in flowers. He took both her hands in his, and the intensity in his dark velvet eyes made her heart melt. This was her man. Her choice. Her forever. She was that certain. She had no idea how she'd gotten to this place, was granted this miracle, but there he was, standing in front of her, looking at her with stark, raw love.

Her heart beat wildly, the way it often did when she caught her first sight of him or when she watched him carrying Gracie, rocking her or talking softly to her. He had a voice that could soothe the most feral of beasts and the calmest energy she'd ever encountered.

She repeated her vows in a whisper, but she meant every single word. Diego slipped a ring on her finger and brought her hand to his mouth before turning back to the preacher. It was those little things he did that captured her heart.

Thank you, Leila, for changing my life. For giving me a family and loving me so unconditionally.

As always when he spoke so intimately, she could feel his emotions. She smiled up at him, love bursting through her. She still had to face their reception, but she felt she could do anything with him at her side.

"I'm going to love you for eternity," she whispered, meaning it.